Joe Rogan interviewing Elon Musk about Neuralink in 2020

JR: Once you become a god it seems very unlikely you'll want to go back to being stupid again . . . I mean you literally could fundamentally change the way humans interface with each other.

EM: Yes.

JR: Yes!?

EM: You wouldn't need to talk.

JR: Ha, ha, ha . . . I'm so scared of that but so excited about it at the same time. Is that weird?

EM: . . . Like, AI is getting better and better . . . Even in a benign scenario we are left behind . . . We're not along for the ride. We're just too dumb. So how do you go along for the ride? Umm, if you can't beat 'em, join 'em.

Chapter 1

"Where are you with getting the software ready for deployment?" Kathy asked Sheila.

"We're not there yet. The code was hacked in a very sophisticated way. I know the system better than anyone and I haven't been able to figure out their methods or the extent of the damage."

"The president wants this operational now," Matt interjected.

Sheila Bloom was meeting with her supervisor, Kathy Owens, the director of Neurodynamic Engineering. The other attendee, Matt Raines, was the head of its Pentagon counterpart.

"What do you need to get this done quickly?" Matt asked.

"We've got all the resources we can use right now," Sheila responded. "Any more would just impede progress. Look, software is like planting a tree. You make sure the soil has the right nutrients, and give it water and light. But you just don't tell it to grow, and it grows. It grows at its own pace, organically, and that takes time."

Kathy and Matt shared an expression of incredulity. Sheila had used this metaphor since she began her career as a programmer. It was always aimed at unreasonable demands made by management who had no idea what was involved in developing complex systems. She'd never won an argument with this analogy but couldn't help using it in situations such as this. She knew it sounded condescending, which just increased her desire to use it now.

"Your current estimate is six months to fix the code and rerun the testing cycles?" Kathy asked.

"Correct."

"The president informed me he wants a subject with the implant operational in two months."

"That's not going to happen, no how, no way."

"I think there is a way," Matt said. "Let me make sure I understand this tree you're growing. It's a comprehensive brain implementation, right?

"That's not entirely wrong," Sheila said, chafing at the crudeness of the description.

"Then let's focus on what really matters. Could you narrow your team's focus to certain areas of the brain?"

"We've never viewed this project that way."

Matt returned Sheila's condescension with a cunning, ugly laugh. "Maybe you haven't, but you better believe others have. So let me lay it out for you. If you focus your efforts on making operational the areas of the software that relate to winning in armed conflicts, and I mean winning at any cost, can you have the system ready to be implemented in two months?"

It was obvious what was going on. Matt was wielding his power, trying to see how far it reached. Sheila's control rested in her knowledge, her unique skill set. Reducing the scope of the project and providing detailed instructions on how to accomplish this truncated approach, effectively reduced the power she exerted over it. She looked at this insecure man and knew that spreading his influence was the only thing he lived for. She was frantic to find a way to undo his plans.

"I would not recommend that. We don't know the impacts of doing that. All of our testing is based on a full deployment of the system."

"That's not what I asked you," Matt yelled. "So, I'll ask again. Can it be done?"

"Yes, we could focus on that part of the code and probably get it operational in two months."

"I think you should make the president aware of this option." Matt said to Kathy.

When the meeting ended Sheila returned to her office and tried to go back to work, but it was futile. She wanted to give her team a heads up but couldn't face them right now. The day was coming to an end. She scheduled a meeting for the next morning with the four programmers and two analysts that reported to her. Pages of reports and programs sat on her desk in unruly piles. She never left her workspace in this level of disarray at the end of the day, but today she felt too dispirited to push back against the chaos. She shut her computer, locked the door behind her and didn't look back.

Back in her apartment one glass of Sauvignon Blanc turned into two and then most of a third. Her mind kept circling the same circumstances and resolved to the same devastating end point. If Matt had his way this wouldn't be a detour but a new direction with horrifying consequences. Once the project was implemented all energies would be devoted to keeping it going. If crucial shortcuts were taken there would be no way to get back to the original intent. There would never be enough time, or will, to get it right if the initial implementation was seriously flawed. The initial implementation always sets the tone for a project, and its care and feeding would require the staff's full attention for a long time thereafter. She reflected on this and knew if Matt got his way, two years would pass before they could manage a major upgrade, one that had a fully integrated neural exposure to the treatments, an eternity in this shifting environment.

She was tasked with having her team assess the effort to scale back the project to the parameters under discussion. Her worst nightmare would be realized if they moved forward with this partial implementation. The rebels' charges against the militarized state apparatus would be given a new poster child, one that she, more than anyone, was most responsible for creating.

Sheila canceled her team's daily 10 minute stand-up meeting, a time used to discuss short-term progress and obstacles. It was replaced by an hour-long meeting and moved to a private conference room. Changes like this tipped off the team that something was up.

"We've been asked to provide estimates for a scaled down implementation. The department heads want us to see how long it would take to get the code related to aggressive reactivity deployed as a standalone platform."

Sheila let this sink in before continuing. "If they choose this path, they said it was only temporary, and that we could follow shortly with a deployment of the full configuration."

Scott Peterson, her lead programmer, responded first. "What do you think the chances of that are? This is what we've been working day and night to avoid. And now, it looks like we failed."

"None of you have failed," Sheila responded forcefully. "That is not a term I would ever apply to any of you, any of the effort you've put forth."

"We know you feel that way, Sheila," Mariana broke in. She was the one who managed the left-brain coding and synthesized human emotion in code better than anyone on the team, better than anyone they'd ever worked with. It was her work that was most threatened.

Mariana continued, "But it doesn't matter. We talked about this before. We talked about this when funding cuts were threatened and most recently when the code was hacked and compromised. We've always been in a race against time. This is the nightmare we've all been living with."

Sheila tried to help them recapture their enthusiasm but could offer little more than a recommendation that they take a wait-and-see approach, and remind them that no decision had been reached yet. She then refocused the meeting on tasks and deadlines needed to complete this deliverable.

The production of the report was a kind of purgatory. They scrambled to assemble the necessary data but their hearts weren't in it and the results were sub-standard. When they were done Mariana tried to return to the difficult task of fixing the neuro-balancing networking software that had been tampered with. The second day into this effort she'd all but given up on making real progress. She spent much of her time searching job posting sites. She wasn't even aware she'd drifted and then looked up at the clock to see she'd just burned 20 minutes on non-work related tasks. At least she found there was a market for her skills. She was fiercely dedicated to this project, as were all her teammates. But each of them experienced the same limbo she felt, and failed to rekindle the passion that had characterized their work on this project up to this point.

Four days after the report was prepared, Sheila was called into a meeting with Kathy and Matt. She sensed from Matt's presence that a decision was reached regarding the future direction of the neuralBlast project.

As soon as they were seated Kathy opened the meeting with the following comment.

"You're not going to like this, Sheila, but the president decided to go with the partial implementation we talked about."

Sheila had kept busy to avoid thinking about how things would shake out, as if she were waiting for the results of a biopsy to see how bad the cancer was. Whatever attention she devoted to the topic convinced her that this new course of action would have catastrophic consequences. So, the news hit her hard and she jumped in without letting Kathy continue.

"This is a terrible direction to move in. If we don't kill the subject, his or her brain will be totally out of balance. There will be nothing to check their aggressive tendencies. And we haven't even finished our study. What the hell was this based on!?"

Instead of Kathy, Matt tersely replied, which surprised Sheila.

"That's not your concern. The president has spoken and it's our job to make his wishes a reality."

Sheila's thinly veiled dislike of Matt was unmasked by her expression. She perpetually shielded her disgust for him because he out-ranked her, but that wasn't enough to hold it back now. "You're happy about this, aren't you? This is what you wanted all along. No need to fully develop all human capabilities if you can turn the subject into a war machine."

Sheila was gearing up to continue her attack on Matt when Kathy cut in.

"There's one more thing. This project will no longer be within my domain. Instead, the work will be done in the Pentagon and instead of me being its senior sponsor, Matt will assume that role."

This was a jolt that knocked Sheila back. She had had a good working relationship with Kathy, her only supervisor since starting in the government. Kathy was adept at managing the politics and she respected Sheila's opinion and let Sheila have her way, for the most part, in the technical arena. She knew Matt would not grant her the same latitude.

"That's right," Matt said, taking over the meeting. "And because of this change, a heightened security clearance is needed. That is part of the overall change in direction that will see greater managerial control, which will allow the project to progress without further delays. Not that these setbacks were anything you could have prevented." His words dripped with sarcasm.

After allowing the news to seep in, Matt continued, "Therefore, all the jobs will be re-posted and will need to be applied for. Current members of the team are welcome to apply. Of course, there is nothing stopping anyone from applying for positions in other departments instead."

It was immediately clear to Sheila that even if she wanted to stay with the project, she was out. The mere mention of the delays was a red flag, a notice that he didn't think she was capable of doing the job. Matt had his own coterie which did not include Sheila, and gaining membership in that club was something she'd never pursue.

Moment by moment, silence brought a new reality into focus. Sheila saw no reason to speak her mind so she listened as Kathy and Matt regurgitated the story they were told and were determined to implement. It was pure fantasy. A quick and seamless transition. Unrealistic project milestone dates that were not allowed to slip. How the project would be truncated, becoming hardly discernible to her and the current team. When they were done, Sheila commented with the only thought to emerge from the wreckage.

"I would like to brief my team on these changes."

"That won't be necessary," Matt responded and seemed happy to see the conversation move in this direction. I've already scheduled a meeting with the current team to go over these details immediately after we're done here. I did not invite you because it will cover the same material we've just discussed."

He was staring at her, his lips twisted in a sadistic sneer. Sheila's gaze darted from Matt to Kathy, who engaged her briefly before casting her eyes down to the papers in front of her.

"The paperwork for the necessary organizational changes will go through in the next few days," Matt summarized, and looked at his watch to indicate their time was nearing an end. "More to come on that."

Sheila returned to her office. This was her home, really, during the last two years. Her adjustment to living in DC after the college town where she built her career was difficult. Her small apartment and big city life were a constant source of dissonance. But she didn't care because it was the work that brought her here and had sustained her.

She left behind a romantic relationship with one of her colleagues. He had been supportive when she was offered this job. They tried to keep the relationship alive but after six months of sporadic contact they agreed to part ways. As she sat in her chair now, she began to seriously question for the first time if she'd made the wrong decision.

One thing she knew was that she was done here. Every scenario she considered was abhorrent. She stayed holed up in her office for two hours and then opened her laptop and wrote her letter of resignation. She had no clear plans for the future but knew she could find something in a research facility or university setting. This was the only path forward for her.

Kathy was in her office and Sheila handed her the letter as she sat down on the other side of her desk.

"Are you sure?" Kathy asked after reading the note.

"Yes I am. And I'm glad I got to give it to you . . .. Before the organizational change hits."

Kathy laughed. "You barely made it. That's how things go around here. You wait for months for a decision to be made and then they're pushed through without taking the time to think about the best way to implement them."

Rarely did they talk about things other than the work, the tasks at hand, and Sheila liked that Kathy opened up in this small way.

"Are you sure you don't want to think this over, sleep on it tonight?"

"No, that won't change anything. My mind's made up. But thanks for putting that option out there for me."

"OK, I understand . . ..We did good work together, made a good team. I'm sorry it's playing out this way. Off the record, I agree that this is too sensitive a project for the military to be the sole arbiter. I made my case but lost. The hacks into the system and the delays they caused were our undoing. Not our fault, of course. But perception is everything and these were the things that led us to not being able to keep the wolves at bay, and the eventual loss of control of the project.

"There's one other development that might have forced their hand. That subject Matt is so keen on for neuralBlast treatments, Milo Garrison, is missing. Disappeared into thin air. They're afraid the rebels who hacked the system abducted him."

"There's no way they have the expertise to administer the software on a live subject," Sheila responded forcefully. "I know more about this software than anyone and I know it's not ready."

Still, they held each other's gaze for a long time, until their embarrassment caused them to break the connection. Each was left wondering if such a thing was possible.

It was noon time and her team was at lunch. They were like family to her, with all the little frictions that come with that. But now she felt an enormous sadness because she was causing a divorce in the family and she had a fierce desire to minimize the trauma that might cause. She scheduled a meeting at 2:00 PM with them and decided to not leave her room until then; food, like everything else, held no interest for her. She wanted to tell them as a group how much she valued their hard work and remind them of their achievements. Tell them that great things awaited them.

At 1:30 there was a sharp knock on Sheila's door. She had told her admin assistant she did not want to be disturbed and was annoyed as she got up to answer it. Matt was there with a box in his hands and two security guards behind him.

"I heard you resigned," Matt said, brushing past Sheila. He was followed by a stern, robotic-looking man and woman.

"There's no way to sugar coat this, Sheila. We're here to escort you out of the building. Your computer security is being revoked as we speak. We'll give you a few minutes to gather your belongings. Anything left behind will be sent to a forwarding address." He placed the box on her desk for her to fill with her personal items.

Matt continued, "You stated you would stay on for an unspecified period of time to perform knowledge transfer.

Because of that we will pay you for the next four weeks, the standard departure notice time."

Sheila was only a little surprised. But it was usually disgruntled employees who were escorted out. Then she laughed to herself when she realized that may be how she was perceived. Still, she held his gaze for an uncomfortably long time before responding.

"Do you really think I'm a security risk?" her sneer turned into a laugh like a slap across the face.

"This is just the protocol we've chosen to adopt," Matt was more than willing to play out this string. "Please, just collect your things so we can conclude this task."

"It's a damn shame. I was going to meet with my team in a half hour. Let them know I was leaving and thank them for their hard work and dedication. If you knew what was best, you'd let me do that before I leave."

Matt briefly considered this suggestion before stating, "No, I think we will stick to the current course of action."

There wasn't much. She had only a few photos of family members and vacations she'd taken. The rest of what laid around held even less meaning but she packed it in the box. What mattered to her was the work, always the work, and the people she worked with who shared her dreams.

She walked out of her room, past her team's set of cubicles and into the hallway towards the elevator. The images of people and marked up white boards on the periphery were parts of the life she was leaving behind. Team members looked up with confused expressions and were drawn to the cardboard box Sheila carried with both hands. It was only after she'd passed them that shock and recognition spread across their faces.

They passed through the lobby on the main level and Sheila started walking toward the exit.

"No, this way. We have some HR matters to address," Matt said, and the four turned down a nondescript passageway that

Sheila had never noticed before. Steel-grey walls reverberated with the staccato click of the group's shoes against the granite floor until Matt opened a door. Sheila followed him in while the other two stood guard outside. Sheila looked around and was surprised to see only a table with a few folding chairs placed around it, which neither of them moved towards. Sheila felt a stab of fear but did not allow herself to be affected by it.

"This has nothing to do with HR, does it?"

"In the strictest sense, no."

Sheila made for the door and Matt yelled, "STOP! Don't try to leave. The guards are under my orders to not let you leave until I say you can go. And you want to hear what I have to tell you."

Sheila stopped and turned to him, wondering how little control of the situation she had.

"You've got a couple of minutes before I start screaming," she threatened Matt.

Matt responded with a snide laugh, an expression she was tired of looking at. "I won't go into how wrong that is on so many levels. What I will say is you have no standing. You are a discredited project leader who was forced to resign. If you try to leak information about this project we, I, will destroy you. People get disappeared for less."

Sheila flashed on all the warnings of the dangers of working inside The System she'd received before taking this job. She ignored them and was wrong to do so. When she did not respond, Matt continued.

"Look, you got skills. You're a talented programmer and AI technician. Get yourself a post at a university. If you find some different outlet for your talents, we won't bother you. You're not unique, you know. The universities are filled with smart people who have been bought off. But don't ever try to redo the work you've done on this project. You won't last long if you do."

Again, Sheila did not respond but only looked daggers into Matt, who was not impressed. Sheila looked around again. Moments ago, she was striding along a major walkway in a busy government facility. Then a walk down a corridor she'd never noticed before that was seemingly off limits and now in this room that resembled a detention or holding cell. Its walls were pocked cinder blocks, and sound proofed probably. She was beginning to sense the danger she was in.

"Do you understand?" Matt asked, and his expression made clear this was the only question that mattered.

Sheila held his gaze for several seconds before nodding just barely enough to be perceptible.

They exited the room without another word spoken and returned to the walkway from which they had departed. When they reached the main entrance to the building, they parted unceremoniously. She felt spilled out onto the front steps, the turbulence of all that had just happened leaving her wobbly. Was she being watched even now, and how much surveillance could she expect in the future? Year after year since the assault in 2021, the epicenter of the US government became increasingly enmeshed with defensive technology and might. The architecture of these buildings was always intended to remind individuals of their own relative unimportance. Independence, the union, the act of continual improvement and justice — these themes undergirded this larger-than-life inner sanctum of power. But now those mythic qualities had been diminished, usurped and replaced by the more basic and honest goal of keeping safe those that had claimed access to these halls of power. Sheila surveyed the drones and mounted infrared scans that scraped every autonomous thing, searching out anomalies, intent on extinguishing threat.

She had never considered it before, not in this way, because she had never been a target. And now she was banned from pursuing her life work of ensuring humans' primacy in the world. She looked out from these marble steps that extended further than necessary in every direction. The hustle continued around her, everyone consumed in the bit part they played, not caring or wanting to comprehend the overarching scheme that Sheila was just exposed to. Then she looked beyond the security apparatus to a hawk or maybe it was a buzzard gliding in the breezy, crisp spring air. Strange, she thought, for such a creature to pass through downtown DC. Or maybe it wasn't. Maybe it's here all the time and I just never saw it. Maybe there are multitudes of them. She smiled as she considered this and it helped her to find her footing, her first steps towards moving on.

Chapter 2

All that was left were the tattoos. His arms were covered in ink as was much of his chest and back. Stories from his years on the road: his first electric guitar, a ring of mountains, a towering Gandalf. But he couldn't hold the band together, none of them could. Not enough money and he wouldn't compromise the message or reduce the eardrum-crushing sound one decibel to placate a venue owner.

He looked down the aisle decimated by the weekend crowd. This is where he'd be working the next 4 – 6 hours. He began at Just For You (JUFY) Foods over a year ago, even before the band, Death's Scepter, broke up. It was the only way he could make rent. The work itself was boring but manageable if he could get into a flow. What he hated were the customers. This was part of the newest wave of healthy food stores. No one working there could afford the prices, and everyone entering through the door knew it.

But he was willing to hang on a while longer because World Transom, a global distribution conglomerate, had recently bought JUFY Foods. They were in the middle of an advertising campaign that trumpeted all the changes to come. The one that interested Milo was expanding the food preparation side of the business. He'd had an interest in being a cook for a while and let his boss, Srini Khatri, know he'd like to get in on it. He had no money for trade school and this would offer him on-the-job training, which felt like his only option.

"It doesn't matter if they're nice or not nice to you. We're still getting barely enough to survive and they have millions, most of which they never earned, that just keeps growing. So, I don't care how *nice* they are," Milo said as he restocked the shelves alongside his co-worker, Jose.

"And most only see us when we get in their way," Jose responded as he reached for another case of extra virgin olive oil, withdrew his knife and cut along 3 sides of the top. Pulling the cardboard back, the green tinted bottles glistened in the newly reflected light. Each bottle fetched $41 and Jose or some other stocker would be back at it tomorrow.

The store was in more disarray than normal as WT was making good on its claim to expand the food prep operation. They had purchased space adjacent to the existing store and were banging out walls and putting up new ones. A continuous sheet of plastic, floor to ceiling, encased the work zone. It looked like a hazmat site, with indistinct figures traversing the debris. But Milo saw it differently. He studied the designs that were shared with the employees, who were now called associates. Corporate reps came in and gave presentations. They were told this store was chosen to be a flagship for how other JUFY food stores would be transformed. Pictures showed gleaming stoves, banks of refrigerators and chic display cases. Milo hadn't been excited about anything for a long time. It wasn't the same as being on stage but he'd get paid for it and hopefully learn a trade. Maybe there was even a long-term career here. All of these thoughts were enough to lift him out of the funk that had become a semi-permanent experience of his waking hours.

He left work feeling good and wasn't in a rush to get home. He'd been staying in a rundown house on the outskirts of town. Revolving roommates was the norm and he found himself now with 2 skinheads. Hook worked for the county. He wasn't sure what Jack did or where his money came from.

Skinheads were part of the audience Milo's band attracted. Thrasher metal was angry music and skinheads were angry. But they weren't the part of the audience Milo was drawn to. He was an outsider himself, and felt rage for how life was coming at him and the few options it offered. And dancing in the mosh pit frenzy to walls of chaotic sound was about the only honest release he and his people could embrace with a sense of honesty.

But the skinheads were different. They would just stand there, frozen. Seething. Doped up. Drunk. They scared him, really. And now they sat in his living room, still observing the same code of behavior, black holes sucking all light and energy from the surroundings.

He walked in on Hook, sitting on the couch drinking a beer.

"How's work," Hook asked.

"Work sucks," Milo replied.

"Tell me about it."

Hook worked outdoors mostly, doing tasks like cutting grass and tree maintenance. He was a vet, served two tours of duty in the middle eastern hegemony the west had been trying to install for the last eight years. He wasn't much older than Milo but condescended to him like he was his younger brother. Hook believed his military background gave him license to behave this way towards Milo, to anyone who hadn't served. Milo did his best to ignore this attitude, but struggled to convince himself that he was Hook's equal. Hook knew Milo's insecurities and made sure to amplify them whenever he could.

Hook continued, "And you can bet it's not going to get any better. I'm lucky I got into the County when I did. The three guys they hired since me are Hispanic. No room for White guys anymore unless you're a doctor or lawyer. And the only reason I got the job was because I was a vet."

Hook let his comments hang in the tense atmosphere, "I keep telling you you should come to a meeting of the White Knights. That will help you get your head screwed on right about what's going on in this country."

Milo didn't want to go down this path again, knowing where it led. This was another part of the way Hook interacted with him. Like he knew how the world worked and would let him in on its secrets if only Milo paid attention. Usually, like now, he could avoid going where Hook led, but not always. The White Knights were a White nationalist organization that Hook was involved in. He'd imprinted its spurious historical reasoning and could recite it back without needing to think about it, which was, of course, the point. But that didn't explain his commitment to the group. The main benefit it provided was the feeling of support he experienced within its ranks, something that existed nowhere else. Milo hadn't sat down and now walked to the refrigerator and pulled out a beer. He continued up the stairs to his room without speaking another word.

Over the next week Milo continued stocking the shelves but kept a close eye on the emergent design of the new wing of the store. The construction was nearly complete and the outline of how the store was transformed could be dimly perceived. Yes, it would essentially be for people with money but it would be like an open market, the parallel aisles replaced by mashed up, attractive displays. It wasn't perfect but it gave him hope that he could be working in this less structured space, doing something that didn't entirely destroy his spirit.

Then the announcement was made that three internal staff members would be joining the newly formed food prep group. In addition to these three, two external chefs were being hired and corporate staff would also be on site for training and startup. Jose was on the list of those who'd been chosen as were two women, both of whom Milo hardly knew. But one thing he noted was, they were both Black.

Milo and Jose continue to work side by side without the normal banter. But Jose was feeling good and finally said, "What's up with you, man?"

Milo could have absorbed the disappointment. He was scary good at shutting down when circumstances were beyond his control. But when asked the question he decided to express how he felt, "I should have gotten that job. I've been here longer than you and work just as hard as you."

They hadn't discussed the job posting but Jose now understood Milo was after the job and wanted it as much as he did. "I don't know, man. Go ask the boss why you didn't get it."

'I think I know why I didn't get it. Seems to me they're looking for more diversity where the customers can see us."

Their shared gaze was now sharper than it had ever been and neither of them could control where this was headed.

"I don't know, man. Maybe they just don't want someone whose arms are all inked up. But you should just go ask them and see what's up."

"It's about my skin. You're right there. But you're finding the wrong message in it."

Jose wasn't happy about having his good vibe blown by this bullshit claim of reverse discrimination.

"Man, maybe you're right. Maybe it's because you're White. I don't know. Maybe it's time you guys stepped aside and let someone else get a chance."

"Fuck off," was all Milo thought fit to say. He pushed past him with a case of industrial, plant-based meat.

It was a Saturday afternoon and the store was packed. Milo was almost grateful for the crowd so that he could blend into the impersonal, transactional environment. After an hour of restocking the shelves, he was called to the checkout area to bag. Twenty minutes in, he finished bagging the order of a tall, statuesque woman. She was visibly upset but not a hair on her salon-generated blond head moved out of place.

"Can I take your bags out to the car," Milo inquired.

Her discriminating gaze scanned him once and he was made to understand he'd failed her test. She was clearly not from this area. Most likely one of the New Yorkers who were gobbling up land in what had been a vacation mecca for New Yorkers for a long time. But this was a different breed. In the past this was the preferred spot for working class people. Monied New Yorkers disdained The Poconos and headed for posher getaways. Everyone recognized this distinction and was OK with it. When the working class atrophied, the same fate pressed into this region. It wasn't pretty as gangs moved in and a generally rough lifestyle took hold. But at least this was still a place for people scraping by.

The destruction of the shorelines accelerated, as anticipated by those looking into these things, in 2030, and in the six years since then the destruction had escalated. Many people with money decided The Poconos was a good place to post-up and they were flocking in. Those getting in now could do so cheaply. The housing inventory from the boom of 30 years ago was mostly crap and could be gutted and replaced with something magnificent at a fraction of what they got from insurance settlements on their prior homes, many of which were last seen being eaten up by enormous storms and ocean incursions. Hence, The Poconos was quickly becoming a home for only those with access to a lot of cash.

She decided he would do, and walked away from the cart which she expected he would push closely behind the path she took. "I suppose. I don't know what else could go wrong in this place."

They walked out of the store and neither uttered a word until midway through the parking lot when he heard her mutter with annoyance, "Why can't the locals do their shopping during the week so *we* don't have to wait in these long lines. I'm going to be late for my exercise class." He offered no response and continued advancing in studied muteness. While she walked, her clothes morphed from shabby-chic jacket and pants outfit to full-on exercise gear. Milo had heard on a Newer Machine report about clothes that could morph by being touched in certain ways but hadn't seen them yet in person. This was explained by credits to buy these garments had only been issued to the very rare Level One Newer Machine accounts. She knew he was dazzled and enjoyed watching his expression of disbelief. He had the look of a dog trying to find the dog on the other side of a mirror. He unloaded the groceries into her Mercedes SUV. She wordlessly held out bills of some denomination, which he declined, a Mona Lisa-like smile curled on his lips his only reply.

Hook was driving and Milo sat beside him. They were on their way to the monthly White Knights meeting. They traveled side roads on the outskirts of town, headed to an old building that was part of a junkyard. When they entered, Milo saw it served multiple functions, part shop, part administrative. The walls were intact but the ceiling tiles sagged and half of them were water stained. A single light bulb hung down through a tile. A wood stove in the corner provided the only heat but kept the space comfortable. There were no computers but there was a bank of file cabinets. For all its backward appearance, there was a certain order to what he looked at.

He was introduced to a small circle of young men, most of whom were a few years older than him. Their main concern was the well-being of one man, Jeremiah, and getting him settled. Jeremiah could walk, but had a hitch in his gait. The same could be said for his speech and other motor skills. The care with which the others attended to him affected Milo. Jeremiah wore an old army jacket and fatigues. Milo surmised these were the clothes Jeremiah wore while serving his country, not a metaphor the Mercedes lady might adopt for whatever situation called for it. Most of the others around him also wore remnants from the time when they served in the armed forces.

"What you been up to?" Hook asked Jeremiah, who had circled back into Milo's orbit, and took a seat next to Jeremiah. Milo stood at a small distance away and studied their interaction. He was struck by Hook's calm, caring attitude.

Hook placed his hand on Jeremiah's forearm, gave it a squeeze, and let it stay there.

Jeremiah shrugged and continued gazing away, downward in no particular direction.

"I'm just trying to get back to normal. Get healthy enough to take care of myself."

"That's right. You'll get there. No need to rush this. In fact, you can't rush it. But until you're better you've got us, your brothers. And that's all you need to see you through."

Jeremiah did not respond outwardly but his body relaxed visibly. Hook got up to say hello to someone across the room and another partially clad military man took his place. All very subdued, quiet restorative motions, simple single-grasp handshakes. The same level of caring played out again and again. These were the deplorables that no one knew what to do with but what they wanted most was to be useful, have something worth caring about, and have the means to live simple, secure lives.

Milo fell into conversation with Ninetoe. He was born with only four toes on one foot and had the nickname for as long as he could remember. The rest of his growth appeared stunted as well. But he seemed to have made his peace with these shortcomings.

"Glad to meet you," Ninetoe said. We're always interested in finding new brothers. "So, what do you do? You working in the trades? That's what most of us do."

"No. Never had much exposure to that type of work. Wish I had. Working in a grocery store right now." Milo purposefully declined saying which one. "Trying to figure out what to do next."

"I know what you mean. I'm a roofer. But work's getting scarcer and scarcer. And pay is worse than I've ever seen during my 10 years doing it. All because the illegals were allowed to come in from down south. Willing to work for nothing. You can't compete with that. This is what we get from the government we spent years in the service defending."

Ninetoe got worked up, his pupils were like pin pricks as he focused on some unseen spot on the opposing wall. He took a deep drag on his cigarette.

"How about you?" Ninetoe asked. "You serve in the armed forces?"

"No, never did. Spent most of my energy since high school playing in bands. Metal mostly. Last band was Death's Scepter. We toured the chum circuit up and down the east coast. Played some gigs in this area. You ever hear of us?"

"No, never did. Too busy trying to put food on my family's table I guess." Ninetoe's tone was not harsh but gave voice to the difference, the distinction between them. Ninetoe doubted this grocery store clerk/rock musician could ever know the day-to-day struggle nearly everyone here waged. The nightmares that followed them from their experiences in the military. The repetitive manual labor that wore their bodies out for an ever-shrinking piece of what was once known as the American Dream.

Milo sensed all this as well and the surprise of the night for him was that he could be made to feel unworthy to join a White nationalist group where he thought skin color was the only prerequisite. . .. But he had seen kindness here and knew he could eventually be accepted if that's what he wanted.

After some moments Ninetoe, becoming upbeat, said, "Maybe you could play at one of our gatherings."

"That would be awesome," Milo said. But the idea sent a shudder through his body as he considered how differently he might someday view the audience they represented.

The rest of the evening was uneventful. If he didn't know this was a White nationalist organization, he would have thought he was at a Rotary or Optimist Club monthly meeting. Mostly he found himself distracted by the idea that there might be something here for him.

Milo met with his manager, Srini, to discuss being passed over for the assistant cook job. Milo didn't say he believed it was because he was White but did say he thought he deserved one of the slots. Srini deflected Milo's assertion but said there would be more openings in the future and Milo would be one of the first to be considered and that he was a valued associate. Milo left it at that. He wasn't surprised by how unsatisfying the conversation felt. Srini was Indian and no matter how hard Milo worked, he never felt like he gained Srini's respect and suspected it was a racial thing. He had seen how White guys who weren't bosses were often assumed to be lazy and incompetent. Milo couldn't shake his anger in the following weeks, as the cooking teams formed and transformed the store's atmosphere. His attitude showed in his performance and if this continued, he wouldn't have to worry about when the next cook opportunity came.

Milo was in his room playing guitar, fingering licks from old Death Scepter songs, but all he felt was what was missing. The clothes washer outside his door offered the only percussive sound . . . monotonous, metronomic. This is what you become, a parody of yourself. Looking back, he wasn't sure how or when he stopped feeling anything. The band had offered him a limited sense of hope and connection to other outcasts. There was no agenda, no plan, just the transcendent experience breaking through the temporal shell when the music propelled them. It was ten months since their last show and the lifeline it provided was all but extinguished. Meanwhile, the-here-and-now was crushing him, while those ephemeral moments mocked him: you're not a heroic free spirit, those days are over.

Milo's phone rang. Hook was calling him, which almost never happened.

"Jeremiah was beat up, bad. He's in the hospital now but will be OK. He's got some broken ribs and cuts on his face."

"What the fuck. How did this happen."

"He was scoring drugs from some Mexican guys and they robbed and beat him instead."

"That's bullshit, man." He'd gone to a couple more White Knights meetings and learned one of Jeremiah's problems was an opioid addiction, which was the result of being medicated after being wounded while on patrol in Af-fucking-ghanistan.

"Yeah, it is, which is why I'm calling you. Some of his brothers are meeting tonight at 10 at Stan's house. We know where their gang hangs out. We're going to pay them a visit. Stand up for one of our brothers."

The line went quiet and then Hook proceeded with his real reason for calling.

"I'd like you to join us if you feel called to do so. Stand up for something you believe in. Maybe it's time for you to recognize who will fight for you when you need it, which means fighting for them when something like this goes down."

The spin cycle in the washing machine was peaking and set off a cacophonous, percussive roar. He told himself he didn't want to move into this world, this cult, this behavior. But he couldn't convince himself because it had become his only support.

"Let me think about it," Milo said.

Hook was satisfied with this. He could sense one more of his clan coming home, one more thread woven into their safety net.

Milo walked the streets of Stan's neighborhood for a half hour, and it was now 9:40 PM. Brisk night air. It was springtime but felt like autumn, could have been Halloween night. His nervous system, starting in his gut, dispersed a jittery feeling through his entire core as he considered how everything had fallen away from him. He'd grown distant from his family in his teen years and remained so. High school friends he'd stayed in touch with were making life decisions that he couldn't, or chose not to. The only thing that made sense was the band and that now was gone, leaving a gaping wound. The world was passing him by and at 24, he felt cut off from it. Each day cemented a new reality that made him feel more alien, more disposable.

Hate was as much a part of what motivated them as brotherhood, and probably would always be. He wondered if he could mellow some of the more strident positions of the White Knights and decided probably not. He'd have to accept the entire package. He came to a street corner. Two street lights cast shadows, his own tilted and pointed in various directions. Stan's was one way, the other back to where he lived. A decision was required but he continued to stand rooted to the spot.

A dark van drove up the street behind him. He noticed it because it was driving too close to the sidewalk, but he looked away and returned to his quandary, hoping his feet would decide for him. The van drove up beside him and instead of turning, the rear-side door opened and three men jumped out. They grabbed him and threw him in the van. His hands were tied behind his back and a mask was placed over his head. His fleeting glimpses of his abductors suggested they were not Hispanic gang members, which was the only reasonable explanation for his abduction.

He tried to squirm and yell but was easily subdued and was actually too scared to do much of anything. He sat wedged between two of his captors and discerned a couple more voices.

"What the fuck is going on?" Milo spat out, hoarse and angry.

"It's OK Milo. We're not going to hurt you. We have something to discuss with you, an offer to make." The voice was coming from the front passenger seat, presumably from the one in charge, as the car sped away. It was a male voice.

25

Because it was measured, Milo was unable to determine the man's temperament or anything else about him. How did they know his name, he wondered.

"Well. Why all this? Do I know you? We could have met over coffee, for Christ sake."

"I get it. This seems extreme to you. But we need to protect ourselves, keep our identity secret. When we're done, we'll bring you back to the spot we picked you up or anywhere else you'd like to go."

Another freaking secret society. But at least this guy didn't sound like some psychopath. Milo would let this play out, cooperate, and hope he'd come through this unharmed. What choice did he have?

"How long will this take?"

"Give us a couple of hours and we'll have you on your way."

They drove for fifteen minutes without speaking. The road was windy which told Milo they were heading out of town, which worried him even more.

When they reached their destination, the only one who'd spoken to him let him know how things would go down.

"We're not going to gag you. But if you start yelling, we'll be on you in a second and will probably end up hurting you. So don't do it. It wouldn't do you any good anyway."

They eased him out of the car. His hands were still tied and the sack still over his head. The air had a dense quality, allowing him to detect only the most immediate sounds. They were definitely in a country setting, but more than that he couldn't say. The ground was an uneven mixture of dirt and grass and someone on both sides guided him around depressions in the earth that could cause him to falter.

They entered a structure of some kind and sat him down.

"We'll take the hood off in a second and free your hands. But don't think about escaping or fighting because it won't do you any good and will just wind up getting you hurt," the same voice he'd become accustomed to informed him.

When the hood came off and his hands were untied, he saw he was sitting at a small table in some type of RV. Lights from the ceiling shined in his eyes and he squinted until they adjusted. Three indistinct figures stood motionless behind the lights. A fourth man sat across from Milo, studying him with a weary intensity. He was about 40 years old, sinewy and muscular. All Milo could think about was why he had become the focus of such attention.

"Would you like something to drink? We got water, coffee and orange juice."

"I'll take some coffee," which Milo hoped would settle his nerves.

He took a couple of sips and then asked, "So, what's all this about?"

"Milo, you can call me Rex. We'll get to that in a minute but the first thing I'd like to ask is if you like superheroes?" Rex's expression brightened as he asked this most bizarre question.

Milo felt blindsided but went along for the ride. "Sure, back when I was a kid, that's what I did. It was the thing I enjoyed most."

"Well, that future is now, or something very much like it. Brain fusion links exist that can connect humans to endless computer networks. This makes learning new skills exponentially faster. It brings the whole world's body of knowledge within the grasp of anyone possessing this link."

"Sounds awesome, sounds like tremendous power to anyone who's hooked up." Milo mused, letting his guard down. It rekindled a flame from his youth that was never completely extinguished.

"Milo, you may not believe this but you are a leading candidate to receive this device."

The shift in consciousness Milo now felt was like a spinning out of control.

"What are you talking about? How do you know so much about me? Shit, how do you even know my name?"

"Which of these do you want me to start with?" Rex said, allowing the first smile to spread across his face. He was not averse to going down any of these paths.

After considering this for a moment Milo responded, "Take your pick. None of it makes any sense to me."

"We know you have a healthy distrust of the government and you're right to believe that they're not looking out for you. We're part of a rebel group that sees signs that civilization is about to come undone and believe we have found a way to combat this evil at its core. We've hacked into the darkest corners of the government and found they're planning to implement a technology called neuralBlast that can connect the human brain directly to computer networks. It allows not just your brain but also your body to absorb information and learn new skills at a rate unknown to humankind. We've downloaded the entire system and made it operational. We've also installed bugs in their version of the software that has set them back months, but they'll eventually get past them. So, we have a window where we can use this software for good. But that window is closing rapidly."

Milo was intrigued. He began believing they weren't going to hurt him, which allowed him to relax and take in the meaning of Rex's comments.

"Okay, you got my interest. But where do I fit in?"

"You remember that car accident you were in when you were 13?"

"Sure, what about it?"

"Even after all the tests and therapies you never felt the same again, right? The headaches may have disappeared but the depression didn't. That's the word they probably gave it but I doubt it explained what you were feeling."

"Fuck you, man! How do you know all this? NOBODY knows this."

"Sorry, relax. I wanted to let you know we'd done our homework. The rest of what I'm going to tell you now will be just as shocking, so get ready . . .. The problems you experienced in your life after the accident was caused by damage done to your limbic system. The doctors taking care of you missed it, had no idea what they were looking for. But we know you have an extraordinary ability to shut yourself down and not feel core emotions like fear and pain. Without proper guidance my bet is this caused you some problems along the way."

Milo wanted to tell Rex to fuck off again, but was too stunned. Rex hit upon the central truth of who he was, the thing that caused him to suffer before he learned how to use it to his advantage. Shutting down these core emotions had become the thing that allowed him to perfect his art, elevate him, keep him free. But it had also caused problems in his relationships and his ability to feel and express emotions.

"But how did you find me, how did you know where to look?"

"You remember the physical you took when World Transom bought out JUFY Foods?"

"Yeah, sure. What about it?"

"Well, they tested a lot more than your blood pressure. That body scan they did got down to the molecular level. Among other things, they tracked brain activity under stress. They've done this for nearly all their 80,000 employees and your scores were off the charts. They probably attributed it to a system malfunction but we dug into your past, which led us to believe the results were accurate. JUFY's database is the largest of its kind, which is why I'm sitting here with you right now."

"Keep talking," Milo replied after mulling over Rex's assertions.

"Your particular condition makes you a perfect candidate for neuralBlast treatments. Subjects need to be fully conscious but disengaged from their emotional response, something out of the reach for most people. There's a lot going on during these sessions. You are interacting with a lot of multi-layered data and your body and mind are changing in real time."

And then, for added emphasis, Rex stated, "My guess is if we didn't get to you first, it wouldn't be long before the government's dark forces paid you a visit. And they wouldn't be as willing to leave the decision up to you as we are."

"You got to be kidding me," Milo spat out. "Here I thought I was being hauled off by a local gang to get the shit kicked out of me and instead you're telling me you can turn me into some superhero dude with a direct hookup to computer networks that can turn me into whoever I want to be."

"That's about right," Rex responded as his body relaxed and a disarming smile spread across his face. "And any one of us here would jump at the chance if we thought we could survive the treatments."

When thinking about technology, the general populous' thoughts turned to The Newer Machine. The ownership of news outlets consolidated until they all rolled up into one quasi-government entity. The internet did a pretty good job of cannibalizing itself, upending every promise it held out in its infancy. The Newer Machine became the de facto platform on every computer screen and mobile device, promising a disciplined approach to disseminating information. The sweeping change occurred shortly after the 2028 election when the dominant party ran on the platform of weeding out corruption and stopping crime. The simple promises offered by The Newer Machine made its acceptance by the vast majority an easy choice. Nothing was as appealing as the benevolent, autocratic rule that it projected through its consistent narrative. Because of the dominance of this scaled-down version of technology, Milo had no idea of the vastness of what he was being offered.

Milo looked up. He still couldn't see the faces of those behind the lights but his eyes had adjusted enough so he could discern the contour of their bodies, which shifted uncomfortably with Rex's last comment. Milo looked back at Rex who had not turned away from him as Milo's gaze wandered. Rex's eyes rested quietly on Milo and for the first time Milo began to believe the story Rex was telling him.

Almost as an afterthought, Rex added, "My guess is you've sensed that there was something a little *off* about you. And then when you'd catch that part of you acting out, you'd shut it down tight but immediately worried about when the next indiscretion would occur and whether you'd be able to contain it."

Milo knew what he was talking about. He ran with some guys on the cross-country track team in high school and had better endurance than them every time because he could push through the pain, even though they always trained and he never did. He was the one driving the van after shows to the next gig without getting tired while everyone else was sacked out.

But these thoughts led to deeper reflections. At key times in his life after the accident he behaved in the most bizarre ways. His younger sister died when he was 15, after being struck by a truck on her bike. When Milo received this news, he felt a little giddy and wanted to laugh and joke around. It took all his effort to put on a show of remorse. He never forgave himself for this reaction and subsequently never dealt properly with his sister's passing. Girls, high school exams, all the things that had given him focus became a jumble of confusion and he simply disassociated from them, something that he did with an ease that surprised even him. It didn't end there and spiraled into every area of his life. No one in his family saw it coming. They tried to reconnect but he pushed them further away. Rejecting their entreaties gave him a sense of personal power.

"So, what would happen to me?" Milo asked.

"You undergo a procedure where a device is attached to the cortex of your brain. After you're stable, we'll slowly increase the bandwidth between you and several arrays of high-speed computers. Think of it as the most advanced search algorithms knowing your thoughts, sometimes before you recognize them, and providing solutions that can instantaneously result in recursive questions and answers until either the absolute answer is attained or the available information is exhausted. This is the part we are most interested in. But the effects on your body are equally profound because it can integrate this diverse information to learn physical skills at extraordinary speed."

Milo found it staggering that his mind could tap into this power. What couldn't he learn and master?

"What type of testing have you done on this? Who else has experienced this?"

It was Rex's turn to cast his eyes away and look uncertain. "It has not been tried on a human yet. We've performed the procedure on rats with great success. We can share the results of these tests with you."

"I'd be the first human to be hooked up. That sounds incredibly risky. Why would I do something like this?"

"Yes, there are risks, which we can go into more when you're ready," Rex said. He allowed some moments to pass before continuing. "Look, you're a good person. I like you. We know about Death's Scepter and how you poured your heart and soul into that band. Since then, your life's been going downhill pretty quickly. We know where you were headed when we abducted you at the street corner. You're better than that. I don't blame you for seeking refuge from your loneliness and alienation, but the answers provided by White nationalists only perpetuate the cycle of violence, and you know that. If you decide to go back to your current life, I doubt you'll save yourself from getting caught up in some type of dehumanizing situation like that.

"What we are offering you is an adventure like none other, one that has never been taken before. It's a chance to help reverse the nightmare so many of us find ourselves in. You'll never get an opportunity like this again. I hope that you seize it."

"What about my life now, as it is?"

"If you decide to accept this offer, your old life, this life, is terminated. We don't know exactly how you'll react to the neuralBlast experience, but we do know it is like stepping through a portal that functions in one direction only. And that's because worlds will be opened up to you that you can't even imagine right now.

"The main thing we expect is that the knowledge you gain will help us take down The System. We're part of the Justice Force movement. Have you heard of us?"

Milo spun through his catalog of groups opposed to The System, but couldn't recall Justice Force. The resistance was such a patchwork of activity playing out at the fringes, he wasn't surprised.

After Milo shook his head, Rex continued. "I get it. The Newer Machine doesn't acknowledge us so we are invisible. If you agree to undergo neuralBlast treatments we expect you to help us gain exposure, find ways to undo the censorship that keeps us from reaching the masses of people who would embrace our message. We have this very small window when we have an advantage over the machine of government. We're not expecting you to be able to defeat them alone. Even with powers as broad as what you will have, that will probably be beyond your capability. But we are hoping for something, a way to allow our resistance to grow and avoid being incinerated in The System's furnace, where everyone who opposes them ends up."

This was real. Milo hadn't believed any of it until this moment. How could he? It had to be one elaborate hoax from which the curtain would soon be pulled from . . .. Except it wasn't. Rex was too real, too determined, too desperate. The System was everything that everyone answered to. The Newer Machine was the interface between the people and the dark forces that few dared to question or inquire about. Moments passed, and the silence was finally broken by Milo.

"So, what's next?" Milo asked in a non-committal way.

"First of all, do you have any further questions?

Milo laughed. "Like a million. But I doubt any of them will make much of a difference."

"OK, then," Rex responded, laughing along with Milo. "We'll take you wherever you want to go. We'll give you a day to decide if you're in or not. Tomorrow at noon we'll text you to see if you have any final questions. If you're with us we'll call you to arrange a rendezvous point. One thing I want to tell you is whether or not you join forces with us, I wouldn't tell anyone about this meeting. We're very good at covering our tracks. Our footprint is even smaller than what the government's dark forces leave behind. And of course, people will think you're crazy. Just like you thought we were when this conversation began."

After tying his hands and placing the hood back on, they drove him back into town but he requested to be dropped off closer to where he lived than where he was picked up. He was less interested in the retaliatory raid and would never know which path he would have taken. Rex left him with this parting comment.

"Take the next day to think about what's being offered to you. You'll be the first person to ever transcend the essential limitations of human consciousness. Certainly, there have been geniuses throughout the ages but no one has come close to the abilities you will have, the ability to integrate information at light speed. Think of the service you could provide. This is what the world has been waiting for, this is the phenomenal endgame of technology, the true merging of human consciousness and computer intelligence. You will lead us into the new future that so many of us have struggled to create."

Milo felt as he did when he was on stage. He walked the couple of blocks to his house enveloped in some type of ecstatic energy. This emotional state was almost absent since his days with the band. What was it that so enthralled him? There was a full moon that displayed the intricate lacy caverns that were so inviting. Humans had found a way to make that journey and we have all benefited from that pilgrimage. Who wouldn't want to be frolicking and bounding along that foreign landscape that, at the first encounter, became part of the human experience. What universes could Milo bring within the human experience if he submitted to the neuralBlast technology?

Astral projection had not accomplished this feat, nor any type of mind-altering drug or religious practice. It was technology's mastery of the physical world that provided this transcendent experience that was shared and now stored in our collective memory. Could he someday, somehow, master these distances with an ease never before imagined?

Were we at a similar juncture right now, he wondered, one even more fundamental and immense than anything that had come before? The moon beckoned, but so did everything close at hand: the midnight air, the touch of the trees' bark that his hand grazed upon as he walked. This was the intoxicant common to all questers, and the cost of being truly alive has always been substantial risk.

He walked the final block where a stone wall abutted the sidewalk, holding back the front lawn of the houses built on this ascent. Street lights lit up the stone, worn down with time. Glass speckles shimmered in the pock-marked mortar like bits of precious stone. He stopped to behold this attenuating street scape that was like the moon and stars that had just captivated him. Then he looked more closely at the bits of sand that had not yet been washed away, and these, too, glistened in their perfection. And then the whole wall shimmered, as if bursting into flame.

Two hours after he left the house, he returned to it. He would never look at abduction stories the same way. Nor would he ever be the same, regardless of his decision, and felt empathy for anyone claiming a similar experience or encounter with the unknown.

He watched TV until he fell asleep. He was exhausted but his sleep was restless. Several times he woke in a cold sweat, caused by dreams of grotesquely shaped marauders chasing him through improbable, claustrophobic labyrinths. When morning came, he got out of bed but was no more refreshed than when he descended into his troubled sleep.

He walked down to the kitchen and turned on the local news as he made coffee. The lead story concerned street violence the night before between 2 gangs. From what Milo could glean the MC 13s had been tipped off to plans of the White Knights and overwhelmed the White gang when they entered onto their turf.

A picture of Hook was displayed on the screen. He was in intensive care having contusions to the head and spine. Milo was shaken by this news and leaned onto the counter. He was angry and sad for the shape his friend was in. But these thoughts were eventually replaced by others that recognized that more reprisals and calls for revenge would follow. And if Milo stayed, he would probably be drawn into them. He walked back in his room and his mind drifted into thoughts of what was worth taking with him.

The house itself felt toxic, filled with things and emotional energy he wanted no part of. He dressed quickly then glanced around his room, wondering if he would ever re-enter it. From a shallow bowl on the bedside table he drew a guitar pick, the one he'd used at the last Death's Scepter concert. He rubbed it between his fingertips and smiled inwardly. At least there was one souvenir, one remnant from his life, he wanted to bring along with him.

Milo walked into a coffee shop on Main St. He had the place mostly to himself and took a seat in the nook by the windows in the front of the store.

Once the caffeine kicked in he felt a little better, a little clearer. He pulled up a messaging app on his phone and scrolled to Cecil, his one bandmate who had been there from beginning to end of Death's Scepter. They had hardly communicated since the band broke up.

Yo, wads up?

> Not much. Caught me good. On a break. Driving truck for my dad.

No shit. Didn't see that coming.

> Yeah, Margie got pregnant. Needed some steady income. You know the gig.

Sure do. Playing any music?

> Nah, no time for that. It's all good though. How about you?

Here and there. Not much... Hey, just want to let you know it looks like I'm moving.

> That so? My turn to say I didn't see that coming. Moving far?

Sort of. Yeah u could say that. Maybe I'll ping u when I get where I'm going.

Yeah, def stay in touch. Good talking to you, man, but I got to get back on the road. My dad busts my balls when I'm late.

I hear ya. Take care and good luck with starting a family.

Dig that. Take care of yourself, too.

Cecil was the last one besides himself. And now he had been co-opted, too. Scurrying to grab what crumbs of the pie he could latch onto. Milo didn't blame him, wished him the best. But, turning his phone over on the table, he decided he did not need any more of these goodbyes. His family was scattered; he'd lost touch with them long ago. He looked out the window and onto the street with its occasional passerby. There was always a barrier between him and them, with or without the glass. This melancholy and loneliness weren't even that hard to take because he at least felt something, even if it was a yearning for something more. He would probably miss this experience, but not enough to make him stay. And when he disappeared, no one would really notice. It happened all the time.

Midway through his third cup of coffee he received the call.

"Morning," Rex began, "Get much sleep?"

"Can't say I did," Milo responded with a little laugh and wondered how much Rex knew about what happened the night before. "I'm exhausted and wired at the same time."

"That's not at all surprising. Before I ask if you made a decision, I want to know if you have any questions."

Milo thought for a minute and then asked, "What can I bring with me?"

Rex laughed, "I guess you cleared the board with that question. Bring what you can carry. Even most of that you won't need in a short while. One last thing, once you have the implant, there's no turning back. You won't be able to recover this life."

"I've come to terms with *it* being dead. But what I'm interested in, is *who* it is that replaces the *me* I know now."

"Exactly right. You'll be more alive than you've ever been, in ways you can't even imagine."

He was told the rendezvous point and got up from his seat. He wasn't sure where he was headed, but was willing to follow the life force pumping through him, which was strong and true. He needed to feel alive and powerful, and that's what Rex offered him. Compared with his aimless life and prospects, this was the better path.

He walked back to his house and hastily packed the few things which held meaning for the 24 years he'd walked this earth. He scanned the house once more and then sailed through the front door and did not look back. In his right hand he held a guitar, and over his left shoulder he draped a small backpack. In it were a few notebooks with his writings, some pictures, a couple of shirts and some precious stones. Too small a trove of treasures for a life, but he did not dwell on this. Instead, he walked, as he'd been told, towards the train tracks on the outskirts of town.

As the rails came into focus he saw an old, rusted RV approach from the other direction. He never got to the tracks. The camper pulled to the side and the door swung open. Rex's head peeked around the corner.

"Step right up," Rex said with a humorous, carnival delivery and made a grand gesture with his hands to welcome Milo aboard. A phosphorescent glow from an unknown source outlined the vehicle. A vortex of energy drew him on; no further effort required for this next step of his transition.

Milo looked about. His captors from the night before now approached him, clasped his hand, and gave him pats on the back. They were comrades now, no hard feelings. Milo stowed his belongings and took a seat. He looked out the window at a muted landscape on this overcast late afternoon. He would have died here, he told himself, much too quickly. He had just accelerated the process, because now he was dead in this land where no one would grieve his departure.

Chapter 3

Back at her apartment, Sheila settled into her favorite chair and considered all that had happened. But her analysis was flawed because something was broken inside and she could not conceive of a way to fix it.

She worked at a furious pace most of her life. Tenth grade chemistry was where she gained focus and determination. She loved the way scientific investigation empowered her. This, more than anything, was responsible for transforming her from the shy girl to the confident woman she was now. Graduate and post-graduate work kept her busy until she was 30, when she took her first full-time job. She was aware of the political divisiveness across the land, but never had time to engage it. Rebellious groups ascended on the left and right and she had sympathy for their complaints, especially those on the left. But their thinking so lacked in rigor that she rarely took it seriously. If she had, she never would have passed the background check, and been spared this devastating chapter in her life.

She worked at her first job for several years. The focus was neural gateway technology and how it could be applied to the newest consumer based, data-mining technologies. Although she excelled and made a name for herself, she was never satisfied because of what she saw as its limited scope and applicability. Lurking behind her success was a dark truth that continued to propel her to this day. She was dissatisfied because the subject of her work, humanity, was deprecated and falling behind. The psychic and mythic energy had shifted to machines as they had eclipsed all but a handful of measurable human capabilities, and these were in the crosshairs of current research.

An opportunity opened up and she went all in. A startup, Titan Computing, was developing software to enhance human capabilities by bridging the human mind with computer networks. A device needed to be implanted in the base of a person's brain to manage the communications. The difference between this and other AI projects was its orientation, which placed the emphasis on the human host. Fixing the world's problems was what Titan professed to be after but there was a somewhat melancholy reason for Sheila's interest. People were becoming obsolete. Machines were taking over. This was the best chance for humans to remain relevant, in control. The procession of technology had forced her hand.

The business model at Titan was flawed. But it didn't matter because they caught the attention of some big investors and when the money started rolling in, they could do the research the right way.

This fortunate arrangement ended when the government started snooping around. At first Titan needed to file reports for ethics investigations. Next, they needed to allow oversight committees to access proprietary information. A year after the initial government inquiry the operation was shut down and all of their work was confiscated by the government. Concerns for national security was the reason disseminated to the media, which barely caused a ripple in the news cycle. This did not come as a great surprise to Sheila and her team. The government scientists kept gnawing and encroaching, becoming more and more interested in the details of their work.

She had risen to the lead research position at Titan and was offered a government job. She agonized over her decision. She knew moving into a bureaucratic, government organization would be brutal, but that wasn't what really bothered her. At Titan, the goal was to increase human capabilities to learn and process data exponentially. Everything she knew told her the government would be less committed to innovation.

The most out of character thing she did was leave the ivory tower of research for a government job. Her colleagues joked about how she would never be able to make peace with the bureaucracy. But she saw a unique opportunity with this project and knew she had no choice but to accept the offer. The quest to alter the brain to take full advantage of its capability was the Holy Grail, and she would go wherever that challenge led. They were on the cutting edge of scientific and ethical thinking and she decided she would lay aside her concerns about whether or not the government could successfully conduct this endeavor.

And they had been close to achieving their goal.

She took a long pull from a glass of wine, and took a moment to appreciate this decent cabernet. But it did not in any way mellow her thoughts.

She'd been over it innumerable times, how the portal had been infiltrated and blown apart by malicious code. They were still seeing cancerous fragments floating around in the system that were only detected after they wreaked havoc. She could never explain how it could happen, to herself or her superiors. And now, it was her undoing.

She had no agenda now, didn't know what her next move would be. She was 41 years old and felt certain she'd already done her best work; any step forward would be a step down from where she'd just been. She had a couple of friends but was not surprised she had no desire to call them and tell them how she'd lost her job today. The people she was closest to were the people she worked with. She'd do anything for them, and already missed the camaraderie they offered. But the basis of their relationship was the work they shared. So their strongest bond was severed.

She was determined not to be a victim and took Matt's threats seriously. The System drew enormous power to itself and reports about the dark side of its power grab occasionally flickered into the public domain before being snuffed out.

Because of this, and the concerns raised by her colleagues, she converted her assets into liquid currency before starting this job. After she began working for the government she figured out how to create a new identity for herself if she should need one. Putting these things in order was what drew her out of her stupor during the first week of joblessness.

The swift changes in her life gave her an increased appreciation for the scope of The System's control. Everyone had a Newer Machine device and it would be hard to imagine life without it. The basic interaction was similar to computers used for the last 40 years, but this incarnation was personalized to a degree that users of earlier models could not relate. When she first turned it on after losing her job it took five minutes to boot, a stunningly long period of time. At first the differences were hardly discernible but that didn't last.

Where previously The Newer Machine searches provided nuanced results, it was now a dull instrument. The more she tried to use her portal, the more frustrated she became. Everything was dumbed-down. Her filter into the world switched from a highly compensated government researcher to that of an out-of-work subversive, and it affected everything.

The change went beyond tracking down information and affected the entertainment and news broadcasts she relied upon. The same people with the same voices provided truncated versions of stories that she'd been following. Today, the conflict at the southern border decried the atrocities of the encroaching horde trying to storm the barricades. Yesterday's news stirred hopes of a negotiated compromise for the same conflict. She realized she was witnessing different permutations of truth for different markets, all of which were controlled by The Newer Machine's algorithms that herded each hierarchical level of society at the behest of the dial twisters who never emerged from behind the curtains, if in fact a human hand was still in control. She stared harder at the news reporters and wondered if they were real or avatars. Words crashed like a waterfall from serious, clenched expressions. But were they sourced from billions of images collected in facial recognition software that could easily be plucked and rearranged. Did the words match the expressions and did those words contain truth and critical thinking? The only thing she was sure of was that The System had done its job very well.

The other thing she did during this first week was reach out to each member of her team. These were the most wrenching experiences of that period. Their lead ally had been whisked away, leaving them alienated and vulnerable. She tried putting a good face on it but it was impossible to give them what they needed. She was told change was happening rapidly and the worst was yet to come.

She left the most difficult of these calls for last. Scott's counsel was the one she most valued. Although he reported to her, that line was often blurred. When technical or bureaucratic frustrations ramped up, he was the one she would likely confide in or vent to.

"Hi Scott," Sheila said, trying for a neutral tone, but wasn't even sure what that was anymore.

"Hey Sheila. It's great to hear your voice."

A week had passed since their world had been jolted and both fumbled for the right thing to say.

"Sorry it's taken this long to call. It's not because I didn't want to talk to you. To tell you the truth, I thought talking to you about what happened would be my hardest conversation. And I just wasn't ready for it until now."

Scott was glad to hear this. His co-workers shared their conversations with Sheila and he couldn't understand why he was being ignored.

"Hey, no problem. You do whatever you need to do, when you need to do it."

Wishing to move on, Sheila commented, "I hear I wouldn't recognize the place."

"Matt's taking a wrecking ball to everything we built. It's hard to watch and not do anything about it."

"Maybe when things settle down you'll be able to redirect the process, put it back on a healthy path again."

"I guess . . . anything's possible," Scott said, but was skeptical. "Until then, I'm at least pulling a paycheck every two weeks."

Sheila felt this had to be a joke. Scott's skills were as much in demand as hers were. And he could make much more in private enterprise than the salary the government was paying. She assumed he, like her, was committed to the project and wondered how long he could work there, but refrained from asking about this.

He queried her about her plans and when she admitted she had none, they returned to office chatter. When they were done and the conversation began to falter, Scott changed the topic.

"Hey Sheila, I'd like to stay in touch. Maybe we could go out for a drink or dinner sometime. More than anything I want to make sure you come through this OK."

This took Sheila by surprise. They had never been out socially outside of work outings, or shared much about their personal lives. They worked together on a deep level but there was no chemistry between them. Considering a relationship outside of work felt awkward to her. But she was in the middle of a difficult period and probably could use input from someone who'd seen her at her best and knew what she was capable of.

"Sure," she responded. "I'd like that. Let me see how things settle out over the next week or so and then I'll give you a call to schedule something."

"That would be great. I look forward to hearing from you."

She tried to not dwell on their fate. The shock was still too fresh and a better time for reflection was yet to come. Physically she wasn't in good shape and was a little overweight. She wore loose fitting clothes like capes and long coats, so it didn't show. But that's not why she wore them. She suspected that her signature dress style had more to do with the swirling motion of the fabric, and this extended her personal power into the surrounding space. Her hair was beginning to show streaks of gray, which she refused to hide; wavy locks that swirled with her outfits. She began taking walks and wondered if it was time to start taking better care of herself.

For hours at a time she hacked through The Newer Machine for suggestions about how to move forward. The rigors of extreme sports piqued her interest. She knew she had the mental strength required, but decided that type of training and discipline just wasn't appealing. The same thought process pushed her away from other activities she'd had some passing interest in: cooking, politics, even teaching. The message she received back from these inquiries was that she no longer knew what she wanted. Her burning passion was the promise of enhancing human consciousness. It was something she believed in completely and aligned with her greatest potential. She had no need for excursions, consumerism, even romance. Now everything she looked into were diversions that lacked meaning or consequence. That was the thing: she believed humanity needed the work she was doing, the work that was now terminated, or at least disfigured beyond recognition.

She hit bottom on the tenth day. Every avenue forward devolved into a misappropriation of her talents and vision. Then a peculiar feeling surfaced when she considered the possibility of abandoning everything. She remembered reading long ago about people with backgrounds similar to hers embracing in-community, subsistence living. The slant of the articles was skepticism bordering on mockery, but their impact never left her. Unfortunately, her new Newer Machine filter now rebuffed every attempt to locate more information about these people and communities. All that returned from her inquiries were watered down eco-tourist attractions, more distractions, like everything else.

On her 15th day of isolation she received a peculiar text message:

> **NeuralBlast is being done the right way. If you want to learn more, be on the corner of 12th and Vine in downtown DC today at 2:00 PM. A man with a silver briefcase will greet you.**

This was a thunderbolt she wasn't ready for. Her body and soul reacted violently to this information and made her realize how deeply wounded she still was. Her daydreams of a simple existence were swept away like debris sent flying in a tornado. This was a rebel group contacting her. It had to be the one that corrupted her software and led to her getting fired. She hated what they'd done, yet harbored a certain respect for them. They were adept technicians with some credible grievances, despite how they were portrayed by TNM. So, she decided she would meet with the man with the silver briefcase and see what he had to say.

Her apartment was a short walk to the appointed destination, which she figured the rebels knew. She spotted him as she approached the intersection. At five feet ten inches she stood a few inches taller than him. His wiry copper colored hair, like his beard, was neatly trimmed. His suit and intense glare made him fit right in with the politician/lobbyist class scurrying around. As she approached, she made a grand sweep with her cape, clearing space around her.

"Sheila Bloom?"

"That looks like a silver briefcase," she said while nodding and then turning her gaze into open space. "And who am I speaking to?

"I go by Rex," he continued looking directly at her even as she refused to meet his gaze.

"No last name?"

"Let's just go with Rex for now."

Sheila could look away no longer. Instead, she glared into opaque sunglasses that rendered his eyes unreachable. "OK, Rex. To start with, why don't you tell me who you represent and why you contacted me."

It was Rex's turn to look away, to consider options and assess the foot traffic around them. "Would you mind if we walk a little while we talk?"

"Sure, lead the way."

After they walked half a block and created space for themselves, Rex began speaking.

"I represent Justice Force. I'm sure you've heard of us."

"I guess, maybe. Word circulates about different disgruntled fringe groups. I really haven't paid much attention. But when I do, my impression is groups like yours can appeal emotionally but lack intellectual rigor. Which is the kiss of death for me."

Rex let that sit for a moment, before deciding how to respond.

"It's easy to get that impression when all the information comes out of The Newer Machine, which is the only game in town for most people. But there are others if you know where to look. And far from being intellectually weak, it is the only approach forward that makes sense, the only one that will free people who are bound in chains, while saving the planet at the same time."

Unconvinced, Sheila had no interest in going down this path. Instead, she chose to press into what mattered to her.

"You're responsible for disrupting my life's work, aren't you? That led to some unpleasant outcomes for me."

"We are, and we're sorry for that. But we just sped up what was certain to happen eventually. I hope someday you'll thank us for getting you fired. But until then, know that we appreciate what this work meant to you, and the good you hoped would come from it. We're sorry for whatever grief we've caused you."

So, he knew she'd lost her job and some of the circumstances surrounding it, things only a small band of people should be aware of. She wanted to know what else he knew. Her look of disdain softened slightly but she chose not to respond verbally.

"Even if we hadn't interfered, you would have lost control," Rex continued, filling the void. "They would have found another excuse to take the technology from you and weaponize it. It's what they do."

"You don't know that," Sheila blurted out. And then with a depth of feeling divorced from these surroundings, "We were so close."

"I think I do. And I'd like to show you why I believe this."

They walked down a side street that had a little foot traffic, enough to support the occasional café they passed.

I'd like to buy you lunch or at least a drink," Rex said. "We could get a private booth in here," he said, pointing to an out of the way bistro as they slowed their pace.

Sheila considered for a moment. She had come this far and decided she would let Rex tell the rest of his story.

"I'm not hungry but will have a cup of coffee."

They slid into a booth at the back of the café. Rex ordered a bowl of chili while Sheila would not be coaxed into more than coffee.

Rex opened his briefcase and removed several sheets of printed email messages. The majority were to and from Matt Raines and various department heads. They contained a steady stream of stinging comments directed at the work Sheila and her team were doing. These emails showed how he'd been plotting for a long time to gain control of the neuralBlast project and wore away the opposition by manufacturing tales of Sheila's incompetence.

"Why should I believe this? This is just paper. You could have put anything you wanted on it."

"That's true," Rex agreed. Losing none of his momentum he added, "We have our sources and know this to be accurate. You'll have to decide whether you believe what you see here. But is it really so hard to believe that Matt plotted against you?"

She looked back down at the emails and read a few of them more carefully. She recognized expressions that were distinctly Matt's and also those of Kathy's in her ineffectual defense of Sheila and her team. She felt disarmed because of the likely authenticity of these documents, and angry because she'd never had the chance to defend herself against these attacks.

"OK, so why come looking for me? How do you benefit from exposing Matt's treachery to me?"

Rex removed his sunglasses and they looked at each other, eye to eye, for the first time.

"Like I said, we have great respect for you and the work you've done. But you've been on the wrong side. The government would never implement your technology the way you wanted. Instead, their emphasis was always on militarizing it; anything else was window dressing. I can give you as many examples as you like of other people having similar experiences. They've normalized this behavior, it's baked into the cake. We supply the despots of the world with the weaponry to keep the people down. Everything else we do is of a secondary concern. NeuralBlast, implemented your way, is a threat to that world order and the people running the government are smart enough to see that."

Sheila drank her coffee and kept her thoughts to herself. It was never easy, hardly possible, to improve people's lives, despite all that science accomplished. And her goal had always been to find a way for all humanity to benefit from neuralBlast's expansion of the mind. Rex was saying the government was creating a monster with the technology she, more than anyone, was responsible for creating. There was no room for the Renaissance women and men Sheila envisioned; maybe it was always a chimera.

Rex continued, "Here's the thing. We ran the neuralBlast process into a subject a couple of weeks ago. He's doing OK but is not responding in ways we expected."

Sheila could not believe what she was hearing. When she left her government job they were months away from running a trial experiment.

"That sounds reckless to me," Sheila hissed, and drew her coat around her unconsciously.

Rex fidgeted and tapped the soup spoon against the bowl before speaking and chose not to respond directly to her comment. "Listen, come work with us so you can see your dreams come to fruition. You want to liberate humanity and so do we. I can tell you whatever you want about our work, and if you join with us you will have primary input into the subject's treatments and therapy."

This was certainly the strangest job offer Sheila had ever received.

"You want me to do what? To go rogue?"

"I want you to join us, embrace our vision which is aligned with your own."

He slid the folder to Sheila and continued, "Read through this. In addition to the emails I've included information about what Justice Force really stands for, what it is you'll help create if you become part of our movement."

For the first time she considered what life would be like as a member of a rebel group, and found the possibility intriguing.   Her mind raced with questions needing to be answered.   She could hardly believe that she was entertaining this offer.

She pulled the folder towards her and Rex suggested a plan for their next rendezvous.

Chapter 4

Sheila waited outside her apartment building. She wasn't sure confiding in Scott was her best move but couldn't think of a better option. She studied the papers Rex gave her and was surprised by their impact on her. Matt had orchestrated a character assassination of Sheila, which was highly successful. Over the last year he had broadcast to all the department heads any misstep in the neuralBlast project and heaped all the blame on Sheila. She imagined him jumping for joy when the software was hacked. His tone was blistering on this point as he blamed her for lax security protocols that were nowhere near within her range of control. She shouldn't have been surprised by the cowardly responses to his broadsides. She even sensed Kathy's defense becoming muted as the tide turned against Sheila. Such was the way of bureaucracies. She had been warned, but was still surprised by how evil it was. As she saw Scott pull up in his car, she fought back against how devastated she felt, determined to present the confidence and leadership she'd always shown at work.

"Good to see you, Sheila. After all you've been through, you're looking good. Way better than I expected."

She doubted this was true but saw no reason to question him as she hopped into the passenger seat.

"Thanks," Sheila replied. "You know what they say, 'Whatever doesn't kill you makes you stronger.'"

This was classic Sheila talking, and Scott was glad to hear it. Maybe she wasn't in as bad shape as he imagined. They sat in the car, exchanging small talk until Scott addressed the reason for their meeting.

"You gave me the impression you wanted to discuss some confidential information. You know there's a high likelihood that we'll be tracked, that our two data points showing up together will light up the surveillance apparatus. We're safe for now in the car because I installed software that obfuscates their tracking signals, but I can't guarantee for how long it will be effective. So, I think it would be safer to head to a less controlled area to talk. I know a place where we should be safe."

This surprised Sheila. Everyone knew, or suspected, these areas existed. But no one knew exactly where they were.

"Aren't they far away," was all Sheila could think to say.

Scott couldn't stifle a laugh. "Not at all. They're really all around us. But The Newer Machine is very adept at masking them, diverting our attention from them."

Before Sheila's Newer Machine demotion they were both in the same rank so Sheila sensed his meaning. Scott was venturing beyond the periphery of convention, and spoke of these things with a degree of candidness that would cause discomfort in normal situations. If it would have bothered her before, she welcomed it now. It was time to throw off the blinders; there was no job to anchor her, there was no anchor at all.

"Sure, lead the way," Sheila replied, assenting to his plan.

They remained quiet for some time as Scott maneuvered the car onto roads that, as Scott predicted, Sheila never traveled or even knew existed. The GPS, which remained permanently on, per the new car standards enacted with The Newer Machine, kept trying to reroute Scott back to roadways prescribed to him. The volume could not be muted so the directions continually disrupted their conversation.

He parked the car and they began walking.

"I'm glad you listened and wore good walking shoes," Scott said.

They were still within the city limits but nowhere she'd ever been. Without Scott she'd have no idea how to get back to her apartment, and she could not deny that she'd be afraid to try on her own. Scott moved with an air of confidence she couldn't match so she let him lead the way, and actually enjoyed the adventure after cocooning the last couple of weeks. She looked at the buildings she passed, some boarded up, most on life support or worse. What spirit they evoked was from a past when they provided good living conditions with an occasional flair: a crest above a door that was still distinguishable, a gargoyle fronting the house that had not been totally dismembered.

The temperature was above 90 degrees and the sun reflected off the buildings before touching her skin. It was early summer and this type of heat still felt alien, although in just a few weeks this norm would be punctuated by much hotter days. But now the heat liquified Sheila's thoughts, softened her step. She assumed the pace of those walking along beside her. They had to have level 7 or 8, and maybe higher, Newer Machine ratings, while hers was a 3 before being devalued to a 5.5, representing a huge drop. Everyone intuited these distinctions but by the third block, with the mass of surging people, she hardly noticed them.

It was 3 PM on a Saturday afternoon and as they rounded a corner, a park opened up to their view on the other side of the street. On the opposite hill sat hundreds of people looking down on a pavilion, still shielded from their view. Scores of people strolled along the meandering paths between food trucks and the sitting area. Sheila and Scott stopped at a playbill that listed the performers that would play deep into the night.

"As bored as I've been," Sheila began, "I've read every local news bulletin, every listing of planned cultural events in the city. How is it possible there was no mention of this?"

Scott let out a laugh, an unrestrained, full throated, masculine laugh like she never before heard come out of him.

"You know the answer. We all do. We just never talk about it."

"Maybe it's time we did," Sheila responded.

"There you go. That's the Sheila I know. I was wondering when she'd reappear," Scott replied, smiling the whole while.

He led her to a section of the hill out of earshot from anyone, but that still allowed a view of the stage.

When they were settled on the grass Scott said, "Sorry, I should have brought a blanket. But no one will be listening to us here. The surveillance apparatus is not elevated here in this neighborhood and our two data points will be scattered by the crowd."

They took a couple of minutes to look around. Hundreds of people turned towards and tuned into the music supplied by a diverse collective of young people. They were playing some retro-reggae music. While they weren't particularly proficient on their instruments the music they made was raw, rhythmic, and captivating.

"So, what's up? What did you want to talk to me about?" Scott asked.

Sheila took a minute to collect her thoughts and then launched into what was on her mind. "The rebel group that hacked our system contacted me. I met with one guy, Rex was his name. He told me about things going on inside The System, inside our project, that I was totally unaware of. Matt's been all over us for a long time. He constantly spread disinformation to undermine all of us, but mostly me. Some of it was outright lies. Lots of them. I probably shouldn't be surprised, but I guess I was taken by the intensity of his attack on us."

"I'm not. The man is pure slime. He'll do whatever he can to get what he wants. He'll keep lying until he doesn't believe he is lying and he's convinced his audience that he's not lying. Then you watch him when he is in the presence of his superiors and he becomes the perfect obsequious mouse. He has no moral core, zero!"

"I see you've been paying attention."

"Have to. It's right there in front of me every day."

Again, she wondered what kept him there and whether he would stay.

"But here's what I really wanted to talk to you about, get your opinion on. I'm sorry ahead of time for involving you, but I had nowhere else to turn. What we've talked about, and just coming here, skirts the fringes of dangerous thought, if not illegal behavior. Where I'm about to go crashes through those barriers. So, if you want to stop here, I get it. I'll still value our relationship and we'll forget this ever happened."

Scott laughed again but with a tenser quality than before. "You expect me to walk away from that setup? But seriously, I can't think of a situation where I wouldn't want to help you if I could. So, please, tell me what's going on."

Sheila took a deep breath before continuing. "They've deployed the full-range neuralBlast treatment on a subject. Not only did they sabotage our work but they downloaded the entire system and reconfigured it. I haven't seen their setup but it sounds legit."

Before Sheila could finish, Scott broke in.

"Those sons of bitches! They stole all our work and ruined our careers, you more than anyone's, but a lot of people's blood's been spilled over this."

"But here's the thing," Sheila said, taking up the thread. "They want me to work with them, go over to their side. Rex explained they were part of the Justice Force movement that is resisting The System. I couldn't tell how organized this group is but it sounds like it has a weak chain of command. Anyway, they're having trouble with their subject. Rex did not go into much detail but he's not responding as they expected. If I join up with them he said I'd have primary control of the neuralBlast treatments and therapy."

Instead of speaking, Scott was reduced to a long "Phew," that trailed off into a piercing whistle.

When he recovered he continued, "So, how do you feel about their offer?"

"I haven't gotten back to them so I guess I'm still considering it . . .. Until I'm not. If that makes sense."

"I get it," Scott replied. "Because you haven't gotten back to them, you haven't shut the door. So, let's look at the pros and cons. Let's start with what you think of them, what they stand for. What did you say their name was?

"Justice Force."

"Oh yeah, I've heard of them. I have access to some back-channel news feeds. From what I can tell they're a major player. Several smaller bands of rebels are joined under that umbrella group."

"Thanks, I didn't know that. Rex gave me some documents that state what they stand for. High-sounding manifestos. That sort of thing."

"So, what did you think? Do you agree with what they stand for?"

Sheila paused before answering, uncertain of how to express her thoughts.

"Sure," she said, throwing her hands in the air as if she didn't mean it. "Everything they said is valid. The System has taken away virtually all civil liberties, the damage they cause to the environment is sending the planet into a free fall, maintaining the borders is a never-ending job that does the most damage to those desperate enough to try and enter. It's a long list. But there's one thing missing. Not one mention of machines making humans obsolete. It's the thing I see every day, the thing I've been fighting against for years. They think their subject can help them, but they have no idea. They haven't thought about it hard enough. There are no guard rails or talk of ethical concerns. They'll screw it up. I'm certain of it."

Scott was looking down at the bandstand as Sheila spoke and now turned towards her, his expression cast into a sly smile. "I think you just decided."

It was Sheila's turn to cast her gaze away, and vaguely peered into the clear blue sky before speaking.

"This work is the only thing that matters to me. My only chance to contribute. I honestly believe it has the best chance of letting us move forward, freeing humanity from the vise that's closing in, constricting us more each day. But to tell you the truth, I'm not sure how or why."

"So you'll become a rebel without becoming a rebel."

"I think so. I don't see another choice. Maybe someday I'll even buy into their whole message. But for now, they have the one thing that I care about, that will make me whole again, and I can't turn away from that."

Chapter 5

Sheila entered the safehouse where Milo was staying. She wanted to meet him alone, without an intermediary or introductions from others. This was one of the pre-conditions she negotiated before deciding to join their program. He sat on a sofa in the living room, his guitar draped across his lap. He did not get up or change his position when she came in from outside.

Sheila, undisturbed by his indifference, walked over to him and reached out her hand.

"Nice to meet you," she said, smiling at him as she studied his face and gestures. He extended his arm and they shook hands briefly. She felt a peculiar quavering energy in his touch, something she couldn't define.

Sheila continued, "I know you've been told I'm the lead developer of the neuralBlast technology. So, I want you to know how fulfilling, how wonderful it is to be here with you. I hope this has been a valuable experience and that you don't regret your decision to have these treatments. I want you to know I'm here to help in whatever way I can."

Sheila had been briefed on Milo's progress. The most vexing behavior observed by his handlers was his fixation on random areas of research, flitting from one to another immediately after each neuralBlast session.

Milo's eyes and expression became thoughtful as he considered the question. "Overall, yes. I'm happy with my decision. Before I got here I was stuck. I wanted to take a vacation from myself, like everyone else I knew. Well, I've certainly done that."

His tattoos ranged up and down his arms and she could see they extended onto his torso. But she did not need to peer at them to decipher something about the nature of this young man. He was an open book. The world coursed through and spilled out of him. His eyes were alert yet seemed to be cast inward.

"Can you tell me what you experience when you're in a session? What learning that way feels like?"

He turned his attention to Sheila and assessed her more closely.   He had become more skilled than any facial recognition software and needed no further introduction. His only question was why her cape was still draped around her.

"I've tried.   It never comes out right, but here goes. Normally, when we try to solve a problem, one thought leads to another and another, pretty much in a linear way. Sure, this is simplistic and there are a lot of other factors at work but there's still truth in what I'm saying. When I'm in a session my brain, or my enhanced brain, consumes information with multi channeled, advanced heuristics.   There is a perpetual winnowing of viable responses based on the most advanced criteria. When a response is determined it is likely to be thrown into another request, or multiple concurrent requests, that I have not consciously posed. Instead, it comes from the prior set of inquiries and combs through altered sets of available data. So, where I end up can be a very different place than where I started. It would take forever to step through all this sequentially if, in fact, that was even possible."

This was very close to the experience she hoped to hear him describe and she found it exhilarating.

"So, truths are presented to you during these sessions that the rest of us can't derive?"

He laughed unexpectedly. "Yes, that's a fair statement. But I can't control it. My thoughts are like a fire hose spraying in all different directions. What I'm left with can be interesting but trivial, or so it seems to Rex and his team. Even when I'm not in a session I retain some of this capability. My canvas, then, isn't data stored in computer networks, but becomes the world around us in all its dimensions and energetic states."

This was what interested her most. Everyone involved in the research had some notion of what the experience of the actual sessions would be. But its long-lasting effects, the impacts felt when not in the midst of the neuralBlast sessions, was something no one could guess at, precisely because it engaged the brain's plasticity. And the potential for how the human brain assimilated this enhanced way of learning was perceived as the most important aspect of this technology.

"So it has long lasting effects and allows you to see things the rest of us can't. Can you give me an example?"

"I think so, but it's hard to explain. Like in the sessions, none of it coheres. There are only disparate insights. But here's one. I can tell you're a good person. I knew it from the moment you walked in. I knew I could trust you. I could see it."

Sheila felt a tear in her clinical detachment, exposing her in a way she did not expect.

"You're right about that," she said and laughed self-consciously. "I'm here for you. You've risked a lot and I am grateful because you allow me to see the fruits of my labor, something I lost hope of attaining. But can you be more precise about what it is you see in me that led you to this conclusion?"

Milo thought about this and as a troubled expression came across his face, he stuttered a stream of incomprehensible fragments. He stopped and after he collected his thoughts said, "The one thing is your eyes. We have been gazing directly at each other since we first made eye contact. I don't usually talk so much and suspect I was doing so just to be able to continue our gaze. And the deeper it went, the surer I was that you have a good heart and came here with good intentions. But if I tried explaining more clearly it would fall apart, which I find very unsettling and disorienting."

"Then don't do it. It will come if it's meant to. You probably need more time to process all these changes you're experiencing, time to let your mind and body catch up to everything that's been thrown at it. I think you've been very clear and forthcoming, which I appreciate so much."

Milo's expression brightened. A minute later he tapped on the guitar body and said, "If you want to know the truth, this is the best thing." And then a small smile broke through the clouds.

"I've been absorbing Jimi Hendrix's work the last several days. Would you like to hear some?"

"I'd be delighted."

With that, Milo turned on the amp beside him and lit into Jimi's signature solos. He played note for note, except where his hands were too small and then improvised admirably.

He played for half an hour and was totally absorbed in the music. Sheila watched in awe at his mastery and absorption. As time passed, she observed her emotions migrate in a new direction. He was like an adolescent discovering his newfound powers and, therefore, capable of making colossal errors. She had some doubts about aligning with Justice Force, but they were quieted now. What replaced them was an overwhelming desire to protect Milo. She didn't fully understand, but already knew she would react with a fury she hadn't known was in her, if that's what the moment required.

She checked back into the guitar work and Milo was in the midst of *The Wind Cries Mary*. She didn't know Hendrix's music, or much of the music from that distant era. But she recognized the melody, and she allowed herself to be drawn into its velvety textures. As she partook of his virtuosity, she began to consider which parts of this interaction she would share with Rex and which parts would remain locked away inside her.

Chapter 6

A week later, Sheila's transition was complete. She settled her affairs, told her few relations that she was going away and left, blending into a twilight that few ever reach or emerge from.

They were in a different part of the safe house, the space where the neuralBlast sessions were administered. The session would start in 30 minutes. Milo lay on a small bed in an adjoining room. It was nearly soundproof and the glass partition framed Milo in repose. His eyes were closed and he rested quietly. IVs were inserted in his arms and electrodes attached around his body to monitor his response. A nurse, Anton, was inside the room with Milo to observe and triage any problems that might arise. Rex stood behind the two technicians who were busy monitoring the server and running last minute regression tests. When Sheila walked in, the activity at the workstations stopped. Rex performed the introductions between Sheila and the two technicians, Marta and Sev.

They both rose out of their seats to shake her hand, and Marta was the first to speak.

"It is such an honor to meet you. Just being able to work with your system has provided us with enormous insights."

This was not the first time that Sheila received praise of this kind. Normally she would engage it lightly, her momentary silence gave her admirers a chance to reveal the nature of the insights she helped them acquire. But not this time, not with a savage hunger stirring inside her.

"I never thought I would see this," her voice was deep in wonder, her eyes lit with fire. She moved closer to the two workstations.

"You know, I wrote a lot of the core code. And the design for this portal is more mine than anyone else's. But until this very moment it was just an academic exercise."

Her life work pulsed on the four monitors in front of her. She touched the side of the closest panels as she analyzed the data on the portal pagelets. But what she really wanted to do was pick up the display panel and shake it in the air a few times and declare to the world that this was her creation and then take a victory lap with it.

Instead, she gazed at the real-time monitoring of Milo, while Sev provided a running narrative.

"I'm in charge of the physical health of the subject while Marta manages the integration between the subject and the computer network."

"Show me how you administer a session. What have you learned from the first three?" Sheila asked.

Marta explained, "He has the operating system and client-side messaging software permanently installed in the wire mesh that's attached to his brain above the cortex. But it remains dormant until the server-side processing unit is paired with the client. After we activate the server, we initiate the Integration Broker, run some diagnostics and establish communication with Milo. If everything is functioning properly, we *seed* Milo's mesh-memory with parameters for him to use during his investigations. We can see when his mind takes up the inquiry. The processors get busy and we allocate more processors, one at a time, to increase the throughput."

"But . . . something happens," said Sev, picking up the thread, "that forces us to throttle down the processing power. Even with his ability to withstand shocks, his vitals spike. The first time this occurred with four concurrent processors, the last time he got to five before experiencing this. We are experimenting with an IV today and have been forcing fluids in him. We also have him on a low dose antidepressant. We're hoping this keeps his vitals stable and lowers the stress."

Rex stood off to the side, not a place he preferred or was used to. He recently became a member of Justice Force's steering committee. His election was proof of just how important this work was viewed by the organization's leaders. There was a chance that its success could catapult him into the position of uncontested leader. Marta and Sev understood his role and treated him with deference, which he accepted with outward modesty. But their deference towards him was insignificant when compared to how they fawned over Sheila. And Sheila behaved like the technical wizard she was, without an ounce of interest in their gushing.

When all preparations were concluded, Marta issued the initial sequence to establish the communication channel. She then seeded Milo's cortex with the parameters for this session: how to link Justice Force's struggle with other organizations nationally and internationally.

Sheila stood alongside Marta and Sev who sat at their workstations. She wore a shawl with piercing orange and blue stripes, one side of which dangled beneath her knee while the other swept over her shoulder and down her back. She braced herself with arms akimbo as though she were ready to set sail on the high seas. This was Sheila's Stradivarius, and her fingers would get to play the instrument for the first time. Her primary interest was with Marta's domain, but she had equal expertise in the physical demands placed upon Milo. There were so many blindspots to watch out for, like energetic health that no instrument could measure. Still, it could be disrupted by the metamorphosis caused by a neuralBlast session.

There was only a faint heartbeat of activity the first few minutes, as if Milo's mind was conceiving the pathways to pursue before taking flight.

"Let's have a look at the app server logs," Sheila said to Marta.

Marta pulled up the log directory which showed activity for the three active app servers. They were advancing in size at a slow rate.

"What level of logging are you running with?" Sheila asked.

"Moderate," Marta replied. "We wanted to capture where he was going, but were afraid all the parsing of a deeper trace would slow the system and put too much stress on Milo. That additional information could also make it harder, not easier, to figure out how Milo's brain was behaving."

"That's exactly how I would have proceeded, and for the same reasons," Sheila responded. Marta, obviously pleased by this compliment, picked up a pen and tapped it against a piece of paper, while secretly reveling in Sheila's comment.

"Of course, that hasn't helped us much," Sev chimed in. "These logs are pretty much spaghetti. We've applied every analysis tool we could find but can't determine how his mind is firing, things like whether there's a generalized approach to his inquiries or whether he is becoming more efficient as he gains more experience."

"I get all that. Makes perfect sense," Sheila replied. She knew she would be spending hours, days, going over these logs, searching for the Holy Grail that so far remained elusive.

"Let's have a look," Sheila said, and pointed to the log advancing at the greatest rate and chewing up the most processor.

Marta opened this file. The editor was smart enough to color code different categories of content, links were active, recursive activity was annotated. Sweat rose to the surface of Sheila's skin as her hands became clammy. She was tempted to rip Marta out of her seat and take over the analysis, but refrained from doing so. This was just the prelude to the main act that was about to begin.

At five minutes Milo remained stable and another processor was added to the pool. A burst of activity registered on all four monitors. His blood flowed up through his cortex at an elevated rate but Milo's beastly ability to remain calm and not overload his brain was on display now.

"He's doing it," Sheila said, mostly to herself. The initial burst subsided and within two minutes his vital signs were only slightly elevated. Anton applied a cool, wet cloth to Milo's perspiring forehead. The logs were getting larger at a highly increased rate.

"Look at that," Sheila said. "It's not just the logs for the new server that are advancing more quickly but so are the servers that were previously active. This is what we thought would happen but had no evidence until right now. He's advancing and he is stable. He is using the new processor synergistically. This is how he will grow, how his learning will enter new frontiers." She almost shouted the last sentences that rose in a steady crescendo and contained frenzied elements of glee and joy.

They waited a few more minutes and when they were satisfied Milo was calm, inserted the fifth server into the pool. The jolt was stronger than last time. A visible tremor ran through Milo's body. Anton applied the cloth and looked anxiously up at the window that separated him from the others. They waited, expecting the integration and balance to assert itself. But that did not happen. Certain servers became dormant while others fired violently; a minute later the reverse was true. This imbalance produced inflammation in Milo's brain and began to register an assortment of unhealthy, potentially serious readings on Sev's monitors.

"I don't like this," Sheila bellowed with a commanding tone, as if she could will the chaotic behavior to reverse itself.

"Throttle back that new server 50%," Sheila commanded Marta.

"No, wait!" Rex interjected, speaking for the first time, and moved closer to the center where Sheila held space. "We've been here before. He will stabilize if we give him a little more time."

Sheila looked at Rex and realized this much: the autonomy she was promised could be challenged.

"If you've been here before and not reversed course, you're lucky you didn't kill him. You want him to stroke-out? Because that's what he's a candidate for right now. And then where would we be?"

"But the leadership expects progress. This isn't even as far as we got the last time. You just said so yourself. This is what he needs in order to expand his powers exponentially."

She looked deeply at him for several moments with a neutral expression but her thoughts were fueled by rage. *The fucking suits, even when they're not wearing suits, always think the same.*

Their attention was turned back to Milo's body which rippled with spasmodic tremors. Anton tried to restrain him, forcing him back on the bed by pushing his shoulders down, while the rest of him jerked around.

"Take that server down 50%, NOW! If he stabilizes, we'll try again," Sheila commanded, and this time Rex did not challenge her. He continued staring at her, but she was no longer concerned with him and turned back to the screen monitoring Milo's physical responses.

They fired up the fifth server to full capacity two more times but Milo went into convulsions while trying to integrate the additional processing power. The session ended at the appointed time. Rex dragged himself around like it was an absolute failure because Milo was unable to integrate the additional concurrent processing. Sheila was in awe of what she'd witnessed and refused to let Rex's peevishness diminish her joy at seeing the embodiment of her work in action. Most importantly, Milo was safe and resting comfortably. There were tons of data for her to shift through, enough to keep her occupied for several days.

Sheila had her own room at the safe house. It was a sprawling, nondescript ranch house, guaranteed to not elicit interest from the casual onlooker. As she looked out onto a secluded wooded ravine, her thoughts reached back, beyond where she usually allowed them to venture. Her public statements about why she'd pursued this line of work she could recite by rote. Her spiel touched upon how the melding of the human brain with machine knowledge was our best chance to advance society beyond what seemed like the intractable problems facing the world. She argued that we, in the "walled in" sectors, were already part cyborg. Our Newer Machine devices were our most cherished objects. Those not embracing this ethos were left behind and made to feel hopelessly backward and irrelevant. But it was all a diversion. The machines controlled the content and were the real wizards, while humans chirped away on their social media accounts, from where any original content was removed or diluted. Humans, she argued, had little to look forward to if they could not liberate the dormant areas of the brain.

But there were more elemental reasons for her committing to this goal, ones she only thought about when her defenses were lowered. Jeremy was a fellow college student she met when they were both freshmen. He was a creative type and ran with the group her friends referred to as "The Smalls". They were called that because her friends, steeped in scientific disciplines, viewed The Smalls as having only their own insights to offer, and these were puny things compared with the ever-expanding body of knowledge available to the scientifically trained mind. And if they, who were the "Bigs", were fortunate, they'd have the opportunity to add a tiny piece to the ever-expanding sum of knowledge that one day

Fred Burton

would contain all knowledge and ultimate truth. If art had any value, it was as diversion, as entertainment.

But Jeremy kept coming around, choosing to be unaware of the cold reception from those surrounding Sheila. Which drew her towards him. He radiated a glow that was preternatural. He came to her with poems he'd written for her and bouquets of wild flowers picked while off on his adventures in the woods. He lived off campus with a group of Smalls who, Sheila felt, mostly earned the epithet because they were simply lazy and uninteresting.

One day towards the end of the freshman year she went to visit him at his house. The door was unlocked and she let herself in, as she always did. He had built a free-standing platform against a wall that rose four feet off the floor. A sofa was placed on it and was seen as a way to view this familiar setting differently. Jeremy was up there, a slight smile spread across her face when she climbed the steps and sat next to him.

There was always a frail quality to him, but now that was all she sensed.

"I dropped out of school," he said.

Sheila felt like she'd been gut-punched. She knew he was struggling and encouraged him to stick with it. At least get through the semester before deciding what to do. And then she felt angry and wondered if what her friends said about him were true.

"You could use the credits. They might help you in the future," her words had more edge than she intended but Jeremy didn't seem to mind.

"I couldn't do it anymore. Each class was like a thousand small cuts. . .. I've been missing a lot of classes," he confessed. "I probably would have flunked out anyway."

"What will you do now?"

"I don't know. Find a bookstore that will hire me, maybe. But all of this is pointless. The System is closing in.

Extinguishing the light of freedom. There is really no hope and the planet is dying."

She heard him speak this way before but wasn't in the mood now. She could not abide his morose thoughts and soon made an excuse to leave, saying she had to study.

Two days later word reached her that Jeremy had killed himself the day before. He was found on the same sofa that she'd walked away from, the victim of a drug overdose.

Sheila was unable to continue her studies that semester and returned home. This was the beginning of the current incarnation of Sheila. But beneath her coarse exterior was a desire to heal and expand human consciousness so that it was not simply a vase that could break and shatter individual lives, particularly those most vulnerable. There would be no Smalls or Bigs if everyone could access their full potential.

She never discussed any of this with her colleagues. In fact, she mostly lost the passion of this calling along the way. Her focus transformed into more tangible goals: generating quantitative results from the neuralBlast technology to justify the expense, effort, and dedication. But Milo embodied what led her to this life work, and he reminded her of Jeremy like no one ever had. This sent her into a tailspin, unmoored her. Both Milo and Jeremy were awakened to a world of wonder that was at times beyond their ability to behold or comprehend. She lost Jeremy. She would not allow Milo to be crushed under the weight of his awakening.

She knew the neuralBlast procedures caused Milo pain and left him in a dissociative state. He chose to sleep and stay secluded in a darkened room for about 24 hours. She'd spend this time studying the logs from this and the prior treatments. One of her main interests was why Milo's investigations veered away from what his handlers intended, causing frustration among the team. Sheila let it be known that she would perform his debriefing.

She walked into Milo's room at the appointed time. This is where he was most comfortable after a session, and where he stayed until he was more stable, usually a few days.

The weather was overcast and the window blinds were partially closed. The little bit of light shining in the room fell upon the desk in front of the only window in the room. Milo sat there working intently. He looked up when she entered and did not seem to mind the interruption. They could barely see each other's face until she approached, and took a seat beside the desk. By then he was back at work, unaffected by her close presence.

She sat and watched, observing his fine, confident movements shaping the paper into the design he pursued. She could have remained entranced like this for much longer, but remembered she had a job to do.

"Have you studied origami for a long time?" she asked.

"Pre-Milo never could have done this, never had the patience to master the steps involved." His hands continued to fold and smooth the emergent design.

This was the first she'd heard this self-naming term that suggested a rift with his prior identity. Avoiding this topic for now, she'd return to it if, and when, his trust in her had strengthened.

"But to answer your question, this was something I was led to in yesterday's session."

He pulled a basket from below the desk and placed it on the side away from Sheila, and opened the lid. One by one he removed 12 origami pieces and arranged them so Sheila could take them in, in all their beautiful and elaborate design. Some were recognizable animals, more birds than any other. But many were not easily recognizable, resembling mischievous gargoyles.

"These are quite extraordinary. I like the impish quality of this one," she said, picking up one of the creatures that could be the inspiration for a statue fronting an old library or state house and rotated it in her hands. "Did you memorize the steps for all these creatures during yesterday's session?"

Milo stopped what he was doing and looked blankly ahead of himself to consider the question. It was a habit of his, one she suspected started when he began receiving neuralBlast infusions. It was the same expression she'd seen on her college boyfriend's face the last time they were together. A look that haunted her on countless sleepless nights.

"It's not really like that, you see. The first few were memorized but . . . I adapted the skill . . . and the vision."

And with that he set back to work. His eyes were like twin moons when he looked at her, suspended ethereally, staring through Sheila in a way that sent a chill through her body.

"That's extraordinary," Sheila gasped. It was her first recognition that the treatments went beyond mere mechanistic knowledge transfer. How much more she'd attempt to gauge.

"Can you tell me if this experience was different from the previous ones?"

He laughed and paused longer than normal before speaking. "No, not really. One thing I would say is there is a growing sense of absence. What *you* experience, what pre-Milo experienced, is a highly filtered learning process that helps you integrate content into an existing context. It is how you make sense of the world and survive. But really that is an impediment to true learning, true engagement."

Her heart melted. These were as close to the sentiments she wished to hear as she could imagine.

"That is spectacular," she gushed. "You must be so happy."

This evoked the longest period of silence yet. When he did answer he said, "Pre-Milo could be spectacularly happy, like the way you were just now when you spoke the word *spectacular*. He played heavy metal thrasher music and the whole world came together for him when he was on stage. This is different. I could do this all day but am not sure why.

It's not like he was when he was at one with the audience. I like doing this. . .. My mind is focused in a way that excludes the type of emotion you were just expressing. But that absence doesn't bother me."

Sheila looked at Milo as he returned to his current creation. She realized she wasn't any closer to understanding what skills he could learn, what joys were within his grasp, or even what dangers he might encounter.

"Fucking origami! Are you kidding me?"

Sheila was not surprised to hear Rex say this. But his level of frustration was more than she expected.

"You know we can't program the way he responds. All we can do is plant some seeds at the start of the session. What we can't do is control where the branching logic takes him. And more to the point, we don't want to," Sheila said, reasserting the approach they had agreed to.

"What we want, and need, are tangible results that can be used in the struggle."

"So, what do you expect? You think Milo will come out of a session with a plan to destroy The System's entire security apparatus?"

"That would be nice. I'd like that very much. But I don't expect it. I know we're in uncharted waters, but we need some concrete examples of how Milo can help us."

"Look," Sheila began, "It's like a plant. You can give it water, good soil and sun. But you can't then tell it to grow and expect it to follow your commands. This is an organic process that must proceed at its own pace."

Rex did not respond immediately. It was obvious the conversation took an unexpected turn, one that made him question whether the methods and techniques employed by him and Sheila could mesh effectively. Sheila was surprised she used this analogy so soon after her conversation with Matt. She was distressed that she felt compelled to employ it here with someone she thought was an ally.

"I never heard that analogy before," Rex said, mulling it over while the color drained from his face.

Sheila's comment caused the conversation to flounder until Rex brought it back to what he was really thinking about. "Things are getting worse every day. We just heard of two more reporters, sympathetic to our cause, that were *disappeared*. Every day, more and more workers have more value as prisoners in the ever-expanding penal market, and are given every incentive to join the ranks of the incarcerated. So, yes, we need something more. Something more than origami figures and Jimi Hendrix guitar licks.

"And time is not on our side. You know The System's dark forces have cannibalized your software. Well, we just learned they've almost completed beta testing it, and will apply it to a subject soon. Our defenses are already porous. If this guy, who they're calling K1, comes online and all we got is origami and Jimi Hendrix it will be very hard for us. And if they figure out how to mass produce clones from him, it'll be game over. People already feel like there is no way to escape. The System has a stranglehold on every thought or action that runs counter to its program. This could be the final nail in the coffin. People's ability to think and act for themselves will be completely snuffed out."

It was Sheila's turn to feel chagrined. "I can't believe they're ready to test the software on a human."

"Why, you think they care about people's safety?" It was Rex's turn to be condescending. "They've never cared and always had a way to turn some sector of the population into sub-humans for experimentation of this kind. They searched the ranks of elite fighters to come up with K1, appealing to their sense of patriotism and daring. Oldest trick in the book."

Sheila did not answer at first but when she did, said, "Alright, I'll do what I can. I'll study the algorithms used to initiate the sessions to see if we can seed more guidance during the infusions. But one thing I won't do is weaponize him the way K1 is being weaponized. That would destroy Milo's humanity. If you do that you might as well kill him."

Chapter 7

"If you think you've been working hard, you're wrong. You haven't."

So began Matt Raines' introduction to the new members of his team.

"And the lack of accountability and failure to deliver milestones on time ends today."

He surveyed the people sitting about him, but none of them could be certain eye contact was ever made. The six former members of Sheila's team were there, together with an equal number of people who were longtime members on Matt's staff.

"Don't get me wrong. You might all be smart and highly skilled. We'll determine that quick enough. The truth is this project was poorly managed. I don't care if saying that hurts your feelings, or if I offend you by calling out your former manager. The door's always open for you to walk through. But if you choose to stay, new rules will apply and you will be held to a whole new set of expectations. As I said, excuses for delays won't be tolerated . . . period.

"For the next three weeks, all of you from the prior team will have someone mirroring you. These staff members are tasked with learning all the duties you perform. Answering their questions and training them is your number one priority because at the end of this period they need to have a complete and thorough understanding of everything you know about the history and current status of neuralBlast. This includes what works and what has been tried but failed."

Matt looked at the members of his coterie and something like a faint, satisfied expression passed over his face and then vanished. "They've been told who their partners are and will walk back with you to your workstations at the end of the meeting. Any questions?"

Several moments passed. Matt was willing to be engaged, but preferred not having to. Then Scott decided to break the tense silence.   He avoided his main thought, that it was impossible to really transfer so much information in three weeks, and instead asked the other question that pressed on all their minds.

"What happens in three weeks, when this knowledge transfer process is complete?"

Matt didn't skip a beat. "At that time, you will be expected to reapply for your positions. If you are not chosen, you'll have one month to find another job on another project. If you fail to find anything, termination proceedings will commence at that time."

This time Matt did meet Scott's gaze and Scott was chilled by the deadened quality and lack of emotion. One thing clear to everyone in the room was that the original team was likely training their replacements over the next three weeks.

Sheila's old team was one week into the knowledge transfer and decided they needed to talk. They assumed they were being monitored separately and their coming together would light up dashboards on multiple agency's portals. This was why they sat in a small room in Ahmed's house. Ahmed was the programmer responsible for securing communications within neuralBlast, and he was serious about security outside of work as well. The room had no electricity and contained an energetic shield that could be activated to neutralize most known probes that spied on the citizenry. Flashlights provided the only light. Beers and snacks were brought in from the outside. A tape recording from one of their previous get togethers played throughout the house to suggest to snooping ears that there was nothing of interest going on here.

Scott, Ahmed, Nigel, Miguel, Nancy, Mariana and Jason were the squad. They were an effective team but not immune from normal workplace behavior. Infighting existed, favoritism suspected.   Alliances were forged that then morphed into something else. All of that disappeared with the incursion of their shared foes, Matt and his minions.

"They are such arrogant assholes."

"And they don't know shit."

It went on like this for a while, a necessary bloodletting, an affirmation that they were the good guys forced to watch their software be defiled, like a pristine pond overwhelmed by industrial waste.

"They are supposed to be interested in the entire scope of our work but all they ask about are the aggression-related data-classes and properties."

"That's because those are the only ones that will see the light of day."

No one knew this for sure but that was the writing on the wall, and no one felt compelled to offer a different opinion.

"There's nothing we can do."

"That's where you're wrong. If we walked in there on Monday and resigned en masse, we'd at least have the satisfaction of flipping them off and watching the expressions on their faces, particularly Matt's. And it won't be easy for them to figure out how the system works if we're not there to hold their hands."

The last comment was spoken by Nigel and jumped the conversation to a new gear.

"But you don't know you'll get fired."

"I know I don't want to work on this truncated, fucked-up project anymore."

"Even if you weren't retained on this project, you could get some other job in the government."

"Don't make me laugh. We all have specialized skills. Our hourly rate was halved when we signed on to work here. We did it because we believed in this project and wanted to work for Sheila. No, outside of this project there's nothing here for us. And *this project* isn't the project we signed up for. If you did find something in another department, they'd have you doing something that would diminish your skills, probably 10 busy-work type things that require little to no thought or creativity. This is the only game in town for us."

Nigel received all the incoming from his initial provocative statement and ably dispatched each volley. Of all the teammates, he was the least social and most volatile. Despite these qualities he was also highly respected because he said what he believed was true and never sugar-coated it.

Ahmed had not engaged in the crossfire up to this point. He was the quiet and cautious team member, always weighing things before striking out in any one direction. So, it was surprising that he broke the prolonged silence that clung to them, and even moreso when they heard what he had to say.

"I'm in. I've seen enough. We all worked hard for something we thought was groundbreaking, something that could set humanity on a new, necessary course. But now that dream has been destroyed and we have to accept that. And what's replaced it is toxic. I felt my disgust grow all week. I'm ready to move on. Unless my thinking changes, I'm resigning Monday effective immediately."

This thunderbolt was followed by others. All echoed this sentiment, and they came from everyone but Scott.

"How about you?"

Scott hesitated before responding.

"I'll think about it, but probably not."

No one would have pegged him as the last holdout. He was Sheila's most trusted confidante, something envied but tolerated by the others. His work was stellar. He had his own ambitions but had been a loyal teammate who refrained from bad-mouthing anyone.

"Why's that?" Ahmed responded first, intrigued by Scott's ambivalence.

"We don't know how things will turn out?"

Caustic laughter rang out.   But before someone else countered, Scott continued.

"And if I don't stay involved, I won't have a chance to change its course."

Louder, more caustic laughter ensued and then Nigel jumped from his seat and stuck his nose into Scott's.

"You little kiss-ass. I guess you had us all fooled. I bet you got your sights set on a director level position."

Nigel grabbed Scott and swung at him ineffectually, just as you would expect from a heads-down programmer. But Scott's reaction was even more bizarre. He scrambled away on all fours as though he was in mortal danger. Uncharacteristic, child-like remonstrations wagged from his mouth. It was an embarrassing display for everyone in the room. Nigel lost his desire for a confrontation and as he walked away, tried to flush the experience out of him.

"You can go fuck yourself, Scott. . .. You do whatever the fuck you want. Because we can all see you don't have the guts to do what's right."

Nigel left the room, followed by a quiet procession until only Scott and Ahmed remained. Scott realized he couldn't delay his exit any longer and peeled himself off the floor. Ahmed shut the safe room behind him and each went their way separately, left to contemplate what had just happened and the very uncertain future of the neuralBlast project team.

Matt Raines was in full control. Sheila left with only a little prodding, although he was prepared to use real force if needed.   Kathy had not made trouble for him when the project was moved out from under her. She was enough of a bureaucrat and professional to know when resistance was pointless and personally damaging, and responded accordingly.

The knowledge transfer was interrupted after a week because of the mass exodus of the prior team members. Scott was the only one who stayed on, but the loss of legacy knowledge did not concern Matt. These were trifles he refused to let slow him down. His focus never wavered from the success of whatever task was placed before him and he surrounded himself with like-minded sycophants who lacked the clarity of vision that guided him. These underlings could be induced to see matters as he did and counted on to be driven by the work itself, all while avoiding any ethical and moral qualms. Matt's only surprise was Scott Menchin. He was Sheila's lead programmer and struck Matt as cocky and impish. He expected needing to sweep him aside too, but so far, he proved surprisingly accepting of the changes. Forthcoming with valuable insights, he was therefore useful. Matt would continue to test Scott's loyalty, but for now, Scott came to work every day and attacked his assignments with vigor. He had a far-reaching knowledge of the software and did not protest against the new direction Matt took with the project.

Scott worked with Matt's lead technologist, Greg. They spent the last week figuring out how to recast the system so that its sole focus was on the reptilian parts of the brain: the hippocampus, amygdala, and hypothalamus. For all its ferocity, it was dull and rigid. The limbic system's fight response was magnificently honed but limited. It did not think creatively and was too much a blunt instrument. NeuralBlast treatments would change that. It made available the vastness of creative enterprise in the midst of a full-on aggressive fight response. When Matt spoke of this vision, he became a little misty eyed. He pushed his glasses up further on the bridge of his nose and wiped his hand across his thinning dusty, brown hair and forehead that glistened with sweat. This made him look even more like a chipmunk rummaging for a nut, than usual.

They are going to meet their deadlines, Matt told them, and that would make him happy, or what passed for happy in

Matt's attenuated range of emotions. In two months, they planned to perform their first neuralBlast session. Matt focused on finding a subject in the elite special ops troops. No one matched the skeletal excellence of the subject in Pennsylvania that got away, but he would make do with what was available. And there was no question about the loyalty of these men and women. They would do what needs to be done without a lot of drama. And if anything went wrong, their profession made it easy for Matt to avoid unwanted scrutiny and delay.

Corporal Zack Turner sat facing Matt, who sat behind his desk alongside an organized pile of documents and folders. Directly behind Matt hung an oversized reproduction of President Meld. Dour faced and unsmiling, giving a palsied salute. Matt's frame obstructed the lower third of the painting from where Zack sat and presented the image of the larger man giving birth to the perfect supplicant. Matt provided parameters to the heads of the elite forces, and Zack was their leading candidate. It was now Matt's turn to see if he fit the specifications.

"I see you've served multiple tours of duty in the ongoing Mexican theater, securing the border, bringing our enemies to heel."

"Yes sir. Three tours, two 12 and the last, 16 months. I applied for a fourth but protocol requires I stand down for another six months."

Matt looked at the man facing him. He was like a caged animal. The anguish he exuded just sitting here was palpable.

"So, what do you go by, Zack or Zachery?" Matt asked, trying to warm up the conversation.

"My friends in the unit call me K1."

"That's an interesting nickname. How did you come upon that?"

"My kill numbers on patrol are always at the top of the list, sir."

Their eyes met and touched lightly. The ultimate bureaucrat and the ultimate killing machine. They would never share anything but they could be effective partners, using each other for what they desired.

"As I said, that is an unusual nickname, but I like it. That's what I'll call you and have others call you, if that's your preference."

"Yes sir, I'd like that," K1 said, a hint of relief entering his voice.

Matt sensed an opening and seized upon it.

"You don't like being here, do you?"

K1 looked confused, uncertain how to respond. He was not tall, but monstrously built. His eyes seemed to lose focus periodically as if the strain of polite conversation overwhelmed his sensory circuits.

"There is nothing here that I particularly dislike. I just would rather be out in the field. It's the only place I feel comfortable. Generally, buildings, especially those with offices, I try to avoid."

Matt had read his record and the person before him bore out what he'd gleaned. A lone wolf trusted with the most deadly assignments. He served with teams that assassinated heads of state and destabilized popular movements. It was only when he was expected to behave like a civilian that problems arose. At those times Zach isolated even further, becoming more rigid in his demeanor, extreme in his training. There was little doubt he was a ticking bomb.

"This is a dangerous assignment we have going on here. But you will be a difference maker . . . if you survive."

K1 was briefed about neuralBlast, and understood the goals and risks of the treatments.

For the first time K1 looked Matt directly in the eyes, and Matt saw something different, something that seemed soft and pleading.

"All I know is danger. I have been seriously injured three times and as soon as I healed, I was ready for my next assignment. I don't expect you to understand, I don't expect anyone to understand. But if I'm not in danger, I don't feel alive."

K1 considered whether to explain further, but backed away from doing so. Instead, he jumped the conversation to the endgame.

"No matter what the outcome, you'd be doing me a favor to choose me for your experiment."

Their eyes met again recognizing the dynamic between them, the value one offered the other. Matt was satisfied. K1 was his man.

"You've got no power, not really. You're nothing but a fly that I could flick away if I wanted, because I've got all the power. But I like you and have been keeping an eye on you. I made sure you got this assignment because I like how you operate, I know you won't accept failure, won't let me down."

Matt was being spoken to by the president of The United States. While he had previously been in meetings with him, Matt never before gained one-on-one access; all his maneuvering pointed in this direction, coalesced in this moment. And now that Matt was here, he'd do anything to prolong the bullying and humiliation. Matt would even buy the whip for the president to use to administer the beating if that was requested.

"I understand and agree with everything you say," Matt stopped himself suddenly and wondered if President Meld took this the wrong way; it exposed Matt's presumption that his opinion mattered in some way. When he spoke again, he tried to cover his tracks, "Which goes without saying."

President Meld allowed his lips to turn upwards at the outer edges briefly. He liked few things better than the fidgety nervousness of self-consciously delivered acts of servility. And that evoked the signature twinkle in his eye that all his admirers sought and responded to as if they'd received a dose of the purest opioid.

Matt hung on the fleeting smile cast in his direction. If he were allowed to kiss the hand of this great man, the great patriarch of a great family, he'd have done so gladly. But of course, this would be unseemly, at least at this, their first meeting.

"You know we don't need this K1 to maintain order. Our order is unparalleled. And the people love us. They love all the entertainment we provide them with The Newer Machine. They love that we have taken all the complicated decisions away from them. They don't even mind that they gave up the charade of voting. Really, who would ever oppose me?"

President Meld let out a soft, velvety peal of laughter that conveyed just how happy he was with the world of his making. But his real reason for this gesture was to show this underling, Matt Raines, that he was willing to laugh in front of him, which he correctly suspected was received as a great honor.

Matt felt elated by the president's sharing of himself in this way. He smiled back at the president, creasing his face uncomfortably. When the president returned his gaze, Matt stopped instantly, again wondering if he overstepped what was expected of him. The president continued staring. Yes, he liked this Matt, his squirming was so charming, so self-deprecating.

"Don't get me wrong, K1 has his purpose." President Meld let his thoughts wander and then proceeded on a different thread of conversation. "Sometimes these people get so uppity. They think they don't need us to guide them. Can you imagine? Can you imagine if they were allowed to make their own decisions? There would be chaos, and that we won't allow. So K1's main use, although there will be others, is to remind them of how, well, insignificant and powerless they are. K1's extraordinary talents and achievements will be touted across The Newer Machine's news feed. It will be the perfect antidote to anyone who thinks they know better than us and has ideas of taking matters into their own hands, like some groups who continue to persist in these activities. These are bad actors that can't be allowed to gain ground. And we will rip them out like weeds if we need to."

President Meld looked off into the distance, contemplating how much truth to extend to this mid-level bureaucrat. He looked at Matt and saw not only servility but a fawning quality that could not be faked. Yes, he decided to draw him one ring closer to the center of power.

"You know," President Meld began to unwind his tale, "We owe much of our success to The Newer Machine's intellect, its grasp and understanding of all things that everyone desires. But here's a little inside information. It's real strength is in manufacturing those desires. Of course, there has always been product marketing, and the capitalist system that was our forebear had many first-rate examples of how to influence people by infiltrating their minds until their neural pathways fired in perfect unison with the marketing messages created for them."

When President Meld got up from behind his desk his mind beheld the glory days that were about to unfold, a part of which he was about to share with this initiate.

"But, you know, there were egregious mistakes. Buffoons ascended to the highest office and very nearly pulled down the whole apparatus of control with them. You couldn't blame them either because the entire process was unhinged. Everyone knew it and by the end of its reign, the genie could not be stuffed back in the bottle.

"That's when work on The Newer Machine started in earnest. The people in charge, who have always been in charge, grew weary of the nation, and by this I mean the economy, lurching inefficiently in one direction and then another. There was enough of a myth of personal freedom, and the associated happy talk to make certain options unpalatable. For instance, they knew there would be resistance if they installed an autocratic leader outright. Similarly, the nation was too splintered for a religious leader to be able to apply the screws the way they needed to be applied. But The Newer Machine was just the right thing for our population, who, let's face it, had long ago lost any real interest in self-determination and caring for each other. Once alternate news outlets were abolished, The Newer Machine established norms of behavior that were crushingly effective, yet difficult to identify. Like water running within a stream, it avoided obstacles while encumbering them. But believe me, very few want to resist the personalized relationship to The Newer Machine that The System provides them."

President Meld paused again and the benevolent expression shifted to one that furrowed his brow, clouded his radiance.

"But there were irregularities. A small, but increasing number of people are finding ways to resist the lures of The Newer Machine. Our technologists are hard at work looking for ways to correct this. They'll figure out what went wrong, what algorithms need to be tweaked. But until they figure this out, we need to take advantage of every tool at our disposal. K1 is one of those tools. When he comes online, we can put him on display. He can calm the jitters of the vast majority and intimidate those wanting to harm us. Basically, he can help buy us time until The Newer Machine asserts full control."

President Meld paused and allowed some mental calculation to unwind before proceeding. "The truth is, the state is not as strong as it could be, and will be. The pandemic of '27 was more vicious than the one seven years earlier. And, between you and me, there is no denying the effects of climate change are here to stay and have disrupted our ability to control the populace. This left people unnerved, uncertain about the efficacy of the state. Points of permeability have been exploited in The Newer Machine, allowing agitators to evade our blanket of censorship and provide false hope with their propaganda. We are working on a version of The Newer Machine to corral these disruptions once and for all. Chips will need to be inserted under people's skin. The Newer Machine will tout all the health benefits of the chip's real-time monitoring of vital signs and alerts when safe limits are exceeded, among other health-related benefits. Your boy K1 will give them a glimpse of what cyborg strength and intelligence can accomplish, but the chip is not intended to give them these powers. Instead, we will finally have the answer that has eluded the various elites since the dawn of the modern era. Dissent will finally be quelled. The Newer Machine will continue to provide the people with their amusements, and life will not seem noticeably different . . . until it needs to be, until the current rulers decide something, some change in direction is required. Then the chips will flood the neural pathways with this new direction and all opposition, all distant memories of contrary living patterns, will drop away.

"The chip won't be mandatory, at least at first, but it will be portrayed as a patriotic act. We have a variety of tools we can use as a second act. Public spaces could become restricted to anyone without a chip because of the health risk they represent. Restaurants will flag people who are not chipped and refuse them patronage. The Newer Machine will ask, in a variety of sophisticated ways, why, if you're not doing anything wrong, are you afraid of taking advantage of all the benefits the chip provides? Over time, non-chipped users will be segregated to serve the purpose that the underclass has always served. They will be a reminder to others of what it means to have fallen, to have nothing. Eventually the majority will embrace even the most intrusive levels of control. It will offer them their primary way to emote, the only thing that releases them from the constriction in the chests, the darkness they sense at the periphery of their vision.

"The System was weakened by internal and external mal-adaptive behavior. This has caused us to scale back our borders. Even in our own cities we have walled off parts of them and they have become ungovernable. The Newer Machine doesn't mention this shameful situation. But once the chip is installed in sufficient numbers, giving us something like herd dominance, we will marshal the strength of those in our fraternity. We will turn them towards those forsaken lands and bring them back to their rightful place within our fold.

"So, can I count on you? Can you deliver this K1 with his extraordinary militaristic capabilities to me, so that he can be held up to the people as a symbol of our might and the future of The System? We will also use him to face down the enemy until we have rooted them out."

"Yes sir, I know you are right in all things, and particularly in recognizing my utter devotion to you," Matt replied with transcendent calm. And then continuing, suddenly unable to contain himself, wanting to bear all, "I don't understand how anyone could disagree or find fault with anything you or your beautiful family asks of us. Your rules are simple and we all must follow them. Anything or anyone that gets in the way needs to be neutralized. I've seen reports claiming that you have been hand-picked by the Almighty and I believe this, have believed it since the time when you swept into power. . . God bless you, sir."

"Yes, yes, certainly. We all have a mission and our part to play is leading that mission," Meld offered, in his best attempt at humility. "Before you go, I want to tell you one more thing. . .. I like you, Matt. There could be a place for you in my inner circle if you accomplish this task. I'm sure you know about the standard levels of The Newer Machine. Although societal norms frown on sharing one's own level, we all know, more or less, a person's level just by looking at or conversing briefly with them. Well, I want to tell you there are more levels than the ones you know, levels that offer opportunities, power and wealth you can't even imagine. And if you accomplish what we have set out for you, these levels, at least some of them, will be within your grasp."

President Meld then nodded briefly to Matt, signaling the end of their meeting. Matt got up to leave but when he later reflected on this meeting, he was unable to recall anything after the final words from President Meld, because of the firestorm of desire it set off in his brain.

"Failure is not an option. Nor is missing deadlines. So, what can we do to get back on track?"

Matt addressed the team in a staff meeting. He was receiving reports that development was behind schedule and that test cases were failing.

The team was now up to ten people, which included three recently hired contractors.

"I know you said more people wouldn't help but that's exactly what you are going to get if things don't turn around fast."

Daphne, the lead tester, responded first. "We have 52 defects logged in phase 1, 2, and 3. When the programmers fix the code, we re-test. There are five more phases to test that we haven't even looked at yet."

Daphne allowed a thought to form before verbalizing it. "It's just that these damn test cases go so deep. They portray a lot of improbable scenarios that contain unlikely safety concerns for the subject. I doubt any of them will be encountered once we go live."

Greg picked up the thread, "And once these defects are found the programmers need to dive into some very complex code, much of it we're still trying to make sense of."

Matt took time to consider this. His first reaction was anger at having to listen to a bunch of whiners. But then his thoughts led in a different direction. "Where did these test cases come from?" he asked.

Daphne responded, "From the prior team. They put together an entire test case library. They had the history with the project and the expertise. We wouldn't have known what to test without them."

Matt paused again and considered this new information. Sheila, it would seem, was persecuting him even in absentia. "The answer, then, is simple," Matt brightened. "We need to streamline testing. Scott, you have the deepest understanding of the project. I want to meet with you and Daphne to see how we can reduce the amount of testing needed. My guess is we can get down to a third of the current test load. Would that help you out, Greg?'

"Yes it would, Matt. It would let us spend less time on maintenance, more on reconfiguring the system."

"Perfect, block out your afternoon, Daphne and Scott. We've got some trimming to do." At this, Matt let out a guffawing laugh, mimicking the sound President Meld had made in their meeting. It contained the same intent: there will be a place at the table for you if you give me what I want and avoid putting roadblocks in my way. Scott smiled but dreaded the meeting. He helped develop the testing scenarios and knew that none of them were frivolous. Bypassing any of them placed the human subject at risk. He knew that by the end of the day two thirds of those guardrails would be gone, and for that he would bear partial responsibility.

K1 was strapped into the chair when Matt and his team entered the room. Matt addressed K1 with an air of congratulations.

"I guess you're ready to become the first human superhero. There's not a person alive who won't be envious of what you will be capable of."

"Only one side is secured." K1 directed his comment to his attendant while raising his left arm, ignoring Matt's comment. "You'll have to tighten this again."

Matt got his way. The testing regimen was truncated. Every test that simulated interactions between organs of the body were scrapped as per Matt's instructions. For instance, the brain's response to a neuralBlast session was simulated but the stress caused to the heart because of the brain's increased activity remained unknown, precisely because those test cases were never run. Similarly, the immune system's response to the external stimulus was glossed over and was anyone's guess. Matt was a bureaucrat who'd acquainted himself with neurological terms and processes. He convinced himself that this rudimentary knowledge made him something of an expert. He thought he had a gift for this particular scientific discipline, and he'd explain why to anyone who cared to listen, of which there were many.

"We'll do that at the same time we connect the other sensors to you. Then we'll run through the diagnostics and be ready to go," Matt responded to K1. Matt's comment was also a cue for the others to get in position and fire up the preliminary sessions and attach the electrodes to K1's body.

As they worked, Matt conversed with K1.

"You'll be on your way in no time. Not only is this great for you but great for our country. You're performing a great service and will help us continue to have superior military might against our enemies both abroad and those hiding within our borders."

K1 could hardly stand listening to Matt babble, which he recognized as the rantings of a mad man.

"Let's get this shit rolling," was K1's only response.

Matt had grown fond of K1. He knew K1 hated him. But Matt had something K1 wanted, so he tolerated Matt despite the extreme discomfort it brought him. It was this restrained hostility directed towards him that Matt liked so much and wanted to cultivate, if the opportunity presented itself. Yes, he'd be disappointed if something happened to K1.

They were ready. Or perhaps it would be better to say there was no reason to delay any longer. Scott was thankful he was not the one to pull the trigger. He worked at the conceptual level and assisted by observing and providing suggestions as they moved through the session. He was principally responsible for developing the parameters used to initiate the session, termed *the narrative.* The narrative Matt tasked him with was to determine the level of threat posed by the various resistance groups within the country's borders and the best way to neutralize them. Scott was flanked by Matt on his left side and Greg on his right. The other four participants were heads-down at their workstations, monitoring K1's reactions and the interactions between K1's cerebral cortex and the computing network it was in direct contact with.

Scott could not believe this was about to happen. Technically, they were months away from when this procedure could be performed safely. The programming had been "stubbed"; so many interactions had been simply turned into empty containers. And no one had a clear understanding of the effect this would have when the system was activated.

"Are you ready?" Matt asked. His doughboy features were hard to read but his face was appropriately flushed. His multi-chinned and bulbous head thrust forward in his best imitation of a mythic general charging into battle.

"Of course I am, you idiot!" K1 yelled as he cast his gaze to an indistinct place.

"Start with two processors, effective immediately," Matt commanded.

K1 needed to remain conscious, which led them to consider administering a mild sedative. But Matt vetoed this option, saying they may miss something in his reactions if he were sedated.

K1's body jumped, pushed against the restraints. His eyes bulged and rotated from side to side without focusing. He clenched hard against a rubber device inserted into his mouth. He made no effort to communicate, as he lost the ability to do so.

All of K1's vital signs were elevated, but not dangerously high. The computer integration showed bursts of activity followed by periods of rest. Five minutes in, Matt issued the following command.

"Bring two more processors online."

This was discussed beforehand and the analysis indicated they should ramp up one processor at a time. But no one breached his command.

Now K1 thrashed and veins popped out on his face. His body tucked in, braced for the body blows it received internally. The techs monitoring the bodily response began yelling out as readings exceeded dangerous levels. Matt seemed to not notice, as the same impassive expression remained painted across his face.

"Bring one more processor online," Matt bellowed.

"Wait," Scott said. "We're already in no man's land. His system might not be able to take it. We can stay here and see what benefits he has derived."

"But we wouldn't know how far we can take it."

Scott couldn't process what lay behind Matt's comment quickly enough to respond before K1 bellowed, "MORE!" as he spit out the rubber device.

Matt and Scott turned from each other and stared at K1. His body jerked with waves of tremors. There was a brutal, far away look on his face that was both captivating and terrifying.

"Bring on that processor," Matt repeated and Scott acquiesced to this directive.

The spasms became uncontrollable and within a couple of minutes K1 lay dead on the table. Later they found that his heart had burst. But now when they looked at him his eyes were wide open and directed towards some distant point.

Scott couldn't contain himself and blurted out, "We could have saved him."

"But then we wouldn't know the upper limits, would we?" Matt had higher goals from which he would not be diverted. He, more than anyone, was fond of K1. But he knew from the start where this would lead. While the others tried to manage their shock, perform the concluding tasks, and address the dead man in their midst, Matt made the final comment.

"He knew what was coming, believe me. And he welcomed it. His sacrifice has given us purpose. His death is something we must honor and measure ourselves against, just like the deaths of all patriots. But did you see the expression on his face just before he passed? It was terrifying but it was beautiful, and the beauty came from the higher cause he knew he was serving. We are duty-bound to apply the same level of commitment. We will forever bear responsibility for his virtuous death and making sure that it was not in vain. You see, we have logs of everything that occurred physiologically. We have gained far more insight into how to manage this process safely than all those ginned up testing scenarios you were wasting your time with."

No one responded, which was good, because Matt would not tolerate dissent. After some moments he concluded, "We will name all subsequent subjects with the 'K' root. So, the alias of our next subject shall be K2." This was Matt's way of memorializing his first, and most precious, casualty. As he walked from the room, leaving the others to attend to K1 and their housekeeping tasks, he believed that his vision was now forged in blood. This cemented a militant quality that needed to be instilled within the team.

Those left behind were wrapped in a new layer of solidarity. Perverse though it was, a blanket of Matt's singular purpose encircled and comforted them. The control he had over them tightened into a knot that would expel competing agendas.

Chapter 8

"There are a few that are bigger and stronger than me. But there's no one more ruthless. When I have a job to do it gets done, without loose ends or messy details. Guaranteed. But if you've got some more tools for me, bring 'em on." Brad Phililps delivered this information to Matt, as a way to introduce himself.

Displays of brashness, where there had been K1's almost desperate quality. Matt was not sure how he liked this new version. K1 was Mt Everest, while K2 was just K2.

"I'm not offering mere tools. We have developed a technology that can download all relevant, forward-militarist strategy and knowledge directly into your brain. You will be the ultimate warrior, able to combine ruthlessness with creativity, brute force and skill like none other. And we will supply you with ample opportunities to use these skills. You should know there are dangers. Your predecessor died in the middle of receiving a treatment. But his experience allowed us to learn how to better administer these sessions, and there shouldn't be another outcome like his."

Brad displayed heightened interest with this turn in the conversation. Others already thought of him as the ultimate warrior, but he knew that was a lie. There were flaws that he was unable to correct. He was drawn to special ops because of how the rules of engagement allowed brutality to range freely outside of ethical norms. But still he yearned for a wider palette. And here was this pasty old bureaucrat offering him exactly what he sought after.

"You've got my interest. When do we start?"

"You haven't been chosen yet," Matt said, and continued to stare at Brad without playing his hand. He wondered if he could adapt to a little mouthing off and decided he probably could, as long as Brad knew who was in charge, who held the whip.

"Tell me something, Brad. What motivates you? To what do you pledge your allegiance?

He considered the question before replying, "My parents lost their lives in the flood of '31. Own fault really. Chose to only listen to their own counsel. Wouldn't move further inland. I never blamed them, either. They died the way they lived, on their own terms. I was deployed at the time and stayed away because there was nothing to come back to. I saw it as a test. If I wasn't strong, I'd be washed away by a tidal rush similar to the one that took them.

"The world is unremittingly brutish. I realized that after losing my parents. And when you look out beyond this world, the environment becomes only more hostile and the silence more impenetrable. The moment I realized this is when it clicked for me. I'll meet this brutishness head on. I will be the more ferocious and effective warrior or expect my foe to vanquish me. I choose to be fully engaged in war because that is the only defense against the crushing loneliness. Each challenge is a way to affirm I'm alive and that my life has meaning. My allegiance is to you and whatever mission you set before me. I am aware of no limit to which I can be pushed."

There was enough here, Matt decided. And time was of the essence. He rose and extended his hand across the desk and said in a grave tone, "Your predecessor was named K1 because he always posted the highest number of kills in his unit. We wish to honor him for his bravery and service and for that reason I confer to you the title of K2."

Brad took the news indifferently. They could call him whatever they wanted because, by whatever name, glory awaited him.

Chapter 9

Sheila drove from their hideout in Harpers Ferry, West Virginia to The Kentlands in Gaithersburg, Maryland. This was her childhood neighborhood. Her parents were so happy when they moved there.   They were in love with New Urbanism and the promise of community festooned upon it. But year by year her parents' displeasure grew as their hopes dimmed.   The depth of relationship to neighbors never materialized because there was no counterpoint to their physical closeness.   The white picket fences, manicured gardens and ample front porches mocked the emergent alienation.   Years later Sheila came to understand that was because the members of the community didn't rely on each other for anything meaningful.   The same pettiness that suffocated them in the upscale suburb they fled infused itself in these closer quarters, resulting in at least as high a level of toxicity.

But as she drove, she was not thinking about this or anything else concerning her past.   She chose it merely because she knew places that provided a suitable meeting location.   It was also conveniently situated, not far from Harpers Ferry and DC. She was driving to talk with Scott who was now her sole confidante. He had continued checking in on her and little by little she succumbed to his inquiries. She shook off the framework of him being someone she managed and placed him on an equal footing with her.

Scott had created a back-channel communication link to Sheila before she disappeared, which involved a dark web messaging server.   These interactions needed to be short because longer exchanges carried the increased risk of being traced. The main reason for this meeting was Sheila's desire to gain a more thorough understanding of how K1 was progressing, to see if the pressure being exerted on her was warranted.

It was a Saturday afternoon and she chose a diner she expected would be quiet. If that was unsuitable there were several walking trails that snaked between the mixed-used structures to provide privacy.

She arrived first and it was only when she looked at the 1950s retro facade of the diner that she reflected on her youth here. It felt like The Newer Machine took lessons from this architecture, celebrating its facile qualities. She entered and was met by a hostess who directed her to a table. When Scott arrived ten minutes later, they asked for coffee and time to look at the menu, but they did not look at the menu.

"So, how are things progressing on the project? Have they succeeded in placing all the blame for any failures on my shoulders?"

Scott laughed before answering. "They buried you a long time ago. Yes, you are the she-devil. Matt Ray-gun, my little nickname for him, actually decreed we were not to reference you by name directly. That is quite difficult as most of the software originated with you."

Sheila shared in the laughter, something she hadn't experienced much recently.

"Hearing Matt won't say my name is something I can't complain about . . .. But tell me, where's the project at now?"

"They're gutting it, actually. It's all shut down except for the militaristic components. They thought implementing that piece was straightforward, and it might be if we'd employed normal coding techniques. But you know how deep we got into the kernel of the operating system. I gave up trying to explain that to Matt and his crew. I see now how fortunate I was when you and Kathy were running things and I didn't have to deal with these *tools*."

"Actually, I'm surprised you stayed on. That they let you . . . and you wanted to."

Scott's eyes strained as they looked to the side and then grazed across the menu. "I felt some obligation. It's hard to explain. Yes, it's hard to watch them dismantle what we built. But if I'm not there, it will be totally abandoned to the worst, lowest features of what we tried to do. Maybe I'm fooling myself and will walk out the door someday. But for now, I'm going to hang in there."

Sheila looked at Scott and decided to leave it at that. She wondered how he managed to get up and go to work every day when there was so little left of what they were trying to accomplish.

"I'm glad you're there and I'm glad you've agreed to meet with me now," Sheila said. "I wouldn't blame you if you didn't. You'd be in danger if they knew who you were with."

"Don't think I don't know that."

"It's good you're doing what you think is right. And what would really help me is if you can tell me how things are progressing with K1?"

Scott paused and became visibly uncomfortable. "Actually, the first subject, K1, died during his first treatment. . .. I believe Matt intended to kill him from the start. My best guess is Matt wanted to use K1 as some sort of baseline, for Christ sake. See how far he could push him before something burst. It happened to be his heart, which seems particularly poignant. It's hard to wrap my head around what I saw, and participated in."

Scott paused again, unable to continue as the nightmarish vision of K1 expiring passed before his mind's eye.

"I've sat in on some interviews of the new recruits who want to be test subjects. They're all the same. Really raw. Special ops types to the max. They don't seem human, don't show any emotion. Perfect killing tools, perfect for what we're assembling. Matt wants to name the next subject K2, some type of fucking tribute to K1. He's mad, I tell you."

Again, Sheila wondered how Scott could stand being involved in this metastasized version of what had been their visionary work, but this time she kept her thoughts to herself.

"That's truly horrible," Sheila began. "And somehow it makes my situation even worse. I'm under a lot of pressure to make Milo productive. I'm not even sure what that means anymore. They want tangible results they can use in the struggle."

"Sure, of course they do. I respect your concern for Milo. I do, really. But you've aligned yourself with rebels who believe they are in a life and death struggle. There's no turning back for them. And they expect the same level of commitment from those in their ranks," Scott said with a surprising level of conviction.

"Sheila, we had a chance to do great work. We did our best but we didn't get it done. The game has shifted now and we need to play the cards we've been dealt."

"You're right, the world has changed and I need to reassess my role in it. But there's one thing I've decided. I won't allow Milo's brain development to be truncated. I won't allow him to be turned into an efficient killer like what you're observing. I refuse to believe that is the way forward for him or this technology."

Scott looked at her closely, trying to determine what lay behind this comment. His expression creased into a frown before he spoke again.

"I am beginning to question what we thought we were doing," Scott confessed. "Were such grand notions of merging computational power with human imagination achievable? I know we had lofty ideals but were we kidding ourselves into thinking we could change the course of history in a positive direction? Or were we just finding an excuse to satisfy our careers and intellectual curiosity while we developed a new Pandora's box for the power elite to misshapen in ways that allow them to broaden their control?"

These thoughts and others like them were also part of Sheila's internal dialog. "I know, I've considered the same questions. But I don't regret our efforts. Not yet anyway." The last part of these comments trailed off, lacking strong conviction.

"These higher-level thoughts don't really matter right now," Scott said with a defeated tone. "The floor has shifted beneath us and we need to get our footing before we get knocked over."

"Be practical. Be tactical."

"That's right. And that may mean compromising our ideals. This translates into me accepting I'm working with a mad man and that you're dealing with an increasing level of militancy from the rebels. Which may mean going along with techniques and procedures you would rather not engage in."

Sheila pondered the unstable ethical foundations holding up Scott's words. She recognized the blending of truths, the ease with which reality-driven rationale beckoned. And then just as quickly she pushed aggressively against this thought exercise.

"I understand what you are doing and I respect it," Sheila said, trying to sound like she meant what she said. "But it's not for me. It will lead to the erosion of everything I've worked my whole career for. And, even more, it will destroy Milo, whose proper development I will defend, even with my own life. Anything less would be a denial of everything I believe in and stand for."

Scott studied Sheila and chose to not respond. She sensed his discomfort but chose to not ask him what he was thinking because she was clear about how she felt. She saw no reason to pursue the topic further.

Their waitress came by once while they spoke and they requested more time, so now they scanned the menu and ordered food. Much of the conversation that followed involved Scott's technical debrief. Sheila relished the details of their progress even as it infuriated her. There were aspects to their approach she wouldn't have considered and laughed at her own blind spots. If she wasn't horrified at the eventual outcome, she would have enjoyed the intellectual challenges this presented. Overshadowing the entire conversation was the recognition that she provided them with the infrastructure to create a monster. It was just a matter of time.

Chapter 10

It took a week for Milo's thoughts to completely unscramble after a session. During the second week Milo was put through a series of tests to determine what newfound powers he'd developed, and work on protocols for the next session was performed. One cycle had passed since the experience leading to Milo's immersion into origami. Prior to the session, Sheila worked strenuously to improve their ability to influence Milo's direction during a session. Rex wanted this session to focus on military tactics to be employed by resistance fighters, and Sheila acquiesced. She sourced David and Goliath military campaigns throughout history, complete with estimates of arsenals on both sides. She also supplied similar data for current hot spots that included imagery of terrain and related information. These inputs were then fed into Milo's neuralBlast connection at the session's inception.

A week after the session Sheila and Rex met to discuss next steps. Their interactions were increasingly antagonistic as each became more outspoken about their incompatible points of view.

"He's almost willfully disregarding what we ask him to do, what we need him to do," Rex told her.

"You know that's not true. He has no more command of how his mind will branch during a session than we do when we are dreaming. Have you tried to control your dreams recently?"

"We don't know that," Rex countered. "All we know is we are sinking a lot of our scant resources into this project and getting nothing in return. Since becoming communicative after this last session all he will talk about is martial arts techniques. We are not grooming him to open a dojo!"

Sheila relented. "I know. I'm frustrated, too. But there's nothing we can do except refine the code. Something will break in our favor." The last comment was delivered with a quavering tone that did not convince even herself.

"I disagree," Rex countered. "I've decided to suspend future sessions until we can see a clear path forward. In pursuit of that, Marta and Sev have gone to work with additional programmers at another location. You will have as much contact with them as you want, but it makes more sense for you to stay here and work with Milo directly. He trusts you the most. Maybe he will open up to you."

"Wait a minute. When I started, you said I was given control of the project. That's not possible with the programmers off-site. This is a power grab and I don't like it."

"Listen, Sheila. I've kept things from you that I'll share now." Rex made little effort to cultivate confidential relationships. What he did cultivate was an air of certainty in his beliefs, which is why seeing him lower his guard felt so foreign to Sheila.

"The Syndicalists we are aligned with are a rag-tag collection of gangs, or worse. Maybe someday that type of decentralization will work but not now, not when we are up against what is still the most powerful fighting machine in the world. I meet with the other Syndicalist sect leaders frequently and have been trying to assert some leadership over these meetings that rage on and on like a freaking cat fight. Only recently have I begun to have some degree of success. And the only reason they show some deference is because of the work we are doing with Milo, the promise it represents. You can imagine the reaction when I tell them how little tangible result we have seen. The blow back towards me is getting strong. These are not all nice people I am dealing with. I, and this team, could even be in danger if they think I've been peddling bullshit.

"So, I'm sorry if you feel I'm being unfair to you, but something has to change. You've been here over a month and have not been able to move the needle. We need to have others with fresh eyes take a look at this because we need to produce results quickly."

"We don't need to break up the team to do this but I'm not going to argue with you."

Sheila did not put up more of a fight because a part of her was happy to be working solo. Directing the other programmers required her to act as project leader, which limited her own investigations. Now she would be largely free to do her own analysis.

After knocking, Sheila walked in on Milo who was performing a series of Tai Chi katas, the apparent object of Rex's scorn. She had seeded military classes of information into the startup parameters and stood observing the results. Normally she'd wait until a pause in Milo's activities before proceeding with her debrief, but she wasn't feeling particularly generous with her time right now.

"Could you take a break from your exercises, so we can discuss the results of our last test?" As she spoke, she moved across the room to sit in one of two chairs angled towards each other. A small night table was nestled between them.

Milo turned his head and acknowledged Sheila for the first time since she entered his room.

"I wouldn't refer to them as exercises, actually. They're really"

Before he could put a finer point on her comment, Sheila cut him off.

"Not now, Milo. I'm not really interested in having an esoteric discussion with you right now."

Milo stopped his motion and appraised Sheila before sitting across from her. "Sure, I'll devote my attention to whatever you need to discuss," offered with the formal demeanor he expressed when feeling the effects of a session. In this instance, he made an effort to sound agreeable.

"I need your help, Milo. I've shielded you from a lot of the discussion around here, but don't know how much longer I'll be able to do that. You may not want to hear it, but people are disappointed in your progress. They expected you to help in the struggle against The System. But so far you've focused on things that they feel are self-indulgent, whimsical. They're considering changes to the neuralBlast software that I think will harm you. I've been able to keep them from shifting in that direction but if you don't give us something we can use, I don't know how long I can hold them off."

Milo came and sat down on the other chair. She was surprised by his bearing. He was about six feet and sinewy, but far from imposing, and never before had he exuded a sense of personal power. He had recently shaved his head, revealing a nicely shaped dome. Scant facial hair covered his face. But what Sheila noticed was his posture, back straight as though the top of his head was being pulled vertically by a string. He was becoming sturdy, Sheila surmised. He would need to be.

Milo's expression became serious in a way Sheila never witnessed before, and he looked older. He sat quietly, engaged in an internal dialog for a few minutes before deciding what direction to send the conversation.

"I know. And I know more about this than you have any idea. I've held the truth back from them . . . and from you. You see, I don't trust them. I haven't been sure about you either, to be honest. I sensed your goodness immediately, but I wasn't sure how strong you'd be when they applied real pressure. When I came here I had bought into their version of what my role was, how I could be used most effectively. But from my first session I perceived more than that. Here's the most important lesson I learned: If you reference problems from within their framework you will eventually become the evil that you are in conflict with. It's happened all the time throughout history, and Rex is just kicking that can down the road. While you and the others were fiddling with the ciphers and parameters used for the session initiations, I inserted my own version into the session-initiation message and that fired instead of what you intended.

"My sessions, as directed by my own search criteria, have sent me down every significant struggle people have engaged in, which includes all the significant points of view embedded within them. I've uncovered every permutation of strife including those fueled by religious, racial and ethnic differences, but mostly the control and exploitation of natural resources. I know more about these things than any human ever has and it has made me wiser. Boiled down to the simplest lesson, the universal truth is that you do not defeat evil when you vanquish it in battle. Instead, you internalize the evil you thought you'd defeated. It weaves its way into the DNA of every person, family, civilization engaged in the struggle. It starts as low-level inflammation that develops into a form of pain that grows exponentially. And it is never seen directly. Amnesia sweeps over both sides but the darkness that's woven into the DNA sows mistreatment that is then normalized.

"My last session was the beginning of a new direction for me. I started scouring the annals for outliers, occurrences that defy this dark trend that leads to perpetual violence and war, where the powerful only relinquish control when they have been overcome by some more lethal force. I'm almost there, I feel like I'm closing in. But I can't discuss it until I have a fuller grasp. They would see what I'm saying as treasonous, or lunacy, probably both. So, instead I express things that are tangential, and that I pick up along the way. Apparently, I could have picked better."

Milo paused and his face lit up, showing a younger, brighter version of itself. "But don't get me wrong. Tai chi and origami have their place and are important. And that's even more true of the Hendrix guitar licks." This comment was a clear sign he was emerging from the spell cast on him from his last session.

Sheila was struck mute by what Milo told her and felt a radiant glow spread throughout her whole body. It was not the attraction to a man she felt, but rather that she fell under the spell of this man/child that she began to feel kin with. And for whom she mostly feared for.

"I think we will forego Purple Haze for now, but I'll take a rain check on that."

"You're no fun sometimes, Sheila. You know that?"

"I've been called worse. But yes, that's certainly the case sometimes." And then turning the conversation back to its primary orbit she asked, "Can you tell me more about this *new way*?"

Milo started and stopped a few times, each time determining that what he was about to say fell short of what he wanted to express. Finally, he allowed the following to escape, "When I am processing at full capacity, when the neural connections are firing in perfect unison, I can feel the depth of any emotion, perceive answers to every problem. The only word I can apply to that experience is joy, pure joy. When I'm there I see no conflict between the earliest Indigenous cultures and the most cutting-edge technological discoveries and adaptations. But those moments are fleeting. Some disruption occurs, stress comes in some unexplained form, and I'm dragged back and besieged by doubt and angst like everyone else except in a much more extreme way. This is why it takes me so long to recover from a session . . . .. So, each time I go under I look to expand those periods of clarity because I'm convinced humanity will embrace this experience, the sense of abundance and coherence presented to me at these moments. Everything else, all the pain and suffering will fall away if I can figure out how to shower people with this beatific experience."

Man Made

Sheila felt the warm glow emanating from Milo. He was gazing beyond her now, searching for how to return to that state, without extinguishing himself in the process. And she understood what it was she must do and assigned herself a new role, that of protectress, mother. No one knew what they signed up for anymore in this world of fluid emotion and cosmic insight that she had helped to birth. Despite this uncertainty, she felt some of the joy that Milo spoke of sprinkling over her like a cool, faint shower of rain.

"OK," Sheila finally responded. "I got it. You're onto something. But until you get there, we need to come up with a plan to keep them from jumping ship on how the program is being administered."

Sheila attacked the log output with a renewed sense of purpose, although she wasn't sure exactly what it was she was looking for. Her primary goal was to find something to convince Rex to restart the sessions with little to no alteration in the methodology. At the same time, she hoped to determine what led to Milo's moments of clarity that quickly frayed before disintegrating. Milo's descriptions were her guideposts, comments such as "firing in perfect unison" and "processing at full capacity". She sought a corollary in the trace data. If she could decipher what those periods of peak insight looked like in the logs, she might be able to recode aspects of the neuralBlast system to help Milo stay in these synchronous experiences for longer periods of time.

The logs conveyed a beautiful, if incomplete, picture of Milo's mind and body interactions. There would be measured searches almost timed to his heartbeat. And then, an explosion of activity erupted. She assembled four monitors and opened the various logs from each of the servers that were hooked to Milo. She lacked sophisticated tools to coordinate the output and was left to her own observations to

115

unlock the miracle of the parallel, multi-processing intelligence that Milo achieved during these sessions. At times a total randomness seemed to govern the inquiries. And then, for no apparent reason, after zigzagging upwards and down into subterranean depths, branching outward, and rebranching a hundred times, each of the four processors resolved to the same data point. She marveled for hours at a time, joyous in these observations, but uncertain she was getting any closer to the underlying principle animating this process.

She became Milo's accomplice, helping him finish the work he felt called to do. And this put her in an uneasy position with the others on the team. If they did not see Milo's actions as treasonous, they were moving in that direction. Out of desperation they became more tactical and would have little patience for Milo's dreamy sounding pursuits of a *third way*. She limited her discussion with the other programmers and thought it best to keep it that way. But she needed to stay in touch with Rex, to see what he was thinking, feel which way the wind was blowing between him and those with whom he consulted. All of these reflections led to an unpleasant sensation of deja vu as she walked into her meeting with Rex, which they scheduled whenever he was on-site.

"So, Sheila, have you made any progress figuring out what young Mr. Einstein is up to?"

"Sure have," Sheila enthused. "It wasn't obvious at first, but he has harvested a lot of useful data."

"That so?" Rex said, while focused on a knot of wood on the headboard of a window frame above Sheila's head, which was as close to eye contact as he was willing to be drawn into.

"Yes it is. He told me he has archived and analyzed every major battle that has occurred in modern history, many of which we discussed in detail."

A flicker of interest passed across his face before he could reassert a look of dull annoyance.

"I see. And what actionable items have we gained from this investigation?"

"He is learning how to neutralize and defeat more technologically advanced enemies by taking advantage of other qualities like the physical terrain and the will of the people."

"How soon can he have this documented for our review?" Rex said, looking directly at her for the first time, trying to assess the quality of the information she was conveying.

"Not yet. He needs another session, maybe more than one to finish his research."

Rex again looked away from her and found the knot on the board.

"I'm not sure about that, Sheila. You know we said we would not move forward until we considered all the options available to us.

"This is big," Sheila said, raising her voice. "What I just told you represents something new because it indicates real progress has been made."

"What you are describing is not real, nor is it tangible. And that is what we need asap or our work gets shut down."

This was new and unsettling information for Sheila, although not surprising.

"How do we move forward without more sessions?"

He looked at her again now and a cloak of some kind spread over his expression, "I'll let you know the answer to that question when we've decided the direction we're headed."

Double-talk and innuendo, deja vu all over again.

"I'll have my report ready for you in a couple of days."

The next evening, working late into the night, Sheila stumbled upon a directory on one of the servers. It was secured but as she had administrative rights on the server, she could access it. These, she quickly realized, were highly classified documents regarding the government's neuralBlast project. Many were from before she was fired but, more importantly, some were written afterwards. She saw among the early ones her own research papers, which she gleaned over the way any author would who felt good about what they had written. But it was the later research that she was most interested in and read voraciously.

After reading through minutes of meetings chaired by Matt Raines she chanced upon the central piece in the repository. This contained detailed plans for truncating the neuralBlast software. After reviewing the specs for an hour she realized this was the blueprint for weaponizing the neuralBlast software. This was the recipe for the deprecated version of her work they planned to implement. She was horrified by the conclusions reached in this document, and the near certainty that it could be adopted fairly quickly.

The author explained how the process could be made to work in the limited technological environment Rex and his crew worked in. It was well thought through and contained a deep understanding of the software, which unnerved Sheila. When she reached the end of the document all the tumblers fell into place. The author signed the document Scochi, which she recognized immediately. One night, late into a drunken outing with her neuralBlast team, Scott and she talked privately. He told her about how he was bullied in school, and how emasculating that was. This went on for years and he decided to find a way to use his brains to defend himself. They nicknamed him Scochi and he resolved to never be embarrassed by that name or allow it to cause him further pain. This was the only time he mentioned this episode to Sheila and she was pretty sure he didn't remember sharing it with her, and now she was sure of it.

It all made sense to her now. She'd been surprised when he initially made contact, but accepted it as one colleague reaching out to another after she got sacked. Somehow, when he ingratiated himself to her it did not raise enough suspicion even though nothing in their relationship predicted that type of closeness.

And she fell right into the trap, confiding in him, telling him she would never allow Milo to be turned into a war machine, that she would sacrifice herself first. After reading through all these documents she could reach no other conclusion but that they were moving ahead with this approach without her approval. She needed to work fast before they had a chance to implement their plans.

Chapter 11

Sheila entered Milo's room. He was on an exercise regimen and was starting to sprout some muscle. She waited until he was done on the pull up bar before motioning to him to sit and saying she had something to discuss.

"I can't keep things together any more, Milo. They're planning to make changes to the software that will harm you."

"What have you found out?"

"You know they're not satisfied with your progress. They want to shut down your full brain activity and restrict the flow to military style engagement."

"I get it. They're in a race with The System and they want me to be the layer of military might that will spur them to victory. They think one more piece of destructive power will solve everything."

"It would appear so."

Milo allowed himself a muffled laugh and Sheila considered how wide-ranging Milo's wisdom had become.

They sat there quietly until Sheila jumped the conversation to where it needed to be.

"I've got a plan. Before I joined the rebels, I withdrew the funds from my savings and converted them to an untraceable cryptocurrency. I also had a fake identity made for myself. These documents are in a safe place that I can access whenever I want. If we go on the run, I could sustain us for a long time."

Milo considered Sheila's offer for a couple of minutes before responding. "What's the point? I'm not done with my analysis. I appreciate you wanting to save me but there's not much point to anything if I can't connect all the dots."

"I'm sorry Milo. I don't see how we can move forward right now. I'm not without hope, though. I have all the neuralBlast software downloaded. There are people at Johns Hopkins in Baltimore who were sympathetic to what I was doing. They may be able to help set up a lab where we can continue our work. But one thing I'm pretty sure about is that if you stay here, they'll effectively lobotomize you, turn you into something that you'll not recognize as yourself. If we go on the run, you will at least be able to take with you what knowledge you've attained. Maybe it will be enough to help you do the work you feel called to do."

Milo again went quiet to consider the options and then simply said, "When do we leave?"

"I'm not sure. I could invent a reason for needing a car but they'd never give one to the two of us. And if you came along secretly as soon as they figured out what we were up to they'd hunt us down because there's tracking devices on all their cars."

Milo thought for a minute before speaking. "I can handle that."

"What do you mean?"

"That's one of the things I figured out, it's one of the skills I've developed. It drains me but I can sense electronic communications along digital frequencies."

"Do tell," Sheila perked up, not sure if she was more hurt or surprised by this revelation that she was just learning about for the first time. "Are you sure you can keep their sensors from finding us?"

"Yeah, pretty sure. I've played with this and it works every time."

"Later I want to hear how you're able to do this. But OK, how frequently do you leave the house?"

"After lunch I usually go for a walk for 30 - 45 minutes."

"That's good. I'll find an excuse to get a car at that time. You'll need to be waiting in the hedges at the far end of the property. I'll pick you up there and we'll get my money and papers in DC and then head to Baltimore and find a place to stay. From there I'll locate my contacts at Johns Hopkins."

The next morning Sheila knocked quietly at Milo's door and was let into the room by him.

"I'll get the car at 1:00," She whispered. "I made an excuse that I wanted to discuss some things with the programmers and it required us to be face to face. They are about 20 minutes away and it will probably be 1:30 before anyone gets suspicious. That'll give us a half hour head start. If you can scramble their tracking mechanism that should give us enough time to get away."

"Got it. Thank you, Sheila."

"So, we both go through the next couple of hours like it's any other day. When you go for your walk, nothing should be different. Don't fill your pockets with things you want to bring with you. This will have to be bare bones, for both of us."

"Sure, the only thing I'll miss is my guitar and I'll be playing it until we leave."

"I'm sorry, Milo. But there's no way to bring it along."

"I know and it's OK."

"Good, so be by the stand of trees at the end of the property at 1:00. Make yourself inconspicuous and be ready to jump in. Then we'll tear ass out of here."

Milo laughed because of how out of character it was for her to say something like that. Catching onto the spirit he responded, "We're freedom bound."

"Something like that."

After she left, he pulled his guitar from the stand. He started with some blues riffs he'd learned from the masters and then blended in his own licks. He would use this time to say goodbye.

Sheila returned to her office but was too keyed up to work. She knew she was putting Milo and herself at risk but there was no better option. She already made sure all the neuralBlast software was safely downloaded on a secure server she'd be able to access when she needed it. This left her feeling buoyant, almost giddy because she was doing something good for Milo. Most of the impacts she caused him she now regretted and she felt guilty about. But there was something else and then she said into the blank void of her room, "I'm enjoying the shit out of breaking the rules." Sure, she had excellent reasons, but just doing it was exhilarating, experiencing the wildness of it, affirming a world outside the ever-constraining forces society placed upon her, upon everyone. It was enough to make her swoon.

She got up and walked to the garage. Usually there would be a mechanic working on keeping their tiny fleet functional but no one was there now. She spied the car she was taking and checked the battery, which only had a quarter charge, probably not enough for what she planned. Energy was in short supply and was rationed accordingly. Just as she was applying the charging cable a mechanic reentered the garage. He looked at her puzzled and annoyed.

"What's up?"

"Just checking the car I'm taking at 1."

"Yeah, I know you reserved a car," he said, perturbed. "But why are you plugging the battery in?"

"To make sure I have enough charge to get me where I'm going."

"You're just going to the "B" House, right? There's already plenty of charge to get you there."

They were squared off with each other. He was in his lair and had grease stains covering his hands and arms to prove it. But she was the lead technologist and that had rank and she decided to use it.

"And if I want to get my goddamn nails done afterwards that's what I'll do. So, if you don't have any more to say about it, leave the battery connected and I'll disconnect it when I'm ready to leave."

She strode out of the garage in a huff, but was praying he would not raise questions to Rex or anyone else who could cause problems.

That little confrontation leveled her off a little, which made it easier to approximate her normal routine. She posted an agenda for the 1:30 meeting that would never happen. At 12:30 she looked outside and noticed the sky was darkening and realized weather was one variable she had not considered and could not control for anyway.

The rain started slowly but by the time she walked out to the car it was a steady rain. The battery was still connected and the mechanic was nowhere in sight. She started the car and headed down the driveway that ran about 50 feet. She turned on to the road and looked ahead toward the rendezvous spot, and her heart sank at what she saw. One of the guards was standing in a threatening way in front of Milo.

"What's going on?" she yelled as she exited the car.

"Not sure," Neil replied. He carried a handgun but still had it holstered. His expression suggested he was being told a story that didn't add up. "Milo, here, says he's out for a little stroll. If you notice, it's raining like crazy. I asked him to empty his pockets and he showed me a bunch of guitar picks and some letters, and some of his origami pieces. . .. Looks like a bunch of mementos to me."

Sheila made to look at the collection but at the same time pulled a can of mace from her bag and sprayed it into Neil's face. He was taken completely off guard and grabbed for his eyes reflexively. She grabbed a large rock from the side of the road and hit Neil in the back of the head, sending him sprawling.

"What the fuck?" Milo yelled.

Sheila was shaking but stayed screwed onto what needed to be done.

"Help me drag Neil to the side of the road. Hurry!"

When he could not be easily seen by passing traffic, they got in the car and drove as fast as they could.

"I'm sorry I did that, but I had to. We're not going to get another chance to escape," she said, more to convince herself than Milo.

"You're right, I guess. You had to do it."

"And I hope you can do something for us now. You're cloaking skills better be good because our head start just got cut in half. Hopefully Neil won't be unconscious for long. But we should call in 15 minutes and let them know he's out there."

"That's the right thing to do. And I'll start obfuscating the signal now."

"We're on our way, Milo. There's no turning back."

"There's nothing worth going back to."

That was one thing they were both sure of. She fishtailed her way around the bends in the road, determined to make it to the main thoroughfare in record time.

Chapter 12

"We should be safe here if we keep a low profile," Sheila said, putting the best spin on what she saw as an otherwise depressing situation. They found a basement apartment in Remington, a small neighborhood in Baltimore. Sheila contacted a colleague at Johns Hopkins who would help set up the computing environment needed to continue Milo's treatments.

But Milo didn't need cheering up. This was the type of place he'd lived in since he was on his own and represented a sort of homecoming. There were usually people about, some of them shady looking but that did not bother him. The safe house from where they had just escaped was so isolated and sterile. Here he could breathe.

Remington gained some notoriety in the early 2010s, when there was still some money and interest in reviving inner city neighborhoods. But all that collapsed after the pandemic of 2027, the same time the decision was made to cordon off and sacrifice the western half of the city. It wasn't that neatly demarcated, but most of the eastern neighborhoods retained a modicum of government support as they were seen as tactically aligned with the northeast corridor which extended from Boston to Washington DC, although much of what was within its borders lay in tatters. Their apartment abutted these two worlds, east and west, and the residents possessed qualities of these different realities. Their landlord asked few questions, and would keep it that way as long as rent was paid on time.

The apartment was listed as furnished, which was laughable. There were two bedrooms but with a railroad car layout you needed to pass through one to get to the other. On the front end was the living room, the far end, the kitchen. A bed and stool outfitted the bedrooms. An old, sagging sofa was the sole item in the living room. They sat in the kitchen which had the only stable furniture, an old table with a corrugated steel apron wrapped around it. The chairs were similarly sturdy without an ounce of comfort. The set would probably outlast the apartment that housed it.

"Nothing a little sprucing up can't fix," Milo commented, spying the pattern left by mold on the walls, illuminated by the harsh light emitted from the single uncovered LED tube in the ceiling.

"Well, I'm glad you feel that way, Milo. I'm going to be super busy setting up the technical environment. That will leave you with plenty of time to do all the sprucing up you want."

She was surprised when he did not react derisively to her comment. Instead, he continued looking around, as if cataloging the changes he'd make. Their escape from the safe house was swift. They headed to a bank in DC where Sheila had a safe deposit box. She gathered her Id papers that defined the new identity she would now step into. She retained her first name but was now Sheila Goldman, a professional in marketing bio-engineering software. She also collected her retirement savings.

"I'm on it," Milo responded, upbeat. "I don't know why, but I feel better than I have for a long time, and more relaxed."

Sheila studied Milo, wondering at the experience going on inside him. None of her research could anticipate what the brain and body did organically after the sessions ended. But he looked better, sharper, clearer now. All she could do was continue monitoring the changes as she readied the lab for further immersion in neuralBlast learning. They were fortunate that Milo figured out how to avoid the state's surveillance apparatus. How wasn't clear yet, and this was something she would study. He explained it as the ability to raise a beacon, like a protective shield or aura that surrounded him, and made him imperceptible to beams issued from surveillance cameras, drones, and related devices. So, he could travel freely for brief periods, although raising the beacon tired him and in a short time became ineffective.

Thus began their daily ritual. Sheila went off to the computer lab and Milo stayed at home to keep house. His interest in these simple tasks baffled both of them at first, but then they sensed he was grounding and preparing himself for whatever the next chapter may be. He set to work disinfecting the apartment, bought basic supplies and learned what services were available locally. The highlight of this initial foray was scoring two used bikes from a local bike shop which they had no choice but to store alongside the lumpy sofa in the living room, which neither of them minded.

One morning after Sheila had left on one of the bikes, Milo was set to take the other and explore the area. When he ascended to street level his gaze was met by a man who appeared to be a few years older than him, sitting on the steps two doors down.

"How you doing?" His voice rang out with an appealing, but nasally, resonance paired with a strong Hispanic accent.

"Good, man, good," Milo wasn't lying either. "Thought I'd take a tour of the neighborhood. See what it has to offer."

"So, you're new to B'more?"

Milo's face flashed with uncertainty before he stammered out, "Pretty much. Came down with my sister. She started a job at Johns Hopkins. I decided to help her with the move. Maybe stay on for a while and find some work around here if I like it."

The other considered, reflecting on Milo's comments for a bit longer than Milo would have preferred.

But then, as if discarding whatever had occupied his thoughts, he said, "My name's Pedro. If you like, I'll take you around sometime to show you the sights. We could take a bike tour."

Milo was surprised by this act of kindness. "Sure, I'd like that. And I'm Milo," he replied. Pedro's most exceptional quality was the almost unnatural friendliness he radiated. His eyes reminded Milo of chipped glass, as if you were gazing into the speckled blue of ocean surf.

"Make sure you check out 'Pedro's Place'. I just opened an eatery a few blocks away. Nothing fancy, but the food is good. First meal, on the house."

"Absolutely, I'll do that. Thanks for the offer."

He took off on his bike, a relic but still functional. He traveled west because the thing he sought was in that direction. Along the way were tell-tale signs of recent history. The rising sea level pushed everything away from the harbor. Those neighborhoods that were still accessible and functioning were mashed together. Merchants who previously had their own shops, now set up clumps of stalls in abandoned alleyways. This was not the thriving market of just a few years before. Instead, people bore the look of those who barely survived, who lived from meal to meal, an experience with which Milo was familiar. He rode past these makeshift markets and the roads and buildings grew increasingly dilapidated. Then, he came upon the barrier. The wall, which was not always a wall but sometimes barbed wire fencing was what bifurcated the city. This was The System's signature policy, a visual enforcer. Every city with a potential for insurrection received the same treatment: physical borders reinforced by high tech surveillance. If you were deemed a significant enough problem, you were conducted over to the walled-off portion of your city, with every intent of being permanently forgotten.

Milo headed south and roamed the desolation. This neighborhood had not seen good times for many years and there was little worth salvaging. The roads were gutted, too, and after a while he turned back. What had seemed distressed before, now looked relatively stable. He better understood why the residents and merchants he passed were willing to band together and make do with their hostile surroundings.

This was the reality imposed by The System, its outward expression of total control versus a framework that constantly needed shoring up. Real want and need were everywhere and The Newer Machine's number one job was to divert people's desire from thinking critically about alternatives to the agendas set forth by The System. And the walled-off ghettos forming everywhere were effective psychological enforcers, reminders of how much worse things could be.

Milo continued riding for a couple of hours. On the way back he spotted Pedro's Place. He was hungry and without thinking about it pulled to the side of the road, found a place to park his bike and entered. There was no one else in there but somehow the atmosphere felt lively and inviting. Milo stood in the doorway for a moment looking around at the sparse surroundings: three tables with a couple of chairs at each, a Mexican flag on the wall surrounded by a couple of posters with pictures of pristine beaches, and poorly laid linoleum covering the floor and curling at the edges. But none of that mattered because of the way Pedro welcomed you.

"Hello, my friend. Come in, come in."

"I bet you didn't think I'd take you up on your offer so quickly."

Pedro's eyes twinkled, "I didn't think one thing or another. But I'm glad you did. If you've been riding all this time, you must be very hungry. So, what can I get you?" The menu was written on a chalkboard on the wall to the side of the counter and cash register.

There were so many appealing items, and Milo was hungry, but instead of choosing he said, "How about you pick. I trust your judgment. Whatever you would like to serve me I would be happy to receive."

"You are a smart man. Yes, I will find something you will appreciate. Please take a seat. These tables are not so nice. Someday they will be better."

Normally Milo would feel uncomfortable with this level of familiarity and graciousness coming from a stranger. But all that suspicion melted away because he sensed how genuine these qualities were.

Milo took a seat and could see Pedro move about his little prep area. He detected oversized crock pots and mini refrigerators, a microwave and a small oven. As he worked his magic, Pedro engaged his new acquaintance.

"So, were you able to see some sites on your bike today?"

"I got around. Toured the boundary, the DMZ."

Pedro was stunned for a moment and searched for how to respond.

"So, what did you think?"

"It was pretty rough, each block closer to the border got more and more deserted and ominous. I feel bad for the people on the other side. Their lives must be hard, without hope."

"I'm sure they are," Pedro mused. "But then again, maybe not everyone on the other side lives without hope for better futures."

Within minutes Pedro delivered the food, chicken stuffed empanadas flanked by a bowl of chili and a side salad. He came back a second time and placed a glass of iced tea next to the food.

Milo's eyes widened. He was hungry, but didn't realize how hungry. "This is too generous of you. You really must let me pay for it."

Pedro pulled the hand cloth from his shoulder and shook it back and forth. "No, no, no. You enjoy the food. Next time, maybe you pay. But now I am just happy to serve you." Pedro made a small wave of the cloth again, coaxing Milo to eat. It was the first time he stepped out of his selflessness, impatient as he waited to observe Milo's reaction to his creations. What a fine way to experience ego, thought Milo.

Milo took a spoonful of chili and areas of taste were experienced for the first time. There was a depth to the spices, a snowballing resonance.

"Damn, that's good. I mean really good."

Pedro beamed and allowed himself to accept the compliment.

And then, without even knowing how he knew such things, Milo rattled off the list of ingredients. "Cumin, fresh coriander, lime, ancho and guajillo chilis, oregano, pecans, bits of chocolate, sesame seeds, and of course onions and garlic."

Pedro was astonished and felt as though he'd been disrobed. He probed his new acquaintance more closely.

"I'm glad my mama didn't hear this. This is an old family recipe for Mole Rojo sauce. Some of these ingredients were hard to come by, almost impossible to find." And then shedding his astonishment, "She would demand I kill you if she heard you recite the ingredients like that." He laughed again, allowing his full spirit to spread throughout the room.

"I don't know where I learned how to do this," a lie. "It's something that just came to me," mostly true.

Since coming to the apartment Milo had moments like this more and more. He regretted spitting out the ingredients, realizing how it might look, but couldn't stop himself. The day before, he knew it was going to rain even though there wasn't a cloud in the sky; a half hour later it was teeming. He thought of it like what a teenager growing into his body experiences, and sensed these changes on a deep, primordial level. The neuralBlast treatments were affecting him organically, long after they occurred.

But it was more than that. He was honing his power to make disparate patterns cohere and from them deduce the next set of occurrences. He'd not shared this with Sheila and knew how weirdly mysterious it might sound. Some would say he could see into the future. But was it any more extraordinary than everything else, like being able to construct and share full sentences which evoked past, present, and future? Of course it wasn't, unless you were not equipped with this skill. Milo was simply expanding the palette of patterns he could recognize, but he wondered if he would alienate those around him who lacked this ability.

"Anyway, even if I can list the ingredients, I couldn't replicate the care that went into the preparation."

"Well yes. There's love in every ingredient," Pedro said, and with this regained his footing.

Milo dug into the empanada and let out a long, sumptuous "Ummmm."

Pedro was satisfied. "I'm glad you enjoy." Pedro's arm swept over an adjacent table and scooped up a condiment tray that he placed alongside Milo's meal. He surveyed Milo's food and accoutrements one last time and then said, "I will leave you alone now to enjoy your lunch."

Pedro went back behind the counter and busied himself with more food preparations. Milo savored this simple feast in the same way he did before his cyborg transformation.

Customers did come in and buy food. Pedro met each one with the same spirit and graciousness that he bestowed upon Milo. What Milo realized watching these interactions was that none of it was false. Instead of tiring him, the desire to serve enervated Pedro. Moments before, Milo was appraising the rise of his own powers but they seemed less grand in Pedro's presence.

The shop went quiet again and Milo's attention turned to the outside. A small group had congregated on the corner and Milo didn't like their look. They dressed in a way unfamiliar to him, all the young men wore some type of clownish, oversized newsboy caps while their lower halves were covered with patterned leggings that he thought may be the colors of their gang. They were the strutting peacocks while the women were covered in black, less interested in fashion but no less angry and hostile. As Milo tried to figure out their angle, two of the men opened the door and walked to the counter, talking all the while.

"My man, my man, my man. What's good? What's popping, today?

"Everything's good, as always," Pedro replied, as nonchalant as he could manage. "You know me."

As the one talked to Pedro, the other walked around the counter, picked the lid off the chili and took a deep breath. He made for the spoon at the end of the counter when Pedro intercepted him.

"You know the rules. I'm the only one allowed back here."

Pedro turned his back and sussed the intruder back to where he belonged. At the same time, the talker reached his hand down the counter and helped himself to a couple of candy bars that he hustled into his jacket pocket.

Milo got up and yelled, "What the fuck do you think you're doing?"

"What business is it of yours," the one with the pilfered stock responded, sizing Milo up for the first time.

"Just pay for the candy bars and leave this man alone and there won't be any trouble."

"We're not bothering anyone. Just ask Pedro. We come here all the time. This is our way of having a little fun with him."

Milo did not wait for Pedro to answer, did not want to put him in that position.

"I don't need to ask anyone anything. I can see what's going on and it's gonna stop now."

The other came from behind the counter and continued straight at Milo. He was the bigger, meaner of the two and was not disposed to chatty conversation. He threw a punch which Milo deflected with his arm. The man lunged but Milo put to use his martial arts training and the man grasped only air. He faltered and Milo assisted his descent with a side kick to the ribs. The other came at Milo with a chair and Milo moved within the round-house arc and delivered several powerful blows to his assailant's exposed midsection. They got up and attacked him a few more times but the results were the same. Milo had never before used his training in combat but moved with masterly assurance and calm. It surprised even himself when the two bodies lay prostrate and unconscious on the floor.

"My friend, what have you done?" Pedro asked in a stunned and concerned voice.

"They should not have stolen from you. They should have shown you and your store proper respect."

Milo was clear about what led to the altercation, but less so about his willingness to take the action he did.

"That's true. That's true. But look outside. They congregate here. I don't like having them around but they are a reality I need to deal with."

Milo considered for the first time the negative impacts his actions could have for Pedro.

"I'll come back and help you again if they bother you again."

"But you can't fight every bad guy that comes in here."

"You'd be surprised."

Milo enjoyed playing the bad ass, a role he never pulled off before. Pedro let out a short laugh.

"Listen, you need to go. When these guys wake up, they'll be getting their friends involved and I don't want you to get hurt or my store damaged. So go now and you can come by my house later and we will talk more."

"And you'll be OK?

Pedro laughed. "You think I don't know how to deal with these punks? I have dealt with much worse. And they're not all bad. Some even pay for their food."

It was Milo's turn to laugh. As he exited the door, it wasn't clear to him if those he walked by were aware of the dustup that had just taken place. But he didn't care if they were. There were six of them, four young men and two women, and he was confident he could take them all on. As he got on the bike and rode away he realized that this was a test, a way for him to flex his muscles instead of his brain. And he laughed when he realized how much he got off on the whole thing.

Throughout dinner Milo worried about whether that gang had caused Pedro more trouble. He knew Pedro's place closed at 7:00, so at 8:30 he walked outside and knocked on his door.

"Hold on, I'll be with you in a minute," he heard from inside.

Moments later the door soon swung open and Pedro emerged. His undershorts peeked out through a robe that covered most of his body and was made of silken material. Whatever concern Milo had for him quickly vanished, and he began to sense some inner strength in Pedro that defied easy categorization.

"You haven't brought those iron fists along, have you?" Pedro feigned concern for his safety and covered his face with his hands, as if for protection. But his expression turned into that gentle smile Milo had already become accustomed to. Before Milo had a chance to respond Pedro opened the door fully and motioned an invitation to enter with his free hand.

They walked through the living room, a mélange of things Pedro loved. Artwork adorned nearly every inch of wall, much of it seascape paintings of his native Mexico. Interspersed with these beautiful but disquieting renderings of Quetzalcoatl and the Ollin symbol. They did not stop there but Pedro continued to the kitchen as if it were the only destination to which he led his guests. There a mashup of pots, pans, ladles and assorted utensils were scattered about, clean and dirty intermixed as if they would only be completely cleaned when needing to be used. They presented a fluid, charmed quality, as if Pedro had done this for a hundred years and would do it for a hundred more. He went back to work, casting a ladle through one bubbling conjuration, the object of his current enterprise.

"Sit, here. I want you to tell me what you think of this."

Pedro drew the ladle through the thick sauce, while sniffing to fire the esoteric calculations to adjust the taste. Milo noted an absentminded, clucking sound that he had heard after the fight, when Pedro was hatching their next move. Now this assisted him with applying the final touches until the desired level of mastery was reached. He drew the ladle across his creation one more time and then pulled a sample that he poured into a small saucer that he placed in front of Milo. As he fished around in the drain board for a spoon Milo lowered his head towards the bowl and allowed his olfactory senses the pleasure of fully engaging what was set before him. Although Milo had just eaten, his lack of appetite did not dampen his appreciation for this food, and his stream of exhortations were not so different from Pedro's. Shredded chicken, in a stew thickened by crushed pinto beans, lime zest, cilantro and assorted chili powder, mixed with more spices to produce a dense sensory experience. Milo accepted the proffered utensil. Pedro leaned against the sink, the only surface not covered with bric a brac and took a sip of Chardonnay from a canning jar. Milo limited his critique to assorted yums and ums. He only spoke when he was done eating and sipping wine that mysteriously appeared before him.

It was a gorgeous eating experience, but it was more than that. He felt wrapped in these surroundings, this small apartment with too many things lying about was more welcoming and comfortable than any place he could remember being.

"So, what do you think? Not bad, eh?"

Milo did not make the same mistake of spitting out the ingredients, and stopped his tongue from delivering the precisely gauged weights and kind of spices Pedro used this time.   Instead, he simply said, "It's marvelous. I can't remember tasting anything so good."

Pedro made a sound like what a throat singer might make, something Milo was sure expressed a heightened experience of pleasure.

"I've been working on this stew for a while, maybe a couple of months, and I finally got it right. I'm thinking of putting it on the menu, to start expanding what I offer my customers."

Milo thought of the clientele he'd observed and doubted they were capable of appreciating Pedro's creation, which turned his thoughts back to this afternoon.

"I hope I didn't cause you problems with those guys," Milo said, returning to his main reason for visiting.

Pedro laughed and then replied. "Like I told you, they don't bother me. I can handle them, have had to deal with much bigger problems.   Before I came here, I worked picking vegetables and working with farm animals out west. I got pinned to a fence by a bull. Broke my back, and I'm lucky I wasn't paralyzed. I was laid up for months with no way to survive. I ended up on the street until a friend in Baltimore contacted me and told me of a job doing food prep in a restaurant. I hitchhiked across the country, which isn't easy when you can barely walk. But I made it and over the years made contacts, which led to this eatery. It's not perfect and if it doesn't work out, I'll find something else."

Pedro stopped to consider what to say next, which was not his style. Even as he was talking about the hard times that brought him here his tone was matter of fact, he had seen enough to not be overwhelmed with whatever life threw at him. But when he spoke again it was with a different tone. "But you, you're different. You come into *the core* from someplace you're evasive about. You recite the ingredients of my chili with pitch perfect precision. You take a bike ride to the deserted zone, which no one does and then talk freely about it. You don't look exceptional and then demolish two guys who look a lot tougher and stronger than you. It all doesn't add up. In fact, I'm not sure if I believe anything you've told me so far. But that's OK. You go on and tell me whatever you want."

Milo was stung by the degree of truth in Pedro's observations. Pedro had been completely transparent, honest to a startling degree, and alternately there was not a shred of truth to Milo's story.

"Like I said, we're new around here and trying to find our way around."

"Yes, yes. Trying to sense the pulse of the city," Pedro said in a mocking tone. "As they used to say before the pandemic and the shore lines eroded away, taking the economy with it."

"Yes, that's me, the tourist with a flair for adventure," Milo said with a self-mocking tone, practically admitting to Pedro's accusations.

"The funniest thing is your story about Sheila getting a job at Johns Hopkins. Just so you know, no one with a research position at Johns Hopkins lives in our 'hood. NO ONE! Not just in this neighborhood but here you are posting up in that skanky basement apartment that's owned by the shadiest landlord around. A place that has seen some badass tenants. Don't be surprised if someone comes crashing through your door looking for their stash. You keep running your story, though. When you want to tell me the truth, I'll be ready to listen.

"Everyone knows the Hopkins elite live behind the wall. But no one talks about *the wall*. I'm taking a chance just mentioning it to you."

Milo was intrigued. "What are you talking about?"

"Damn, how naive are you? Haven't you noticed the neighborhoods in the central corridor are walled up. They have even been erased from maps on The Newer Machine, the only ones that exist anymore; these places only exist if you have the right security clearance. The System decided that Johns Hopkins was the only institution in the area it was interested in, so it insulated it and all the tony neighborhoods that support it. If your Citizen Card is not properly digitized there's no getting in, which accounts for everyone I know, everyone around here."

Milo considered for a minute and then said, "I can get you in."

Pedro stared at Milo and then the light came back in his eyes and a laugh emerged from deep within him.

"I had a feeling you had more tricks up your sleeve." Which set off in Pedro another round of laughter, mischievous and electric.

"Get your bike. Let's go for a ride," Pedro said when the laughter faded away.

They got outside and headed to Milo's to get his bike.

"Baltimore is the perfect set up for The System. East and west have always been cut off from one another by the center cut, the prime real estate. There is hardly any mass transit running east to west." Pedro was providing a civics lesson to this recent transplant.

"So, when they decided Baltimore needed cutting up, it was easy. Preserve the center cut, which was anchored by Johns Hopkins. Make the eastern neighborhoods marginally livable, which were valuable to the northeast corridor. Everything west of The Tenderloin would be cut out, forsaken."

Sheila was out when they entered Milo's apartment to get his bike.

"I'm telling you," Pedro said, a frenzy in his voice, "I know it's there. Been told stories of these beautifully appointed homes, the lovely gardens with endless flower beds that alternate between spring's boisterous colors and the more subdued patterns of summer and then that bursting fall foliage. But it will not admit me or anyone else without the pedigree, the secret codes. You drive up and think you are getting close but you're not. Every road heads straight towards it and then bends, leaving you in some outlying place. It is impossible to penetrate. You'll see."

It was only a couple of miles, starting in neighborhoods much like the ones they lived in. Some row homes were boarded up with broken windows looking like punched-in eyes. But still a pulse registered and life existed beyond the decimated facades.

Three-quarters of the way there, they weren't yet in The Tenderloin but its tentacles were coming into focus. Garlands lined the streets as if for a holiday, gleaming shops gave purpose to people strolling by in the latest fashions, immaculately clean streets, street lights that worked. That was the thing: everything was neatly choreographed, everything fit together as they were intended. Too well. Milo looked back and saw Pedro lagging behind and stopped his bike to wait. When he looked again Pedro was gone. He quickly returned to the prior intersection and saw Pedro riding in a perpendicular direction to the one they needed to follow. When Milo caught up, Pedro looked surprised.

"What brings you here, my friend?"

Milo was taken off-guard and responded, "Don't you remember?"

"I . . . I thought I was just out for a ride but seeing you is causing me to remember something, something very unpleasant."

Milo was aware of it too, but hadn't been conscious of it. The mist and fog rising to surround them was not the effects of an approaching storm. This had weight and an unnatural quality. The further you traveled into it the more you sensed its displeasure and its desire to disgorge you.

"I remember now. It was terrifying," Pedro began. "I could not speak or cry out for reasons I can't explain. But even if I had been able, I had no words to describe what I was feeling. Each time I pushed on my pedals it was like digging deeper into quicksand. The voices in my head said I could save myself only by choosing a different path. And as soon as I made the turn the entire experience was stripped from my consciousness. It only came back to me because of you and the fact you were not affected."

"We were headed into The Tenderloin, the gardens of color you told me about. And I was affected, but not in the same way. Listening to you talk about it made me aware of it."

Pedro's eyes grew wide and his face grimaced with fear, as he was unable to shake off the horror.

"What were those voices saying to you?" Milo asked.

"I can't say exactly, except they made sure I understood a couple of things: that I did not belong here, that everyone knew it just by glancing at me, and my condition was stamped on me and would always be there. They were like worms digging into my brain, my whole body. Brother, I don't ever want to feel that bad about myself again."

"I understand. But if you don't confront this they will always be there, ready to kick your ass whenever you push too hard against The System. They will always have this over you. You will always be servile, never free. Listen, if you start to feel that way again, drive up alongside me . . . put your hand on my shoulder if you have to. I'm strong enough to get us through this energetic field or whatever it is."

Pedro hesitated. After a minute, he smiled wryly and said, "OK, brain boy, we'll give it a try."

They rode back to the intersection where their paths split and got back on the trail, heading due north. Pedro kept his gaze down and focused on his breath, his physical exertion. At the same time Milo cast a protective, energetic cloak around them without Pedro realizing it.

They sailed headlong into The Tenderloin. By now the reality of tumbling mortar and brick gave way to towering elegance, archways to the sky. The brilliance of The Newer Machine displayed its bounty to those it deemed worthy. Brownstones, as finely appointed as anything New York ever served up, sat alongside New Orleans style honky tonks and Nordic ice palaces. But Milo could see into them and realized they were nothing more than manufactured facades. The apparent disconnect did not register on the strolling inhabitants.

And then they emerged on the other side of the electric storm.

The sensation for Pedro was like ascending from the depths of the ocean as he shed layers of pressure against his body. When Milo sensed they were safe, he loosened the bonds of the protective cloak. No intruder was expected to emerge through The System's shield and once inside, the turbulent cloud was gone.

They found that the nightmare was replaced by a much more pleasant dream as they pedaled along, criss-crossing and passing one another. Milo watched Pedro put on a show as he sped by. His pale blue windbreaker flapped in the wind like wings. He rode without holding the handlebars and interlaced his fingers behind his head. He could see that Pedro was balding, a monk's spot starting to show, and the hair was probably more thin and frizzy than it had been when he was younger. For the first time he wondered how old Pedro was. He was more childlike than any adult he'd ever met but already conveyed more personal stories than most claimed in an entire lifetime. Milo's reverie vanished when it was his turn to accelerate and experience the slingshot momentum they caused for each other.

The road ascended, dipped and curved so many times that both lost their sense of direction. It folded up like an accordion and then released them as if they rode a wave, their tires gliding over a frictionless surface. The houses they passed varied in design but not perfection. They did not dwell on the fact that none of this would ever be theirs because the drug of opulence was upon them.

They sped along and rode straight towards an impressive structure up ahead. The stone siding peeked through layers of exotic ivy. The front was a hundred feet across and then they saw the sign: Betterworld Academy Institute.

As its true purpose still confounded them, they took a path that curved around the structure to a small incline that allowed them to see most of the surrounding land. Banks of lights blanketed ball fields stretching in every direction. Every manner of equipment for every imaginable sport glistened in the artificial light. The grass-like surface was an unnaturally vibrant green, a carpet cut to of a precise, uniform length.

"It's a goddamn school. A school for kids." Pedro fussed and fumed. He was angry and Milo got to see what that looked like, and decided even that was OK to be around.

"Sign says it's an *Academy,* an *Institute.*"

"Sure, sure," Pedro said but would have none of it. "And the teachers don't have co-workers, they have colleagues. I've been around this block before. It's all a way to set us apart, make those on the outside feel 'less than'. Makes me sick."

The games and practices proceeded. Milo and Pedro sat on an adjacent stretch of grass and watched without real interest. Just when they were about to get up to leave, whistles blew from all directions. Individual activities ceased immediately. The noise and chatter also stopped and the children, ranging in age from 5 to 17, hurried to the center stadium. Quickly, rows of children formed that spanned the entire playing field and each stepped mindlessly in place on their spot. Even the youngest acquired an air of practiced seriousness.

"The next generation of controllers," Milo said.

Pedro understood perfectly. "There isn't an ounce of fun out there. . ... They haven't a fucking clue."

Then, as if by some prearranged signal, they started performing their patterns. In an instant their stepping became more intense, rigid, precise, while the dehumanized quality of their facial features advanced accordingly. Milo and Pedro glimpsed the dead eyes of politicians who offer no support to the unwashed and still found a way to go to sleep the same evening. These movements entirely lacked athleticism and beauty. What they did instill was unity, purpose, and discipline. Arms move to the one side and heads jutted in the opposite direction with a synchronicity that would rival a flock of starlings.

"It's a religion, a cult. They are determined to completely erase their spirit and replace it with something malignant," Pedro said.

"The beauty of the machine," Milo marveled. "They will never be the ones holding the guns, but they are learning how to believe they have the right to force others to do so."

"I've seen enough."

"Me too, let's head back."

As they were reorienting their bikes they spied one of the groundskeepers coming towards them and decided to engage him.

"How are you, my friend," Pedro said in the tone Milo found irresistible.

The man was also Hispanic and Pedro expected to feel some commonality.

"I'm fine, sir, just fine." The man smiled back at Pedro in a formal way that lacked any intimacy.

"I hope they treat you good here, and that you enjoy your work."

"Oh yes, we are all in the service of the children. Everything is done to promote their growth and education." The man's expression turned blank and he seemed to forget Pedro was there, and returned to the task to which he was assigned. It was as if saying these words reinstated him in the matrix of expectations placed upon him and crowded out any, and all, distractions.

"You get what's going on here, don't you brain boy?"

"I think I do."

"They're harvesting."

"How's that?"

"Until The System can clone the next generation of the elite class, they need to do it the old-fashioned way. Layer upon layer of brainwashing. Look at all this." Pedro paused and panned the perimeter until his gaze stopped on one example, a faux multi-turreted stone house with thick lead glass windows that could have been built 300 years ago. "They used to rim castles with a moat. But that's not necessary anymore."

"Did you notice that once we broke through the turbulence at the border everything was calm?" Milo asked.

"Yes, I did."

"I thought it was because they didn't think intruders would penetrate it, but now I believe it's because they figure anyone inside the barrier is sufficiently indoctrinated. As I was analyzing the energy that affected you on the way here, I realized you don't need a secret code to get past it. What you need is to have mastered the ability to shut down parts of your brain, the empathetic parts. If they are active, the worm will enter, and it will bore in until you can't stand it."

"That's what separates the elites?"

"That's what separates the elites."

Pedro looked around one last time to confirm that all that sparkled had lost its luster.

Let's get out of here," Pedro finally said.

They pedaled alongside one another and did not speak until they emerged on the other side of the energetic curtain.

"Alright," Pedro said, as if just deciding something. "I need to do a food run to pick up vegetables for my restaurant. If you want to join me, there's something I'd like you to see. If you're interested, meet me outside my apartment with your bike tomorrow morning at 8. I'll show you some things hardly anyone gets to see."

Milo jumped at the offer, the same way he partook of The Tenderloin, accepting the food placed in front of him and any other suggestion that Pedro made. They continued riding but said little more as both processed the long reach of The System and the death grip it held on anything that defied it.

The next morning Milo walked up to Pedro who was busy attaching baskets to each side of his bike.

"So, you going to tell me where we're headed?" Milo asked, after their initial hellos.

Pedro laughed, "Not the final destination. But I will tell you we are headed back in the direction you were riding yesterday."

That was enough to whet Milo's curiosity.

They rode much the same path that Milo had taken, but did not stop when the road gaped open and the buildings became uninhabited. Most of the time they rode single file and Milo was surprised by the pace Pedro set across the pockmarked terrain. Even Milo was affected by the remnants of the world that once existed here. Ghostly emanations ranged about, searching for that which had been torn free unwillingly, mercilessly. Occasionally Pedro motioned for Milo to drive up alongside so he could tell him something about the sites they passed. There was a museum, a playhouse, hospital, all in tatters, crumbling buildings that no longer held their defining spirit.

They traveled along the wall for half a mile and then Pedro took a road that ran perpendicularly away from it. Just as quickly he darted into what was once a parking garage. They descended along a cylindrical passageway until they emerged onto the subterranean level. One lane was cleared of debris and they followed it 100 yards or more. The area was luminescent, the source of which was unknown. It was noticeably cooler than above ground and Milo was seized with a desire to stay down here and study the flickering light and peculiar perspective permeating this underground border space. Because that's what they were doing, crossing under the border. So, of course he would continue, journey into the area where only the castoffs and irredeemable gained access.

The ascent was continuous, a straight slope up. Soon, they were looking at the same sun that shone on the land The System deemed worthy. But here there was no need for obfuscation, as the state of disrepair was nearly complete. Many areas of the US have long had parallels to life in third world countries, but now, none so much as those that were cordoned off. The roads consisted of matted dirt with interspersed sections of tar, a tattooed hieroglyph. Fortunately, the road they were on was still passable with a bike, less so with motorized vehicles.

"It's amazing," Milo said.

"What's that?"

"I drove up and down the coast many times while I was with the band. Thought I knew my way around. How is it possible I didn't know that this part of the city was turned into a sacrifice zone?"

Pedro laughed, clearly enjoying himself again, now that they made it across. "We call this area X-Zone, or cut to XZ, because it has no identity in today's culture, it's been erased. But to answer your question, obviously you don't know anything about X-Zone because they don't want you to know. They couldn't have these places if they couldn't conceal them from general observation. The Newer Machine has absolute power. If it wants to erase you or your family or the western half of a once thriving city, it can be done without much effort. It simply flushes that thing from virtual reality. Once you are unseen you are dead even if you are sentient, upright, and can scream and shout. But because you are invisible, you will grow tired of screaming into a vacuum, become despondent and soon decide that you won't fight anymore. So, you allow yourself to be muzzled. This is all The System wanted and it's the fate you can count on if TNM dissolves your identity. It is indefatigable in its pursuit of clearing inflammation and debris."

Milo looked around at a neighborhood that was now mostly rubble, a tipping point reached with no turning back. The few people he saw were moving about in the distance with no discernible purpose, somnambulant. A great gust of wind blew up from nowhere pushing at him; until then the air was leaden and dripping hot. At this point, he became lightheaded. What he saw before him in mid-distance was the procession of decay, the future awaiting this space, but that's not what captured his attention. He tried to control his thinking by making it more linearly focused, but it refused and continued to branch and jump. His steering became erratic and he pulled the bike to the side just in time and pitched over onto the ground.

Pedro rode back when he heard the crash, and set to work untangling Milo's legs from the frame of his bike. He then pulled a towel from one of his containers, rolled it up and put it beneath Milo's head as he lay there unconscious, but there was really no way to make him comfortable on this rugged terrain.

After a couple of minutes Milo's eye began to flicker.

When he was able to focus, Pedro said, "How are you doing, my friend?"

The words pierced through the ether in waves that needed decoding. But with each moment it became easier to think, and then, communicate.

"I saw things. I can't tell you why or how. But everything was aging like in a time-lapsed movie. Most of the buildings disintegrated to dust, nothing left on the ground but graying concrete and the earth shifting in a wave with an intelligence I couldn't identify. But one structure stood apart, in the distance, different from anything I've ever seen. That's what I was trying to see better. The force drawing me to it was so strong. Until the strain was too much. Still, I don't know why it was so important, why I felt such a yearning to connect with it."

Pedro continued staring at Milo, a different type of concern emerging as the color came back into Milo's cheeks. "You're one wild cat, you know that?"

"You don't know the half of it," Milo said, lowering his guard.

"You want me to call your sister, or whoever she is."

"No need to call Sheila. Nothing to tell her. I'm feeling better already," Milo responded, avoiding the innuendo in Pedro's comments.

But he was still groggy, and as he struggled to clear his vision the first thing he focused on was the pendant of the Virgin Mary, dangling from a chain hanging around Pedro's neck.

"Why do you wear that?"

"What do you mean? It was passed down from my mother. She gave it to me when we all lived together in a small village in central Mexico."

"That's nice. I'm glad you have that to remind you of her. But that's not what I'm getting at. Mary's a symbol of oppression. It has been totally co-opted by The System. It has helped to enslave your people."

"Don't be so sure of that," Pedro said, and now chose his word with precision. "My people were smart enough to merge with what would have killed them if they hadn't. But at the same time, we always held onto Madre Tonantzin. She is the ancestral archetype in our culture for the mother of creation. She has always been there and will last forever."

"So Mary is fake, something you don't believe in?"

"That's not really true, but we view her through the lens of our ancestral saints that pre-date the Christian incursion."

"So, you can see through Mary to something grander, older, more tied to your culture?"

"Yes, that is a good way to understand it."

Milo considered this before responding, "Which will work as long as you don't lose track of your roots and that bigger, grander vision."

"You are very correct. And every day I fear The System will accomplish just what you are describing."

They sat with their own thoughts until Pedro circled back, "Can you tell me more about what you saw before you went down."

Milo decided to not hold back because it was the only way for him to make sense of it. Besides, he was grateful to Pedro, who he already considered a friend, someone who deserved his trust.

"You see that tree, there?" Milo said and pointed to an oak 30 yards in front of them. It had rooted itself into the middle of a section of pavement that was losing its form to this resurgent natural process. But the tree itself was still small and unassuming.

"Well, all of a sudden it started to shiver and grow big, right before my eyes. And then the surrounding landscape shifted, undulating, differentiating. The buildings, most of them, went to dust and were covered over by soil that was fertile, vibrant looking.

"But further off," and now Milo pointed into the distance, which contained only an obstacle course of dilapidated structures, an abandoned construction site's stew of materials, "I saw a building of some kind, although its sides were mostly transparent. Round, probably, and large, the size of a city block. Contained within it was a fiery presence with lightning and an electrical presence firing multi-directionally and without apparent order. It was beyond normal experience and I sensed a deep knowledge contained within it. I wanted so much to reach it but just looking at it was such a drain of my energy. I pushed but it was like quicksand until I fell and blacked out."

"I take you for a little bike ride and you see flying saucers," Pedro joked, as he did with most things. "I'm cool with that. But what do you think it was there for, what's its purpose?"

"I don't know, man. I wish I did. More than anything." Milo looked again in that same direction but now saw only the accumulated debris, tumbleweed, the earth's slow winning formula against man's mania for building upon, and desecrating, nature's regenerative powers.

Milo stood up, dusted himself off, and righted his bike.

"You OK to go on or should we turn back?"

"I'm definitely fine. Let's head on. I want to see what you brought me here for."

It was true he was fine in a physical sense, but emotionally he was spent. He continued to marvel at the vision and the energetic presence it had projected, while everything around him no longer held his interest.

But he did not have to consider this for long because about a mile up the road, they encountered the outer edge to what was once Leakin Park. Here, the ravages to the land were not so severe. Its lushness was never completely destroyed and had taken on a sub-tropical quality as temperatures climbed. Everywhere vines enmeshed with their hosts, draped in stillness.

They pulled their bikes into a small covey of trees and walked a hundred yards into deepening woods. What Milo saw when they stepped into a clearing surprised him. The sun's rays were absorbed by fields of vegetables that covered a couple of acres. Off to the side were pens where a few animals grazed.

"My friend, my friend," Pedro said to a man coming towards Pedro from the fields. His dark skin glistened with the sweat of his labor. They embraced and then Pedro introduced Milo to Jamal. Jamal was unassuming, short in stature and what hair he had left was braided into dreads. He wore loose fitting brown cotton pants and a tan colored shirt whose arms had been cut away exposing a muscular, wiry frame.

"Glad to meet you," Jamal held out his hand and offered it to Milo and Milo sensed both gentleness and strength in the handshake, and in the energy space surrounding Jamal.

"If you have a minute, could you show my new friend and I around a bit? I think he will be blown away by what you're doing here," Pedro said.

"Sure, I'd be happy to," Jamal responded, and started walking towards the vegetable beds.

"This is our third year here and we expect some of the crops, like the asparagus and berries, to start producing with this year's harvest," and pointed in the direction of those plants.

"When we started, we debated whether or not to plan long-term. We knew The System could come in and shut us down, torch the place. But so far, they've left us alone. We are pretty much off their radar. They've chosen to consolidate and not care what happens in those areas they've turned their back on, and we hope it stays that way."

Milo was confused by one thing. Although the vegetables looked healthy, the crops were not in straight lines. Even tree roots, risen above ground, surrounded some of the plants. The ground was unlevel. Weeds grew freely.

Jamal sensed Milo's observations and addressed them. "We're using permaculture techniques. This is a no-till farm. Cheaper and easier for us, and better for the land, which is a living organism and benefits from not having its composition broken up and destroyed. Think about how our own bones, muscles, and tendons would do if they were disconnected from each other every year and had to be put back together."

Jamal walked over to some plants and plucked a handful of snap peas. He extended his hand and Milo and Pedro each took a few. Sweet, Milo thought, and biting into them was like the raucous chatter of firecrackers.

They stopped in the middle of the fields and took in their surroundings. Milo was enchanted by this space and what they were trying to accomplish here.

"So, how did you learn all this? You grow up on a farm?" Milo asked.

Jamal laughed, "Hell no. City boy through and through. But I got caught up in some things and ended up in The Pen. Spent 5 years in The System's purgatory. I was all but forgotten. The only good thing was getting assigned to working in the gardens that provided the only fresh fruits and vegetables for the inmates. They were into some amazing shit. The staff, especially the guy managing the gardens, knew a lot about working with the land and wanted us to learn as much as we could. He knew some shit was coming down. Knew people were going to have trouble surviving and made that his mission."

"So, you're passing it forward."

"How I see it."

Three people worked in the gardens. Adjacent to the fields were two simple but sturdy structures, like those Indigenous communities might have lived and worked in, Milo guessed. The sun had risen to its zenith and the rhythms of a late-summer day were in full swing. The crush of life under The System peeled away, leaving what has always been, and hopefully will be again. The lush, green fronds encroaching upon the crops made him think of magical rainforests in far off lands. Milo felt that was a perfect way to describe what he felt about this place, and was something none of them felt compelled to disturb.

Finally, Milo asked Jamal, "You live here, don't you?"

"That's right. So far there's about 10 of us and, like I said, we pray The System leaves us alone. Hopefully, we can keep homesteading until we figure out how to be wholly self-sufficient. Until then, we rely on the help from brave people on the outside, people like Pedro."

"What I'm doing is very small, but thank you Jamal. And I get better produce here than I could find inside the controlled area."

"Pedro comes by a couple times a week during our growing season and picks up vegetables for his restaurant. We use the money to pay for supplies we can't make on our own yet."

Milo reflected on the desolation he encountered during the bike ride. "How do you use your money over here? I didn't see any shops. I didn't see much of anything."

Jamal laughed. "You'd be surprised. There's an active black market and dollars are still in high demand. You didn't see them, but there are small outposts scattered throughout this territory. We are starting to network but that is still in the initial stages."

"I'm glad you got to meet," Pedro piped in, happy with the way the conversation had gone. "But I know Jamal has things to do and I have to get the restaurant ready to open."

They turned and headed back in the direction they came while Jamal listed the vegetables available for purchase. Pedro made his choices and when they had returned, Jamal filled Pedro's baskets.

"The vegetables you packed for my salads look beautiful, but the herbs, they're special. I can see I'll be using a lot of cilantro this week, so it will be a very good week."

"I believe you," Jamal responded. "This is the best harvest we've had so far. We are learning how to build healthy soil, which mostly means not trying to improve it artificially. It is as good as it could possibly be when left alone and amended with natural material."

Before they got back on their bikes Milo turned to Jamal and said, "This is great what you are doing here. I have some free time right now. If you like I could come by and help out. I have some skills that might be useful to you."

Pedro laughed. "Yes he does. I haven't figured this one out yet. He destroyed two of the worst tough guys I have to deal with at my shop, then recited all the ingredients in my chili, which no one is supposed to know, and generally seems to tell me things before they actually happen."

Jamal regarded Milo slightly differently, weighing benefits and risks, then said, "Sure, you are welcome here to get to know us, and to learn and teach."

"Thanks very much," Milo said as he returned Jamal's gaze. "I would be honored."

They started their ride back single file but Milo was eager to discuss what he'd just seen so came up alongside Pedro.

"What they are doing is awesome," Milo gushed.

"Yes, I wish them best luck for their survival," Pedro responded, more soberly than Milo expected.

"You don't sound too hopeful, Pedro. Back there it was all about, 'this is the best harvest ever.'"

"Which is true. But you didn't see what we were comparing it to. The fact is they are barely making it. Even though their methods are sound, the soil is so depleted. They don't have a way to get commercial fertilizer and I'm not sure they'd use it even if they could. They struggle to grow enough to feed themselves."

"So, you think they will fail?"

"I'm not going to say that and don't believe it. So much can happen especially because their spirit is pure, their conviction strong."

They grew silent again and rode back along the same cratered roadways, which did not look so desolate as before to Milo. Out in the distance, stirrings from nascent outposts, unveiling a sort of life.

When Milo returned to the apartment he felt agitated in a way that was eerily familiar. Sheila came home a few hours later and found that in that short period of time Milo had created and spread his drawings everywhere. She had not seen this type of creative mania in him since his days exploring origami.

"What's up?" Sheila said. She carried a full book pack over her shoulder which she dropped on the floor as she entered the room.

He acknowledged her by raising his gaze from his current piece but did not greet her with a friendly word or gesture. The drawings were all some variation on a spherical orb. Some slightly more substantial than others but each with a transparent quality that made them alien, disquieting.

Finally Milo said, "I had a vision of something, and don't know what it was. Pedro took me to the X-Zone. That's what they call the area on the other side of the barricade. He knows a secret passage there."

Sheila's eyebrow raised. She had stated her desire that he keep a low profile until she got the lab running and he resumed his sessions. Their goal was to enhance the areas of human intellect that had not yet been the subject of neuralBlast technology. She knew it unlikely he would comply, that he would instead venture out, take risks. But this far exceeded what she expected from him. People who were expelled to the X-Zone were expected to stay there, and anyone could be detained if caught trying to reenter. More than anything, the rumors of death, devastation, and depravity in these demarcated territories were shadows that crept into her thoughts.

"How'd you manage that? Your friend Pedro is a magician?"

"No," Milo replied, and then reconsidered. "Maybe. But that's not how we got there. He knows of a parking garage that links to a tunnel that comes out on the other side."

Sheila considered this news, another example of The System not having things locked down the way they wanted you to think they had. If you poked around, there were lots of cracks in the edifice.

"So, what did you see while you were over there?"

"At first look, it was what you'd expect. Most of the buildings gone to rubble. Roads were bad. Other than walking, our bikes were about the only way to get around. But there was a weird energy and stillness, which was almost sacred, like what you'd feel in an ancient burial ground."

Sheila took a seat now, and listened intently. He had that post-session vibe about him, like he had plunged into a vortex of knowledge that would leave him unmoored until he could integrate it. But he hadn't had a session, not for several weeks. So, if she was correctly interpreting what was going on, he was using his extraordinary powers to grow organically. This was something she wondered about, but did not expect would occur. While the possibilities intrigued her, they also raised concern for Milo.

"I had a weird experience. Time sped forward. I saw the remaining structures ground to dust with fast-forward imaging. It was like those old-timey flip cards that show progressive change except that it was all around me, with the ground shifting everywhere. But it wasn't just that things were disintegrating because at the same time I witnessed a resurgence. The land returned to green pasture, slowly but perceptively. Cement pods disintegrated as wild flowers pushed through them. It was engaging and left me feeling hopeful. But then this distant image presented itself in front of me. It was large, forceful, and conveyed a heavy vibration.

"These are replicas I keep making to try and understand. It kept beckoning me to enter and experience what it concealed, but I couldn't pierce through its barriers. It was willing to withhold its insights, its charm. Even as it acted as a magnet, it repelled me. I went down in exhaustion trying to reach it, blacked out. But the vision remains."

"It sounds like an enchanted thing," Sheila replied, when she realized Milo would say no more.

"Oh, it was," Milo said, a trill entering his voice. "But there was more. Something daunting. For all its scope there was an exclusionary quality to it, as if it knew that what it embodied could destroy as well as create."

This remembrance tripped the cyborg part of Milo's mind and in an instant he was back at his drawing, oblivious to everything except his desire to crack the thing's source code.

Sheila understood what was happening, saw the same activity after each session. The hope she felt was offset by familiar misgivings: what had she wrought, what dangers lie within the gifts she bestowed upon Milo, could she act quickly enough if great danger overtook him?

He got up from the floor and announced he was going to the store, and let the door flap open as he moved down the street with purpose. He didn't consider the architecture, shady characters, the moist summer air evaporating off the cement and building facades along the way. He popped into a bodega a few blocks away and purchased two, five-pound bags of flour and every copy of every newspaper on the rack. On the way back he was oblivious to the light rain starting to fall on him and his parcel. Even the wind, starting to pick up, buffeting him on his way both to and from the store, failed to register; the storm brewing inside him was the locus of his attention. He returned 15 minutes after departing, the space of time it would take if he were in a race.

Back in the apartment he pulled a tangle of metal hangers from the hall closet, which he separated, one by one. The breeze outside stiffened and reflected the torrent of energy returned into the house. First, he connected the wires according to the specifications of the circumference of the drawings. Then he attached lengths of wire perpendicularly to the sphere. He worked furiously as Sheila sat on the other side of the room, glancing up from her computer from time to time. She placed her fingers back on the keyboard and received a shock as she started typing again. Her right index finger raised to her lips reflexively and she soothed away the residue of the electric charge. A jagged rumble of thunder approached, as though determined to roll its fury into their misapprehended quarters. So much had already happened to them that Sheila would not easily succumb to worry. She took off her glasses and cleaned them, making sure not to miss any part of this unfolding whirlwind event.

Although his hands bled, he did not stop working until a framework of wire supports fanned out and left the orb self-standing a foot off the floor. He pulled a screen from one of the windows and cut lengthwise sections from it, and then attached them to the frame. An hour passed before he was satisfied with the enclosed screen that rose above the top edge of the wire hoop and met in the center, forming a dome-like shape. But he was not done, nor was the storm that raged outside.

He ripped open a bag of flour and threw half of it in a pot, started adding water and then strips of paper. He flexed the gooey substance through his fingers that clenched and re-clenched into fists.

When the proper consistency was reached, he returned to the living room and started molding the sides into a structure. Around him, wind blew sideways and rain entered the house through the window that no longer contained even a screen to sluice the air. When a light layer of paper mache covered the lower part of the shell it no longer needed to be handled delicately, so he could do what he wanted all along, which was to hurl the goop at the object. Each frenetic toss brought him closer to what this thing represented, even as it withheld its ultimate meaning and purpose. The lightning, thunder and more lightning creased the sky and collided with and transformed the energetic space within. But when he was done, spent, exhausted and bloodied, he felt only a little closer to what this thing wanted from him, even as it activated every neuron in his brain and heart.

They stood beside each other, gazing at the dome, the dim light recording the cratered surface. The wind had abated but it was too soon to tell if they were merely in the eye of the storm.

"It looks like a yurt, or maybe a flying saucer," Sheila said.

"It is neither. Those things wouldn't have these jagged surfaces."

Milo was referring to the canopy. Where the gobs of material hit the surface, they splayed erratically. Sometimes these tendrils touched, sometimes not. It was really rather ugly but intriguing nonetheless.

"So, what is it?"

He gazed at it; the same desire held him fast but with a less consuming flame. "I'm not sure, but it is important." He also felt how this searing passion had transformed him, bathed him in a blue energy that disconnected him from his surroundings. He did not mind the sensation but would have not been able to alter it even if he had. The greater mystery lay on the table before them.

"The top looks less substantial than the sides," Sheila observed. "I can see bits of wire protruding through the material. It's almost like the higher surface is meant to be transparent, conductive."

Milo sucked air through his teeth and into his lungs in a spasm, as if Sheila's comment caught him off guard, hurt him in some way.

He turned and appraised her. "Not everyone would notice that, but you're right. I think the strands are trying to make contact."

She assessed him more closely, wondering if he knew more than he was saying. Before she had a chance to probe the meaning behind his words, he concluded, "But don't ask me why, because I have no idea."

The next two days Milo gave way to restlessness. He pondered his creation but it refused to yield more of its purpose, even to the one whose hands had created it, leaving him to feel like a mere bystander. Although he considered it from every angle, as it dominated what passed for their dining room, it remained remote, secretive. Did it really have significance? He was beginning to doubt it, doubt that he had any power, extraordinary or otherwise.

Chapter 13

Milo knew he was supposed to stay away from public places. Surveillance was always lurking. Even though Sheila assumed a new identity and Milo could shield detection with an energetic field that he draped around himself, there lurked the very real possibility of these defenses being penetrated. But he couldn't keep looking at the orb that grew more remote and inert with each passing hour. The temperature dropped from 75 to 45 degrees after the storm two nights earlier and stayed that way. It was only the middle of September; no one tried to predict weather anymore. At 10 PM he walked the streets. The vibe was more urban and diverse than he was used to, and he felt good being in the midst of it.

He came up to North Avenue, and depending on the perspective, it was an amalgam of a budding art center, a rat-infested urban war zone, a speculator's dream or nightmare. He passed a bar, The Birdcage, and then retraced his steps. It was Wednesday, open mic night. The window was uncovered, but it was too dark inside to see much. He walked in, bought a beer, and listened. Rap, spoken-word mostly, a form of creativity that survived for decades. Not what he did, or listened to, but he was surprised at its appeal. Everyone telling their story, the pain in their lives, the injustice they suffer. The same, in concept, as what he did with Death's Scepter.

There was a lull in the entertainment. Before he realized it, he was talking to the bartender. He was told the guitar on stage was amped and available to anyone wanting to use it.

He wanted to play songs he'd written during his days with Death's Scepter but felt he shouldn't, that he was no longer worthy of them, that since he'd entered the world of speed learning, they belonged to someone other than who he had become. Then he laughed because he was pretty sure this crowd would hate that music, not seeing any connection to the music he'd just listened to.

Instead, he uncoiled bits from the neuralBlast sessions. The archives of Hendrix, Vaughn, and Paige streamed through his fingers. The crowd, only partially aware of the previous performers, suddenly stopped their conversations to focus on the stage. Milo played for 20 minutes. Occasionally he experienced emotion, but it was more as a listener than a performer.

Milo completed the set and was greeted with a raucous round of applause. He smiled, feigning appreciation and modesty. The showman was still there inside of him. When he returned to his beer a few people came up to him and offered their thanks. One guy came up and asked if he could sit and talk to Milo for a bit. Milo motioned to the vacant chair beside him.

"My name's Nathan. Have to tell you, that was pretty amazing guitar playing. Lick for lick you nailed it."

"Thanks," Milo responded. "They're some of my guitar gods. Just felt like paying homage to them tonight."

"Definitely, and you did right by them, did them proud. Memorizing the solos for all those songs had to be a lot of work."

Milo searched for something to say, a way to explain without explaining.

"It's like flipping a deck of cards. Just play along as the cards flip past."

"You make it sound like you're a digital decoder," Nathan joked.

Instead of returning Nathan's smile, Milo turned back to his beer and took a long pull.

"You must have written some of your own music. Would have liked to have heard some of that, too," Nathan said, sensing that Milo had taken offense for some reason.

"Sure, I've written some," Milo responded, but offered no more on the topic.

When Nathan realized this, too, was going nowhere, he turned the conversation to what was on his mind.

"I play keyboards in a band. We play some covers but want to do more interesting material and we're looking for a lead guitarist. I think you'd fit right in. I think you could help us get to the next level."

"I really appreciate you saying that. You know, it's nice to be considered . . .. But I don't know. I've got a lot going on right now."

Before Milo could continue, Nathan jumped in, "It's OK. You don't need to give me an answer now." He'd pulled his wallet out and grabbed a card and extended it to Milo. "My contact info is on it. If you want to check us out, give me a call."

Milo looked down at the card. He liked the band's name, Crewsome, emblazoned along the top.

"Thanks, I'll think about it. Again, I want you to know I really appreciate the offer."

Milo was alone again, alone with his thoughts. He knew he couldn't join the band. But it went beyond that. Neo had it all wrong. When he got martial arts infused into him, he was ecstatic. "Let's do this again," he intoned breathlessly.

But reality was far different. His musical dexterity left him listless, as was true of the other talents he obtained from neuralBlast sessions. The simple truth was he'd done nothing to earn these skills, nor this adulation. He would rather be playing his three chord, amped up anthems than blather on with all this virtuosity because the former was his, hammered out and served up from somewhere deep within him. And the more he played this way, the more alienated it made him feel.

He got up and departed, leaving his half-finished beer and the business card on the bar. The air outside was cold and felt like a slap on the face, an experience that brought him back to himself.   The drama in the bar still haunted him, as did the unpleasant truth that it revealed.   He walked along these streets where crime visited frequently, but it was not harm to his body that he contemplated.   It was his mind and the effects of the neuralBlast sessions. He knew they would make him smarter but did not understand how they would separate him. He had developed in so many ways, like his ability to be in any setting and see it in a different season, a hundred years before and even the approximate conditions in the future. But these skills gave him no joy. The human need to struggle to move forward in the world with only the most meager guidelines to create one's own story, was missing. And now he saw how vital this was, even for him. What was left for him, he wondered?   How does he, given his extraordinary circumstances, satisfy this yearning, which could no longer be measured by normal, human successes and failures?

Milo turned a corner on his way home and without warning was slammed against the brick wall of the adjoining building. He knew his assailant immediately, and was surprised he was not already dead. K2 was in full command and with his right hand, wedged like a vice around his throat, lifted Milo off the ground.

"I've been tracking you for a long time. I can't believe you'd be so stupid as to live out in the open, in plain sight this way."

The danger of the situation caused Milo's mind to race and the *cards* to start flipping. The scenery around him started to advance at an increased rate.

K2 lowered him to the ground and loosened his grip a little, something Milo did not expect.

"Does it really matter that much? Are there any regions where surveillance isn't conducted?"

K2's eyes shifted sideways, indicating something, a recognition he'd rather avoid. "The System does what it has to do to secure its people and its borders."

"You really believe that?"

K2 faltered inexplicably. Milo wondered if K2 picked up on the same trippy effects that he was experiencing. He knew that if this was true, it held out his only chance for escape. K2, indeed, was affected. Moments before he was bearing down with incredible force, but now he needed to contend with kaleidoscopic images bursting and rearranging around him.

"Look, I know they tailored your sessions to only certain parts of your brain," Milo continued. "But I doubt that's all you've seen. My sessions were cut short too. But, that's not the end of my story. My powers have grown on their own, organically. I bet yours have too. They might have shielded things from you but that doesn't mean it stopped you from gaining knowledge of things outside of their protocol."

"You don't know what you're talking about," K2 snarled unconvincingly, while a look of betrayal passed across his face.

"Tell me the truth. You've seen things, right? You know there's more."

Milo studied K2's confused expression. That's when he saw it, beside K2's left ear. A slit appeared in the advancing and receding scenery that he sensed was a portal into interdimensional space. He was drawn to K2, drawn to his indecision, the questions etched in his face. They were, he realized, his questions as well. Questions to which he knew he had to find answers. He did not want to leave K2, not now, but knew his safety depended on it. If the portal sealed before he passed through it, K2 would probably end up killing him.

Milo pushed K2 aside as hard as he could and hurled himself through the opening. He gained his footing and moved away from the portal entrance. To his surprise K2 followed and was coming at him hard. They hurtled from one roof top to another, strands of energetic filaments tracing their pathways.

When did it stop being a chase laced with danger? Milo didn't know. What he knew was that bedazzled look on K2's face as he explored the passing epochs and the intelligence of nature's design.

Then they stood beside each other, beholding an iridescent cliff, an ancient city deep in the valley, faint lights poking through the braided cloud separating them from it.

Milo launched himself across the gorge, propelled by the bolts of energy emanating from his extremities and sense receptors, particularly his eyes. He bounded across the landscape and then looked for K2, and saw he hadn't moved from the other side. Instead, K2 took a knee and cast his head down. His face was beet red and veins bulged from his neck and forehead. Milo retraced his steps until he stood beside K2. He felt for his pulse and clocked it at 140 beats per minute. The strain of living in this dimension was too much, and he needed to get K2 out of here before he ruptured something, had a stroke, or died.

This meant reversing the deck. He grabbed K2 and g-forced them back to the entry point. Milo navigated them to be in front of the University Hospital emergency room. K2 staggered groggily with Milo's support. Milo made a snap decision as they progressed to the doorway and established a linked pathway between the neural processors within their brains. He pinged it and received a response. There was some risk it could be traced but he was pretty sure he could obfuscate the energetic telemetry. But he wanted this connection more than anything and the ping was proof it existed.

He made another decision and sent another message into K2's overheated neural laced OS, instructions for contacting Milo. This was more risky. He needed to open a port in his own messaging platform, which left him vulnerable. He knew there was a good argument against doing this, that Sheila would read him the riot act if she found out, but he wasn't going to give up on the connection he made with K2. Milo knew he couldn't stay here any longer. He sensed the surveillance cameras and evaded them. He placed K2 down at the entrance, hit the emergency alarm, and then ran back into the darkness, away from the pull that K2 exerted, one he did not understand, but tore at him as he abandoned K2.

Chapter 14

Even before K2 wondered where he was, he wondered how long he'd been here. His brain felt like mush as he looked around to examine the small cell, which contained nothing to disrupt the white, sterile surroundings. His focus shifted to the bed he laid on and the concentric straps that secured him to it. With his normal strength he could have busted free, but when he tried now, the straps wouldn't budge.

His mind tried to review all that had happened. The strange journey with Milo was an episodic, psychedelic whirl that merged with the viciousness of white coats beating him, shocking him, narcotizing him. None of these experiences formed a coherent whole, and when he tried to place them in a framework, the results grew even murkier. But he remembered enough: that he was K2, the enforcer needed by The System to maintain order. The rest would fall into place.

"Hello, I'd like to talk to someone," he yelled into the void. To his surprise, a group assembled around his bed within minutes. Four guards in riot gear and two doctors whose white coats blended into the background, along with their pasty faces. The faces were familiar but indiscernible, caught in a whirlpool of images disconnected from any comprehensible narrative.

"We're glad to see you're awake and able to communicate," one doctor said as both he and his colleague kept their distance from K2, and studied him closely.

K2 tried to return the gaze but his vision was blurry. "Can you increase the contrast in here? The white on white on white makes it hard to figure out who I'm talking to."

The doctors were amused by this request, and the one who had not spoken yet used this opportunity to enter into the conversation. "We'll see if we can find some dimmer lights, but I suspect all you need is to let your eyes adjust another minute."

As K2 regained his senses, he became annoyed by their intrusive glare.

"I'm glad you're doing better, able to carry a conversation," the doctor said in a more friendly tone, which did nothing to lessen K2's need to be on high alert.

"If we've met before, I have no recollection of it," K2 replied, on a fishing expedition of his own but still with no idea where to throw the line.

"Yes, we have talked before but I'm not surprised you don't remember. You've been pretty agitated and not making a lot of sense. But you seem calmer now, after we adjusted your meds. What can you tell us about yourself, what do you remember now that you're feeling better?"

K2's mind ranged about. He retained the bare outline of his existence. He was a cyborg. He volunteered for this assignment because of the challenge, because he was bored and he hated being bored. Above all else he remembered that he had to do everything possible to avoid allowing the neuralBlast technology to fall into enemy hands.

Then other memories asserted themselves, closer, dream-like, indecipherable. Somehow they bridged time and space. Landscapes outlined by a fiery red at the furthest reaches of the horizon. Bolts of translucent, multi-colored light descending from the sky. This streaming memory was cut short, leaving him to wonder if it was more hallucinatory than real, a technical error manufactured in his brain. But these were not the things to dwell on now, not when he was strapped in so tight to a gurney that he couldn't move.

"I remember, I'm David Timmerman. I work as an account rep for NorthQuest Corporation. You need to let me go. Why do you have me chained up like this, anyway?" His voice raised up angrily for the first time.

The doctor who remained silent since his initial comment now took charge of the conversation, as if that transition was planned all along. "Hi David. It's clear you don't remember us, so let me reintroduce the two of us to you. I'm Doctor Grimes and this is Doctor Stark."

So, he had talked, probably in a state of delirium and had no recollection of these conversations. This put him at a distinct disadvantage, but one he had no way to gauge.

"I see," K2 responded warily. "I must have made quite an impression to get my own padded cell in what I assume is a psych ward. But I don't remember either of you at all. Maybe you could enlighten me on what we discussed."

Grimes leaned in closer to K2. He was in his mid 60s, fit and active. He still had a full head of hair that would grow unruly if not tamed by a military crew cut. A bow tie was all that peeked out from his lab jacket.

"I'll say you did. And we'll be happy to relay those conversations to you. But first, what more can you tell us about your life, your work with NorthQuest?"

"Sure, we can talk about that if you want. But how about you loosen the hold on me first. Then we can all sit down and have ourselves a nice little chat."

"I'm not sure we're ready to do that. You see, you got quite unruly the last time you were free. You weren't coherent but had a lot to say. I'm not surprised you're unable to recall those conversations. Because of this, these precautions are necessary. For now, anyway."

While this conversation took place, Doctor Stark moved over to a monitoring device that was connected to electrodes hooked to K2's body. K2 registered the awe/horror passing over Stark's poorly masked expression, as he monitored K2's reaction to Grimes' comments. He knew all of his vital signs would be off the charts, especially now that he was engaged in this game of cat and mouse with Grimes. Stark motioned to Grimes and they both observed the results, pointing at screens this way and that, wordlessly.

"You are extraordinary. We've never observed brain function like what you possess." Grimes conceded after disengaging his attention from the monitors.

"That so?"

"You don't seem surprised to hear me say this."

"I was in a car accident as a child. Barely survived. Brain damage shut down some parts of my brain and accelerated others." So was the line he was instructed to say in a situation like this.

"That so?" Now it was Grimes' turn to express skepticism. Tests were performed during his stay, for which K2 was heavily sedated. The activity in the basal ganglia, the "lizard brain" in humans, was unimaginably high. It scared Grimes and his colleagues when they reviewed the results. Their investigations began after the patient was dropped off outside the emergency room. No identification, but looking more like a marine or a linebacker than a homeless indigent. They placed him on a stretcher because he was unconscious, and knew something was wrong as soon as they checked his vital signs. Everything was spiked. He should have been dead for any of a number of reasons.

When K2 regained consciousness in the intake room he immediately became disruptive, not unusual in this setting. But when orderlies tried to restrain him, he displayed superhuman strength. He injured four orderlies and kept another eight at bay. The outcome was anything but secured until they got a shot of Propofol into him; at least he wasn't pharmacologically immune. But their subsequent tests indicated how compromised his system was, and now that he was regaining strength, they wondered what type of deterrent would be required to control him.

He'd been in this seclusion cell since his initial outburst and the mystery of who he was only deepened since then. They pulled him out of sedation twice before, but the meds were not right and his delirium left him murmuring incomprehensible stuff about cyborgs and neurologically expansive technologies. He related the narrative he'd just repeated but alternately called himself K2 and demanded to be released to the authorities at Homeland Security.

This was the first time he was coherent and the doctors were intent on learning how much of this fantasy the patient believed when he was fully conscious. The troubling part was his fantastical ravings had basis in his metabolism. If it didn't, they would have chalked him up as just another delusionally wrecked human being that required heavy doses of antipsychotic drugs. But even after sedation and days of rest his vitals were off the charts, dangerously high. And now, as his stress rose because they did not set him free, the cortisol levels and blood flow to the basal ganglia were a fire storm that both frightened and intrigued.

"OK, David. We know how uncomfortable it is for you and we want to make you more comfortable. But you have to work with us a little too. Before we let you free, we need to make sure we're safe and know who you are." Grimes said while Stark continued to scan the monitors.

"Not much to tell. I live alone in Rockville Maryland. 2802 Jones Rd. # 34. Small condo, nothing fancy. I spend most of my time working for NorthQuest Corporation, a military contractor. That's all I can tell you because the work is classified."

"What else can you tell us, what can you tell us about your personal life?"

"What the hell's going on here? You got to let me go. What right do you have to keep me tied up like this?"

"We can keep you here for as long as we deem you a danger to society. So, it would be for your greatest good to cooperate with us."

K2 considered his options. He doubted he could break free from these restraints and neutralize the guards. He surveyed the room more thoroughly. The door leading outside was reinforced metal. It, in itself, did not present a challenge but he did not know what lay on the other side. All of these factors caused him to conclude his chance of escape was slim. As much as he hated the idea, he would play it straight and see where that got him.

"There's not much to tell. I grew up in Wichita, Kansas. I got a scholarship to play football at Princeton. Moved to the DC area six years ago. Started as an analyst in the DoD but then shifted into the public sector with NorthQuest about 2 years ago."

"And friends, family relations?"

"Not much to say there. Family's back in Wichita. Go out for beers with the guys at work. A girlfriend here and there but nothing along those lines right now."

"So, outside of work there's no one we can contact about you locally."

"Afraid not. Sorry if I don't live up to your idea of what's an acceptable level of socializing. But I'm sure you know that's far from unusual these days."

"Do you like your job, David?"

"For fuck's sake. What does that mean? I like making money. I like not being poor. But I don't sit around the campfire singing Kum-ba-yah with my clients."

"Of course you don't, David, of course." Grimes said as he walked back over to Stark. They conferred privately for a few minutes, and then Grimes stepped away from the devices until he was midway between Stark and K2.

"While you were providing the autobiographical information Dr. Stark was verifying it online. Let me show you what he found."

A holographic display appeared above K2. Two rows of display screens each contained 3 panes of search results.

K2 could see what was coming, and plotted as he listened.

"We didn't ask your age but assumed you are in the 20 – 35 year age group. There are no David Timmermans that are unaccounted for, none that would place you here. Moving to the last pane on top, there is also no record of a NorthQuest Corporation at the address you provided, or anywhere else. The office building you mention has been looking for a new leasee for 4 months. Moving to the right on the bottom, you can see the condo you said you owned was purchased by a Margaret Noonan two years ago. So, based on these government supplied databases you don't live or work where you say you do, and don't even exist as the person, with the birthplace you say is yours…. How do you account for these discrepancies, David?"

"How long did you say I've been in here?"

"I didn't, but it's been about two weeks. Why do you ask?"

K2 knew what happened. The agency assumed the worst, that he was killed or captured. He knew they'd wipe away all references to his alias if they believed that happened, just as they had with his pre-cyborg identity. So, he was indeed a non-person, imprisoned in this psych ward. It looked like his new reality included doctors who inflict pain to further their research along with the goons who inflict pain for the fuck of it.

"Ok, I'll come clean. I'm involved in a top secret military program. My brain has been programmed with highly sophisticated software that connects directly to computer networks. I am the most advanced warrior that has ever been created. I was recruited from the deepest levels of espionage affairs and you will be in a world of trouble if you don't turn me over to Homeland Security immediately."

Doctor Grimes had been watching impassively as K2 told his tale. When he was done, he turned to Doctor Stark.

"Wait, I'm not done!" K2 screamed, sensing the energy in the room turn hostile.

Instead of heeding his command, Grimes spread his lab coat like a cape and pressed his opened right hand behind him, signaling K2 to be quiet. This gesture made clear to K2 that Grimes had decided that K2 was delusional and dangerous. He began thrashing at his restraints with incredible force, bursting one and then another of the metal fasteners. His arms were starting to break free, but the rest of his body still held fast. Grimes moved towards him with measured quickness. He injected a sedative cocktail into K2's thigh. The thrashing continued, but with less force. Right before consciousness broke he looked at Grimes' expression. There was cruelty in it and he realized he'd just become a new lab rat for Grimes' experiments. K2 lunged at him but the narcotic had already taken effect.

He came-to groggily, infrequently, over hours, maybe days. He'd been moved and was in the center of an examination chamber that was more like a crypt. Towering banks of computer hardware lay on a far wall, laser-like scanners were scattered about the ceiling and were pointed at him. Dampness in the air suggested they were far below ground level. But of prime interest was the steel cage surrounding him, which was 8' x 8' x 8' containing only a bed, small wash basin, and toilet. He could look through the bars only with some difficulty because they were set so close together. What he saw was Dr. Grimes walking towards him from the other side of the room. As he did, K2 sat up on the side of his cot and watched the doctor's advance.

"I hope you are well rested," Grimes began. "We've needed to keep you sedated while we readied your new accommodations. Nothing fancy as you have no doubt already deduced. But you are such an unusual case that we needed to take extreme precautions. We're not sure just how strong you are, so we built in some advanced security features. You can touch the metal bars but if you apply pressure, they will emit an electric current that will increase as the assault upon them increases. Before you could break free, assuming you could dislodge these bars, you would electrocute yourself . . .. As I say, you are an unusual case."

"So what do you want from me?" K2 asked, deciding, for now, not to test the sturdiness of the cell's restraints. "You saw through my alias and then didn't believe the truth. Where do we go from here?"

"We are interested in what you have to say, but are more interested in what makes you the way you are."

After a moment's pause, Grimes continued, "We'll be running some tests. Some will be uncomfortable, but we'll try to make this as painless as possible for you. You see, science beckons and you are a prized specimen whose secrets we mean to unlock."

"I'm telling you, you need to contact Homeland Security. They'll verify my story. I need to get back to my post. The safety of the nation is impacted by my being here and not protecting our borders, our defense against internal and external terrorists."

"You are exceptional," Grimes responded, with more feeling than he'd ever expressed to K2, "But not for the reason you mention. David, that's what we'll call you for now unless there's another name you would prefer, we have done what you asked. Homeland Security has no record of you, or the project you claim to be a part of."

"Of course, they don't know who I am. I'm part of a top secret program that a front-line customer service rep would have no knowledge of. And call me K2!" he commanded. "I have sacrificed everything for this country, for your safety. I have secret codes you could pass onto Homeland Security that will lead to my identity being verified. You are obligated to seek my return to where I can do the most good."

"I am under no such obligation K2, if that is what you wish to be called. And what will it be next time? That we need to contact NASA because your self-propelled launch to the moon has been delayed. You have extraordinary powers, that is true. But you are delusional. You are not the first one to have that mix. And we will help you recover, but need to make sure you don't harm others in the meantime. Your powers do inspire awe, make no mistake. And it is to the end of uncovering their source that you will submit to our evaluation." With this last sentence Grimes became stern, harsh, resolute. K2 glared back, not giving an inch.

K2 launched himself towards the doctor and grabbed hold of two adjacent bars of his prison cell. As he tried to pry them apart an electric shock radiated through his body, just as Grimes had promised. He flinched away, powerless to do otherwise.

A faint sneer passed over Grimes' face, and then it was gone. "You're here and you're not going anywhere. If you work with us, things will go better for you. You may even be freed someday. But don't fixate on that. We have a lot of work to do before then. Until then, you'll do as we say."

He remembered almost from the time he'd gained consciousness, but pushed it away. Milo was his sworn enemy. All his training and upgrades were intended for one thing: to neutralize threats to The System, and Milo was the most potent of all. Milo's ability to cut through The System's controls and provide the Resistance with confidential information raised concerns. Worst of all, they had no idea how far Milo could extend his power, so his threat could not be properly gauged.

Memories trickled back in. The encounter when K2 should have neutralized Milo. But Milo slipped away and led him into that universe of ever changing landscapes, nature bursting against azure skies and turbulent seas. It was beautiful and breathtaking. He tried to push the significance of this encounter away, to avoid seeing his own misstep in allowing it to happen. But what he had felt was freedom, something he realized he had never felt before. It was a freedom perfectly aligned to his cyborg nature, the only thing that he'd ever encountered that was equal to it.

Grimes finished working at his computer and then got up to address K2. "We will be taking some samples from you and examining them. It will cause you discomfort, more than most people can handle," Grimes said, his face twisting with curiosity and anticipation. "But seeing how you react to extreme conditions is one of the things we are most interested in, so pain is unavoidable."

Grimes placed a gas mask over his head and returned to the computer. Soon a stream of gas shot out of a nozzle above K2's cage. When K2 realized what happened he covered his face in a blanket, but it was ineffective and he lost consciousness moments later.

When Grimes was convinced K2 was unconscious he called in a surgical team and guards. After K2 was strapped down, Grimes made incisions into both bone and muscle, beginning what he believed would be the study that cemented his place in the forefront of the New Eugenics that had shed its historical references and gained a sizable foothold in the scientific community. Whether K2 survived was of less significance. But he needed to last long enough for his research to be completed, and findings published.

Two weeks of torture ensued. K2 was subjected to extreme, cruel levels of pain and deprivation. His stoicism only fueled Grimes' malevolent desires. There were more cuts, more scrapings. K2 was weakening.

Why Milo decided to implant the communication link in K2's brain was something K2 couldn't comprehend. He was surprised that Milo decided not to neutralize him, but installing the connection went far beyond that. He grew angry whenever he considered using it, that it was even there to tempt him. But the anger was supplanted by the thought that he would probably die from this humiliating and painful torture.

He opened the port in his brain, the part where the neural mesh fired. He had not felt this flow of energy in a long time. This is when his physiology really spiked and he needed to shield this from Grimes and his team, who had no idea that this could be brought on by voluntary effort. They had seen it during his early fits of rage and he'd not engaged these powers since then. But he could feel his limbs pump fire now, his brain engorged by the neuralBlast technology. If it wasn't for the electricity in the bars he would burst through this prison; but they had lucked upon one of the few strategies that could keep him contained.

A single pulse pushed through the energetic, neural pathways. It passed beyond the electric fence that ensnared him, the walls of concrete and steel. Wondrous energetic pulse, as unknowable as it was unquantifiable. And it dropped into a single brain that was open to this transmission, a beacon in the cosmos poised to welcome this unique neural signature.

Chapter 15

The message came into the Homeland Security Special Ops hotline. The transmission was received on a secured line, through an untraceable source. The message revealed that K2 was detained in a maximum security ward at the Reeducation Psychiatric Hospital in Bethesda Md., where K2 was transferred when they decided to detain him. He was under the direct care of a Dr. Grimes. The physical description and the reference to his alias, David Timmerman, were a perfect match.

When Matt Raines saw the message, he sensed this might be his last chance. Weeks had passed since K2 disappeared. In addition, two days ago they suffered a cyber attack that seriously damaged their software. Matt tried to hide these developments, but word reached the president. Meld issued orders to shut down the program. He would not tolerate losers and this had *loser* written all over it. Raines requested an audience with President Meld to plead his case but it was denied. Matt knew his career was in freefall, leaving him depressed and prey to suicidal thoughts. But the news that K2 might be alive invigorated Matt. Everyone in the president's inner circle slipped in and out of favor. Meld liked that level of chaos, fed on it, and everyone involved with him accepted it as the price of admission. If Matt could resurrect K2 he might, once again, improve his chances of inching closer to the president.

Matt assembled a team to make an unannounced trip to liberate what was rightfully his. Three hours later, they descended on the main entrance of the hospital after disembarking from two impregnable military vehicles. Six FBI agents flanked Matt and his assistant, Frank Stern. Matt flashed official documents at the overwhelmed and frightened front desk clerk, Anita Huston, and demanded to see the most senior administrator immediately.

"Whom should I say is calling?"

"Don't give a name, just read across the first line of the document I gave you."

Anita dialed the number, said hello, explained the situation as best she could, and then read from the paper, "Members of the FBI are here to retrieve a government agent who has been detained here without cause or justification." She received a response, cupped her hand over the mouthpiece and said to Matt, "I'm sorry but Dr. Carney has a full schedule today and can't fit in any more appointments. He said "

Before Anita could complete her thought, Matt grabbed the phone from her and took over the conversation, "Dr. Carney, you have no idea how much worse your day just became. I have the authority to detain you and anyone else from this hospital who does not cooperate fully. If you know what's good for you, you will clear your calendar for the rest of the day, and tell this young woman to grant us access to your office. But really it doesn't matter what you do, because we will find you one way or another."

Dr. Carney had a change of heart and decided he could, in fact, fit one more meeting into his schedule.

They dominated whatever space they strode through. They walked right through Carney's waiting room and barged into his office. Two of the guards posted up prior to entering Carney's office, conforming to some learned protocol, and four guards and Frank followed Matt into Carney's office. Matt immediately slammed official documents on Carney's desk.

Carney popped up from his seat and bellowed, "What's the meaning of this? Is all this really necessary?"

"You tell me, Carney. Why don't you start with the isolation wards you're running here without oversight or controls?"

Carney hesitated and assessed the phalanx of gray suits and hostile attitudes that descended into his office. He decided he could better deal with his adversaries if he knew who they represented, so took a minute to scan the documents before him. They looked official, had the seal of the FBI and some other markings he did not recognize, principally a man with a snake-like creature wrapped around him with bits of matter like tiny sine waves surrounding them, all of which were encapsulated in a sphere. The long and short of the letter was that agent Matt Raines was to be afforded full access to the hospital facility and its records.

"I suppose you're Matt Raines."

Before Carney was finished with his comment, he was looking at Raines's ID which he flipped open six inches from Carney's face. When Carney nodded, Matt reinserted the ID in his inner coat pocket.

"I'll need to make some calls to verify the story you're telling me," Carney said, trying to gain back some degree of authority.

"No, that's not going to happen," Raines shot back with only slightly restrained fury while placing his hand on top of Carney's phone. I don't care what you think is going on here, but if you make one misstep you'll be removed from your job and disappeared into a re-education camp. You haven't reached your level without having some understanding of how things work. You are looking at an emissary from the deepest dark place in The System and that is a place you don't ever want to look at directly. You may think you're aligned with some power structure but it will crumble. If we need to crush you, we will do so with impunity, without a second thought. Do I make myself clear?"

Carney did know how the game was played, but not at this level. He was a harsh, at times, cruel boss and enjoyed wielding his power. But he also knew how to act when the tables were turned on him. Groveling in these situations did not offend. To survive and flourish in The System required a certain type of obsequious behavior in the face of superior power.

"Yes, abundantly clear. What do you want from me?"

Raines saw that the charade of resistance was removed and advanced his inquiry to the next level.

"You have been holding a patient for some time. You may know him as K2 or David Timmerman. We need to take him with us now. Further, you need to remove him from your computer systems, any record of him must be expunged. We will have data analysts come by in 24 hours to perform a sweep through your systems to ensure full compliance is met."

Carney was aware of K2. Grimes had alerted him to his incredible powers and the fantasy he'd dreamed up about himself. Their running theory was that K2 was using his delusions to tap some dormant areas of the brain. Carney agreed to keep him in a high security isolation chamber and allow *unconventional* methods be used to study him. There was also an implicit agreement that these studies would not be recorded in the normal patient tracking systems. Yes, Carney had agreed to all this but only through dialog between the two, so it would be possible to throw Grimes under the bus if need be.

"Before freeing him, I would like to talk with the attending physician who's responsible for managing K2's treatment. Please call him into the office now."

"You are referring to Dr. Grimes. He may be unavailable now but I'll try to contact him."

"For your own good, you should avail yourself of every means possible to bring him here without delay."

Carney placed the call, which Grimes answered. After some attempts to divert this intrusion into his schedule, Grimes relented, influenced by the seriousness and uncharacteristic threatening tone of Carney's voice.

The two fierce looking bodyguards he passed on his way into Carney's office confirmed Grimes' suspicions. The group in the office had said little since the call was made, and now Raines swiveled his body and observed Grimes step through the door and did not wait to be introduced.

"You have been holding a subject who is a high value agent responsible for our country's security. I need to know what tests you've performed and what you've learned."

"You need to tell them everything you know," Carney said to Grimes. "They are coming from an area of the government I didn't even know existed, one that could make our lives difficult, cause us a great deal of harm."

Grimes did not consider subterfuge. It was clear Raines and his crew had crawled out from underneath some rock and he would do whatever he could to hasten their return.

"He is an interesting subject, you must admit that," Grimes started, attempting a collegial attitude. Raines was unfazed, would have none of it.

"What tests have you administered to him? What is his current status?"

"We have biopsied most of his organs and taken bone and skin samples. He's had a full battery of toxicological, neurological and related testing. He has been through a series of procedures that test his strength and ability to withstand pain and deprivation."

He went on, providing details of the test they'd performed. Despite the obvious danger confronting him, Grimes could not hide a level of exuberance as he relayed the sadistic regimen K2 had been put through.

He concluded, "As you are aware, he is capable of super-human strength and endurance. But it still doesn't make sense. We haven't come any closer to understanding what makes him tick."

"No matter what you threw at him," Matt responded.

"Yes, yes, that's correct. He is an amazing specimen. Because of that we needed to keep him confined. It's the only way for us to be safe. Metal bars with electric current are the only thing we've found to secure him."

"You won't have to worry about that anymore," Raines replied, signaling an end, as he had heard enough.

The thin smile on Grimes' face was quickly erased when Raines continued. "But you better hope you didn't damage K2. If we learn you treated him inhumanely, you'll have a chance to experience your techniques yourself, with some of the sorriest mother fuckers you ever laid eyes on. Because you'll be down in a pit alongside them. Now, take us to K2 so we can release him."

Real fear penetrated Grimes and he plotted his escape.

"I'm very busy. You pulled me from my rounds and I need to get back to my patients. I'll send an assistant to take you to him."

"Not a chance. I want to see him with you standing next to me. In fact, I want both of you to escort us to K2 . . . the person responsible for his care and the hospital's lead administrator. Now, let's not waste any more time."

Raines motioned to the door, a gesture that was more of a command than a courtesy, which the two white coats understood. As they moved through the hallways, the doctors were squeezed into the middle by the bulky security guards who rejoined the group from their positions in the outer chambers.

The party of ten were shoulder to shoulder in a maintenance elevator. Grimes pressed the bottom knob, LL3.

"I'll bet most elevators don't have access to LL3," Raines said, anger pulsating in each word.

Neither Grimes nor Carney chose to answer or say anything at all, even after they disembarked. The corridor led to a single room. Grimes placed his thumb on a pad and the door lock disengaged. Two guards turned and straddled the door while the other walked through it.

The changes in K2 were startling. Rage boiled inside Raines as he took in the diminished character, imprisoned like a lab rat, in the middle of the room. He had not shaved in weeks, nor had he bathed during his time in captivity.

"What the fuck have you been up to, Grimes? You trying to figure out how far you could push him before you killed him?"

Turning back to K2, he could only look at the withered frame, gashes and marks along his body, blood-shot but still fierce eyes and expression.

"What took you so long?" K2 said with the barest trace of humor and sarcasm.

"We looked everywhere for you, except down in this fucking dungeon."

Raines turned to Grimes and said, "Let him out . . . now!"

This was Grimes' worst nightmare and he tried to resist. "I don't think that's a good idea. Based on everything we've seen he is fundamentally dangerous and delusional."

"I'm not in the habit of repeating myself. Do it!"

Grimes moved to the gate as did K2, from the other side. K2 tracked Grimes and his movements while Grimes turned his gaze downward.

K2 stepped out of his cage for the first time since he arrived. Even diminished, he was a frightening killing machine. He stood silently in front of Grimes who failed to lift his gaze from the floor, who until recently had complete control over K2 and applied that power mercilessly. K2 lifted Grimes by the throat and raised him with both hands above his head. He threw him hard against a wall and let out a scream of primal rage, a sound like nothing any of them had ever heard before. Carney tried to retreat to the door but was restrained by two guards. K2 continued his assault on Grimes, picking him up and heaving him multiple times, long after any life had left his body, like a baboon thrashing an unruly pup.

He seemed to only get stronger as the beating went on, and made his move for Carney when there was no more play in Grimes' body. But his progress was halted when Raines stepped in front of him.

"We need this one," Raines said, and seemed disappointed at having to say it. He'd enjoyed the blood lust and wanted to see more but there were other requirements. And Grimes' sacrifice was calculated. Matt had no idea how K2's captivity affected him, if he still had it in him. He needed to see K2 attack with zeal. K2's thrashing of Grimes was sufficient proof that his aggressive potential and thirst for violence was untamed, even after prolonged torture.

"Carney needs to make sure he wipes you clean from all the hospital's systems. If he fails in any way, we'll let you pay him a visit." Matt said to K2 in the way of consolation, while patting him on his shoulder as a way to welcome him back.

He turned from Grimes' lifeless body to Carney and said, "I'll let you come up with an explanation for this," while pointing to Grimes without taking his eyes off of Carney. "Next time you think it's OK to torture a patient, maybe you'll think about how it worked out for you this time. Might not be worth whatever you expected to get out of it, whether it was papers published or new grants money."

Raines looked at K2. Yes, he'd been brutally mistreated but was still alive. A depleted version of himself but still capable of awesome strength and fury. K2 had been tested and Raines hoped the challenge of these last two months would leave him a stronger, more ruthless warrior.

Raines walked up to K2, looked him over one last time and said, "You look like hell," and clapped him on the shoulder. "Let's get you out of here."

K2 looked back at his cell one last time and then turned and walked with Raines towards the door. They halted while passing Carney. "Remember, a team from the agency will be here in 24 hours. Make sure you're ready for them."

K2 broke from rank and went face to face with Carney. He picked him up with one hand, lifted him above his head, and studied his terror stricken face. The effort of smiling was foreign, and confused the muscles in his jaws and cheeks. He tossed Carney away who went flying across the room until he landed on his back. Raines was, again, enthralled by this playful display of savagery.

They took the elevator to the ground floor and then walked towards daylight and freedom, each step for K2 stronger than the one before. No words were spoken until they sat comfortably in one of the military vehicles, heading back to their home base in The Pentagon.

"One thing I still don't understand is how we got notified of your location," Matt mused. "From what I can tell they kept everything about what they were doing to you pretty buttoned up. Yet someone reached out to us and did it in a way that was very sophisticated, a way we haven't been able to source yet. You have any idea who may have wanted to help you?"

K2 knew this was coming and had a response ready. He hesitated before answering, as if giving it thought for the first time.

"They brought in some assistants to monitor me from time to time. I told anyone I thought may help to reach out to Homeland to verify my story. I'd bet it was one of them, but I really have no idea."

K2 turned back towards the window, deciding this was the best way to conclude the deceit. Milo was his nemesis. The fact he was the one that rescued him infuriated K2 as much as anything. The kinship he'd felt as they gamboled across landscapes of immense natural beauty now seemed like a bad dream, a stupid diversion, worthless. Or so he told himself.

But Raines could never know about this. Because he would never understand, make something of it that it was not, see in it some weakness in K2, a lost opportunity to strike. And when K2 was asked how he ended up in the hospital, he conjured up a story of treachery gone bad, the type of thing Matt would feast on when K2 served it up. In that way, Milo would remain his private and primary target.

Chapter 16

Milo was tired and frustrated with trying to decipher the meaning behind his obsession. He contacted Pedro and found he was making a run to the farm that morning. Milo had just finished breakfast and rode towards Pedro's shop 15 minutes later.

It was a week since his first visit and the X-Zone looked a little more hospitable. This time he noticed a few wires on a couple of streets that he assumed were functioning. The drip of electricity connected them tenuously to what The System promoted as civilization.

There were three other workers at the farm, and Jamal was deep in discussion with them. They were disagreeing about something that neither Pedro nor Milo could hear clearly enough to figure out. After a minute Jamal broke free and walked towards Pedro and Milo.

"Sorry for keeping you waiting, but I needed to clear up some matters."

"Sure, sure, no problem, my friend," Pedro reassured. "It allowed us to admire the progress you're making around here."

Milo had studied farming methods this past week and recognized the permaculture features employed here. No-till beds of plants and plants of different types grown together, being the most prominent. But the soil was undernourished and wouldn't likely produce much of a harvest.

"I'm glad I did not completely waste your time, then," Jamal responded. And then, almost more to himself, "We are trying to bring this land back, but it can be a slow process and the lack of progress can cause some to question our methods."

Their conversation faltered, a victim of the disagreement that left a charge in the air.

"So, what can I get you today, Pedro?" Jamal asked, his voice recalibrating to a more pleasant tone.

Pedro handed him a list of items and Jamal, after looking it over, retreated to fill the order. Milo strayed from Pedro and continued to take an inventory of his surroundings. He returned as Pedro and Jamal were concluding their transaction.

The three spoke for a few more minutes and then Pedro said it was time for him to return. Instead of following Pedro, Milo told him he would like to stay behind and see if he could help out. Pedro smiled because nothing made him happier than connecting two disparate points of light, which apparently he had just done.

"See if you can figure him out, because I can't." Pedro said this in the direction of Jamal as he pedaled away. A strong gust of wind pressed against him, raising his beret off his head. One hand held the hat down while the other was on the handlebars, and it seemed as if he was waving back at both Milo and Jamal as he pedaled away.

"So, what's this secret Pedro thinks you got locked up inside you."

"Nothing really," Milo said and hesitated before completing his thought. "Sometimes I guess I can see things sooner than most people."

"So, you're sensitive to vibrations that others can't feel, is that it?"

"Yeah, that's as good a description as any."

"Have you had any premonitions about out here in the X?"

"Hmmm, there is one. You know I fell off my bike the last time I came?"

"Yeah, Pedro mentioned that. Did it happen again?"

"No, once was enough. But the thing that got me in trouble the last time keeps coming back. I keep seeing something like a dome being built around here. It doesn't make any sense to me. It's big, elevated off the ground, spanning a good portion of the sky. Too weird for me to make sense of."

"It doesn't sound like any development project I've heard about," Jamal laughed. "But this land has been forsaken for a long time, so it could use all the help it can get."

"Yeah," Milo responded. "I don't see any Faux-na developments going up around here."

This was the new housing fad being touted by The Newer Machine. The private spaces people lived in were little more than warehouse units. The public spaces took their inspiration from amusement parks and did a digital makeover seasonally, featuring everything from urban chic to desert oasis. The kinks were still being worked out but already the neighborhoods were transformed by digitally managed facades along the walkways. Underlying it all was The System's absolute control of messaging, from advertisements to political commentary and entertainment. The Newer Machine reported long waits to buy-in, but orders were still taken and prioritized based on the applicant's perceived loyalty to The System.

This made Jamal laugh. "You won't find many people in these parts busting down the doors to get into one of them. Things are tough here, but many of the people in the XZ are self-exiles. Many had been part of The Resistance, but that didn't work for them, either. And most of those who were banished here, would choose to stay even if they could go back."

"Why's that?"

"Because we're free spirits and we see what being on the other side does to people."

This was exactly what appealed to Milo about this place, but didn't realize it until Jamal expressed it. He decided to pay close attention to what was going on here to see if it offered a new wrinkle, answers to the questions he'd been asking.

"So, what do you want to help with?" Jamal said, bringing the conversation back to the question of Milo's stay on the farm. "The main things going on is work in the fields and repairing the Big House, which is where most of us live. It still needs a lot of work to make it habitable. Cold weather's not far off and we need to prepare."

Milo considered the options before responding. "If it's all the same to you I'd like to take a look around. I have some skills that are hard to describe. But if I spend time helping in different ways, I think I'll find where I can do the most good."

Jamal was satisfied with this and said, "Suit yourself."

They parted and Milo spent the next couple of days surveying the encampment. Pedro's assessment that it was barely hanging on was correct. Ten adults and two children comprised this outpost that was barely scratching out an existence. Milo assisted with cutting boards from trees and placing them over missing siding. He also assisted in the gardens, mostly hauling water from the only well on the property.

In both cases he was struck by the listlessness of those with whom he worked. He improved the processes of both of these operations and received little thanks for doing so. They were depressed, he reasoned. When he ate with them, he came to understand the root cause of their ambivalence. They were hungry and malnourished. On the third day Milo strode up to Jamal who was surveying green beans that needed to be picked and expressed a thought that was percolating since he began his rounds.

"You need meat!"

"Of course we do." Jamal responded angrily. He was in no mood to respond to stupid assertions that conveyed an obvious truth that was simply beyond their reach. He had kept an eye on Milo who he had to admit was helpful. But he expected Milo's visits to slow and then stop, as was common among those Whites who were not condemned to the X-Zone, but still came to sniff around until it no longer titillated them. Jamal tried to feel grateful for whatever help they provided.

But there was always a slight revulsion at the dilettante quality of their assistance. So, Milo's assertion didn't surprise him.

The vision that haunted Milo on his first visit was replaced by one akin to it. Over the last few days Milo sketched a series of portraits of the landscape in its current state. They exposed its desolate and soil-poor conditions, and the difficulty of getting anything to grow on it. Weeds and grass penetrated chunks of cement left over from enterprise run amuck, the only thing in abundance. The barrenness was daunting, needing decades to pass at the current rate before its recovery could be claimed. But his new vision spoke of an accelerated repair.

"I can help."

"How's that?" Jamal asked, more skeptical than interested.

Milo gazed out at the landscape that had inspired his vision. Life, sprawling in every direction. The desecration giving way.

"Out there," he said haltingly, unsure of how to describe his unfurling vision. "I can set up four quadrants, maybe five square acres each, all connected in a large square. I can fence them in energetically, I'll explain more later. I can call in some cattle. Don't ask me how, but I can do it. You rotate the cows from one quadrant to another. They graze and defecate in one. Their hooves breaking up the ground and then move on. The beetles go to work on the cow pies, driving the nutrients deep within the ground, where the bacteria get to work bringing the soil back to health. Healthy soil sequesters tons of the carbon spoiling the atmosphere. You can't regenerate the land without animals. Can't!"

Milo was stunned again, overtaken by a vision more powerful than the one that haunted him previously. This time no artistic representation was required. Instead, when he perceived the flipping deck again, it was not just over there but here, beneath his feet. The ground undulated around him and he fell on it when he could no longer retain his balance.

For several minutes he watched the cement break apart, give way, as long grasses grew up in the newly formed rivulets, sprouting skyward. The ground only stopped shifting when it returned to the grassy knoll it had been for millennia. And then it all dissolved away and he was returned to the devastated present.

Jamal tried to settle Milo as he thrashed into and out of a trance, but was unable to lift the spirit from him. Jamal knew shamans, he knew mystics. And now he sensed the same great power emanating from Milo. Finally, Milo did settle and he sensed Milo was ready to speak.

"You OK, man?" He kneeled beside Milo and rested a hand on Milo's arm.

Milo would not yet let the image free, not until he could pull something from it, some way to express what it represented. He struggled to a sitting position and crossed his legs in front of him. From this posture he looked out at what had just been disclosed to him.

"Five, eight years from now this place will be a lush, beautiful woodland, like it was before we thought we knew better. The food the cattle provides will be a side benefit to the resurgent, bio-diverse landscape they help give life to."

Jamal now appreciated what Pedro was talking about. "Sure, bro, knock yourself out. If it's land with scrub grass you want, that we got plenty of."

They both looked out. Milo had the advantage of the recently departed vision, but both saw more than what was normally disclosed when peering in this direction. There was already grass, pressing up through the fractured cement and tumbling structures, making it difficult but not impossible to imagine what Milo envisioned. With each scuff of beating hooves, empire would chip away, eventually to dust, and replacing it, a reclaimed wilderness.

Milo returned to the apartment and set to work making good on his promise. During the morning of the third day he was in the basement hunched over a dozen metal rods of various sizes, until Sheila appeared.

"What's up?" she asked, coffee in hand. Milo already told her of his plan to re-wild a portion of the X-Zone for grazing animals.

"Need to be able to make a fence that's big, cheap, easy to build and maintain."

"Your cows better be pretty small if you expect these to pen them in." Kidding him, again, which was often an effective way to get him to express what he was working on and thinking about. But he was too deep in to be aware this was a joke.

"Their size can't matter."

"How's that?"

"I don't have the materials or time to build a traditional fence. So, I want to create one that is charged energetically, and think I can do it with these poles."

"How do you propose to do that without a consistent energy source?"

"I'm not sure, but I believe the metals are capable of doing this. Maybe they need a little help, which is what I am trying to learn from them."

"Why do you believe this? What are you basing it on?"

Milo was back in his strange zone, his untouchable zone. Cyborg intense. But then came a most unexpected confession from Milo.

"I am communing with the metals, trying to dialog at a base metallurgical level. It's alive, you know. Everything that has not been wrestled from its essential state is alive and conversant. Shaping the metal into rods has dimmed its self-knowing, but did not extinguish it. I can sense its exertions to communicate with me."

Man Made

Sheila was stunned by this. She had never heard him speak in such near-mystical terms. But again, his cyborg nature was evolving independently. She observed how he handled these objects, not like utilitarian objects but cradling them like living, sentient beings.

She wanted to ask more but sensed his desire to return to this thought experiment, so she stepped away quietly because they both had work to do. He remained awkwardly hunched over the seemingly inert objects, placing one and then another in his hands, trying to decipher the archaic code that pinged between them and him.

Milo remained sequestered for two more days trying to figure out how to build a fence for the cattle, and lurking behind that was the challenge of *calling in* the cows. He continued working with metal rods made of different ores and mastered the ability to move rods that were made of a single metal. Like a magnet, he aligned his energy and dragged it towards him or pushed it away. But, still, he experienced total failure when trying to enable direct communication between two rods.

"I need to get back in the lab," Milo asserted as he barged into Sheila's room. "I'm stumped and need to learn everything I can about electromagnetic energy and the movement of energy between inanimate objects, from Sufi mysticism to quantum physics."

Sheila felt the blood rush to her face, her forearms tingle with a similar sensation. It had been a while since she'd seen this level of passion in him. He hadn't had a neuralBlast session for a long time, and she wondered if his desire for it had waned. This was the type of inquiry she hoped would result from her work, not the militaristic aspects she was pressed to focus on.

199

"I wish I could hook you up right now but I still have more than a week of work before the lab is up and running. Until then, you're on your own. Keep communing with those rods. See if they can help you figure out what you need to do."

He turned from her and went back to work. This was not what she envisioned when she started down this path many years before. Back then, she had visions of human intelligence taking advantage of the vast array of digital information to unleash the birth of a human-centered technology. But here was Milo sitting on a broken down sofa in this shabbiest of apartments, the apex of her work, the likes of which she would probably never see again. And instead of her hi-blown dreams, he was shifting lengths of metals through his hands, looking for some sign, an act that could only be viewed as mystical. She was learning just as he was, learning to be quiet, to not try to change the direction of what she had engendered but no longer laid claim to, now that it was set free in the world. But she was also learning to enjoy the ride, which is all that any of us can wish to do.

After two more days of seclusion in his room, he sat on the living room sofa, cradling the same metal rods.

"Welcome back," Sheila said and smiled as she watched Milo lay down the metal and rub his eyes, accepting that it was time to take a break.

He attempted a smile and tried to make small talk, which was difficult so soon after the intense work session.

"Glad to be back. The world is beginning to regain its contour." As he said this, he unconsciously examined one of the rods. Sheila was caught by his attitude towards it. In general, his movement and bearing had an unusual lightness. Before, he was hunched over, studying, growing frustrated at his lack of progress. Now there was a relaxed smile behind the intensity, a clearness of vision, a sense that he was getting closer to reaching his goal.

"Is there anything you can tell me, anything you've learned?" Sheila asked.

Milo took a minute before speaking to establish himself within the meditation that had consumed him during his time in his room. Which led him to the current moment, and then the next moment, and so on; rendering the smell of coffee, the gentle breeze entering through the windows, their own energetic pulse expanding and contracting the space he and Sheila shared.

"All animate objects wish to serve."

"Even these?" Sheila picked up a piece of metal and considered it with an expression that betrayed her skepticism.

"Even these. But there needs to be reciprocity. They will gladly perform the metallurgical tasks I'm requesting but must have their needs met too. That is what I need to understand, it is the key to fixing all problems. And it is that which I will meditate on, with good spirit and hopefulness . . . for as long as it takes."

Unconsciously he began to fiddle with the variously sized pieces of metal, all heaped together like a stack of pickup sticks. This was her toddler Sheila mused, and chuckled to herself. His hair was longer and all tousled together, giving him a juvenile quality. But the image also projected a subversive edge because Milo embodied the toddler's boundless curiosity and determination to bend all creation to its will. Just now he considered the possibility of intercepting satellite transmissions and using them to establish communications between two bars. He stayed with this for several hours, moving to different places within the house trying, unsuccessfully, to get one to ping the other. He used alchemical processes involving both fire and ice, trying to detect when transformation occurred and then insinuate his request as the material transmuted into a new form. In these moments he sensed the metal's openness, but there was still its unwillingness to act upon his request.

There was a small backyard and he brought six of his companions with him. He immediately sensed a lightness, a coming alive. Like Mexican jumping beans they wiggled around, or so it seemed to Milo's highly attuned senses, and he felt his heart beat harder with the suggestion that his understanding was about to grow richer.

With a hammer he drove one stake into the ground. He knew that he was on the right track because the metal continued to vibrate long after he had set it in the ground. Then he witnessed a blue aura encasing the metal shaft. All of this was a prelude to what he sensed was a greeting and interest in deepening their communication.

He grabbed another metal post and drove it in the ground two feet from the first rod. It, too, radiated energetically and sent recognition and thanks to him. He imagined the two rods connected and projected those thought constructs to them, along the same pathways that carried their prior communications. But they remained languid, their little blue orbs unable to share their signal, despite his feeling that they were capable and willing to do so.

Several more stakes were placed in the ground at increasingly closer intervals, but the results were the same. With each successive failure the thought that something was missing continued to form. He tried aligning them differently, even having them touch, but they still would not make contact with each other.

He put his hammer down and sat with them, listened to them, touched them, still believing they would comply with what he asked them to do. Hours he spent in this way, communing with the metals, and what he felt surprised him. There was a sense of yearning, almost human. Although they were happy in their way, they were incomplete. But that was all he could learn.

He sat there meditating, reflecting on everything he learned and felt. He considered the profound knowledge he acquired in these sessions. Everything shared the same energetic pathways; everything was aligned with the greater good. How could anything be missing? And then it came to him like a thunderclap.

He got up and grabbed his bike. An hour later he returned from a local nursery. Standing alongside the metals he opened a bag of biochar. He plunged his hands inside and pulled out a handful of the grimy soil and placed it around the base of two pieces of metal, and they immediately began to twirl energetic flares. Milo realized that reciprocity extended further than he first conceived; first and foremost, a gift to the mother was needed that would allow her skin to be pierced with these metals. Milo fell on his knees as tears formed in the corner of his eyes and he prayed to no god in particular as the current flew between the metal rods in an ecstatic dance.

Milo fashioned a come-along to his bike, ladened with supplies. What passed for roads in the X-Zone were generally not passable with his load, so he was forced to walk much of the way, pulling his cargo along for a couple of miles. How his perspective had changed during the course of these few trips. There was nothing left to salvage he'd told himself the first time. Nothing more nor less than what you find in any deserted, discarded place. Untold cement and tar forever altering what lay beneath. The glint of sun over these unnatural landscapes projecting oasis after oasis in the distance that were never reached, never replacing the ruination at his feet. But now each step suggested something different, as he saw up close the twisting of crumbling infrastructure entwined in nature, turning the landscape into something else. His slower passage exposed the reemerging outposts. Tarps were fashioned to structures that were still partially intact. A few families, with children in tattered clothes playing among the rubble. They cast around him a protective bubble, he and the heavy weight he dragged along. His sweat and exertions were well suited to the X-Zone, and it prepared him for what lay ahead.

Jamal saw Milo approach, stopped what he was doing and walked to greet him.

"Yo, my man! Been a couple of weeks since you laid down those visions and plans on me. I was starting to wonder if I'd see you again."

"I'm here. Been busy figuring things out." Milo mopped sweat from his forehead but did not feel tired.

"You bringing us presents? What you got back there?"

Milo pulled back the sheets that covered his satchels to display metal rods, hammer, and bags of biochar. He was ready to begin his work.

"You're looking at your fence."

Milo had never heard Jamal laugh, not like this. Full-throated and saturated with a deep bass rumble. When he got control of himself he responded, "Don't look like any fence I've ever seen." The seriousness of their previous talk felt distant and he examined Milo with friendly skepticism. He would have enjoyed poking fun a bit longer but had work to do.

"So, what's your plan?"

Milo registered Jamal's skepticism so instead of responding he started moving again towards the area that was designated for his use.

"Let me show you."

Milo drove one stake into the ground along the perimeter of one of the quadrants. He scattered a handful of biochar around it, placed his hands on top of the biochar and spent a minute performing a meditation. He did the same within another bar ten yards down the perimeter. When he was done, he told Jamal to stick his hand between the bars.

Jamal found himself giving more credence to this charlatan's magic than he wanted, and Milo smiled when he sensed Jamal's hesitation.

"Fucking hell, what was that!" A charge ran through Jamal's body, causing him to pull back his hand.

"That is what is going to keep the cows penned in. Won't take them long to figure it out."

Jamal understood the words, but otherwise lacked comprehension.

"How does this work?" was all he was able to get out.

Milo responded, "We have an agreement. Me, the metal rods, and the earth that supports all of us."

A bit more comprehension filtered in but it was still overshadowed by utter amazement. As words failed Jamal, Milo went back to unloading his bags. In the middle of his preparations he stopped and relayed one more piece of information.

"When they are in the ground the charge they carry is self-sustaining. As soon as they're removed from the soil, they're inert. So, if you need to move or disable them you can touch them while they're *hot* with man-made materials. Milo pulled a rubber glove from his pocket and put it on. First he touched the rod and then waved his hand in the same area where Jamal had experienced the charge. He took the glove off and handed it to Jamal. Jamal waved his gloved hand there too and now felt nothing at all.

"I think you're right, these cows of yours will find out soon enough where they can and cannot roam." Upon delivering this comment, Jamal conceded there may be something to the fantasy Milo was weaving together.

Milo sighted down the lines of the perimeter and got to work. He tested the charge and found that it could easily hold at 10 yards. He was 5 posts in when the only worker besides Jamal at the farm today walked up to him.

"What are you doing?" She asked.

Milo looked up from pounding stake number 6 into the ground and replied, "Building a fence."

She'd been following his progress and looked back on it and then let out a roar of a laugh. His attention to what he was doing was still high, but the laugh had such a radiant quality that it redirected his focused concentration onto her.

"I hope you're not planning to keep anything more mobile than plants in there." She offered in a playful way. "This non-fence seems like non-sense to me."

Milo chuckled before responding, "Sorry, but I'm going to put cows in here," and declined responding to the editorial part of her comment.

The laughter she let free before paled in comparison to the spasm unleashed from her now. She wasn't sure which seemed more ludicrous, this non-fence or cattle grazing on this wasteland.

Milo continued to gather his impressions of her. She could match him tat for tat. But he couldn't make out most of them because her skin was too dark, which intrigued him even more. She clearly enjoyed her laugh and something about the sigh at the end of it suggested she didn't do it often enough.

"We'll get to the cows later, but first I'd like you to explain this fence to me if you wouldn't mind."

"Sure, these metal rods are communicating and creating a force field. If you stick your hand between them, you'll get a little kick."

She looked at him, incredulous. There was no energy source, so how could that be? But he had a look of absolute certainty. She raised her arm and pushed it forward, searching for something she didn't believe existed. The flash of silver sent through her body convinced her otherwise. She looked back at him; charlatan or madman, or something else entirely.

"Wow, that's wild."

"You'll be OK. Just enough charge to keep those grazers in."

Milo then explained to her what he'd just related to Jamal.

"It's unbelievable. You're a magician, or have some special power," she said with a sly twist. "Glad to meet you. My name is Onyinye."

He loved the sound of it, O-NEE-NEE, and reflected on it before replying. "I'm Milo, but you can call me Merlin if you prefer." He held out his hand, which she grasped and gave a measured shake.

"I'll go with Milo for now, but I have a feeling Merlin will find a way to filter back from time to time."

They made small talk to allow the more important communication occurring with their eyes to not be disturbed. Both were in their mid 20s and had traveled very different paths to get here. Her's led through the north African desert and the final immigration from that diaspora out of Nigeria. She was old enough to understand the images of suffering she left behind as a young girl, but not so old that she knew how to protect herself from the lives trapped inside those faces, for whom there would be no rescue. But resilience was also one of her qualities, and over time she learned to smile again, as now while looking at this stranger's face.

But something else was working on Milo, something so strong that it forced him to drop to a knee.

"Are you OK?" Onyinye asked, coming closer, surprised but ready to assist.

"I'll be fine . . .. I've been working so hard figuring out how to do this that I didn't consider how much it would take out of me when I started laying the stakes in the ground consecutively." As he said this he began feeling worse, so he sat down in the dirt, legs stretched out, arms bracing him from behind.

"It's harder than I thought it would be. You see, I am brokering a trust between these pieces of metal, the earth, and myself. Mostly I am asking permission to allow each stake to remain in the ground.   I clear my mind until I sense the necessary connections, which requires honesty, openness, and attunement. I learned this process through," he scuffled a little before completing this thought, "some advanced training. But until today I had only performed this procedure as discrete experiments.   Now I see how much effort is involved and am beginning to wonder if I can get it done."

She continued looking at him from above, uncertain as to how to interpret this strange man and the stranger story he had to tell.

"That may be the wildest thing I ever heard. And I wouldn't have believed a word of it if I hadn't singed my fingers on your *fence*."

She let out another laugh, different this time for its lightness, playfulness, which he hung on for every catch in her breath that was followed, again, by another peal of laughter.

After only a brief reflection, Onyinye spoke again, this time with conviction.

"You'll get it done. We'll get it done together."

"Be careful what you sign up for. I'm aiming to stake out the perimeter of a 20 acre spread. Then I need to create an XY axis through the middle to establish four, 5 acre sections. I brought thirty metal stakes with me and hope to get them in today. But the whole job will require more than 150."

He looked at her, sweat forming on her forehead from her labor and the late morning sun. She wore a faded green, lightweight muslin house dress.   While hand-made and crudely shaped, her movements gave it an almost elegant quality. She was not tall or particularly muscular, but evoked a spirit of being able to do anything she set her mind to. And it was clear from his condition that he could use the help.

"Well then," she said without missing a beat, "we got a lot of work to do, so we better get started as soon as you're able."

"I'm ready and grateful for your offer . . .. Could you give me a hand up."

With Onyinye's help Milo stood upright. He had already marked the place where the next piece of metal should be inserted and Onyinye picked up the hammer and started driving the stake into the ground. When she was done, she watched Milo pull from a bag a bit of biochar and disperse it on the ground that was stirred up around the metal pin. He went to his knees, covered the biochar with his hands and became lost to her as he communed with these natural elements until their spirits were aligned, the bond of trust formed.

They proceeded, one stake at a time, stopping and resting as Milo required. They came to appreciate the needed breaks for the opportunity it afforded them to talk.

"So, if you don't mind me asking, how did you end up in the X?" Milo asked.

Onyinye hesitated to consider what part of her story she would divulge.

"I'd been living on the fringe for a while. Word filtered to me about what Jamal was up to. I found a way to get through the border. I liked what I saw him and the others doing here, so decided to stick around and help out."

Milo wanted to know more about why she was living on the fringe but decided not to press her on it. Instead, he responded in the following way.

"Thank you for sharing that. Anything you tell me will be held in confidence, and I'd like to hear whatever you are comfortable telling me. And I love your accent, it's song-like quality. So please speak, both for what you have to say and just for the sound of your voice. Your name, which I know means 'A gift from God', seems well deserved."

"You are the first to know the origin of my name," she said. Although she felt exposed, it did not upset her or set off alarms. "I have a feeling you will be providing me with more surprises."

By some unspoken signal they decided it was time to get back to it. They settled into a rhythm of work, talk and rest and were satisfied with their progress. As the day wore on, the duration of the work sessions decreased. This gave them more time to talk, something both valued more each time.

On one such stop they sat on the ground and he gave his face to the sun, which was making its way to the horizon.

"This gig isn't getting easier. I figured once I got into a routine, I could knock them out pretty quick. I just wish I could get my ass up and moving again." He laughed, grew quiet and then laughed again.

"So, you're upset because performing miracles drains your battery a little bit? Damn, I still can't believe what I'm seeing. You've got yourself a little challenge here, don't you Merlin?"

"I do and I'm not complaining. But it is definitely different from what I expected. Yes, I am approaching the rod and soil with respect and asking them to engage in a way that benefits me but conforms to their nature. This is no surprise and what I expected. But there's more. . .. Each rod possesses the accumulated experience of the prior rods that were set. And the ground and the rods learn from each other. Again, all of this is only moderately surprising. But they are also learning about me! I have become both subject and object. I can feel them working their magic on me as mine works on them. But they are more knowledgeable of how this transfer works and I still don't understand what is being requested of me, what it is they wish to impart to me. Each successive stake and each piece of soil commune a bit more directly with my soul. I just hope I come to understand the wisdom they wish to impart."

Onyinye felt thunderstruck. From the first, the scope of what they were doing lay far outside of anything she understood.   And now it seemed they were only on the threshold of what was to come.

At the twenty-third post something different happened. The ground rejected it. Milo placed the metal rod in different locations and provided multiple offerings, but the results were always the same. He took it in his hands, studied it, and noticed something.   He could feel there was some other material mixed in with the metal. He examined further and could see that an acrylic was woven into it. While only a small amount, it was enough to alter its composition, enough to make it unnatural and unsuited for what he was asking of it.

Milo tossed it aside, but it continued to linger in his thoughts.   The mood that had buoyed their work and conversation was disturbed by this failed rod in a way he couldn't explain.   But they muscled through and completed the remaining posts, and then walked back to the Big House.

Onyinye's sleep was restless. She walked along the fence the next morning, and a couple of more shocks proved to her that this thing was real, although she still had no idea how that could be or what was its significance. She contemplated this until Milo showed up with more metal rods and they worked together preparing the worksite. But she couldn't shake feeling agitated and finally asked, "How long will the charge between the metal rods last?"

Milo was focused on getting back on task. When he turned to answer her it was with a surprised look, as if he expected her to understand. "This is who they are and will be until they are called to a different purpose or transmuted into some different form."

"So, they radiate from within and no external energy source is required?"

"That's a close approximation. But to understand you need to dig deeper, and dig where words can't go. It's the place where energy flows and stimulates all things. Tap into that and the idea of external and internal energy sources becomes meaningless pretty quickly."

"How can that be? I've heard physics plays games on a theoretical level with ideas like this, but no one really believes it because we can look and see all the things, actual THINGS, around us. You're not me." And then picking up a random chunk of cement, "And I'm not this piece of shit, like all the rest of it that's choking off real life from emerging around here."

Milo began to speak again but stopped himself and smiled. Finally he offered, "If you believe that, you will never understand what's happening here. In fact, you will never understand the most important lessons of what it means to be alive."

Onyinye wanted to get up in his face but held back. Her years off the grid had hardened her towards charlatans and would-be saviors. Mostly White guys so full of themselves that it was easy for them to project that charismatic, glowing bullshit. They were self-inflated usurpers of a common dream they attached themselves to like leeches to a host. Was Milo one of these? She wasn't sure. He worked quietly and steadily, one metal bar at a time with a focused, selfless determination. But isn't that the way it always started? Then something gets cross-wired and any chance for a breakthrough gets corrupted by *the sacred one's* uncensored belief in himself and the adulation received from others. Her parents were truly committed and the deaths dealt them, the likely outcome for anyone standing up to The System.

Milo was caught up in his preparations and unaware of the firestorm he helped set off in Onyinye. The previous workday ended sourly because of the bad metal rod and his night was disturbed because of it. So, he checked this new batch over and over and made sure he could ping each one of them. But still, he didn't understand why that experience bothered him so much.

"Let's get started," he said. She was more than ready to move on and walked in silence to the next site along the circuit.

Each stake edged them one step further down the path of discovery. He did not take breaks as he had the previous day and he worked at a quicker pace. Occasionally his mind wobbled and he fell into a trance. He once saw himself bounding down a steep mountain, shape-shifting, suspended like a seahorse or a prancing marionette. But when he returned to normal consciousness, it was the side of the barn he stared at with lichen spilling down its north side. Even this did not slow him down for long. He knew he must commune with the next rod, and the one after that, until he found what they were trying to impart to him, or, alternately, he dropped from exhaustion.

The rods and soil knew, knew of the injury he suffered in the car accident as a teen, and the effects it had on him. And each rod and patch of soil guided him back to before the trauma. He saw clearly the disability it caused and also how he falsely perceived his malfunctioning brain to be the source of his personal power. Now a sense of calm flowed through him in a way long forgotten. It was not an uncommon story: well adjusted, normal kid one day and a pariah the next. The schism was complete because the flow, the emotional connection, was cut as if by a surgical procedure. But now the experience of placing the rods reawakened in him those sensations and a world that he felt drawn to. Finally, he could push himself no further and stopped to rest. It was then he noticed the violent distancing from all things was hushed.

"I'm a cyborg?"

"How's that?"

"I'm part machine."

"I know the definition of a cyborg. But what do you mean?"

213

"I had a wire mesh placed inside my brain that allows me to communicate directly with computer data and intelligence. When I'm connected, I can absorb and cross-reference information hundreds of times faster than normal people."

"That explains a lot."

"But it doesn't explain what's going on right now. The reason I'm able to survive these sessions is because I can disassociate from my emotions. Normal people's bodies would become over stimulated and burn up if they were exposed to what I absorb. The thing is, performing these repeated rituals out here, is healing me. There was a shell covering my heart I wasn't even aware of until now, because it's been cracked open. My brain has opened pathways that collapsed because of an injury when I was young. And now I'm able to feel in ways that I was incapable of experiencing. It's breathtaking and almost more than I can manage and process. The blinders have come off."

Onyinye let these comments settle and everything slowed around them. The uncertainty she felt for him disappeared. A gentle wind pushed at them, touching their cheeks along the way. This wind pushed open a door inside her that she always kept guarded and secured.

"I know what it feels like to be cut off," she said, referring to the events that torpedoed her life.

"My parents were diplomats in Nigeria and I was their only child. We left on one of the last planes out of there nine years ago when I was twelve. They said they were employed at a university but I never believed that was all they did. My mother, who could be so much fun back then, was the one who would be the first to make time to play with me, but I could tell she was also experiencing tremendous stress. I believe now that she was a high ranking official and The System drained every ounce of information out of her they could after we fled. The methods of persuasion they used must have been horrible. She grew very depressed. My dad and I tried to make her feel better but nothing we did helped. One day I came home from school and found her in bed, dead from an overdose of narcotics.

"My dad set me up in a safe house run by a resistance cell soon after my mom committed suicide. Before leaving he told me what I had suspected, that they were both double agents and The System was closing in on them. It was too much for mom. He said he needed to tie up some loose ends but then would return and take me away. He left some provisions and money and said he'd be back in a week, two at most. But it was the last time I ever saw him. I've made my way in and out of the secured zones ever since. This feels like home to me now but I will probably move on if I can find a better way to resist The System."

Milo said nothing at first and then offered, "I'm sorry for your loss, really I am. I can only imagine what it's like to be a refugee and then have your only family taken from you." A few moments later he concluded, "I feel honored that you share your story with me."

"You're welcome, magic man. I don't know why I trust you. But, you have a good heart, and seem to get that the more you know, the more you don't know."

She placed her hand on his and both welcomed the connection that helped beat back the demons that had been set free and still lurked in plain sight.

They continued working and by the end of the third day were closing in on the square. Word spread among the disparate outposts. Small groups with their tribe's colors approached the fence, tested it and walked back to their clusters muttering. Milo did not seem to notice and Onyinye was only slightly more interested in the onlookers. They were wary inhabitants of this depleted landscape who ventured out only when word of something extraordinary reached them through infrequently used communication pathways.

RusticMark got out of his land cruiser, a traveling device with a primitive engine but whose suspension was well suited to the disintegrated roadways. He was big. Long, golden hair was held back by a tattered bandana, the right side of his face was discolored either from birth or injury. His attire had a military aspect like those with whom he traveled. At the conclusion of the third day of fence building he introduced himself to Milo.

After pleasantries were exchanged, RusticMark said, simply.

"Cows?"

Which was met with an equally impassive, "Cows."

"But this land isn't naturally grazing farmland."

Milo laughed, "Shit, this land isn't anything anymore. It will work just fine for grazing. And the cows will bend the land to their purpose if managed properly."

Like for everyone else, it was the shock received from the fence that upped Milo's cred for RusticMark. People came up to it like dogs sniffing out a scent, mulling over it until their curiosity was satisfied only by putting their bodies in harm's way. Milo wondered why it was necessary for so many of them to hurt themselves, why they couldn't trust what others told them. They would randomly stick their hands into the hot zone and get what they asked for. Some were not satisfied with that. They would raise their hands as high as they could, quite ingeniously sometimes, hoisting bodies on top of bodies but this sent a shock through them all and jangled the human scaffolding. In the end, they always gathered around the metal posts, analyzing them, conjuring theories to explain what they didn't understand.

"We could use some cattle up our way. We've got a camp on the other side of Leakin. Better land than what you're working with here."

So, Milo's services were in demand. He assessed RusticMark who was probably in his late 30s and had obviously been traveling on the outer fringes for a while. He was ripped but his arm muscles conveyed a fatigued quality; strength and ill health spoke in this single image. There were teeth missing and a scar beneath one eye.

"Sure, I understand. Let's see how this works out. If all goes well, I don't see why we can't replicate this elsewhere."

RusticMark clutched Milo's arm. He wasn't a man used to begging. "I got people who are hungry, barely hanging on. Babies, young ones. This would be a big help."

Milo wanted to offer RusticMark something more, but was uncomfortable with the expectation placed upon him. He began to see all of those on the periphery through that lens. They continued walking towards Milo's bike and saw a small crowd had formed, awaiting the maestro.

"I understand, I really do. Let's get this done and then we'll see where we want to go with it." He held out his hand to RusticMark who grasped it and pulled Milo to him and wrapped him in a bear hug.

Milo, his work done for the day, hopped on his bike and pedaled away.

"So, you've become a cow farmer." Sheila was pouring the wine a little earlier today. She sat at their only table that was no more than a rickety surface for playing cards. Milo poured a glass for himself and then sat slumped onto their couch, the only posture it would allow.

"That's me. Working for the dispossessed, the exiled caste."

"That's good I guess, for now anyway."

"What do you mean? Have you learned something?" Milo had observed that Sheila wouldn't offer too much information unless he showed proper interest.

"I've read reports of The System's having trouble maintaining control. They are being pecked at from a hundred directions. They're not in danger of losing their grip, but it's impacting them. A mutiny here, a slowdown there. In the scheme of things it's not much, but it's something, it's a start."

"I know. I need to get back to that, back to dealing with the bigger question of how to use my power for the greater good. But I need to finish what I started first. I figure I got another 2 - 3 days of work. Hopefully they'll have enough spikes at the salvage yard for me to finish the job. But it feels good to be helping them. And I am gaining power, Sheila. I can feel it growing every day."

Sheila was encouraged every time he spoke like this, every time he found a way to express his sense of becoming, like shedding the outer husk to display the gossamer threads of insight that lay beneath.

The next three days passed in much the same way. Milo would have attained wizard status if he was not so dismissive of the notion. Others approached him in the same way as RusticMark had. He learned to listen with a calm, attentive attitude, which is what they needed as much as anything. There was more life popping up in these remote outposts than he could have imagined, and he observed that many of the people he spoke with were not in regular contact with anyone outside of their group. But it was the prospect of beef cattle and the abundance of healthy food it would provide that caused them to turn out and, for now at least, share their stories with him and each other.

But there were still no cows. What there was was a 20 acre square enclosure, with several flags demarcating the enclosed space. The same held for the crisscrossing lines that ran within the square, setting the larger space into four, five acre square lots.

When the last metal rod was set, Onyinye and Milo gathered their tools and began their trek back to Milo's bike.

They proved an effective work team but still it took six long days to complete. The midday heat was always above 90 degrees. When they started, she didn't think he'd make it. He tired easily and often. She had to help him get to where the next stake needed to be worked. But even at those times he remained in good spirits and joked about how he needed to get into better shape.

Before they reached the bike Milo said, "I'm not going home tonight."

"Why's that?" Onyinye asked, genuinely surprised.

"I need to be here for the cows, be a beacon for them."

She laughed. She was charmed. She felt a cool breeze against her face that seemed to emanate from Milo. *Maybe it is that beacon casting out its signal.* Whereas before his approach had been workmanlike, now he exuded a boyish excitement.

"If you like, I could stay here with you."

Milo considered the offer before responding. "I'd like that very much. But once I start, I won't be very good company. That won't be for a couple of hours, though." And then, after considering it a bit longer, he concluded, "We can spend the first part of the evening getting to know each other better. Mostly we've only talked for short bursts, long enough for me to get to know you but not enough to unlock the mystery surrounding you."

She laughed, "You're kidding me, right? You, with all your crazy power and half-mystical jive, are calling me a mystery. I guess we've both got things we'd like to learn more about."

"I'll need to send out my call from within the paddock but there's not much shade here so why don't we head over to those trees for now."

They walked to the spot that Milo pointed out, a stand of old maples that were still holding on despite the higher temperatures. But they were probably the last, as their seeds failed to root, except for those pushed further north. Instead, the earth, here, was gradually becoming covered with more heat tolerant species.

The shelter of the trees provided the cooler shade they desired. They drank from their canteens and ate from the provisions Milo brought with him. Then they laid back and rested. When they both felt refreshed, Milo spoke again.

"I don't think I ever thanked you properly. I don't think I could have done it without you."

Onyinye laughed, "You could have done it alone. But I wasn't so sure in the beginning if we were going to make it, even with me helping. It was strange watching you through the whole process. You got stronger as you went along. It seemed like you gained mastery of some new-found skill. It was a fascinating thing to watch unfold."

"You're right, I've been learning about my powers but it goes way beyond that. Since that breakthrough on the second day everything coheres and is compelling. But I want to tell you something, too. When you first volunteered I expected you to only stay for a little while, a couple of hours maybe. But you never stopped working, even though I'm sure there were other things you needed to attend to."

She remained silent because he touched on something she always kept sheltered. And then she decided to open that door a little more.

"That first day, I overheard you say something to Jamal. It was something like, 'You can't fix the soil without animals.' This is the same thing my parents told me when I was young. This was one of the primary messages they wanted me to carry forward. It came to have deep meaning for me and I wondered if what you were doing was important for me in some way. Hearing you say this brought me back to them like I haven't felt in a long time, and it's what prompted me to ask if I could help you."

They sat close together, close enough for her to put her hand on his. Hers was the first woman's touch, other than

Sheila's, he experienced since he took on this cyborg identity and he felt renewed by it. He was still human, he told himself. He was still a man.

"I believed in you from the start, although I didn't show it. I defended you against the claims of you being a snake oil salesman performing some sleight of hand, just as I believe in you now, that soon we'll have cows penned up in these yards and they will nurture us and heal the land."

She rose up on her knees and slowly drew him close to her and pressed her lips onto his. He did not expect this and hid his tremendous desire for her from himself. So, he took her gift and returned it, and they stayed locked in the giving and receiving that a kiss can uniquely provide. When it ended, Milo's words contained a confessional tone.

"I used to play head banging music. You would have hated it." They both laughed, which was better than the response he expected.

"Don't be so sure. You'd be surprised by what I find pleasure in," she said with a coy inflection and studied him, enjoying the effects this provocative comment had. He felt her eyes on him, eyes straining to discern more about this man she had just kissed. But this didn't hold her attention for long, as they came together again in a long, more passionate embrace.

"But that's not all I wanted to say," Milo continued, when their hold on each other loosened. "I already told you about my cyborg treatments. What I haven't told you is that they were stopped before I was done. I am halfway into something new which means I am also half who I used to be."

"What happened? Why did they stop?"

"It's hard to explain. I was undergoing a lot of treatments but they ended abruptly because my handlers, part of The Resistance, weren't satisfied with my progress. They were going to change the program to turn into a fighting machine. The woman who ran the program disagreed with this approach and the two of us fled. We've been on the run ever since."

He saw Onyinye's eyebrow raised and he interrupted his narrative to say, "It's not like that. Sheila's more like a mother-protector than what you may be thinking.

"The main point is I'll soon be starting these sessions again, and I'm not sure how I feel about it. I've benefited from being out of the lab because it gave me a chance to develop on my own. At this point I can't tell you how I came up with this idea for the fences and cows. My powers are growing, but growing in a mostly organic way. This half-cyborg, half-human existence is the fuel, but I also sense it could consume me."

She drew away from him slightly as she considered what she was hearing. The fingers on her left hand touched and stroked her cheek as she listened. Onyinye measured her life by the amount of courage she could muster against The System. She'd been on raids to loot warehouses containing weapons and attacks against federal buildings. Part of the reason she was holed up with Jamal and his people was because she was on the run. But even with all these experiences, she had trouble imagining the path Milo had chosen.

"What made you do it? Why'd you let them rewire your brain?" she finally asked, enthralled by the story she was being told.

He laughed. It was a question he'd never been asked, although it was one that haunted him.

"I was tired of being me. It's worse than that really. I was horrified by who I was becoming, how my brain was being molded by hate and a meaningless existence. And I couldn't stop the slide. Except by putting a bullet in my head, which I didn't have the courage to do. So, I chose this when the offer was made. My world has become a different place as a result of what I've learned, more interesting for sure. Jury is still out about whether I like it better or not. But I have no regrets."

They sat in silence which Milo preferred because he could only talk for so long about how different he was. And then he decided it was his turn to learn more about this woman for whom he'd developed feelings. "So, tell me about your tattoos."

Onyinye laughed. "You can't see them, right?"

"Not too well."

"Even with that superhuman vision you must have?"

"Hmmmm."

"I like it that way, really. I know who and what they are and like having them close. And this way I can share them with who I want. Like when you could have tinted glass in car windows. Only sharing with those you want to let into your private space."

Milo's eyes asked the question of whether he would be let in, and Onyinye's smile assured his right of entry.

"Here is my mother and my father," she pointed to the prominent image on one and then the other arm which were brought into focus for him, allowing him to see the details of the images.

"I have images of an equal number of men and women because I align with both feminine and masculine energies. The separation of the two has caused so much harm, and reuniting them is the thing I feel most driven to accomplish. When that happens, healing can begin."

"So, if you want to think of me as a magician, I will think of you as superwoman-man, something The System will never find a way to defeat," Milo replied. "I think that is what I'm learning too. I am being pulled towards various types of energy that, when I examine more closely, spring from the same source. My destiny feels drawn to apprehending that unifying energy."

Onyinye's face broke into a broad smile, setting off feelings of warmth and love in Milo. He reached out his hand and stroked her cheek. At first, they moved imperceptibly closer and then quickly came together in an embrace that began to convey knowledge of the other's lips, hands, and bodies. When the kiss ended, they laid down on the ground, embraced again and allowed the sun to caress them as well.

"So, what's next, Merlin?"

"I do hope that's the last time you call me that?" he said, but was unable to stifle his laughter. After a moment's reflection he continued, "I'm not sure, really. You know, I've never done this before. I'll reach out to the cows using some of the same techniques I used to pair the metal rods. But of course, it'll be on a much larger scale. I'll send my call out into a vast space that will hopefully be recognized and answered. One thing I feel certain of is that I will need to sit out there in the pen that I'm drawing them into."

It was Onyinye's turn to laugh. "You have a talent for making these magical actions seem mundane, as if they were always there within our grasp . . .. I'll be there with you to provide whatever support I can."

Milo felt she had touched upon something important but wasn't sure exactly what it was, and tried to work his way back to it.

"Maybe that's because once you can do something, it is no longer mysterious in the same way. On the other hand, everything we do contains some essential mystery. Every breath, every movement, every encounter like the one we are sharing right now."

They held each other quietly . . . feeling no need to say more for several minutes until Onyinye broke the spell.

"When do we start?"

"Tonight. But I want to rest here for a while first. I've scoped out a little gully that suits my needs, provides a little shelter. I wish there was some shade for tomorrow but I'll just have to prevail against the sun and the heat. And, for whatever time you would like to join me, I'd like to sense your presence with me."

Side by side, they let their bodies relax. The ground was not soft, but there was a lightness to their spirits that allowed them to rest easy on the ground. Milo fell into a drowsy sleep and Onyinye followed once she worked out the logistics for erecting a lean-to to shelter him from the direct sun the next day.

At 2:00 AM Milo woke, the effects of a dream still lingering. He'd been running beneath an eagle that was gliding right above him. But he couldn't keep up, and raised his arm in its direction, just as it moved out of his range of vision. The dreamer's inability to soar projected a familiar sense of yearning onto conscious reality. But the vision soon faded as the sluggish dreamer peered up at the moonless sky, dappled in stars. He felt alert and happy, and looked forward to performing this final part of his mission. He tried not to rouse Onyinye but she heard him stir and was soon up on an elbow trying to shake free from her abbreviated slumber.

"What's up?" she managed.

"It's time," was all he said, like a child finally let free on Christmas morning to receive gifts that were ephemeral up to this point. He knew that this frenetic excitement would burn him out, make it difficult to do the necessary work. But for now, he was powerless to rein it in, and really, he had no desire to.

"You looked pleased with yourself," Onyinye said after she sized up the glow surrounding him.

"I haven't done anything yet, helped anybody, even though I can do all these things. That's about to change. So, yeah, I'm feeling good, have a little kick in my step."

"Sure, let's do this thing. . .. Let's see what you got."

The stars were almost enough to light their way but not quite. "Here, take my hand. I can drop my vision down to night vision spectra. It's not pretty but I can get us there safely."

So, they ventured off, hand in hand. He, joking and cajoling, she, not so sure because her vision was clear only to her thighs and the ground held jutting outcroppings of unnatural materials that could cut and bruise. But she trusted him, trusted his glib descriptions of the detritus they passed along the way.

"This is good," Milo said. He had guided them into the center of the northwest quadrant after removing some spikes at the corner to allow them to enter. The night air was good, alive. He twirled slowly, looking in all directions.

"Are you ready?" Onyinye asked.

"I am," he said. Milo turned to Onyinye and hugged her with the strength buzzing through him and she sent that same energy back at him.

"Then you should do this now."

"Ok, I will."

Milo sat on the ground cross legged, his hands fell to his side, touching the ground softly. Within minutes his eyes closed and a peaceful hum escaped from his lips.

Is that the beacon? Will that be heard across the land? Will the call be answered? These were Onyinye's thoughts, along with realizing there would be no more sleep for either of them on this night.

The sound was not the beacon, he was the beacon. The air communicated the needs of this community and the ground shimmered with that same message. Like a beating heart, he pulsated as one with all life touching the earth. But also like a beating heart, it was not a simple pump action. The beat was to provide a cadence so the entire body could pulse as one and extend his reach with each repetition. Like drops of water falling into a pond from a leaf's edge, each pulse collected and then rippled out further and further.

For hours Milo followed the spreading tentacles, spreading along synapses both seen and unseen. He was drawn by their unity of purpose that was far greater than anything he had ever experienced, with a cohesion grander than anything his cyborg mind could conceive of. By the time the sun began to rise he could no longer say where the message extended because of its vastness. The broadening scope did not increase his physical strain because the beacon only needed to stay steady and true, nature's network would do the rest. But the messaging feedback increased exponentially and his focus was pulled deeper and deeper into this wild conversational hub.

By mid-morning Onyinye erected the simple lean-to she envisioned the night before. Milo was in a deep trance, and did not hear her digging to set the posts for the covering they would shelter under. It concerned her that he was so far removed, but would not let her mind consider whether he was doing himself harm. She hoped he could resurface when it was time to do so.

Interested spectators ringed the periphery as word of Milo's endeavor spread. Most did not stay long, for them it was an amusing sideshow, a diversion from the constant struggle to survive. But there was a small contingent who stayed longer, uncertain why they felt compelled to do so. Except that some yearning was quenched by that figure removed from the horrors that were the X-Zone's shared story, because the story he was engaged in seemed beyond what was possible. Soon a few of them came within the circumference, entering through the section of fence where the charge was deactivated, and sat around Milo and Onyinye. They were not shielded from the sun, but felt less in harm's way here than in their lives beyond the fence.

They watched in contemplative awe. Only in the absence of stress do you see it clearly. Only when there is a tear in the suffering, does the pressure it places on you ease. A handful of men and women felt compelled to stay, and soak in this new experience that provided healing for a sickness that had no name.

Because what they felt was Milo channeling his pulse deep into the nature sphere. More importantly, they experienced the pulse that connected the seen and unseen world. There was no discussion because they needed to meditate upon that pulse, caress it, follow it.

Milo stayed deep within the pulse. Onyinye got up to cover the food she brought him but for which he showed no interest. She left the water uncovered, hoping he would take some. In this heat it would not be long before he became dehydrated.

Morning turned into afternoon and then evening. Milo had not stirred, nor was he just Milo any longer. He swam with the mitochondria of the earth, the energetic waves binding the atmosphere. He would be forever marked by this experience that spoke to him of the connectedness of all living things, which most of us suspect but don't experience. The stable of followers solidified, and were almost as immovable as Milo himself. Into the night, first twilight and then full on. Bursting mystery. The small group of 9 all fasted in support of Milo's effort. A little water, no conversation. Attunement to the sanctity of this event. Through this night which might continue for an eternity or an instant.

But morning did come, as did slumber for the observers, but not for Milo who remained steadfast. Onyinye was the first to see and then others followed the direction of her gaze. A black and white-spotted heifer was approaching from the north, stepping quickly over the land, which was not entirely hospitable. The others were up now, dumbfounded, except for Milo who stayed in the same position he had assumed since this started. It was years since large animals roamed here, especially on this forsaken section of land. And the extreme joy it brought exceeded any rational explanation, exploding with a sense of reunion.

She reached the gate and then entered the enclosure. Those standing around Milo cheered as did the few who returned to the periphery. At the moment she crossed the threshold, Milo returned to consciousness.

He looked at the young cow with satisfaction. "More will follow," is all he said as he reached for the water goblet. He sensed it seep into his body, rejuvenate him and then travel out into the space where he had just been communing. Then he pointed towards the horizon to land that was decimated, denuded, and saw two older cows ambling towards them, not in any rush like the younger cow who was already getting the lay of the land. The first cow was met with stunned silence by the crowd but when the next two joined her they were ready for them and jumped and yelled and hugged each other. People looked around and sightings were made in all directions, except those gazing towards the region controlled by The System. They walked and mooed and seemed generally pleased with themselves. This easy pleasure spilled out over everything and everyone. Even the limited, decimated landscape appeared wholly different, ready to recover itself. Spirit-blooms erupt when regeneration can be imagined.

"You done good, Merlin," Onyinye said and wrapped her arms around him, tentatively at first because she wasn't sure of his strength, but when she felt him respond she went all in.

He smiled, allowing her this little joke but said, "Last time?" To which she responded in accord, "Last time."

But she would not hold back from giving voice to what brought on this comment. "Can you sense what's going on here? Do you realize you've given these people their first ray of hope in a very long time? It's a gift you've given them, a marvelous gift."

Milo accepted the compliment humbly and then said, "I want to name the first cow that entered, Lagos." This was the city that was Onyinye's home in Nigeria before they fled.

"I would like that," she said. "It is not just their spirit you have touched. I feel my own blossoming in ways I thought were no longer possible."

She put her hands on his face, drew him towards her and they kissed tenderly.

Chapter 17

Two days passed since the cows, 12 in all, were situated in the paddocks. Jamal put his considerable knowledge on display by taking charge of providing the herd with water and setting up a rotational grazing schedule. Milo was feeling the afterglow of doing something worthwhile. He was returning from a visit to Pedro's restaurant where he was treated to an all expense paid gourmet lunch experience. He wanted to work off some of the meal and took an indirect path to the apartment. When he turned a corner of a deserted street he was met by a nightmare and a dream. K2 straddled the sidewalk, a wry, corrosive smile curled the edges of his lips.

"Don't go running off into that tear in the sky I chased you through last time," K2 said, as the smile spread across his rugged face. "They may want me to kill you but I'm not going to do that, not now anyway."

Milo thought about escaping but didn't move, because he knew he wanted to see K2 again.

"Well, that's good to hear. I wasn't sure how healthy it would be for me if we crossed paths again."

Milo assessed K2 and although he was still powerfully built, he was clearly diminished in some way; a loss of muscle, a narrowing of his face.

"How did it go for you in the hospital?" Milo asked.

"I was in a coma for days. They ran tests on me, and sensed I was different . . . you know what I mean. Then when I came out of it, they treated me like a lab rat. It was pretty harsh. My handlers expunged all references to me when I didn't return. So, the doctors thought I was a psychopath when my alibi didn't check out. Decided I was good research material. There was no other way out so I contacted you. You may have saved my life so I want to thank you for that."

Milo let himself relax a little, more than he ever expected he could in the presence of this killing machine.

"You're welcome. I sent word as soon as I received your message. I knew I could be exposing myself but had to do it, and am not sorry I did. I guess it's because we're the only ones, we share something, even as we've sworn allegiance to opposite sides and you're sworn to eliminate me."

"Your side, my side," K2 said and then emitted a guttural laugh. "You really believe that shit, don't you? You liberators will create a new order based on justice and all those other lofty ideals."

"I do, I have to," Milo responded, aware of the mild discomfort saying that caused him.

"It's just different heads of the same monster, if you ask me."

"Not true. There are seeds of resistance that are founded on better principles. But we need to come together before we can act boldly to destroy our oppressors."

"The overwhelming majority of people only respond to what they can see, what they experience with their own senses. That's even true of the smart ones in your orbit. Average people respond only to the towering images of President Meld, The System, The Newer Machine. You will never be more powerful than the ingrained images that they superimpose on the back of people's brains. This conditioning has had hundreds of years to weave its way into our DNA, and now we're wired to be disconnected from each other in any type of meaningful way. We've *progressed* to the point where we simply don't need each other, for anything. Any other belief system has been cast so far out of the mainstream as to not exist in any meaningful way. Sunday church for the few who cling to that illusion, traditions that offer nothing substantive. So I say, hitch your ride to whoever is in power because it doesn't matter who that somebody is."

"That's some cynical shit. I'm not going there, man. Can't."

"Suit yourself. Maybe even your eyes will be opened to what's real someday. Then you'll see how impossible your goals are. How, to be honest, embarrassing they are," K2 said with disgust and a sense of finality, which allowed him to move the conversation in a different direction.

"I wanted to give you something to show my gratitude for saving me because, to be honest, I wouldn't have done the same for you. I wanted it to be something you'd find useful and now that we talked, I know I made a good choice."

Milo listened and was unsure what to make of this. Before he could pose a question, K2 proceeded.

You're going to have to open up the port that connects us. I have information I want to share with you. Information you'll find interesting.

Milo looked at K2. This could be a trap. He could introduce a virus or trojan horse. But he decided he would override these concerns in favor of the trust he felt and wanted to believe in.

It took only seconds to reconfigure the portal security and when he was done, he shook his head slightly in K2's direction to signal he was ready. The surge was hard like an angry flare. The portal's processor tried to throttle back the throughput several times but each time he reopened the connections. At some point they both reached out and took hold of each other's shoulders with outstretched hands to ground the transfer and stabilize the packets of information flowing from the wire mesh in K2's brain to the one in Milo's.

For 10 minutes this went on and then the final handshake was sent and the transmission line grew silent.

"You'll decipher it quick enough, but I'll tell you now that that is the entire architecture of The Newer Machine. I'm not sure what you'll do with it, but I'm looking forward to seeing what you come up with." He paused and let out a coarse laugh. "And don't waste time. They have plans for changing it and are moving quickly. Once The Newer Machine is upgraded these schematics will be much less accurate."

Milo's mind raced, deconstructing the information from the feed. But this process would take hours, possibly days. Until then his questions would be scatter-shot and of little value. Plus, he was bone tired, drained by this data feed that he had not prepared for.

"Thanks, we'll find a use for it. And I hope it never gets traced back to you."

K2 laughed. "They have no idea. I mean too much to them for them to consider I'd do something like this. But I have to split. They keep tabs on me and I don't want to raise their suspicions."

They held each other's gaze and K2 unexpectedly gave Milo a brief, powerful hug. "You might not want to admit it but you and me, we're brothers. There's no one else like us in the world. We're tied at the hip, or really, by the wire nibs attached to our brain stems. I'm not crying or complaining about it. Just sayin'."

"Yeah, man," Milo replied. "I didn't want to admit it but I've known this for a while. Just didn't know what to do with it. Still don't."

"Like I said, just let it roll." And then before ducking down the alley way, "See you on the wire."

Milo was left to wonder what future interactions with K2 would lead to.

Chapter 18

"What's up?" Sheila greeted Milo. She was sitting at her makeshift desk, four tray tables with computer hardware that she could rearrange any way that suited her. She was able to do some work remotely and was performing regression tests on portions of the neuralBlast software that had received system upgrades.

"I met him weeks ago and just saw him again."

"Who's that?

"K2."

Sheila stopped what she was doing and studied him before asking, "How'd that go? I'm glad, and a little surprised, you're here to tell me about it."

"The first time I thought he was going to kill me. That's what he's programmed to do, but something held him back from executing that directive. He grabbed me by the throat and threw me against a wall. But then he started talking to me. We didn't talk long, but it was long enough for me to feel like I understood something about him, and I'm pretty sure he felt the same about me.

"What happened next still freaks me out. The cards started flipping and then there was a tear in the fabric of normal experience, big enough for me to jump through. It elevated me into what I think of as *interspace*. But K2 was quick enough and followed me into it.

"At first, he chased me with the same fury that I felt when he dug his fingers into my throat. But after a couple of minutes I could tell he was digging it. We were cloud dippin'." Milo made motions like swimming underwater, except what they discovered was how to be free from the constraints of gravity. Milo continued to describe their journey and then how K2 got sick, and how Milo dropped him off at the hospital.

"I know it's not your style, but you should have killed him. Because I don't think you can ever trust him to not take you out. His mind is imbalanced, intoxicated by violence. His humanity is shattered."

Milo considered the recommendation. "I don't think he's the killer you make him out to be or that they want him to be. I sensed that when we made contact the first time, and even more today. He recognizes there is more to our power, his power, than they intended. He's asking questions his handlers would certainly censure if they knew. And once I picked up on this, killing him wasn't an option. In fact, I helped get him rescued." His gaze turned from her, as he realized this was something he didn't want to explain further or justify to her.

Sheila was shaken by this news and it made her uncomfortable in a way she couldn't explain. How much had he kept from her, how much did he continue to keep to himself?

"There's another reason I wish you'd taken out K2, and that's because I don't think K3 will be coming online anytime soon, or maybe ever."

This was the nightmare they shared. Managing the threat K2 posed was hard enough. But they were afraid The System would figure out ways to create even more diabolical monsters, or devise a cloning process. If that happened it would be harder, or impossible, to keep Milo safe.

"I didn't want to tell you before I was sure what I did worked, but it has. Before I left The System, I planted time bombs in the software. Before I set them off, I needed to make sure all the backups were destroyed. For the last 2 months the deep system backups of the file systems related to the neuralBlast project were redirected to null source locations.   It took two months for all of these to be permanently deleted. That milestone just passed and the software bombs were set off. By now The System has a pretty good idea of how bad things are. My guess is it will take them

1 – 2 years to get back to where they were, which is an eternity in this field. The project will likely be disbanded before then."

"But how do you know this? How do you know they didn't find and remove your bombs?"

"I can't be 100% sure, but almost. Deep within the code I sent an encrypted message to an untraceable site when the mission was accomplished. I received that today. It contained a detailed audit of what I just described. From what I can tell it was 100% successful. Bottom line: It is just you and K2 for the foreseeable future and maybe forever if they can't get their funding renewed. And you just squandered a chance to neutralize the only force on earth that rivals yours. I just hope you never regret it."

"Listen," Milo said, his voice rising with frustration. "Say what you want about K2, but he just gave me the entire architecture of The Newer Machine. I haven't resolved it fully but I'm betting it's legit. You know what we can do with this? We could bust them up good."

Milo thought for a moment and then said, "I see now how important it is to strike against The Newer Machine. The System's capacity for evil had me by the throat and I sensed the malevolence it's capable of. I've been studying TNM since I realized what a hold it has on everything and everyone. It's been a full year since the last upgrade was applied to TNM. A glitch in that upgrade process went undetected and caused outages and loss of functionality. The damage was contained, but still sent shock waves through society. Markets collapsed that are just now recovering. It made clear to anyone still able to think critically that The Newer Machine had threaded its way into every crevice of our lives and controlled many of the things people rely upon."

"That's outstanding! If what you say is true this is a once in a lifetime opportunity!"

Sheila considered all she was told and then concluded, "And now we've got to do the work. Go and analyze what K2 gave you and then we'll decide how best to proceed."

Milo nodded his head. It was good to have reached this agreement with her and get past the parts about K2 he thought she could never understand.

After a couple of days of processing the download, he strode into the kitchen and announced to Sheila, "How soon can you hook me into the network at Hopkins? I need another session to figure out how to break through TNM's security," Milo told Sheila.

"Probably in the next few days. But I'm hesitant to say that because the last 10 percent of the work can take 50 percent of your time, if you know what I mean . . .. What are you planning to do with this information?"

Milo hesitated and chose his words carefully. "I've been studying the process used to upgrade The Newer Machine. The only time The System saw its control really threatened was after the last upgrade was installed. They are all about what an aberration that was, how all the glitches have been worked out, and doing whatever they can to calm people's fears. The new features in the next upgrade are being hailed as awe inspiring, life-changing, affecting every aspect of people's lives, blah, blah, blah."

Milo paused and looked directly at Sheila with a conviction he'd never before experienced while interacting with her.

"I bet," he continued, "that if you get me hooked into a neuralBlast session I could figure out how to disrupt the upgrade. I'm not sure how yet, but the system should be most vulnerable when it is cutting over from old to new. If I can listen in on their activities I might be able to interrupt them at the very least, but potentially I could do real damage. And the schematics K2 gave me provide insight into every nook and cranny."

Sheila put her coffee mug down while continuing to assess Milo. Her image of him was like a lock whose tumblers suddenly aligned into place, a slot machine resolving to the highest prize. Even with all his talents and computational skills his thought process had lacked maturity, and because of that he had not earned her deepest respect. Until this moment. So much about this plan developed outside of her purview, like the interactions with K2, which she would not have condoned. She didn't have the imagination to conjure this scheme. It was a plan that evolved organically, culled from experience, both human and superhuman. She beheld this young man, sensing his emergence in eyes that burned with desire and purpose. At the same time, she sensed a lessening of her own vitality, a fault driven through the tectonic plates of her layered self, as she was left to observe a drama to which until moments before, she played a leading role. Maybe someday she could feel like she was not such a monster for fundamentally changing Milo. But that glacier of self-incrimination would not yet yield.

"It would be wonderful if you were able to accomplish this."

"I'm really happy you feel that way," he said, still not fully sensing the depths of meaning that lay below her words. And then, returning to the thoughts crowding his mind, "I've got plenty of prep to do for the session. There's a lot of information on the shadow web about The Newer Machine. Some of the programmers involved in the original build went rogue and posted enough for me to gain valuable insights. Hopefully, the failures and glitches in the last upgrade disrupted its web of security in ways that haven't been fully stitched back together. Before I can damage it, I need to find ways to infiltrate it. But if this all comes together people will sense freedom for the first time in a long time. And once they sense it, The System won't easily be able to clamp the lid back on."

"You're a soldier now, we both are, stepping up to take down the machine," she said, as if just realizing how far down this path they'd traveled. "I didn't see this coming, but am thankful that you took the initiative. This has become way bigger than anything I imagined, but that doesn't mean we should shrink away from it. Let me know if you run into any roadblocks. I'll do what I can to get you what you need."

Milo got right to work, which meant repackaging the information provided by K2. He retrieved the data in manageable chunks that he scanned and stored in regions of his brain made available by neuralBlast technology. His first area of focus came when he learned about The Deep Eye, the government program that managed all the State's clandestine operations; he placed all of its network configurations in a highly accessible area of storage in his brain.

But an unexpected diversion occurred when he analyzed the mountain of information describing TNM's psychological underpinnings and its accretion of power. He learned how every effort was made to mold citizens into ciphers. Even Milo had trouble keeping track of the myriad ways people were kept from the state's intent, for fear of what would happen if enough people realized their brains had been hijacked.

The primary mechanism for ensuring control was to periodically create a choreographed "chaotic" condition and then manipulate people's reaction so they end up back where The System needed them to be. The iconic image of the melting pot, originating hundreds of years before, was back in vogue. But this version was much more aggressive, expressed in images of a smoldering cauldron, and the wisps of humanity cast out of the churn were dealt with harshly. These manufactured events usually required injury and death. Once joined with the System's self-righteous narrative the outcome, sealed in blood, was nearly assured. This approach proved to be enormously effective, but not entirely.

TNM was extending its power across more and more of the technologically advanced world, nurturing it with news, sports and art, much of it accurate and entertaining. TNM provided people with ways to safely experience virtual adventure. Matters related to sex and other human drives were given ample, if more discreet, outlets. The System smothered expressions of moral outrage because it learned, after an epoch-spanning period of missteps, that they made people less malleable. Everything bent to TNM's true intent: changing the way people act and behave, and devaluing all other sources of information, entertainment and spiritual sustenance.

Achieving these goals was possible because of the maturation of the artificial intelligence under-girding The Newer Machine, the so-called Algorithms of Life. This was something Milo needed no introduction to. It was the brute force backbone that everyone referred to, a system of numbers and categories that encapsulated every aspect of human experience. Virtual games showed people that The Algorithms of Life knew them better than they knew themselves. It was championed as the better arbiter of information and was nearly universally accepted as such. And for those that did not acquiesce easily, there were an abundance of tools to expose, humiliate and silence them.

Sometimes the new directions helped the general populace, usually not. But TNM would never allow the hardships caused by these directives to be the dominant narrative, and sometimes force was required to reestablish order. When this happened, the masses were expected to look away from the spreading violence and respond indolently. Their news feeds were filled with insipid, TNM-inspired controversies, which had the effect of vaporizing deeper, unpleasant thoughts that might have crossed the barrier into consciousness and resulted in action.

This level of compliance could be traced back to TNM's predecessor, the free internet, and the way it was disbanded with the assent of the vast majority of the population. At the end, all anyone could see was the insidious effect it had. The "free" internet was anything but, as it was programmed to maximize profit and its search algorithms designed to fulfill that goal. Which meant keeping people connected as long as possible so they could ingest advertisements, register clicks, and satisfy related metrics. Which meant feeding the news and points of view that <u>each individual</u> found agreeable! The level of granularity of siloed information found a whole new level of efficiency. When people were forced to pull out of their insular warp of information, they were confronted by chaos and mayhem, when they expected a mirror of their siloed universe, which they knew to be correct and righteous. This set off an avalanche of infantile wails and screeds, overwhelming any attempt at critical thinking. The free internet simply had to go, and nobody grieved when the plug was finally pulled.

During the free internet's death throes the country descended into such a state of chaos that there was widespread agreement that any shared point of view was better than the anarchy unleashed in surges of violence and brutality.

What better invitation could there be for The Newer Machine . . .

The free internet, for all its faults, still encouraged the top performers to think critically about important questions. But these issues received a full blackout with the rise of TNM, followed by a near perfect amnesiac stupor. To be clear, this was what was always promoted for the vast majority for a very long time. The tools prior to TNM were less sophisticated and correspondingly less effective. They included chaining students to crushing debt so they could be cowed until they sacrificed their freedom in return for debt repayment. The less educated were held in line with the well documented levers of eternal economic instability.

But these older techniques were seriously flawed because the hands that controlled the machinery were identifiable, observed directly. This direct gaze could and often did become a critical gaze. Puppet leaders forgot the playbook for convincing citizens that the degree of freedom they were allotted was just the right amount. Flare ups that threatened the old order were rare but not without precedent.

The Newer Machine fixed much of that. It provided convincing evidence that it was able to make better decisions about our wants and needs, freeing people from the responsibility of making these important decisions themselves. Everyone knew that we could not compete with the prowess of technological data-gathering and processing power. This was a gateway to allowing TNM to decide a range of issues such as which social justice issue had the most merit, who were the most deserving candidates, what health regimens should be followed. At its most insidious, it invalidated personal experience and any ritual that connected individuals to a larger community such as an ancestral past, the natural world, a unifying presence. This was never explicitly stated as a goal of TNM but for the few people whose vision wasn't totally co-opted, this truth was undeniable. The vast majority, and this includes all but the very highest strata of society, felt insignificant, beholden. No individual could match, or even conceive of the consummate talents that reigned within The Newer Machine. Here was a religion that announced itself by displaying its mastery of the known world to everyone all the time. And no individual, by him or herself, could match its majesty. Once revered, artists were now seen as providing a primitive form of entertainment with no greater purpose or message and, in fact, had become something of an embarrassment.

Milo kept digging, determined to understand what The System wanted and where it was headed. These questions confounded him even as he plowed through more data than any human could. But then the answer came to him from a knowledge-engineered paper produced by The Newer Machine itself. The lead engineers asked it to define what it believed was its primary mission, and its response was simple and elegant. It existed simply to allow The System to do whatever it wanted, whenever it wanted. People needed to believe they were free, but that freedom needed to be regulated as if it were a tourniquet that could be tightened or loosened at will. The modalities for achieving this needed to be deployed surreptitiously. When The System didn't require compliance for acts like declaring war or stiffening economic sanctions, The Newer Machine loosened pressure and served up a cornucopia of manufactured enjoyments, whether in the form of new moves to old dances or old moves with a new flair. The content really didn't matter. What did matter was keeping the zeitgeist bright and shiny, the thing The Newer Machine compelled all participants to worship and defend.

But then the paper pirouetted and landed awkwardly. It criticized itself and its handlers and delineated a series of botched exercises of power. The reason was TNM had reached the limits of its effectiveness. The simple truth was that too many humans would evade sufficient levels of control given the current toolset. If the toolset was not enhanced, current trends indicated control would decrease and resistance would eventually gain an upper hand. But there was, of course, an alternative.

People needed to be controlled directly. Even with all its technological wizardry, The Newer Machine was aware of a deep pulse within human consciousness it was never able to silence. Its origins and purpose were just as much a mystery to it as it was to any sentient being roaming the earth. Milo read these sections and was taken by the tone of indignation rising above the scientific liturgy. Control needed to be meted out more directly if The System's goal of total dominance would be achieved.

Eighteen months following the publication of this paper, word spread about the capabilities that would be available in this version of TNM. There was nothing organic about the way the message was dispensed, but every effort was made to make it look that way. Infomercials, which were the main staple of news broadcasts, promoted a narrative about the revolutionary chip that would soon be available. Inserted at the base of the skull and beside the spine, it could be utilized to create extraordinary experiences. The news broadcasts contained scenes of someone said to be the recipient of a prototype of the chip, and who remained masked through the episodes. He performed incredible feats of strength and endurance that required heightened sensory and computational capability. Even before Milo heard the voice, he knew it was K2. But the chip would not be used like neuralBlast technology, which was a ruse and sales pitch. The chip would be used as an agent of control, pure and simple.

Chapter 19

Two days later Onyinye infiltrated the border and reconnected with Milo. She did not need to worry about surveillance scans as long as she stayed within his orbit of obfuscation. They sat close to each other on the sofa, reading from their devices when Sheila walked in, just a couple of days after Onyinye got settled. Sheila was taken by the casual comfort they displayed with each other. Onyinye was fiercely independent, just as she was, but also found it easy to show her affection for Milo and handled him gently when necessary. Sheila was glad to have her aboard, another ally in their struggle.

"We're ready for your next session. We can do it as early as tomorrow, if you like," Sheila announced.

Before Sheila walked in, Milo had been reading a news release about future plans to insert chips into people. The article advertised how it would allow people to acquire new skills, perform health diagnostic tests, and connect with each other on numerous virtual platforms. The tourniquet was tightening.

"Great, let's do it tomorrow then."

"OK, I figured that's what you'd say, so I started putting the pieces in place," Sheila responded. "It's interesting how you've come to look at these sessions. They used to drain and disorient you so much. It was like you were getting chemo. But you're different about it now."

Milo reflected before answering. "You're right. There are things about it that are very unpleasant. You go in so deep, it feels like you could blow yourself up in the process. But it's also a rush. . . all that information and emotion churning through you as if you were riding a monster wave. But more than that, I have a reason for doing it now, whereas before I was searching, trying to figure out what I was fishing for."

"Back when we were on the farm you gave me a different impression of these sessions," Onyinye reflected. "You seemed concerned that they were robbing you of your humanity."

Milo stiffened at the memory of this conversation. "You're right. I know I said that, but I'm not so in touch with that right now."

Onyinye probed further, "So, is it the rush, pursuit of knowledge, or is it a sense of purpose that caused you to cast off your concerns?"

"It's all of those things, but more, too. You see, I have a job to do, something no one else is capable of. So, I need to keep grinding, pushing into it and hope that I'm not damaged along the way."

Onyinye looked at him as he spoke, as concern and admiration spread across her face. She then nestled up to him and drew him to her, wrapping him in her arms, sending out all the love and energy she had to give.

The next morning he was back at it, locked and loaded, determined to figure out how to take down The Newer Machine. They entered the computer lab that was converted for their use. It was down a very long corridor on the building's lowest level; it was easy to see how their work in this subterranean chamber could go unnoticed. There was a cot barely long enough for Milo to lay on and a couple of IVs that contained electrolytes and a mild sedative. Two computers sat on tables a foot away from the cot. Jack Robbins, Sheila's colleague, who made this clandestine setup possible, was working at one of them but stood and exchanged greetings with Milo and Onyinye, who he had not met before.

"We're going bare-bones here," Milo said, having completed his sweep of the layout.

"You were expecting The Ritz, maybe?" Sheila joked back.

"I guess I was hoping to not feel like the network that was going to pour gigabytes of data into my brains wasn't held together with duct tape."

"Baling wire, maybe, duct tape, never."

Truth was, Milo had all the confidence in Sheila he needed. If she said they were ready, then he would go, but not without a playful jab or two. Milo laid down on the bed, and was strapped in. Onyinye took a seat close to him. She felt something like a rock star's girlfriend, aimlessly waiting to see what magic would be wrought by this session. It was a role she did not enjoy but did not balk at. Milo, himself, reinforced the rock star motif. He felt cocky, already anticipating the rush of experience coursing through him, leading him down paths he could not anticipate. And Sheila played the producer, confidently modulating the tempo, establishing the framework within which explosive energy would be allowed to career freely.

Sheila started the IVs and attached electrodes to his body. They monitored him for 15 minutes, enough time for him to register a sense of calm.

"You ready, Milo? Because we can start as soon as you are," Sheila said. She sat beside Jack, and between them, they worked the software that monitored Milo's body's responses and the connectivity to external data stores.

Milo softened for a minute and motioned to Onyinye with his free hand. She came over to him and placed her hand in his, and then guided his arm back to his side.

"You'll learn what needs to happen next. And then we'll get it done together," Onyinye whispered soothingly to him.

She did not wait for his response, but instead hovered close to his face, and then kissed him gently on the lips.

"Everything's happened so quickly," Milo said with a bewildered tone. "I hope someday we can slow down and just focus on each other."

She smiled in the vibrant, coy way that made his heart leap. "We will, my Magic Man, if that's what's meant to be. But until then we will live the way we are called to live and soar in harmony every moment we are together." Her hair fell across her face and as she brushed it away, she leaned in and kissed him briefly again, so softly he was not sure when it ended and when he was left with just its tingling effects.

Milo took a deep breath and lingered another moment, and then bellowed, "Let's go Sheila. Rev those engines!"

They started with two processors, flaring Milo's nostrils as he took in long draws of breath and dove in. The parameters of his deep dive were focused on The Newer Machine, and there was no reason for him to do anything but glide along with the information being fed to him, even as the twists and turns presented surprises.

The history of control sped past. When The System first rolled out The Newer Machine it had global aspirations, and grew accordingly. It proposed a global dialectic aimed at harnessing all things. But regional problems, caused by artificially imposed borders, occurred with sufficient frequency to force the elites to rethink their approach. This resulted in the current balkanization of the world. President Meld consolidated power in what was the eastern half of the United States. Similar fiefdoms were established around the world and communication between them, except at the highest levels, was severely curtailed and closely monitored. These smaller parcels were slowly coming under control. But the broader plan was to tie them back together when the right technology came online. The chip was being promoted as a game changer, the leading candidate for achieving this goal.

Each fiefdom asserted control in a similar fashion, and something like The Newer Machine was being used in all developed enclaves. When the processors available to Milo increased to three and then four, the additional parallel processing power allowed him to pursue these various agents of control, their relative effectiveness and evolution. Then his inquiries hit upon the recent advances in The Newer Machine. The software was initially created to support a single instance. But over time, the software became much more sophisticated and could run multiple instances. This was the new game, and TNM was a leading contender. It was being sold to other governments as a way to maintain control at a fraction of the cost of doing it themselves. The core software ran the majority of the system but "exits" were inserted at key junctures, and this was where local bits could be inserted. Here, local customs and celebrity gossip were given a small window of exposure, enough to give people something familiar without diluting the essential messaging significantly.

The multi-instance capability was the game that held everyone's attention now. Those first out of the gate with it, did everything to enhance their position. A few in the second tier tried to distinguish themselves with "best of breed" features, while the rest of the countries lagged behind with little hope of being able to compete in this most crucial of games.

His mind flipped back to TNM's upgrade process. His extensive knowledge of its current-state allowed him to grasp the upcoming changes, and what steps would be performed to accomplish the upgrade. He traversed the areas of TNM's network that allowed access, which conformed to the schematics provided by K2. He found a backdoor to a new server array and ascertained it would be brought online to manage the new features. These servers were to lay dormant with the newly installed software and be brought online when the upgrade assembled all the necessary peripherals the new features needed to be operational.

His inquiry shifted to the revolutionary intent of this upgrade and then he learned of the role he, himself, was supposed to have played in it. This last bit of intel sent his vitals rising to levels never before seen and, if not for his dissociative skills, would have fried his brain. When Sheila saw the sudden surge and strain on his body, she incrementally de-accelerated the computing power to safe levels. He remained unconscious, even after they disengaged him from the machines. After an hour he was able to move so they rented a vehicle and got him back to the apartment. Once he hit his bed, he did not move for 24 hours.

Sheila and Onyinye took turns sitting with Milo. Sheila was there when he first stirred. Onyinye heard him moving and Sheila motioned to her to come and take her seat. She went to fetch a fresh glass of water, but that was a ruse for relinquishing her seat, and both women knew it. Their eyes met momentarily and a recognition passed between them. They already respected each other and it was reinforced by this gesture.

After several minutes of letting his eyes roll this way and that, Milo displayed some interest in conversing.

"Who hit me with a sledgehammer?"

Onyinye laughed and Sheila responded, "Whatever it was, I think it was self-inflicted."

"Oh yeah, now I remember," Milo said, peeling back the remaining layers of slumber that still blanketed him. "I lost my shit when I realized they wanted me to be the mascot for the chips they want to insert into everyone."

"How's that?" Sheila responded, the comment seizing her attention.

"You think you had control of the project until the very end, but you didn't. They've been planning this chip for a long time. It's why they kept funding your neuralBlast project. They were looking for me to *wow* people with my magnificence. They wanted me to make the people comfortable with the idea of being a cyborg. 'See all the cool things he can do. See how smart he is.' The fact that the neuralBlast technology and the chip have nothing to do with each other is irrelevant. I was supposed to normalize the cyborg experience. And this would have aided them in their real quest for domination through technology, and with this chip in particular.

"But when the project faltered, they lost faith in your ability to deliver on time. They decided to trade in the Renaissance Man motif for Super Warrior. He would be simpler to manage and be brought online much faster. And with a little alteration to the messaging, the warrior could provide almost the same level of usefulness."

"Fuck!" Sheila said, after a moment's reflection. "I knew I was being played, but I had no idea what the game was. I never trusted anyone with all of what I was doing. But, I believed we could have helped save the world if I could have continued working with you. Hearing this reminds me of another revelation I had: the idea that I could pull this off by myself was hubris. In fact, I thought I was the only one who could get it done."

"You're both doing good work now," Onyinye jumped in, reassuring. "The cows in the pasture will show people what's possible. And now you are plotting your next attacks against The System."

This segue activated Milo. "I think you're right. But it's the three of us in this together now. And I have the outline for a plan."

"Whata ya got?" Sheila asked, glad to be moving beyond this difficult topic.

"In two weeks the TNM upgrade will lay down the computing infrastructure for the chip. They will be making sweeping changes to the user interface but even more significant are the backend network upgrades. They won't be able to deploy the chip right away, but they need all the server-side software operational well before then. The airways have already been exposing people to what the chip will allow them to do, and from this time forward it will be an all-out blitz. Once the infrastructure is in place, it will be nearly impossible to tear it down. But there will be a small window during the cutover to the new software when they'll be vulnerable.

"The project is called Operation Nightshade. I cataloged the entire series of rolling patches and upgrades that will be applied. I know I can disrupt the process.

"Some of the intel I uncovered paints a more vulnerable picture of The System than the one we all have. It's true that the chip will give them a level of control that could probably never be defeated. But it is equally true that real threats to The System's control come at them every day. They are being suppressed, but inside the circles of power are questions about how long they can be held off if they don't take radical action."

"Sounds like if we can't stop it now, it might be 'game over'," Onyinye said.

"But if we can, there is a chance. We got our work cut out for us," Sheila mused as she felt the rumblings of inspiration.

"There's something else that happened during this session, something important," Milo said. He then became reflective, cautious.

"Up until now I've been a node on the network, able to receive and send packets of information, much like any device. But right before you pulled me from the session I felt my power accelerate, my experience change fundamentally. I was no longer a node residing outside, but instead, some part of my consciousness was pushed within the network. I didn't receive a pulse, I was the pulse, traveling at the speed of light, approaching simultaneity."

Onyinye and Sheila glanced at each other and found expressions of fear that neither would admit to feeling, while Milo remained wrapped in his own recollection until he jumped to a new topic.

"I found an array of servers that will be brought online as part of the upgrade. They will be off the network except for a single backdoor port that I found. It keeps a heart beat on the servers but they are mostly dormant, which means system scans won't be running until the upgrade brings them online. If I can be resident on this server I could hide there until its network connections are established. When that happens, I'll be able to wreak havoc before they can react. They won't know what hit them.

"We'll need as much access to the computer lab as we can get. Sheila, you and I will need to dig into the details and devise a plan. I understand what needs to be done, and between us we can figure out how to damage TNM for a good while, long enough to let people shake off the chains that hold them down.

"Onyinye, you can't help us with the technical tasks because that's not your background. But you have studied visual arts. And you have the stories of immigration and the devastation you left behind. Maybe you can weave these together into a video that describes how The Newer Machine has canceled our freedom and desire for justice. If we are able to take control of The Newer Machine, we'll be able to send a short transmission to its entire audience, which, as we know, is just about everyone. If you would do this, I, and I'm sure I can speak for Sheila, we would be grateful."

"That's a great idea," Sheila affirmed. "You and I will be 'heads down' getting things ready. If we have the chance, we need to send out a message saying the moment for liberation is NOW!"

Over the following days, Milo and Sheila worked side by side. She put to use his vast understanding of the computing infrastructure of the omnipresent Newer Machine. He diagrammed its structure, going as granular as needed. Together, they studied the array of computers that formed the backbone of the system. They looked for weaknesses, gates, as they referred to them, that could be pried open at the appropriate time. These lightweight snippets of code were

Sheila's specialty. She'd rather be building something but finding ways to destroy, or at least damage, *the machine* was nearly as satisfying. There were a handful of viruses she knew that could be deployed, that wasn't the problem. Breaching all the walls and obstacles was the challenging part, and Milo's encyclopedic understanding of these computing defenses was the only way to derive the steps needed to unleash the viruses.

Step by step they defined the strategy they would employ to unleash the attack. Their problems were two-fold. The first challenge was finding a way to make Milo resident on the server. The second, far more difficult, was providing Milo with the tools to perform his assault once the server was fully connected to the network. As consummately solid as TNM was, there was no amount of architecting that could remove all vulnerability during the upgrade. If they were successful, the viruses would spread to every node in the system, choking off its malevolence for a very long time.

They worked feverishly, even sleeping at the lab sometimes. As they were wrapping up after one long session Sheila said to Milo, "I could do this all day and night."

"What are you talking about, you just about are."

Sheila laughed, "I guess you're right. That's about all we do. When I lost control of the neuralBlast project I thought I'd never have another chance to make a big impact. What we're working on now isn't exactly what I had in mind but maybe it's what's most needed. Once we bring The Newer Machine to its knees and people see how The System has kept them in chains, I expect spontaneous revolts to erupt. Rebel groups will find common ground."

"That may only happen if we have inspired messaging. . ... How are things going over there, Onyinye?" Milo asked.

Onyinye sat at a workstation on the other side of a cubicle wall. Milo had made available to her vast amounts of classified information that was all but impossible to get your hands on. She spent the first several days reading about The System's deliberate destruction of the natural world and Indigenous cultures. She read widely but focused on her birth place, Nigeria, and the African continent. It transformed her understanding and was something she still processed.

But the thing that riveted her attention was the cache of information devoted to her parents, Nadia and Hasif Sani. They lived lives of agents and double-agents, their allegiance scatter-shot and unpredictable. They were coerced into aligning with The System and when the truth of their past was uncovered, they were detained by Nigerian authorities. She read detailed accounts of the awful interrogations that followed. The System interceded and gave them an exit plan, and brought them to the eastern US enclave.

When she did not respond, Milo got up from his seat and looked at her from over the divider. He saw her crying and trying, unsuccessfully, to conceal it.

Eventually she managed to say, "The information you pulled back contains extensive information about my parents. There were lots of things I never knew about them and it answers many questions."

This caught Milo off guard. He'd forgotten he had included information about them in the arguments that catalyzed his neuralBlast session. Sheila quietly got up and stood in the doorway of Onyinye's cubicle.

"I'm sorry, Onyinye. I was so caught up in what I was doing I never reviewed them after they were downloaded," Sheila said, trying to comfort Onyinye. "So, you have learned things?"

"They are very detailed. So many things. Things I'm sure they would have shared with me if there was time. They walked a tightrope their entire professional careers. I'm sure they were trying to do good, but it all became so muddled for them. Their last interviews sounded like confessions. They were sorry for their mistakes, their short sightedness. I'm sure they were pressured by The System, but they were clearly aware of and felt guilty for the harm they caused.

"After we got to the US my parents would sometimes talk about Nigeria. Their training was in agricultural science and they told me about how, despite their best efforts, the land was increasingly unsuitable to grow crops. The farmers were locked in a thirty year contract with international petrol-fertilizer-seed companies, which led them to stop using, and forget, their age-old farming techniques. At first my parents were ardent supporters of the new technology and the yield it provided. But it never worked as advertised; all it succeeded in doing was destroying the structure and health of the soil itself. That and lining the pockets of the elite class. When the plagues hit the west, the lifeline to these addictive products was cut and utter devastation overwhelmed most of the African continent because the people had lost their traditional ways. My parents turned their support to the Indigenous farming communes when they recognized the devastation that was coming, but it was too late. We fled before the worst effects were experienced. But they kept track of the suffering and it killed their spirit long before their bodies died. They died believing they had failed the people they tried to serve."

"I get it," Sheila confided. "I lived in a cocoon similar to the one you are describing for far too long."

"I thought of you, Sheila, as I was reading this. You would have liked my parents. You could have been friends."

Sheila placed her hands on Onyinye's shoulders. After a few moments Onyinye rose from her seat and the two women hugged.

"They're gone now," Sheila said. "But we can do this work that I think they would like to have been a part of."

"Yes, we can. And we will do it together. That was their problem. They didn't let anyone in and that, as much as anything, led to their failures."

"I know . . . you're right," Sheila responded. "And that is something we won't allow to happen here."

"Reading this made me want to focus on the harm done to my native country; the desertification, the starvation, the destruction of traditional ways. These were the things I wanted to express in the message that we'll broadcast. But then I realized we need to tell the local version of the same story. Because like it or not this is the land we live on, and we are the ones who must be its stewards. We must see and name the destructive forces that wish to weaken that bond. We have to work our way back to an Indigenous sense of the world in the place where we are."

"That's perfect," Milo said. "Everyone out there is living lives of shady double agents, siloed and secretive. We'll show them that they can live differently, without the deceptive filters placed on us by The Newer Machine."

"Your parents would be proud of you." Sheila followed. "I'm sure they would see what you're doing as a way of continuing their work, finding ways for everyone to be cared for."

"I believe you, I believe you are right. Thank you both for your kindness," Onyinye responded, speaking from the depths of her heart. Then, surfacing from these deep emotions, she said, "But we have a lot to do and not a lot of time. So, let's get back to it, back to what we have been called to do."

They knew she was right but lingered in communion, allowing what they shared in this emotional space to play itself out. But soon they were back to work. Onyinye scoured the archival information Milo unearthed, determined to create a video that chronicled the harm done by The System to all living things. The more she looked, the more inspired she became. She assembled decks of images that described the assaults directed at place and people. Mountains before and after their tops were blown off, some of the richest farmland in the world now nothing but dust, once vibrant urban areas

Man Made

turned into corridors of despair and homelessness, denuded landscapes and waterways. She layered all of this on top of a narrative describing the covert policies that set people against each other.

"People need to see these things," Onyinye blurted out. "How can they react when the reality of The System's impacts has been hidden and misrepresented? These images, and what we will say about them, will force them to see the truth."

Sheila and Milo were back in their seats but looked up from their work towards each other. Smiles spread across their faces and thumbs up were given and received.

"And we're going to blow up the thing that's keeping the blinders on," Sheila asserted. "People will be flying free and that might scare them, but they'll be free. And once they get a taste of it, there will be no turning back."

They went back to work with even more determination. Sheila found a way to crack open every gateway Milo identified. In order to derive the location and properties of the locked gateways he simulated the network in his mind, letting sections of it fire and noting its behavior. He inserted himself into the neural pathways, becoming more of an energetic pulse than a human entity. Something was changing inside Milo's body. Previously, his method had been to analyze the metadata gained during neuralBlast sessions. But now there was no need for interpretation; he related directly to the language of machines, became the light that knew all things about the network because it was one with the network. It was him, as much as his own flesh and blood. He careened from one host machine to another before returning to consciousness with his latest findings. He found it to be exhilarating: its speed, how it diffused his being across multiple tiers. These exercises drew him closer to the heart of a machine, the clear unwavering logic, the certainty of its path and the solutions it provided.

Sheila watched him grow into his power. During long sessions he sat Buddha-like, recreating complex computing networks. The attitude settled the air around him with bands of energetic pulses, like billowing smoke rings roiling the air. They contained a tidal presence, a powerful flow, the nature of which was unclear. Milo would awaken, bolt upright from these meditations and with a sense of urgency, walked over to one of the white boards. He provided strings of information about the new vulnerability he detected: IP addresses, reverse proxy information, encryption algorithms employed by these servers, and any other helpful information he had pulled back.

These were the building blocks Sheila used to write her snippets of code that would allow The Newer Machine's defenses to be scaled. Each penetration brought them closer to unlocking the most tightly guarded computing infrastructure the world had ever known, one that was thought to be impregnable.

Sheila admired the precision of Milo's findings. "Pretty nifty. You're keeping me busy."

"That's the idea. We're getting close."

"One of my biggest concerns is being found," Sheila said. "We can obfuscate the locations of our workstations and servers but they will come looking for us, tracing every tell-tale sign. It will be hard to get our work done before they shut us down."

Milo let that sit for a minute before responding. "That won't be a problem."

"How can you be sure?"

"Because we won't have to work from this site. In fact, we won't have to launch the attack remotely."

"How's that? Whatever presence you have on the web will contain some originating address." Sheila stated, uncertain where this was headed.

"No, I won't. There is no way for you to have grasped what I've learned how to do. In fact, I'm still figuring it out myself.

But once I've established my presence energetically, I am my own protocol that can be detected as an intruder but not with the attributes that contain a point of origin."

"That's not possible," Sheila objected.

"Is too," Milo joked. "I've already done it. Not in the TNM network but I've been practicing on other, less restricted, networks. I can be tracked and identified but am always an independent agent. You just need to keep your ports open and I'll find my way back here."

"Is that what you were just doing? We sensed waves of concentric energy coming off of you. You were out there in that digital, energetic space you're describing."

"It's exhilarating."

"It's too dangerous to not be tethered to a home address. What if your abilities are compromised?"

"That's a chance I'm willing to take. This is our best chance of success while keeping you safe and this lab undetected. You know this is best for everyone, Sheila."

She tried to mount a counter argument but couldn't find one, because he was right and she knew it.

They worked day and night until their work was done, only a couple of days before they needed to carry out their plans. Sheila and Milo decided on the best time to launch their attack. During the upgrade The Newer Machine would be running just a bare image of itself, enough to give the general populace a sense of continuity. At the same time the core, backend software would transition from the old to new system, at which time it would be most vulnerable to attack.

"The old and new systems will be like two bugs flipped on their backs," Sheila said

"They'll be easy for me to skewer and set on fire," Milo said, imagining the destructive digital fireworks he'd soon cause to erupt.

"How sure are you of being able to retrace your steps to get back here?" Onyinye stepped around the cubicle wall and joined the conversation.

"Not sure at all," Milo laughed. "Never did anything like this before," he sounded like a cowboy and felt like one, too. "In fact, I'm not sure how any of this is going to go down," and laughed again, this time a little too loud and raspy. "There's a risk. There's a chance they'll be able to detect my activity quickly enough and reconfigure their security apparatus so I can't get out, even with Sheila's bag of tricks. But I'm almost positive I can make their software inoperable for a long time, and pretty sure I can transmit your message. More than that, we'll just have to wait and see."

They were left to their own thoughts until Sheila broke the spell. Turning her attention to Onyinye she asked, "So, how's your message coming?"

Onyinye laughed. She had withheld information about her progress. They were her compatriots but engaged in a totally different activity. While they were plotting to blow something up, yelling and pumping their fists every time they inched their way deeper into the evil labyrinth, she was imagining a better place where humanity, and all living things, could thrive. So, it was necessary for her to not mix their spirits together until her work was done. And that time had now arrived.

"Here, come look," her first invitation to a viewing since the earliest video clips were mashed together. It had been almost too easy. The archival images came in historical sequence and the degradation of one landscape after another was a script played over and over. It was the story of scarcity and competition for the few remaining resources, the only story that most people understood in their framing of the world.

And then there were images of something else, another story struggling to emerge. The few natural places that were not plowed under stayed very much intact, continued to thrive. But more important were the still fewer places where humans lived in harmony and enhanced the natural world. These pictures contained even a more vibrant quality than the ones that were untouched by human hands. . .. These images showed how humans could actually play a beneficial role for all living things.

Embedded within the visual display was Onyinye's soft but powerful voice reciting her message.

"There are reasons for our depression and ill-health: the last heat wave or hurricane, the next deadly strain of virus, shortages of essential items. All problems and circumstances requiring expertise we, individually, lack. So, we look to The Newer Machine, which promises deliverance from situations we believe are beyond our ability to solve. We worship it because we believe its story of how it is the better arbiter of our lives and futures. The effects of this belief are more damaging than what anyone could conceive, and everywhere the same message of our helplessness permeates our lives. But in order for that singular message to succeed, it must smother everything that runs counter to it, and when this happens it will have achieved its singular goal of controlling our minds. Along the way, our little bit of freedom is pulled back the moment it gains traction and poses a threat to The System. So, there is no freedom at all. And the prizes offered by The Newer Machine, when compared to what we have lost, are meaningless trinkets.

This is the cause of the depression you feel. The body knows this, both our own physical bodies and the body surrounding us, of earth and nature, which is no less a part of us. Disconnected from the root, we grasp at all the trifles The Newer Machine makes available, according to our rank within its hierarchy. So, throw off your chains now that The Newer Machine has been silenced. Join us and find deeper meaning in community and in service of justice and freedom. Popular uprisings will soon erupt everywhere. This is the time to join in to recapture your freedom, your brilliance. You may never get another chance!

"Beautiful! Exactly what needs to be said. And it is short enough so it should finish before they can shut it down," Sheila spoke, while Milo, who could not find words to express himself, sat with a big smile painted across his face.

"You don't think it's too idealistic? I never before gave voice to what it is we are fundamentally missing in our lives. And now that I have, it seems so obvious."

"Sure, it's idealistic, every manifesto is," Sheila responded. "But the message will get through to most people. They will see that the deals society has forced on us are the chains that enslave us."

The smile on Milo's face now contained a fierce quality, as the conversation reminded him of what they, what he, was about to do.

"So, we're ready? Ready to blow the lid off The Newer Machine, the mouthpiece to all the madness?" Onyinye asked, her voice rising with emotion.

"Their upgrade starts tomorrow at midnight. Twelve hours later, if things go as planned, those two bugs will be lying on their backs with their bellies fully exposed, ready to be eviscerated. I'll be in their network long before then, embedded in one of their servers. I'll ping out to the network every five seconds. When I sense the server is online, I'll perform some tests to make sure the old and new versions are unstable and vulnerable. I'll strike as soon as they are!"

"Yes, that's what we've been working towards. It's our best chance to bust a hole in The System. And hopefully, it will spark the drive for liberation that we know needs to occur," Sheila said, bringing the conversation to completion, and setting them all back to work on their final preparations.

Back in the apartment, Milo and Onyinye laid in bed, not expecting to find sleep but courting it in an indifferent way. It was mid-October and the oppressive summer heat was making a comeback. The lone window in his room allowed a thin, sweet breeze to caress their exposed bodies. They were aware of the fleeting quality of these moments, which multiplied the tenderness they felt for each other.

"So, what's it like?" she asked, uncoupling herself from him and sitting up while looking out the window at a sky brightened by artificial light.

"What's *what* like?'

"You know, buzzing through computer networks. Or whatever it is you're doing."

Milo had to think about this because he wasn't sure what he experienced at these times, but then he blurted out, "I have to forget who I am, lighten the load ego puts on my energetic self. When I've done that, I can transform my being into electrical impulses. I've learned how to energetically travel along computer networks so far, but I don't think that's the end of it. It feels more like it's just the beginning."

This was as unimaginable to Onyinye, as it was enthralling.

"Do you enjoy it?"

"I don't know," Milo responded. "It's a rush, sure, racing at the speed of light, sending out tracers multi-directionally. Of course, who wouldn't get off on that. But," and now came the thought that he was unsure how to express. "Each time I come back I feel different, and it takes longer to connect with myself and with others, to just feel normal again. Truth is, I'm not sure I know what normal is anymore."

Onyinye looked back towards him and saw his worried expression. "I'll keep you connected," she turned her body towards his, lowered herself and grinded her hips slowly into his. He was still human enough to be reached by physical touch and passion.

Milo awoke the next morning from his dreams and the sweetness of their love-making. But that afterglow was soon displaced by the recognition of this day's significance. They got ready for what might be their last session in the lab. They loaded up on food and water, and brought a few blankets along. Their expectation was that once they entered, they would not leave until the mission was accomplished or they were discovered, hauled off and arrested.

After they got settled in, Milo performed his initial reconnaissance. He queried TNM's upgrade devices and observed the expected behaviors. Pre-upgrade audits and setup tasks were being performed on the servers that would manage the upgrade. The pathways taken by these processes were all mapped and internalized in his brain, and the viruses he possessed would be sent down these same pathways at the speed of light, waffling everything it encountered along the way. The biggest question was, how far it would get before it was discovered and neutralized.

"They're scurrying like bees," Milo said as he emerged from his inquiries.

"I've been on that side of things many times," Sheila said. "You put a lot of work into an upgrade like this. Egos and careers are on the line. The entire upgrade gets broken down into categories and sub-categories, and so on until what you've got are discrete, measurable tasks. They've all been run and rerun on test systems, and placed within a master plan. The leaders will be keeping their focus on predefined milestones, while their staff manage the more detailed tasks. I'd hate to see their reactions when you set fire to the entire upgrade and their dashboards turn red or stop functioning all together. Check that. . ... Actually, I'd love to see what happens when we turn their world upside down."

"Sorry, visuals of that kind haven't been written into the script," Milo joked.

"You're forgiven," Sheila replied and performed an incidental inspection of her fingernails.

Milo made his way over to their meager rations and said, "I hope we don't have to stay here more than a day or two, because this stuff will kill us for sure." There was no refrigerator and a microwave was their only cooking device. He was opening a can of chili when Onyinye responded.

"You expecting Jamal to deliver a steak from one of those cows you rodeoed into the pen?"

"That would be nice," Milo mused. "I hope it's not long before we have a feast with all of them back on the farm."

"Which reminds me," Sheila jumped in, "You ever going to take me out there and introduce me to your human and bovine friends?"

"I have a feeling we might be going out there and not just for a pleasure visit," Milo responded. "Things could get really hot for us here. It might be the safest spot for us."

"They'll be happy to give us shelter," Onyinye said. "Our struggle is their struggle, and you have already done so much for them."

And so, a probable escape route had been decided upon, if one was needed.

The banter waned as time drew nearer to midnight. Milo tried to stay calm, but was restless and ended up lying on the cot trying to numb his mind. There were no windows, no sense of life beyond the alabaster walls, just the hum of computing devices. How had he, with little ambition outside of playing sonic guitar in a band, become the most dangerous tool to confront The System? His mind drifted to his dad, who he rarely thought about. He worked at the fringes of society when he worked at all, and to this day Milo could not say what his hustle was. But that's not what he thought about now. Instead, he focused on the vacant expression on his father's face that disappeared when he was ten. He was a drifter by circumstance, not choice. The few memories he had broke into consciousness and lit up the back of his retina; a montage of flying a kite, a camping trip, a trip to a theme park. But there was always something wrong. This was an old feeling he had about the man, and one that still saddened him. Each event falling short of expectation. His dad raised his voice and tried to bellow as he believed dads should. But he could not fool himself, and could see in his son's uncomfortable expression that he was not fooled as well. Milo felt he better understood his dad's unhappiness now. His father felt like a fraud, knowing he was an empty vessel unable to pass on meaningful traditions and knowledge, incapable even of having fun, bereft of gateways to life-affirming emotion. And finally, there was nothing inside him to cause or feel attraction. The disappointment caused his father to thrash with anger. He could no more stay within the family structure than atoms can stay intact during the explosion of an atomic bomb. Milo never felt so close to his dad as he did right now, nor felt such love because he was in touch with his shattering alienation from the world.

He jerked himself up with a violent motion because he knew what he had to do, as did Onyinye and Sheila who felt a blast come off him, like a gust of wind pushed along by a gathering storm. He wasn't sure how his father's depression and estrangement was tied to The System, but he knew they were. And destroying The Newer Machine would be a gift from the son to the father, a tribute to someone he knew had passed long ago, because few could carry that great a burden and sadness for this long.

"I'm going in!" he declared.

It was only 10:30 PM and Sheila and Onyinye shared a look of surprise. They were not expecting Milo to make his first inquiries until after midnight.

"I'm not resting anyway," Milo explained. "There won't be any rest for me until this thing is done. I've got things to do, we all do."

He laid back down on the cot and Sheila got up and walked over to the cart that had the devices to hook onto Milo for a neuralBlast session.

"I don't need that anymore."

"What do you mean? Getting you started with a neuralBlast session was always part of the plan."

"I can do it on my own."

He reached over towards the desk where Sheila had been sitting and closed his eyes. Moments later the desk raised six inches off the ground and just as quickly returned to the floor.

"My powers are developing in ways I'm not even aware of until I stumble onto them."

Onyinye and Sheila looked from Milo to the desk and back again.

"Trust me. It will be safer for everyone. If I need your assistance I will send you a message. But I realize now that any encumbrance, even a neuralBlast connection will slow me down, introduce an unnecessary, artificial quality to what I can now do organically."

Sheila and Onyinye glanced at each other again, and then signaled their assent with their silence and down cast eyes.

So, Milo closed his eyes. He spun out his web until its tendrils touched the more expansive, artificial web, and then continued to increase his contact points in number and strength. He rode the pathway to the gates of The Newer Machine's blocked entranceways and then threw key after key from Sheila's bag of tricks at the locks until he gained access to its inner sanctum, and then he saw what was not on the script. The upgrade was already in full gear. The two bugs would be lying exposed on their backs sooner than he expected. They had started early, maybe to throw off would-be attackers.

Light whizzed by, but he was light, and its digital wisdom entered into him, which he consumed whole. Here and there he darted until he was fully conversant with all the parts that he would set on digital fire. When he completed the inventory of targets, he retreated to the dormant server farm and entered the backdoor of the lead server in this group. The upgrade would be in its final stages when these servers were brought online and he would stay locked in here until then to avoid detection.

Time passes slowly when you are nothing but an emanation trapped in a single system running on life support. He loved mastering speed; the speed of light, quantum speed, as close to simultaneity as possible, indistinct from it. But now, he crashed into boundaries every time he stretched in one direction or another.

He reviewed his plans for wreaking digital mayhem. With wildfire speed and intensity, he would turn the digital devices in The Newer Machine's network into death zones. They would lose their ability to communicate bi-directionally, and the information they currently stored would then become inaccessible. The devastation should be so thorough that the actual server machines would become inoperable, as if a massive magnet was pulled across each disk.

He was excited, he was ready. But a rehearsal can only be performed so many times. And his pleasure in imagining what was to come decreased with each rendering. The digital wind whipped past him, which was something he could not feel but only hear; its empty low howl, emptier than any prairie wind, devoid of life, unchanging.

All he was left with was a stillness beyond anything most people could endure, an emptiness that forced upon Milo an overwhelming sense of separation. If he could survive this, regardless of whatever else he would be, he would not be a fraud. And in order to overcome this legacy, he must now be a warrior.

His time out here shrunk his heart, and gathered strength to the rational part of his being. *A fair trade?* He meditated on this proposition, which was an essentially meaningless dialogue. Because what mattered was the onslaught of what he had become, a mind wired to and capable of pure rational thought, which was at once both exhilarating and deadening. The dying parts would be jettisoned, interesting artifacts that had been vibrant just a short time before. The lingering tenderness in his heart could not be reconciled, so it had to be excised.

He sensed this change, saw it off on the horizon, recognizing it as a necessary step on the road to reaching his potential and achieving his goal. He was, after all, a cyborg and if he could graft his cyborg strength onto every part of his being, he would be unstoppable. So, he silenced the dialectic and let the winds of this lifeless womb pass through him, each like a microscopic shard of glass cutting at his heart, something to which he had grown indifferent.

When that was done, when he knew his cyborg nature was in control, the dominant "I", he was without fear, without longing, in full control. Then he knew that he'd crossed over into something. That even when his consciousness was reunited with his physical body, the recognition of what he had become would dim but never be extinguished. This was who he was, and now his being absorbed this knowledge. He would never again be tethered to conventions imposed by human emotion.

He checked in and saw the two systems ripen, growing fat. The old with decrepitude, the new with a resurgent malignancy, cyber-blood flowing into its limbs that still lacked purpose, not yet woken to its intended use: disseminating the demon seed of mass truth-altering coercion, every cell poised to administer and manipulate chaos in the pursuit of control.

Seven hours from when he entered the labyrinth, the moment they'd been waiting for dawned. The server was coming online. Programmers and engineers struggled to stay focused as they rolled out the new features and ran tests to ensure the new functionality performed as expected. No one was looking for the firebolt that was about to be unleashed. The digital wind grew in force, waking up the machine housing Milo, synchronizing its pulse with the entire network.

It was time to strike!

He buzzed the network like a fighter pilot and dropped his charges inside the upgraded system's core devices. A cannonball of light scoured the digital landscape. He then directed his scalpel to the code, messaging, and data components and laid waste to them in their entirety. The digital forest provided a fuel-load that would rage like the coal fires in Centralia, Pennsylvania. Before the lights were shut off completely, he hurled Onyinye's message with a global destination signature down the throat of the last messaging server and watched it burn through the wires. He then turned his attention to the deprecated system, and let free his mayhem. Sparks flew but not as magnificently. He investigated and noted the explosive force was diminished. He looked further and saw that some of the servers housing the old system were already offline and there was no way to access them; his success would not be as thorough as he had hoped.

The gateways were shuttered. He had tarried too long searching out the remnants of the old system. He threw everything in Sheila's bag of tricks at various gateways but they had been placed on high alert and would not respond to these keys. Furiously he spun through the network's fiber, searching unsuccessfully for a leak in its defenses.

The nightmare reached a new level when he sensed the network changing. Large sectors of it were shutting down. He would be extinguished if caught in one of these shutdowns and never emerge. Speed was his best defense, so he pushed himself to the borders of what was possible.

It was a breakthrough of knowing, of clarity, of a human mind dispersed across a plane of machine coherence. There was no "I" left as he spread himself to all available points.

Until he sensed a port on one of the new servers had not yet been brought onto the network's overarching security framework. And like a genie submitting to ventricular force, his dispersed form constricted and passed through the opening. He headed home, but his progress was slowed by exhaustion until finally his eyes opened. His consciousness reconstituted itself incrementally, as it reintegrated with his corporeal form. He blinked and licked his lips. Sensation and physicality contained a certain pleasure that he realized he missed. He again presented as a sentient being. He knew he should be happy, but as he reattached to his earthly shell he was aware of what he'd left behind: emanations of perfection and unrestricted access to whatever he fancied, experiences he felt were pulled from him as he regained his physical form. But within moments the experience of loss did not long consume him because his consciousness was adapting to new circumstances. When the dreamer awakens, the turmoil of the dream's certain truths is replaced by a neutralizing consciousness, so too with Milo.

The smiles on Sheila's and Onyinye's faces were overshadowed by their concern. He looked around at the familiar, sterile surroundings. Was he happy to see them? Was he happy to be back? These questions did not yield easy, direct answers.

"How are you?" Onyinye asked. "If you don't want to speak yet, that's OK. Just shake your head to show you understand us."

He shook his head and then whispered, "I'm OK."

He turned to the screen they were monitoring while waiting for his return. The sound was muted, but images of urban destruction tumbled across the screen.

"It's started," Sheila said, sensing the thing of greatest interest to Milo. Her voice contained the power of undertow caused by wave after wave crashing upon the shore.

"You were able to broadcast Onyinye's paean. But moments after it completed The Newer Machine's broadcasts were cut. Instead, we have this. Scenes of chaos all over the country broadcasting on unofficial frequencies until they are shut down. The people are taking to the streets, demanding their freedoms which they realize have been taken from them, demanding a world that is essentially fair and just.

"This may not be the way we wanted to do it, but it's the best we could do. We've thrown a wrench into the machine and now all we can do is help move the struggle towards a better life, one that will never again be dominated by The Newer Machine."

Chapter 20

Onyinye, Sheila and Milo decided to stay holed up in their apartment. Two days after Milo's tear through TNM the screens on their devices continued to blink on and off, proof of their extraordinary success. Depleted by his efforts, Milo could not have ventured back into the wire. Even if he could, they would not risk going back to the lab. It would be under surveillance if the attack was tracked back to that location.

So, they waited, secretly trying to ascertain the impacts of what they had done. Sheila opened back channels to the nascent reports that started to emerge. With old-style devices and communication protocols, assorted voices from the fringe filled the airwaves; anarchist, alt-right, religious jihadist, all the outliers who were never fully silenced seized this opportunity to fill the void with their message. The quality of the transmissions was poor and rarely did the entire content arrive without drops and distortion, but at least they weren't being flagged and neutralized by The System before reaching an audience. The System posted messages in the simplest plain text format on the TNM channels, which resembled old-school mainframe monitors with their green, one-size fits all interface. Milo reasoned this was cobbled together from the parts of TNM he was unable to destroy before it was shut down. They urged people to stay calm, saying The Newer Machine would soon be operational. But fewer and fewer people held faith in this, as hours turned into days without the return to normalcy.

Then on the second night the messaging changed dramatically. Flares illuminated the night and three bombs exploded in different parts of the city. These were a prelude to larger detonations and sporadic rounds of gunfire.

They listened to 20 minutes of gunfire edging closer and closer to them.

"Well, it started," Milo said. "I'm not sure what *it* is, but whatever it is it needed to be unleashed and I'm glad we did it. People are angry, as well they should be. We need to let it play out and then join forces with the best option that emerges."

Before anyone could say more another blast occurred, this time only a couple of blocks away. The concussion moved things around, and rattled them further.

"That came from the direction of Pedro's shop!" Milo blurted out. Then, a moment later, "I tried calling him earlier but he didn't answer. I'm going over there to make sure he's alright."

"That's not a smart idea," Sheila said.

Milo let out a huff. "I don't care if it's a smart idea or not. All I know is Pedro might be getting caught up in this and I'm going to help him if he needs it."

Onyinye spoke next, "I'm going with you."

"You shouldn't come. It's going to be dangerous."

"Stop trying to be a hero that needs to do everything by himself." Onyinye replied in a way that made clear the isolation was getting to her also.

"But that's what I'm supposed to be. That's what everyone's been telling me since they started putting lightning in my brain," he said in a half kidding tone.

"Well, I'm your girlfriend, and you don't want to get my lightning stirred up."

They all laughed and Milo saw that in this conversation, his logic had little standing.

"I'm going to pass on this expedition," Sheila offered. "I'll try and see if I can get better information about what's going on around here and the rest of the country."

It didn't take long for Milo and Onyinye to see the impacts of the last 48 hours as they threaded their way through the wreckage. Garbage cans spewed their contents; bits of fire incinerated them instead. Signs of looting everywhere: murals desecrated with spray paint, broken windows, shuttered stores, the smell of smoke seen billowing from adjacent streets. There was a quality to the air that left a metallic taste on the tongue. The few people on the streets moved even more furtively than normal, chins pressed hard into chests as though to fend off danger they feared lurked around the next corner or shadowy storefront.

They reached Pedro's shop and it, the least deserving, was the hardest hit by the violence and mayhem. The front windows were gone, large and small shards littered the exterior and interior of the store. Pedro had been bent over and raised his body when he saw who it was.

"Sons of bitches," Pedro said, walking out from behind the food counter in a daze. He held a broom and dust pan in his hands but did not seem to be putting them to use. Even someone with his determination was stymied by the amount of destruction surrounding them.

"These creeps have been waiting for something like this. They have nothing to do, especially now with The Newer Machine down. So, they come after me, because I don't sound like them, because I try to be nice to them."

Milo broke from Onyinye, approached Pedro and placed his hand on Pedro's shoulder.

"You can't do anything about it, not now," Milo told him.

Milo assessed the damage. Food from the pots splattered the walls and the pots and pans lay scattered about, the food in the refrigerators strewn across the floor and the refrigerator door ripped from its hinge. One of the tables, smashed to pieces.

"Come back with us. You'll be safe there. We'll figure out what to do next," Onyinye reinforced what Milo had started. She'd met Pedro on the farm so there was no need for introductions.

"I can't leave my restaurant looking like this," Pedro said, turning and looking again. But he'd already taken an inventory, a fuller inventory than Milo's and that was the source of his heartache. "If I run away leaving it this way, they'll think they won, that they chased me out, stripped me of my dignity. This is something I will not allow. But I also will not put you in danger. The two of you must leave. This is not your problem."

Milo looked around, uncertain of what to do next. It was dangerous outside and the explosions were getting progressively closer and louder.

"Yes, Pedro, it is my problem. I am responsible, we are," he said motioning over to Onyinye. 'We are the ones who took down The Newer Machine."

"Whew," was all Pedro could muster, and this news was the only thing that could shake him from the desolation that held him like a death grip. "And your *sister*?"

"Yes, and she's not my sister."

"I knew that."

"I know you did. . .. I have special powers that I can tell you about later."

"I knew that too."

Milo did not respond directly. "I was able to infiltrate The Newer Machine's network and destroy most of it."

"I'd be impressed and congratulate you if it didn't hit me so hard."

"I know, I can see that and am very sorry."

They all remained silent, letting their emotions filter through them and distill the available options.

"If we help you clean, at least the worst of it, would you be willing to go then?" Onyinye offered, trying to find a path forward.

"I got here when they were finishing up their rampage. Desperate Boys they call themselves, which is a good name because they are children. I asked them why they do this and they responded that when The Newer Machine went down everything they cared about and believed in went with it. President Meld has been heard on sub-frequencies rallying all those who believed in him, believed in The System, to destroy their enemies, the intruders who have come to do them harm. That's when they came here to give rage to their infantile drives. I hate The Newer Machine, hate it as much as anyone. But it anesthetized almost everyone, and now that that's gone, it's unleashed all their suppressed ugliness."

Milo and Onyinye looked at each other as a feeling of terror gripped them. Finally Milo said, "Let's hope it's not all that is unleashed. Let's hope people sense their freedom and use that experience to break free from The System's dystopian control."

They looked again at their surroundings and wondered if Pedro's comments more accurately reflected the effects of their actions.

"I will go with you," Pedro assented.

"Then let's get to work," Onyinye replied. They would do what was necessary to return sufficient dignity to the restaurant, and then decide how to ride out the storm.

They spent an hour cleaning the worst of it. They bagged up the food strewn along the floor, a recent batch of chili and vegetables purchased from Jamal two days before. Milo cleaned up the glass around the window and watched small groups of marauders pass by. He could keep them out while they were here but had no illusion about what would happen after they left. Once the glass was cleared, he and Onyinye used some plywood he found at the back of the store, and with a hammer and nails, fastened a porous defense against the next wave of looters.

When Onyinye and Milo were done, they looked at each other and then at Pedro who was up on a chair washing down the walls.

"What do you say, Pedro?" Milo said. It was not really a question. "This can wait until after things blow over. We'll do all the rest of the cleaning then. But we need to get out of here before things escalate further."

Pedro looked at them blankly. If it was up to him, he would not leave. He would clean, make the food, provide as best he could, even sacrifice himself if need be. But these two in front of him pulled him in another direction, with their friendship and concern. He threw the rag into the bucket and leapt off the chair.

Pedro turned the key in the lock, which still worked. When he passed beyond its storefront, he never looked back. Block by block the city changed. A major assault was launched near Pedro's restaurant and danger permeated. The dark forces overwhelmed everyone in close proximity.

But they made progress. They navigated the sidewalks, the buffeting wind, the dangerous calls lurking in darkness. By the time they reached the apartment, the atmosphere was not so desperate. They were tempted to feel safe, but knew this was an ephemeral moment.

Sheila welcomed them in.

"Here, this is for you. They destroyed most of my food, but they spared this." Pedro never let go of the package. He then withdrew it from Sheila's hands and walked into the kitchen with it.

The three left in the living room smiled, but briefly.

"They made a mess of Pedro's place," Onyinye said.

"There's a much bigger mess brewing out there from what I can tell," Sheila responded.

"What did you find out, Sheila?"

"I was able to get feeds from different cities. There is widespread rioting."

Milo and Onyinye took the information in stride as they expected this was the case.

Sheila was not finished though and relayed what else she had uncovered. "There's more to it and you're not going to like it. They're not taking advantage of the opportunity to attack The System, now that it's been weakened. They're not raging against The Newer Machine but, rather, demanding it be reinstated! They are attacking government buildings because they think The System intentionally withdrew TNM from them!"

"That's crazy," Onyinye said. "You mean they are protesting to have the chains reasserted, placed back on them? How could they desire that, prefer it to being free?"

"It's hard to understand, but that's what I'm seeing across the board."

"All of the reports?" Milo asked.

"Yes, from what I can tell."

"And you believe them?"

Sheila frowned. "I learned long ago not to fully trust anything I can't verify with my own eyes."

"And that is coming from someone with a lot of experience and education," Pedro continued unwinding the thread as he had returned from the kitchen. "What do you think it will take to change the minds of those thugs who tore my restaurant apart? Whatever it is, it will have to be strong medicine and yes, they won't believe you if they can't see evidence of the better reality you are pushing. The strategy can't be to just pull off the scab; you need to show them the real cure, too."

They didn't want to hear what Pedro said, but that hardly mattered. He was correct and this analysis could be pushed further: the rebels needed to take advantage of this opportunity quickly or it would fail, and fail spectacularly. If The System regained control, it would throw the people a few crumbs and spin the narrative about this act of 'terrorism' that it would crush cruelly with the full support of the people. Sheila went back to her computer, intent on finding any legitimate seeds of opposition. Pedro went back to preparing the food and Onyinye followed him, as both needed some distance from the disturbing turn of events.

Milo sought his own council and drifted into the little patch of green behind their apartment. He sat on the ledge leading to the basement, casting his legs into darkness. But it was more than his legs. It was zugzwang, the state of having no good moves. The move he searched for was for a game, a world, that he questioned whether he wanted to play a part. But weirdly, he did not mind. He felt as he did while on the wire before he destroyed The Newer Machine, but without the abject misery.

The mass of humanity took the easy route, rarely saw or acted in its own best interest, preferred facile emotion over the pursuit of knowledge. Better to fawn over some strong-man leader when things got tough. All through recorded history the same thing. He witnessed it all during his sessions. Now, its bile regurgitated, and the bitter taste welled up in his mouth until he spit it into the pit of darkness.

*Because they needed to **see** the truth. . .* And when there was a truth that was not observable, as were all the most important truths, they were hijacked, challenged, deformed, denigrated, watered down, ignored, lost to all but the few who wouldn't fall prey to the tricksters and charlatans.

He didn't care . . . that they were shooting each other up right now for the wrong reasons. There were sirens piercing the air with their waves of circular sound that careened off and were frenzied by the still solid walls of this crumbling neighborhood. The helicopters swooped in and out of sight, casting lights into the hovels that no longer provided refuge for their inhabitants.

Because his now clear, unbiased vision was enough.

He didn't care . . . that he'd spent his whole life locked on this tiresome treadmill, that was grounded on nothing substantial, and left him susceptible to whims and conjurings.

Because his now clear, unbiased vision was enough.

He didn't care. . . that he wasn't sure that he ever loved anything or anyone.

Because his now clear, unbiased vision was enough.

But he would not give up on humanity, not yet, both the battle in his own being and those marching towards peril and self-destruction. And in pursuit of that connection, he had one more trick to play.

Milo got up and strode with purpose back into the house. As he emerged into the dimly lit kitchen Sheila said without looking up from her device, "It's real. Every contact I make confirms the initial reports. The people are taking to the streets demanding to have the instruments of oppression be reasserted, instead of demanding their freedom as we had hoped! How could this have gone so wrong; how could we not have seen this coming?"

"We need to leave; we need to go to Jamal's now. We figured they'd eventually be onto us but expected the uprising that developed organically would be our shield," Milo responded. And then continuing somewhat evasively, "I've got some ideas but need to go there to work on them. It is the safest place for us and it is about our only chance to turn things around."

The other three looked at him, not sure how they felt. But something in his manner projected they needed to trust his judgment.

"As long as you don't ask me to create any more docu-mercials. Didn't exactly work out the way we'd planned."

"I'm the one that figured out how to unlock the gates," Sheila said, as a sign of solidarity with Onyinye.

"Yeah, but I've got you both beat," Milo said, joining in the playful self-flagellation. "I came up with this brilliant idea and was the one who doused TNM with lighter fluid and set a match to it."

"You did that," Onyinye said, smiling now, "You seriously did that!"

"And all I was doing was selling a new chili featuring chorizo sausage," Pedro said with Chaplinesque sadness. "People, you have to tell me up front the next time you go spelunking around the enshrined holy place."

"You're a part of us now, compadre. Not going to do anything without you again," Onyinye said. She had warmed to Pedro. How could she not be regaled by his stories and the warmth of his character?

Chapter 21

They made it to Jamal's and were welcomed as heroes. Not because they crushed The Newer Machine, but because of the herd of cattle and the rotational grazing enclosure that the cows were happy to comply with. They decided to not share their role in shutting down TNM, uncertain of the effect it would have. But when the topic came up, it was generally agreed that it was good that it happened.

"Why don't those fools throw off the chains that oppress them and rise up and demand liberation," Came the comments from the long term, expelled castoffs. But there were some who were not so far removed from society, and they well knew the pangs of dislocation when first cut off from the only thing that gave pleasure and security.

The four of them got settled during the first few hours and then Milo went off on his own.

"What do you think he's up to?" Onyinye asked. They sat in a lean-to that was unoccupied.

"Not sure," Sheila responded. "Since he announced he had an idea, he's been acting strange. I couldn't place it at first but then I realized what it was. He acted this way when Rex and his allies tried to manipulate him. He was smart enough to see it before I did but he kept his thoughts to himself. He made like he was distracted by trivial matters, like he's doing now. There is the same aloofness. Whether he is using it as a way to keep us from getting close to him, I can't say. I don't even know if he is conscious of putting up a wall between himself and everything around him. But I can bet there's something churning in his head that has him fully engaged, and more than anything else, that's the cause of his strangeness."

Onyinye threw off the blanket she huddled beneath and got up to look around. The fields were in their final harvest. A small fire burned to provide warmth for those working outdoors and to heat water for the tea that was a staple here. The provisions they brought would carry them for only a few days. But they didn't dwell on this and instead, turned their attention towards figuring out how to survive here. Onyinye said she needed to stretch her legs and walked toward the area where the cows grazed contentedly.

Onyinye spied Milo in the quadrant where the cows were grazing. He had a casual way with them and as he walked between them, he occasionally let his hand graze over their backs and along their flanks. She laughed to herself when she saw how much more comfortable he was with the cows than he had been with them. Her mind never strayed far from wondering why he needed to come back here. He would tell them in his own good time and until then he would behave in this spaced-out sort of way. Aloof and disengaged, but more sensitive than any man she'd ever known. Taking on the weight of suffering humanity, but only connecting with those closest to him and even that required enormous effort. She turned back and headed away from Milo and his small herd of ruminants, because she accepted that he had to grow his magic in solitude. Only once did she look back to see his recently shaven head and the beginning of a salt and pepper beard. He gazed into the night sky, appearing to be lost in some esoteric calculations.

Instead of returning to their tent, she walked over to where she stayed prior to teaming up with Milo. She was hoping there would be room for them in the Big House.

Milo was glad to be back. He felt he could breathe again, partially because he'd accomplished something here, something he was proud of that helped the community. That was before he unleashed his power to destroy The Newer Machine. He'd become very good at creating and destroying things and took time to consider the effects each had on him, as he walked within the paddock. This internal dialogue restored him the way a low, steady current recharges a battery. He felt the charge most strongly when he walked the perimeter. His fingers tingled when he drew close to one of the energized stakes. The sensation increased when he placed his hand on the ground. He remained in this position for half an hour, meditating on the transacting current. He turned the tickling feeling over and over in his mind, providing it with different psychic add-ins, like mixing paints and then starting over with an unaffected base. Then one of the filters acted as a translucent elixir, and the connection radiated a phosphorescent glow along the ground. He studied the mystical ray of light, flowing between his hand and the metal post. After some minutes he moved his hand away, attempting to lengthen the emanation, but as soon as he moved, it disappeared and did not return. He held the hand that was involved in the communication and stared at it, marveling, wondering if this was what he was looking for.

Onyinye was able to make arrangements for them to stay in the Big House. It was once the centerpiece of the park that had existed here. It contained several large rooms, and they were allowed to set up in what had been the ornithology wing. A few desks remained along with emptied display cabinets. Murals of birds, most from the deep past, covered the walls and ceiling. They were the only indications of its former use, dulled by a rusted patina from years of neglect. Those epochs portrayed in the murals felt less removed than they would have only two decades before, and, in fact, felt eerily familiar. Now sheets and assorted material hung from the ceiling, creating whatever private space there was to be had. It was well past dark when they had settled in. Milo had still not returned.

"What do you think?" Sheila asked Pedro and Onyinye.

"I think we may not see him for a while. When he was calling in the cows, he wanted me to be there with him. But this time he didn't, and seems more distant," Onyinye said, and tried to not show how hurtful this was.

"You two don't worry," Pedro responded with lightness and song in his voice. "Brain-boy knows what he needs to do. But maybe you should bring him a parka, Onyinye. And we should heat up the chili I was able to salvage. It won't last long without proper refrigeration. He loves him some of my chili, that I'm sure of."

He was right, they knew. Not just that Milo would like some chili but more importantly that they were essentially powerless to help him; whatever he was into was his own to struggle with unless he asked for their involvement. They would follow Pedro's suggestion and Onyinye would bring him something to eat and something to wrap himself in, along with the hope that he would allow her to help shoulder whatever burden he carried.

From the moment he saw the spike of energy radiate along the ground, he was hopeful that there was something important to be gained from it. It set off a vibration occurring deep within his body that made him think of a glacier just before an ice sheet calved, throwing off tumultuous energy that was waiting to be released.

He raised his arm and sparks radiated through his fingertips. He was not ready to share what he did not understand so cloaked these emanations. He'd learned long ago how easy it was to do this because people generally saw what they expected to see and, with only minor adjustments, a mesmerizing vision could be replaced with something commonplace.

He raised his arms again and the light trail from his fingers flared into the firmament. But it was the sparkle, the jolt when he plunged his fingers into the ground that was most captivating. They sent spiky trails wildly in various directions that collided and then spun a new course only to connect, weave, and then diverge again.

It was tiring because the light was sourced from him, and that required him to concentrate his energy. He rested and changed his location from time to time, before again unleashing the light energy into the ground and watching it spread throughout his surroundings, pushing it further and further each time. He studied different pockets where the light waves swarmed, trying to understand them, wondering what purpose guided the precious spirals of light.

Hours passed as he tried to define and wield this new-found power. He tinkered with the energy currents and realized he could modify their path and force. When he sent this pulse through a single finger, he could bend it in a particular direction until it weakened and broke apart into filaments of lesser light as if it refracted through cut glass. Then he found he could harness the clear blue ray of light emitted when two fingers pressed together. It was stronger and held to its course better than any other he'd set forth. He brought it to within inches of a cow who slept while standing. He brought the current to one of its hooves and then the miraculous thing happened. The current leapt into the cow's body and for one glorious moment everything inside it was illuminated. Every organ pulsed with movement, but more important was the attuned rhythm of the entire body and the red pool of light surrounding each hoof that emitted their own rays down into the ground. Just as he was exploring the wondrous image and its connection, it flared out and disappeared. He continued these investigations over and over.

Unexpectedly, Onyinye called out to him. She walked to the edge of the electrically enclosed space before speaking. She could have entered but felt better staying on the periphery of what felt like his private lair. After a couple of minutes he walked towards her. There was enough moonlight in the sky for them to make out each other's image, and maybe there was even some light emanating from within them to outline their features in this darkened, quieted world.

He looked transformed, opaque. She was concerned, but also beyond concern.

"How are you?" She asked. "Have you found what you are looking for?"

"I've found something," he said with sardonic laughter. "But how can we be sure that what we find is what we seek after?"

Onyinye considered the question he posed in response to her question. The wind was bracing but Milo seemed unaware of its force. His head was exposed to the elements, his eyes were opened wide but unfocused.

"I think you know. I think YOU know right now what it is that guides you," Onyinye said, tapping into the spirit ranging about this place.

"There is something, something right here that I'm following, trying to unearth. It's too early to talk about. But I believe it may be useful, may be important."

"And you need to stay here alone until you figure it out?"

"I think so, yes, that's right," he regretted saying what he knew would hurt her.

They looked at each other from across the fence for several moments and then Onyinye returned to mundane matters.

"I brought these. Pedro wanted you to have some of his chili. It was hot when I walked out here but it's only warm now, so you should eat it soon. And here's something for you to wear to keep warm."

"That's very nice. Here, wait, let me deactivate this post so you can enter the pen."

This area of the paddock was already energetically active and when Onyinye entered she was unknowingly engaged in his experiment. He looked in awe at her and she returned his gaze with a perplexed expression.

"You are beautiful, Onyinye. You belong. Your ideas of being an outsider, a refugee, are all fabrications. Every cell in your body, in every person's being, is rooted in something grander than you can imagine."

"That's so very nice of you to say," Onyinye replied. She was surprised by the sudden seriousness and emotional depths, but had seen this in him before. "I feel that sometimes, but not too often. I wish that was my normal experience of the world and my place in it."

"Someday soon it will be."

Onyinye wondered how he could be so sure, but her thoughts shifted when she saw he was shaking. She set the food on a stump and walked towards him. She placed the parka around him and rubbed her hands up and down his arms and back, creating friction, inciting warmth.

"You should eat what Pedro sent you," she said, but he continued to show no interest in the food.

"I don't deserve such kindness from all of you. It's you and your needs that I should be looking out for."

She took hold of him and wrapped him in the firmest embrace she could offer to which he melted, succumbed.

"I'm sorry for being so secretive, to have you think you don't play a part in what I'm doing. But nothing could be further from the truth."

Onyinye studied him and what she saw terrified her. Before there was an ecstatic expression that was fragile and complex. But that was dashed, and she feared he was in a free fall. She asked, again, what she promised she wouldn't ask, "Would you like me to stay here with you, like when we laid down the fence together? Maybe I could help you now, too."

He hesitated before responding but that did not change the direction of his thoughts. "I don't think so. Not this time. This feels like something I need to work through on my own. But thank you, thank you so much for your offer and the love you have shown me."

Milo began walking back towards the fence and she followed, as she knew she must. When they reached the enclosure, they turned to each other again.

"I will leave you because you need me to go. But I am still here with you," She placed her hand on his heart, with a firm, reassuring pressure. Then she withdrew her hand, gathered herself together, turned from him and walked back to camp.

His loneliness was overwhelming as he turned and headed to the center of the paddock, leaving the chili untouched, and so much more that would never again be within his reach. He was unhinged with sadness and approximated a four-legged creature, his hands digging into the land setting off angry energetic pulses as he made his way as far from the humans as possible.

But banishing Onyinye opened him to the energy field in which he was immersed. Because he needed to learn all it had to offer. Because it was a mother. Because it was a father. Because it wanted to give up its secrets but he had not yet learned how to fully converse with it. Because he felt free and wild and powerful here, and knew these feelings could grow exponentially if he just stayed true to his calling. So, he dug his hands deeper into the soil and harnessed his energetic pulse through the space above and below the ground that radiated like a tsunami, like the wave coming off a nuclear blast, and plunged onward towards a destination that still concealed itself.

"So, how's brain-boy doing?" Pedro asked Onyinye, with equal parts concern and humor.

She thought for a moment and then responded, "I wish I knew. We talked and he said he is making progress. But I don't know. He's in the middle of something big that seems to be changing him in a fundamental way. He had that blitzed-out yogi thing going, but I don't believe that's the direction he's headed."

Before they could continue sorting out their prognosis Jamal walked over to them. He hadn't had time to talk before now and was eager to hear what was happening on the other side of the wall.

"I hear The Newer Machine disruption has caused the anesthesia to wear off. That could lead to a pretty big meltdown," Jamal said, firing the first salvo.

"We can only hope," Sheila responded. The two had never met but had heard enough about the other to form a positive impression and feel a willingness to speak freely.

"Maybe we'll see people rise up," Jamal said, allowing a dream to float to the surface that he rarely allowed to bloom or be fully extinguished.

"They're pissed off enough to," Sheila replied. "But it's hard to know how they'll express that rage, in what direction it will propel them."

"Nothing comes from nothing," Jamal intoned, verbalizing a silent mantra.

"I agree. But we were getting reports that did not sound promising. Tapped into some back-channel feeds. People were out on the streets, alright. But they were mostly vigilantes wanting more control from above, because that's what keeps in motion the only mode of existence they've ever known."

"Or can imagine."

"They've been spoon-fed a world view of scarcity and the fear of scarcity. A singularly effective feedback loop."

"And if they don't quickly embrace a different ethos, one that embodies justice and regeneration, it won't be long before they're under The System's thumb again."

They looked at each other and knew they could go on, but felt too tired to do so.

"The thing is," Sheila said in an attempt to quell the litany, "that's all they know, all they can see around them. So, their reaction shouldn't surprise anyone. It looks like they are placing the handcuffs back on themselves and handing the authorities the key . . . and the whip."

"I hope you're wrong, I hope it's different this time."

Sheila shrugged her shoulders and then said, "So do I, but I don't think I am."

Jamal shrugged his shoulders in reply, mirrored Sheila's shiver of resignation, and left after explaining he had some tasks to get back to.

They were welcomed in large part because of the wonderful gift Milo had bestowed upon them. But they would tax the already low levels of supplies. The black market they relied on to provide items they couldn't make or grow would see prices spike because of the unrest. They knew they needed to do everything they could to not be a burden so the conversation shifted to finding ways to contribute.

They made dinner while they continued to talk about the future. They hoped within the next few weeks the heat would be off them and they could return to the other side. They had not heard from Milo, which wasn't a surprise. Onyinye said she would take food to him and check in to see how he was in the morning. She wanted to go back and see him again this evening but resisted the urge.

The next morning when the sun had barely risen, Onyinye was back at the paddock. She did not breach the enclosure but called out to Milo several times without receiving a response. The bowl of food she brought Milo the night before lay on the tree stump where she left it. She noticed only a few bites were gone and then saw something beneath it. She entered the enclosure and saw that it was a handwritten note. After reading it she headed back to the Big House, filled with competing emotions.

Onyinye stood in front of Sheila and Pedro and read Milo's letter which began, *"I have achieved a breakthrough, but it is so big that I can't face its significance yet."* He went on to say that he needed to go back within the controlled zone because he had unfinished business. He would be back in touch with them soon, and they should stay where they were until he reconnected.

"What do you think that's about? Did you see anything else out there?" Sheila asked, as she searched her own mind for what it might mean.

"I didn't see this coming. And no, he didn't leave any more clues than what I've already told you."

"My guess," Pedro mused, "is whatever he found out there made him look deep inside himself, and it was more than he could process. Maybe there's something back on the other side that he needs to confront, some missing link."

Chapter 22

Milo walked past Pedro's store and was glad to see no more damage had been done. The boards they put up over the broken windows were still intact, but were now covered with the colors and insignias of local gangs. He was getting good at distinguishing them and had seen them in large swaths of the city during his travels since he returned from the X-Zone a couple of days ago. A battle for control was underway in sections that the officials didn't care much about. The System was particularly unconcerned because of its struggle to reassert itself with its limited toolset. The Newer Machine sprang to life sporadically, but its content was abbreviated. The news items were all locally produced and downplayed the amount of damage done to TNM. Progress reports on when life would return to normal were sketchy. The degree to which TNM wove its way into every area of life had been understood by only a few, but that reality was now on full display. The societal response Milo gleaned from TNM and anecdotal reports on frequencies normally shut down were not significantly different. Demonstrations and bloody riots demanded the return to normal, which was synonymous with a full-on Newer Machine. The power elite were overjoyed by this unforeseen response, but knew the tide could turn against them with tsunami force if they did not manage the situation correctly.

Milo rounded a corner and spied what he was looking for and walked towards it.

"Pretty nice wheels they give you to roll with. I guess The System takes care of its superstars."

It was a high-end convertible that screamed power. Twenty inches of off-road, angry looking tires. In fact, everything about the car was angry looking.

"What matters is what I get to do with it," K2 responded. "Hop in."

Milo looked back warily. "You're not going to throw any of that jujitsu shit at me, are you?"

"If that's what you're worried about, you probably guessed I could have had you for lunch by now. But then again, maybe not. Maybe you could find another crease that you disappear into." K2 stopped and his look grew unfocused, lost. "That was some kind of weird shit, man. A day hasn't gone by that I haven't thought about it."

Milo let it pass. There would be a better opportunity to talk about their trip through interspace. Instead, he pursued what he'd been thinking about as he got into the passenger seat.

"You look a lot better than the last time I saw you. Glad to see you recovered from that experience in the hospital."

K2 reached back to when he was held captive and then responded. "They tried some very interesting techniques, torture really, to figure out what made me tick. If it wasn't for you, they'd probably still be peeling me like an onion." Milo sensed the gratitude but before he had a chance to acknowledge it, K2 finished his thought. "But when my handlers came and freed me, I made sure the doctor in charge paid for what he did to me."

K2 looked absolutely menacing as he spoke this last sentence. Milo wondered, again, if he'd made a mistake initiating this meeting. There was still time to escape.

"C'mon man," K2 sensed Milo's discomfort and brightened. "I've got no beef with you, not today at least. Relax."

They sat side by side, looking out the window, still figuring out if this was a good idea for either of them.

"I didn't expect to hear from you, especially so soon after you demolished The Newer Machine. They figured it was your work. May even suspect I played a role. Don't care really."

"Yeah. We lit the flame and are watching the fire spread."

"Taking some interesting turns, don't you think?"

K2 turned towards Milo and flashed a sardonic grin. Milo grudgingly admired him. His brilliant white teeth, chiseled features and hair standing straight up, an inch from his scalp. But it was the bulging muscles expanding across his torso, arms, and legs that energized the space around him. He had an undeniable presence.

"It is," Milo conceded. "I didn't expect it. I thought people would rally around it and push to take back control, but it looks like the exact opposite is happening."

"Sounds like a conversation we had a while ago. Maybe you need to stop seeing what you want to see in people and start seeing what's really there."

"I don't want to talk about this, not now." Milo hesitated before continuing. "Mostly because I don't feel that connected to the struggle right now."

K2 looked over at Milo and his expression became softer. The taut muscles that supported his massive frame relaxed and became more fluid.

"You're right. Their struggle may not even be their struggle anymore, but it is certainly not yours."

"What do you mean by that?"

"You're a cyborg, man! Color it any way you want, but you've *stepped out*. And that's obvious. The people I work with, my handlers, they've stepped out too. What isn't so obvious is these people you're trying to help. But my guess is they're no more connected than anyone else. I bet they don't even know that's important, that it exists. And that means evil will emerge the moment they gain power, but there's little chance of that ever happening."

"Sorry, man. I'm not ready to go that negative." Milo paused to check how closely K2's comment corresponded to what he believed. "I risked everything and things won't get better. In fact, they might even get worse. Makes you wonder."

"Hey, man. You're bumming me out. I'm used to you being the knight in shining armor."

They sat there a minute, lost in their own thoughts. K2 was the one to move the conversation forward and he did so in a big way.

"Fuck it! There's nothing you or I can do about the mess they've gotten themselves into. So I say, let's have some fun instead!"

"The world is falling apart and you think this is a good time to have a little fun?"

K2 ignored Milo's reaction and reached behind his seat, grabbed and tossed a football into Milo's lap. "What you told me last time was true, right? That you detoured a neuralBlast session and learned how to throw a football. That you could throw it 65, 70 yards on a dime. If so, I'll be the one catching up to it.

"The Ravens scheduled an impromptu 'one day open to the public' tryout today, which is largely a publicity stunt. The System has been pushing organizations to schedule local events to divert attention from the chaos you created and this is their way to curry favor. Nothing ever comes of these tryouts. But today Coach Hamburg will get an eyeful. Today he'll think he's witnessing the second coming. So . . . you in?"

Milo felt coils he did not know were there, loosening around him. He didn't expect the day to take this turn but was absolutely cool with it. K2 flashed a bit of red meat in front of him and he wanted to consume it whole and raw.

"Fuck, yeah, let's roll!" Milo replied.

K2 let out a gruff, raspy laugh that was as big as he was, that crashed against the glass surrounding them, threatening to burst it apart.

"After you calibrate how to be coach's next wet dream, find yourself a helmet. I got a few in the back seat. We got to keep them on all the time. Your people and my people wouldn't be happy seeing us playing pitch and catch together . . . or, for that matter, doing anything together."

"Got it. Let's do this."

Milo swiveled around and started trying on the helmets while K2 put the car in gear and then crushed the accelerator pedal.

"Haven't had one of these on since pee wee football days. Coaches used to make us keep the helmets on throughout practice back then, too. Made no sense. Just a bunch of cruel bastards."

"What they were doing was trying to toughen you up. Because they knew that's what you'd need when you got in a game, in the middle of battle."

"Maybe, but it was still stupid."

"I'll bet you only played a year or two in any sport and then packed it in. Asshole coaches, not enough playing time. Whatever excuse you could come up with to flick them off and walk away."

"Fuck you, man! What the fuck are we talking about here, anyway," Milo reacted. "Sure, I wasn't a jock. Never said I was. But I did my thing. And I'm not interested in listening to you telling me to man-up, either."

"Suit yourself," K2 responded and laughed when he realized how much fun and how easy it was to get a reaction out of Milo. He turned the corner on three wheels and headed straight for the stadium.

They walked on the field, in the direction of the mass of dreamers. They were the only ones helmeted and that caused a few derisive expressions from the onlookers. K2 dropped a duffel bag and fished around for a pair of cleats that he slipped on and laced up. Milo remained standing, wearing his standard jeans and sneakers. They stood looking up and around in The Ravens' football stadium. The field was beyond immaculate. The stands empty, but still majestic. All of it together projected a consecrated space. It was impossible not to imagine the rush caused by all those seats filled with fans cheering you on, something only the elite athlete gets to experience.

Two reporters with TNM credentials circulated through the crowd. But even here Milo's work was in evidence, as there were only a couple of cameras hoisted on men's backs to capture the action; no drones or simulating machines as part of the entourage.

"You ready?"

"Been waiting for you?" Milo responded in his best gunslinger monotone.

K2 pulled a football from the bag and tossed it to Milo. Milo's passes were at first wobbly, but his body quickly recalibrated the learned techniques. Twenty yard down-and-out patterns, the hardest to throw because of the angle a defender could take on it, were delivered on a rope and with pinpoint accuracy. Anyone standing along the path of the ball heard the wind scissored as if a bullet had passed through a wind tunnel.

The larger group began to take notice, and other activities attenuated. Milo took a casual approach to the attention. It didn't matter to him that the skills hadn't been acquired honestly. He was standing in a professional football stadium having fun playing out a fantasy that he didn't know existed.

K2 returned to the line of scrimmage and set up as a wide out. He had been running a series of ins, outs, and button hooks for about 10 minutes. The passes were delivered and received perfectly each time. The routes were run with nuanced precision.

"Let's cut the crap with the short stuff. You're warmed up now. I'm going to run a post. Let's see what you can do when you air it out."

Milo dropped back and waited 2.2 seconds before letting it fly. It landed in K2's outstretched hands 50 yards down the field 1.5 seconds later. The focus in the surrounding tryout activities turned to them. The coaching staff jotted notes on their clipboards or remained motionless and disbelieving of the story told by their stopwatches.

K2 and Milo were having the time of their lives. The spooked faces on the observers were priceless, but they found more value in what was going on between them. Each pass and catch placed them back in a carefree youth neither had experienced, with brothers they never had.

"That all you got?" K2 would say each time he trotted back from his jaunts down the field, not a bit out of breath.

"What do you think?" Milo responded, channeling the greatest quarterbacks whoever played the game. What fun this mock seriousness was, Milo thought. How much better than everything that had recently confounded him.

K2 was off again. Milo waited an extra second and let it fly. No one here had ever witnessed something like this before. When gravity finally asserted its force, the spiral continued to stay true, until the moment when it landed in K2's outstretched hands, 70 yards down the field. They were invincible.

They shed the role of quarterback and receiver at this point. Instead, they made the field into a round, widening the dimensions of the stage on which they played. Now that they cast off the role of passer and receiver, they became both and were intertwined. They abandoned straight line runs, embellished their movements, one-upping each other with stunts like somersaults in the air just before catching the ball fractions of an inch from the ground; gravity be damned. All of this was met with laughter and applause from everyone else on the field.

What was different about this display of super human ability than playing killer guitar at the bar? It was K2, of course. Milo could calculate distance, velocity, and vector end points with precision. But he was much less able to anticipate the excitement, adrenaline, and pure joy he felt as K2 pushed him harder and harder every time. There had been no pleasure in being exceptional until this moment that had been engineered by K2, and sharing experiences like this made them real. It left him feeling a wildness and attitude that reminded him of his days in the band. They rounded back to the starting point and were set to go through a new set of improvisations.

Coach Hamburg dislodged himself from the athlete wannabes and watched at a slight distance what started as a casual pitch and catch. The speed and precision of the routes were of an order he'd never seen. But the thing that really caught his attention, that he couldn't let go of, was the sound of the ball penetrating and clearing the air as it moved through space. There were myths about how the quarterbacks with the strongest arms could evince this sound, but he'd never heard it. And now that he could, he was reluctant to trust his senses, no matter how many times they returned the same message.

"So . . . where you boys play ball?" Hamburg said, as he advanced toward them, still uncertain where this conversation would lead.

"I was military until recently, sir. Straight out of high school. I had a couple of colleges show an interest but decided to serve my country first," K2 explained.

Milo liked the sound of this subterfuge. "That's pretty much my story, too," he replied.

"I wonder if you could do me a favor," Hamburg began. And then pointing to K2 he said, "I'd like you to run 40 yards down field and cut to the far sideline." He then turned his attention to Milo and said, "I'd like you to hit him at a dead run just before he goes out of bounds."

K2 shrugged his shoulders and set off on a sprint just as Hamburg pressed his stopwatch. Milo threw the pass that even at this distance was on a rope and caught K2 in mid-stride just before stepping out of bounds.

Hamburg had seen enough, and stepped in closer to converse with this dynamic duo. He began speaking after K2 jetted back to them.

"It's hard for me to believe what I'm seeing," Hamburg said, and pointed at K2. "I consistently clock you running sub 4.0 40s, but I know that can't be right. And your passes are traveling at a rate that's also like nothing I've ever seen."

Hamburg paused, still unsure of the direction to take this. His time was valuable. Tryouts like this were photo ops he was forced to walk through. But they were inconsequential. Every exceptional athlete was on somebody's radar before the age of 12. So how do these two diamonds in the rough show up here on his doorstep, out of nowhere, self-possessed, cocky, looking for game.

K2 and Milo took a step closer to Hamburg. They entered his personal space and were willing to stand there mute for a very long time watching Hamburg fidget, a man rarely wracked by indecision.

"No college ball, none at all?"

They did not verbalize a response, but shook their heads while continuing to peer directly into his eyes, giving him no respite.

And then, making a decision he knew he'd regret, he let the door open just a little. "You know our roster is just about sewn up. Weren't expecting any last minute surprises." He paused again. K2 and Milo continued staring at the coach with an unfazed lack of expression that haunted Hamburg.

Coach pressed onward, casting a glance at the football field he recently commanded, but that was now littered with landmines. "How about we put some coverage on you," he said, nodding to K2. "We brought a cornerback along, Michael Smith, for a situation like this. He's not a starter but one of our better man-on-man cover guys."

"Sure, coach. That should make it a little more interesting," K2 responded, with cocky nonchalance.

Michael was called over and introductions made. Michael was wary but put out that he was not impressed. His appearance did nothing to diminish K2 or Milo's confidence or demeanor. Game on.

The throw and catch proceeded apace. Coach continued to marvel, and allowed himself to dare, in small increments, to consider what was unfurling before him. Poor Michael never got a hand on the ball or K2. He tried stuffing him at the line of scrimmage but K2 was stronger than him and after beating off the feeble attempts, blew by him into open field. Each route, perfectly choreographed. Each pass, delivered with pinpoint accuracy.

Coach made up his mind. They would be invited to camp. He wasn't sure how it would work but knew he was watching something special, something that occurred only once in a lifetime, if you were lucky.

"Take one more and then bring it in here," Coach commanded.

K2 and Milo had already planned this out. K2 ran a 30 yard post but not at full speed, staying only slightly ahead of the defender. The ball was delivered short of its target. K2 executed a perfect pivot, placing himself behind Michael and caught the ball with one hand. With the other, he pulled back Michael's shorts and stuffed the ball into them. . .. And that's when their escape commenced.

K2 grabbed his bag and then he and Milo ran for the exit. Coach took a few seconds to collect himself and snapped out of it in time to see what he suspected was his legacy vanish into a darkened corridor leading to the parking lot.

"After them," Hamburg bellowed. He led the charge with his assistants in close pursuit.

But they were gone, not to be seen or heard from again. Hamburg seethed and after noxious protestations to the gods, vowed never to speak of it and commanded those around him to never broach the subject with him. He confiscated a few snippets of video documenting these impossible feats, but a few slipped between his fingers and became the stuff of urban myth. Hamburg rubbed his eyes, as if to remove sleepers. Just another day in the world of professional sports where there is only one winner, and it was, again, not him.

K2 and Milo jumped into K2's car and were through the exit gates, leaving coach and his minions far behind. Inside the moving cannonball, K2 fishtailed all through the tony neighborhood by the stadium until they reached a sort of no-man's land, where the real fun began. The testosterone levels inside the car were erupting with the same force as what was coming off the angry car's burning rubber and screeching paranoia.

Milo continued to wear a smile that hadn't relaxed since he took his seat beside K2.

"Did you see the look on his face? You're right. Hamburg couldn't believe we were so good. We were the answer to his dreams that turned into a nightmare when we disappeared through the tunnel. Best prank ever."

"That was *the shit*, man. I can't remember having so much fun. That last play was utter perfection. Couldn't have choreographed it any better," K2 responded, which was accompanied by bellowing laughter, a horn that he pumped just because it felt like the right thing to do, and high fives riffing in the air.

They rounded a corner and K2 navigated around debris, car parts, and a road surface straining to remain passable. Up ahead a scuffle. Six guys surrounded and pummeled one guy on the ground, who was trying unsuccessfully to protect himself. K2 drove right for it, causing the scuffling mass to pause the beatdown and assess the statement made by the mad roadster coming at them. This was surprise enough for Milo, but then K2 threw the car into park and jumped out of it, running directly at the closest perpetrators. He slammed one to the ground, but two more were on him. Milo jumped from his seat and entered the fray. He pulled one of the guys from K2's back and sent him sprawling to the ground with a kick to the chest. He turned and was back-to-back with K2, taking on anything that came at them. To Milo's surprise, his blows landed with precision. He took his attackers' force and turned it against them. And if that didn't work, he cracked them across the face with lightning fists, and that always worked. Two of their assailants produced knives, which resulted in the hands holding the knives being broken.

Soon there were no more takers. The victim of the ambush righted himself. They wondered what he'd done to deserve this beating but didn't ask. They checked him over. Nothing broken. He was thankful but distrustful and just as happy to disappear into the semi-abandoned buildings once he realized they would let him go.

"Quite a day for a couple of outliers," Milo offered.

"As much fun as I've had in a long time," K2 agreed.

They kept looking down the silent, vacant street, at the shuttered doors and broken window panes. The setting sun lengthened the vista of brick and mortar. Milo felt his experience in the wire return. Passion without boundaries, simultaneous awareness. But now he was in his body and it was his flesh and bone that had delivered this experience.

"You know, man, this is all there is," K2 said, not turning from the road. "You and the resistance want to change the world. But it's not going to change. There will always be little specks of light and a lot of darkness. And we, right here, created another bit of light. And we did it with our fists, with our muscle."

Milo could have argued that it was The System's overarching control that caused scenes like this and the only meaningful action was to work to defeat The System. But he sensed how lame that sounded. They had done good and helped someone who couldn't help himself. Milo wasn't going to get bogged down in the endless debate, not now. He savored their success and adopted the spin provided by K2.

They got back in the car and returned to the spot where K2 and Milo met. K2 pulled the car to the curb but Milo did not get out. Instead, he looked out the window and his laser vision considered his surroundings. The occasional street light that still worked reflected the dangerousness of this city, a danger that consumed vast stretches of the world, a danger he felt responsible to fix but couldn't, and now had little desire to try. Instead, Milo felt more connected to his fellow cyborg than the whole rest of the world. He and K2 were masters of their universe, but he had a premonition that this was short-lived. Everything felt in motion and he didn't know where he would land.

"Let's keep driving," Milo said, looking straight out into the darkness beyond, that even he could not make sense of.

"Where to?" K2 said, a small snicker tracing along his lips.

"Some place . . . dangerous, some place wild."

K2 stomped on the gas. Black smoke and tire tread were all that was left of them at this spot a moment later.

"And where would that be, professor?"

"Not sure, Pit Bull." They laughed hard and long. These nicknames would be their preferred monikers henceforth. And then, continuing the thought, Milo concluded, "You've had all the answers up to this point."

K2 pulled back on the gas, didn't stop but slowed to almost a safe speed. Apparently, he wasn't always the raging psychopath, the destroyer, and instrument of war.

"Low on answers right now," K2 said, lowering his guard. "I've gone a little off script. They send me on errands, like jobs to eliminate their enemies. My main overarching task is to track you down and neutralize you. Ha, if they knew we had contact again and I didn't take you out, they'd probably eliminate me."

"Then why did you put us in a public space earlier? Some place where they will probably figure out it was us marching up and down the field."

K2 slowed the car again, traveling below the speed limit and practically making a nuisance of himself. He did not answer for a considerable space of time but when he did, said, "Because I don't really give a fuck anymore. Because I'm tired of their games, of their bullshit. You think I don't know The System's only goal is to retain control, that they will do and say anything to maintain the status quo? That nothing and no one is off-limits to them in pursuit of this goal?"

Milo was surprised by this. Honesty and vulnerability were not expected. He would not have guessed K2 was capable of sharing such things.

"You could come join us in the resistance," Milo offered.

K2 slammed on the brakes and the car skidded to the side of the road, stopping at an oblique angle in relation to the curb. With his hands firmly gripping the steering wheel at the 10 and 2 position, he torched this idea.

"You're kidding, right? Those crazy bastards are worse, way worse than the people I work for. If they get organized, any notion of order breaks down. Way worse food security and armed rebellions of all different persuasions will break out across the country, bringing chaos and anarchy. And if your friends happen to take control, they'll end up being at least as ruthless as what we have today. No one likes bureaucracy and the corruption that comes with it. But no one's figured out a better way to manage the mess of civilization. So, why would I want to join up with your sad comrades?

"And I know what you've been up to," K2 continued. "Building that cow palace in the X-Zone. I bet it felt good providing for all those cherubs. But if it was so satisfying, why did you leave to come meet-up with me? Anyway, the point is if those clans got their shit together and became unified, they'd turn into the same sort of organization you first hooked up with, the ones who wanted to turn you into me.

"C'mon now, you know all this. Why else would you put yourself in so much danger and come calling on me. They suffer a major hit if they lose you. Me, I don't mean that much to The System. With or without me they hold all the cards."

Milo looked out the window. Homeless people ranged up ahead. Small fires burned that drew skulking packs of three or four. What a waste, Milo thought. They were beyond hope or repair. He felt a desire to sweep them all from the face of the earth and start over with a clean slate.

"Why did I come looking for you? Because I'm not one of them anymore. And when I realized that, I had to get away."

"The System has its faults, but it has strength," K2 replied, advancing his argument. "It enlists science for the control it gives them, but also uses it to benefit those people who abide by their rule of law. You and I are their finest creation and because they can't make new ones right now, we would continue to be highly valued. They will worship you, but the resistance will resent and eventually destroy you."

"They'll worship us until we are replaced by the new shiny object," Milo countered.

"That's true. But if you come in with me now by the time they've found new deadly toys, we could amass enough power that we could adapt to whatever they throw at us."

Milo was shaken by the direction of the conversation, which he interpreted as K2 trying to turn Milo. Who was the fox, who the hen?

"It's all bullshit," Milo spat out. "The resistance might not ever get its shit together but The System is covered in blood. Countless victims who didn't deserve what they got."

"Most of the time you're only a victim if you let yourself be one," K2 responded with a sneer.

Milo felt himself drifting in a way that felt both familiar and alien.

"What really matters," Milo said, trying to unwind his thoughts, "is we're not the same as them. We're exiled by the strength of our minds and bodies. We try to make contact but it's exhausting and ultimately unsatisfying. Eventually that will become too much of a burden and we'll stop trying. We are a tribe of two, you and I."

"Well, well, well. You finally figured this out. It's what I've been telling you all along, but you didn't want to hear it. I let you go on. Let you spin your revolutionary claptrap. Ha, welcome to your life! You've found your way to the main event."

Milo was not quite ready to embrace this fate. Instead, the following burst out of him, "Fuck this, man. The whole thing. Your side, my side. Everything."

K2 sighed in a way Milo had never heard and then said, "I know." Then, after another pause, "Even with the helmets my handlers will figure out it was you and me out there. If I went back without you, I'm not sure what they'll throw at me. But I'm not telling you this to pressure you. I wanted to see you. Like you said, it's just the two of us. I decided a while ago that if you contacted me, we'd meet and I wouldn't do you any harm regardless of the consequences to me."

Milo sank back into his seat and let his mind clear. He hadn't thought deeply about the danger their meeting posed to K2, and was embarrassed that he had to be told. It wasn't just the danger he heard, but the affection he was willing to express. All of this called for Milo to force a reset, and consider an expanded set of options.

"I figured out teleportation," Milo finally said in a cautious tone. "It's not perfect but I can avoid danger and get close to the desired location."

Milo had succeeded in turning K2's world upside down again.

"How the hell you do that?"

"It wasn't that hard. When I worked on the project at the farm I explored the energetic nature of things. First, I learned how to move objects. Next, how to dematerialize and then rematerialize them within a small space. I used my experience on The Newer Machine network to figure out how to create an energetic tunnel between me and where I wanted to go. When I put it all together I was able to travel through space at nearly the speed of light. I've done it several times. It works."

K2 was gobsmacked and mute, and could only shake his head and chuckle quietly.

"I got to get out of here. I can't make sense of this place anymore," Milo confessed. "I want to go surfing. I want to go to Hawaii. If you're in, all you need to do is grab my hand and we'll jet our way the fuck out of here."

K2 laughed again, harder this time, like the way Milo was used to. They were still sitting in the car when K2 grasped Milo's hand and both leaned back against the headrest of their seat. Moments later their essences were turned into energetic crystals that rocketed to the other side of the world while the engine still purred in the driverless muscle car.

They landed on a tropical beach on Moloka'i. Their bodies twirled like leaves blown in by a gust of wind. They came to rest on their backs, looking at a sky of uncheckered, ancient, pure blue. K2 was the first to sit up. He looked around and laughed again in much the same way he had moments before on the other side of the world.

Milo was up next and on his feet, shaking sand from his hair, picking it out of his ears, flicking it from the corners of his eyes. "I'm going to have to work on my landings," was all he said when he regained his senses.

K2 looked at Milo with a renewed sneer and then doubled over in laughter as though that was the funniest thing he ever heard. "Right! We'll stick it next time."

They looked around. Neither had ever seen such majestic beauty. And as they took in this lush oasis, they left behind thoughts of the rupture their departure would cause their allies. Once their AWOL status was confirmed they would never be trusted again.

But it was the ocean that commanded their attention and desire. Endless, or at least as seemingly endless as the blue sky above, with which it merged at the horizon, establishing a continuum. They decided they would stay at the tip of this island where the waves came in full and hard, a decision that required no cyborg intervention.

Money wasn't a problem when credit cards could be fashioned out of strips of plastic. So, they spent the rest of the day getting set up in thatched huts. They were built in the jungle abutting a steep cliff, overlooking endless ocean with primordial surf crashing against it. The serenity of the place was dashed when the two of them drove up on old-style Harley Davidsons. The engines screamed a tear in the fabric of idyllic nature but the joy of riding these hogs was too great a prize for them to regret their presence.

It was late when they settled in. The fire they built provided light, heat and a way to cook the steaks, which was the lone item on the menu, except for the beer staying cool in an ice chest. They had bowie knives and shared one mess kit they'd purchased in the general store where they found the few things that they were now outfitted with. They embraced the lack of civilization and comfort their surroundings provided.

The next morning they were up, perched in the same spot where they witnessed the onset of darkness that was pierced by hundreds of specks of light emanating from the firmament.

Milo was first to talk, but spoke to that which captivated both of them. "What occurs in people that have lived here all their lives and were aware of no other way to live?"

"Then all they would know is nature's charms. They would be surrounded by Shangri La and believe that was the normal condition of the world."

Milo pressed on, "But if this is all they knew, if they were removed from want, removed from the destructive lures and obscenity of The System, would they appreciate what they have?"

"They would, beyond what we can imagine," K2 responded. "Because goodness and abundance are on display everywhere you look, it would be a constant presence and would seep into a person's DNA."

Milo gave this time to settle and then replied, "But not for us."

"No, never for us."

"Because we stepped out."

"That's right. We stepped out and there's no going back."

If they were saddened by this revelation, they did not show it. Instead, they were glad to have each other. Together they could withstand the loneliness as they considered where their capabilities, the scope of which was still unknown, would lead. They looked away and contemplated how the abundance they were in the midst of would never be enough for them.

"Let's find some surfboards," K2 suggested.

"You read my mind," Milo replied.

They rode into town and stopped in front of a surf shop and were soon outfitted with a couple of boards. They asked the shop owner some rudimentary questions about surfing and soon were carting them down to the water's edge. They used the bits of information from the store owner to seed their neural receptors to gain the necessary skills. They were both becoming fluent with this process but the differences in their neuralBlast sessions caused them to experience and learn differently; K2 with sheer force and Milo with panache.

"You heard the man, 'When you are the wave and the ocean, you can ride any wave in any ocean,'" Milo said.

"Sheeeet! He was so happy to sell his two most expensive boards he would have said anything you'd have liked him to."

Soon they were paddling through a heavy surf. Milo used his telemetric skills to navigate the way of least resistance, which still taxed his strength. But he was aware of something else, which was that he felt wild and free in this intense setting. That was important because it freed him from the burden he carried that had been inescapable. If extreme experiences provided relief, there would be more of it. K2 surged ahead, smashing himself against monster waves, his laughter echoing before he entered the wave and again when he emerged on the other side.

And the waves were huge; monstrous tubes of water surrounded them as they barreled along. They had come to the island during the peak surfing season and the gods of Hawaii were flexing their muscles for them. They continued engaging with these superb forces of nature until their bodies ached and even then, took a few more rides. When they were physically spent, they paddled back into shore and draped themselves over their boards.

"Could you hear them, the ancients, rattling through the wind as you played on the knife edge of these killer waves?" Milo asked, and looked out at the rhythmic onslaught of waves that continued to blow in from the west and pound the shore.

"Not sure who I heard, but I heard something," K2 responded and then did something unexpected, he let down his guard. "It was incredible. I'm not going to say it changed my life, but . . . maybe it did. Thing is, when I'm not experiencing life like this, with this level of engagement and risk, I feel disconnected, like I'll go crazy."

Their gaze met and they felt the danger raging at the borders of their wondrous adventure.

"I know," Milo replied. "I didn't always feel this way, but more and more that's where I find myself."

Silence overtook them again and when K2 broke into it, he did so with his old spirit, "So what you got on the agenda tomorrow? Hunting tigers in Borneo? Scaling my namesake, K2?"

They laughed and considered the possibilities.

"We could, I suppose." But Milo found the question disquieting. "Not sure, not sure of anything right now."

"One thing seems pretty certain, though. The longer we stay out here, the harder it will be for us to return to our respective sides. I'm betting both have learned of our football exploits, and they're not going to like it. Your people or mine. You might see a difference, but I see their similarities. They'll never trust us again, so we're on our own. And you can bet on one other thing. They'll be coming after us, at least The System will. So, your juju better be good, because we're going to need it."

Milo wasn't ready to accept K2's analysis.

"The resistance has a lot of good people and are fighting for what they think is just."

"I could say the same for The System, but I won't because it will just lead us to the same dance, play-act around the divide that has entertained people throughout recorded history. But look at yourself. You helped build that little nirvana, that supposed safe place, and you couldn't wait to flee from it because me and you, we're different. Maybe it will work for them, but I doubt it. They will find some way to corrupt it. Humans, left to their own devices, always do. And their adaptations over the last 500 years are not pretty. When they're left to choose, they choose badly, they choose against what's in their best self-interest. They've abandoned listening to any higher calling and replaced it with *reason*, which can be manipulated and as self-serving as any other framework. If you go back, they'll find a way to make you the cause of their problems, they'll demonize you.

"You thought you were doing something good, something noble. But how did that work out for you? I bet you weren't even done with your handiwork before you started chafing, ready for something different, ready to exploit your power that keeps extending outward in ways that dazzle even you.

"That's not the main point. Right now, you think their actions are tied to some high ideal. But what are they really in service to? Nothing much, some vague notions and flimsy ideals. Those things will get derailed by internal or external forces that don't even need to be that strong; a personal slight will set off an outraged response in the person believing he's been done wrong. People will disappoint you, entropy will kick in. You will never be able to thrive in a world that is so deeply flawed.

"That's why The System will always prevail. Control and discipline are the things that keep the wheels from falling off. Next to that, nothing matters much, which is what I tried to tell you the first time we spoke. The fact that you haven't focused a single neuralBlast session on effective ways to administer and maintain control, tells me how out of touch with the real world your training has been and because of that the potential danger you pose to everyone."

Milo turned away unable, or not wanting, to respond.

They did not scale K2, nor visit the Kalahari or Amazon rainforest nor any other worldly attractions, all of which could have been served up with a snap of Milo's fingers. As effortlessly as those destinations could be attained, the act required human agency, the quality most diminished by the beating surf and spirits hidden within. Instead, they let several days pass, lost in the ocean mists and a denser fog that was harder to define.

They rode their bikes from one end of the island to the other, and surfed most of the rest of the time. They bought daily provisions at the local market and one night went into a bar where they ran into a local gang. But even the dustup that followed did not break through the lethargy that became palpable.

They leaned against their bikes off to the side of the road. They were at one of the overlooks they had come to favor. But a mist had rolled in, obscuring the enormity of the ocean and the high peaks jutting up along the coastline.

"So where to next, professor?"

Milo laughed and perceived the absence of laughter the last couple of days.

"I don't know. Different places sound good but nothing stands out right now. And there's nothing wrong with staying here a while longer."

"Wait a minute. This is the same conversation we've had a bunch of times. All the places in the world are not the same. And as far as staying here, you're getting weirder and more depressed every day. Talk to me, man. You're starting to creep me out. This is our fourth day here, and you just keep drilling into yourself more and more. It's about time you checked in with me and let me know what's up. And we're vulnerable, you know. You can bet The System is sending its assassins out for us. We need to stay sharp so they don't get lucky. So, let's hear what's got you in this funk."

Milo let K2's comments turn over his mind and then said finally, "It's a few different things but mostly it's them. I just keep feeling like I failed them. I don't want to be the reason they didn't figure out how to act to set themselves free."

K2's laugh was loud, forced, and aggressive. He swept away the spittle that had formed at the corners of his mouth.

"I hope you're kidding, or at least you see how naive that sounds. The overwhelming majority of people don't want the responsibility of having to act on their own, think for themselves. They are more than happy to perform the tasks laid out for them by The System and be kept alive in return, and given enough pleasurable experiences to not be bothered by reports of hardship in some far off place that do not affect them. And no matter what the actual proximity, it will always be portrayed as far off. This is who they are and how they'll always be. And nothing you do will change it.

"But there are the few that have escaped that underling role. Wernher Von Braun was celebrated, made into royalty on both sides of the bloodiest conflict of the 20th century, because of his special talents. He could walk over the dead POWs, who were starved and overworked until their bodies gave out while building the catacombs for his V2 rockets. And then be lionized in those same countries from where those dead bodies had called home, not many years later.

"So, what's really important to us is how we choose to fit in. Your people will never know what to do with you. You will always be a sideshow freak. The only way you wouldn't be viewed with distrust is if you find a way to strait-jacket your immense talents."

K2 took a moment to collect himself before continuing, "It is all about power and control. When you have it there is nothing you can't do. It is the only thing that can engage and satisfy your cyborg spirit. Don't you see that as soon as you had your first session you were on your way to becoming aligned with The System? You accepted an unnatural state of being in return for an exponential increase in knowledge. Knowledge equates to power and that is the fuel that ignites The System. Try as you might, you are perfectly attuned to them. It is time for you to see your false allegiance to The Resistance for what it is.

"But if you came over to The System, they will provide the means for you to develop your full range of talents and capabilities. Instead of herding cattle, you could be the master of entire civilizations. Instead of being scorned, you'll be the guiding light of a new age. And don't worry about controlling the people, limiting their choices; they would have it no other way. Because even if they like and admire you, they have no interest in being like you or I. They have no interest in having power and control. They like this arrangement of being told what to do, how to behave. As long as we take care of their basic needs and don't throw in their faces that they have ceded their power to us, they will be living the lives that suit them, the ones that they prefer.

"You've sacrificed everything but now you've broken free and your engine is turbo-charged. Your momentum is unstoppable and that is something you can't run away from. You can't share it with them or pass it on, either. You either make the most of it, or it will tear you to shreds just like these waves will do if you don't utilize your cyborg powers."

Milo's heart rate accelerated and felt ready to burst from his chest. Since his first neuralBlast session he was aware of feeling something transcendent, which K2 now alluded to. Milo had sheltered these feelings, obscuring them even from himself. He knew he was supposed to use his powers to help guide people against tyranny, because they were the good guys and he was expected to be one of them. But how could he remain good and humble with such overwhelming power? No one could and he knew that. So, he had suppressed all these feelings and sheltered his potential because, he knew now, he was afraid of his power, afraid of how it separated him and where it may lead.

Since he came to this island he'd been haunted by a report he heard years before. A climber was trapped in a storm on the top of a mountain and was in radio communication with his wife. She and other family members encouraged him to keep walking towards safety and into the storm. It was an uproarious outpouring of support and an exhilarating display of shared energy across space. Until they realized his comments and descriptions were in a loop. And then they determined there was no progress, and that he was delirious and would be forever separated from them. As a final act of bravery and love they continued the charade until his transmissions became attenuated and then stopped. Milo wasn't trapped in a snowstorm but he, too, would never be able to find his way back.

"Still, these places all seem the same to me." Milo said, returning to the initial topic. He looked out across space but could make out no discernable images. "And none of them feel like places I want to be."

"You don't know that. There is a world of adventure waiting for us, whatever we want."

"For you maybe. But for me it just feels like one big comic book. Which is why every time you ask what I want to do next, I shut down. I feel like we're at the end of the line with nothing calling us to a place where we belong."

K2 sucked in air through his teeth and then said, "I get it. But we chose to do this and can choose to undo it. The System will still take us in and, whether you want to believe it or not, your people are not implementing anything that can engage you. So, even with all its warts, it's the only game in town and offers you the best opportunity to use your skills and power."

Milo was softening and he could barely believe he was considering this offer.

"Let's ride!" He called into space, wanting closure to this conversation that was leading to an unwanted conclusion.

They rode their bikes for a couple of hours. But instead of circumnavigating the island as they had done before, Milo took them on the back roads. When the pavement vanished they took it off-road, Milo leading the way. He was driven by desperation, a feeling of being trapped in a box and no way out, that he was destined to annihilate himself or harm the people closest to him. So, he pressed onward through swamp and over log covered paths until they reached immovable objects or sharply jutting terrain. When that endpoint was reached, they retraced their steps and searched for another tortuous path they would be tested by.

At one juncture, just before civilization dropped off, they spotted a little canteen. It was as unexpected as it was shoddy, a cinderblock oasis of commerce poisoning the otherwise pristine setting. Milo pulled his bike into the small parking area and K2 followed. The shutdown engines uncovered a myriad of bird and wind sounds. All around, a thousand hues of green. They stepped through the door and were greeted by a middle-aged woman from behind the counter. She held a deep energetic presence and offered K2 and Milo a measured smile. She wore a traditional dress with bright, contrasting colors and her hair was pulled back with a tie and then held in a bun. They walked the aisles, surprised by the variety of merchandise. There were field guides of native plants and books containing local histories and myths. Local handicrafts were also on display. Colorful garments with patterns of exotic fruit and plant life with which the inhabitants shared the island. It was the statues and figurines whose fierce expressions made Milo realize the local culture was aware of how they needed to defend these wonders from outside contagion. But most of the aisles were stuffed with confectionaries you would find in any corner store and displays bursting with bags of chips of every kind and size.

They hauled their purchases to the counter and then saw what they wished they would never see. A boy, her son presumably. Thirteen-fourteen years old but dressed indistinguishably from any teenager on the mainland. More disturbing was the look in his eye which was a soul cry of teenage angst known to every culture. Most disturbing was the picture behind the woman. Already curled at the edges but still distinguishable was the new hulk, the modern warrior, none other than K2 himself from one of his advertisement campaigns for the chip, masked and triumphant. He held a machine gun the size of a bazooka like a toothpick across his body. His arms and torso were exposed, and presented ripped, lean muscle. Sweat glistened and mixed with the grimy soot of war. A bandana like a crown of thorns wrapped through and around his hair. Myth making on steroids.

Both Milo and K2 knew this woman and her people were screwed, and now understood the reason for the concerned downturn at the edges of her smile when they entered. They would not withstand both the overt and covert pressures exerted by The System; few Indigenous cultures could. Her son had already been abducted.

They paid their bill wordlessly and left the store. They jumped back on their bikes but before heading off Milo said, "We have another option."

Chapter 23

Sheila returned to her cot and was resting between chores. It was mid-afternoon and she was working her way into the routine at the farm and finding ways to be useful. A week had passed since Milo's departure and she was beginning to think about how long she'd stay here waiting for him. But it was her lifeline to Milo and she had not given up on his return.

Reports filtered to them of conditions on the other side of the wall, which continued to deteriorate. They had done their work well. The Newer Machine was still in disarray but the "revolution" they had unleashed was a brand of reactionary populism that leaned towards fascism and stoked societal antagonisms that The System knew how to play to perfection. At its core was the demand for The System to take measures to increase their level of control on society, which they were only too happy to oblige and responded by enacting even more Draconian laws than the ones they replaced. Pedro and Onyinye had also heard these reports and agreed that there was no reason to return to this enhanced subjugation.

Sheila realized she'd made the right decision when the space above her cot began to flicker. Within seconds the crystals of light congealed into a hologram of Milo. She had worked with technology of this kind, but had never seen an image so life-like. Milo looked around as if he wasn't sure if he had fully materialized. She passed a hand through his image and it was pure space, no different than the air around it except for the articulated image that she wished she could touch and feel.

"Hello Sheila," the image spoke, as clear as if Milo himself was speaking. "I could sense you were alone, which is why I appeared. But I can't tell exactly where you are on the farm.

Sorry if I caught you in the middle of something where you'd rather not be disturbed, like taking a pee."

This disembodied image laughed lightly, appropriate enough for the potty reference. After a moment more where Milo appeared to be looking about, he said, "This is prerecorded because I wasn't sure of all I wanted to say, or if I'm ready to respond to your questions. I've experienced a lot in the last week, and I want to share it with all of you. But there are still some details to work out. Could you be out in the southwest paddocks tomorrow night at 7:00. Please invite Pedro and Onyinye to join you. We will have a proper talk then and I will explain everything as well as I'm able.

"I'm sorry to leave you with so little information, like telling you why I took off without saying goodbye. I couldn't explain it then, to you or even myself. But I know what I need to do now and want to let you know what's going on. I think of the three of you all the time and I placed your well-being at the center of my plans.

"Goodbye for now. I can't wait to see the three of you."

And then slowly, pixel by pixel, he disappeared.

Hearing and seeing Milo left her feeling off kilter. Sheila was giddy and felt this reaction inappropriate. But he was alive and did not hate her, and knowing this let her regain some part of her sanity. And he had a plan, a plan she saw satisfied him, even through this holographic facsimile. He looked different, aged. But how much can someone's appearance change in a week, she reasoned. Still the question lingered. She got up and cleared her area and then was off to find Pedro and Onyinye to tell them of this encounter.

Milo and K2 returned to their huts, and within minutes of dismounting from their bikes Milo announced he needed to go into the forest to think through his plans. K2 looked at Milo as he said this, and smiled when he was done. "I trust you," was his only response. He turned his back and set to work starting a fire, which they did not need but acted as a diversion, and proceeded with this task until he turned and saw the empty space where Milo had been standing.

The next morning Milo emerged from the forest. He looked weary but not distraught. In fact, everything about his demeanor suggested a clarity of purpose. These were the things K2 noticed as Milo strode up to the fire he had just restarted.

"You're looking pretty good for someone who's missed a couple of meals and slept in the woods last night," K2 said, not taking his eyes off Milo.

"I'm doing pretty good, but could use a little of whatever you got cooking on the fire."

K2 placed a couple of scoops of the bean mash he cooked in the bottom half of the mess kit and handed it to Milo. They sat quietly as Milo nourished his body and when he was done, he began to speak.

"You know, you're right, we could keep up this globe trotting. We could have limitless fun."

"But that's not what you want, is it?" K2 said, anticipating and coaxing Milo along.

"It's not. Our time here has been fun, amazing really. But it would get old real fast."

"Oh, yeah, right . . . unbearable fun. A big part of me would like to try that out instead of watching all this angst-driven drool oozing out of your mouth since we got here."

This brought a laugh from both of them but did not sidetrack Milo for long.

"But you know what I mean . . . .. These are human level enjoyments. It won't take long before they lose their appeal. It's started already."

"That's not the only option on the table," K2 said, joining back to the conversation the night before.

This was the opportunity Milo was looking for and he seized it.

"I know. I've been considering that."

K2 was engaged now, but was surprised by the direction Milo took the discussion.

"I've heard you say that interspace is the greatest thing you ever experienced. Well, that's where I was most of last night. My powers have expanded and I can exert them fully in that realm.   I traversed terrestrial time and saw unimaginable things: 100 foot tall flora and dinosaurs eating from their tops. I can smash worlds together and speed up evolutionary forces that will create unimaginable hybrids and then wipe the slate clean and start all over. This is the type of adventure that can satisfy superhumans such as us."

"How do you do this?"

"It wasn't that hard. I still don't know how we entered it the first time. The rupture in the fabric of reality was caused by the stress you laid on me. If you remember, I was pretty sure you were going to rip my throat out.   So, some self-preservation instinctual force caused the tear. Although I can't explain its origin, I can recreate the necessary conditions. The next step was figuring out how to manage the trips into this realm. What I learned was that the same mechanism for neuralBlast sessions could be applied to interspace.   That means I am able to "seed" interspace travel. The parameters I feed into a voyage create a world for us to explore. But it only establishes a base scenario which can, and does, spiral into wild and magical directions."

K2 was enchanted and speechless until his thoughts made it back to his prior experience. "And it's safe?"

"It is!   That is what I wanted to make sure of before I suggested it to you. I can create a private network for us that will keep our physical bodies protected from the radiation and gravitational forces that bombarded you the last time. So, we can stay as long as we like. From what I experienced last night,

I doubt we will ever want to return to this single level reality. This world, even with its limited attributes and range of experience, is besieged with problems that are beyond even our powers to fix."

"I experienced my life in a whole different way when I was there with you before I got sick," K2 admitted. A day doesn't go by when I don't think about how boundless it was, sensing elemental forces with all their power, magnifying every second. Tell me more of what it's like, what you experienced last night."

"Ha, you'll be surprised. Instead of breaking ground in new worlds I went back and played out the fantasy that enchanted me as a kid. I seeded my journey with what I knew of King Arthur and his men. I was with him as he pulled Excalibur from the stone and rode along the heath at his side as he defended his kingdom against the despised Saxons. I sat at the roundtable with his loyal knights and planned how to protect his kingdom and expand his empire. I watched as the passion between his most favored knight, Lancelot, and his queen, Guinevere, became a thing so hot it could not be contained."

"You got me," K2 said. His heart raced and his nostrils flared as they struggled to suck in all the oxygen his body craved. He was ready to go. He was ready to colonize interspace again and again and again. The wildness, the fury long held in abeyance escaped like a lion surveying his dominion and reveling in it. The beast would not easily be cowed again. "When do we go?"

Milo observed K2's transformation, but this time was not horrified by it as he was when K2 first leapt at him and exposed the warrior that neuralBlast had turned him into. In fact, he felt a similar reaction inside himself and wondered if K2 held up a mirror before him that he had never allowed himself to peer into before now. He was coming to accept that this was the true outcome of an artificial brain, no matter how it was configured, what it was influenced by.

"Soon, we go this afternoon. But first I need to speak with my friends who I will leave behind. And that will happen in one hour."

They stood together in the paddock, sharing space with the cows who had settled in for the night. This was the first extended break they allowed themselves. Although the work here was hard and long it was done at a slower pace. They had been at it for only a week, but already their bodies were being conditioned by the harsher demands placed upon them. These were well known to Onyinye, and Pedro had a zen-like relation to changing life experiences. Sheila chafed the most at first, not because of the hard work but because she only knew how to move with frenetic energy and the slow, steady pace tired her more than anything the land or animals could throw at her. But she was beginning to heed the natural rhythms and approached them as an opportunity for meditation and something akin to penance.

They stood there waiting in quiet, as the what-if scenarios came into focus and then were extinguished, like shooting stars in their brains. Milo would soon dispel the mysteries and they would decide if he simply went rogue or if his actions could be justified. So, they looked up at the sliver of moon on the horizon, and the occasional star piercing the darkening sky.

At 7:00 the glittering fragments of light coalesced and within seconds Milo's full image was there with them, elevated and lit as if from some internal source. Again, he waited, but now his sight was focused on his three friends, whose expressions he breathed in like an intoxicating fragrance.

"Thank you so much for coming. It's great to see you. Better than you can imagine," Milo said, overcome with emotion.

"Of course, we'd come, brain-boy," Pedro responded first. "We're your people."

Milo rubbed his eyes and dashed away a tear that began to form. He sensed how this simple comment could have the power to derail all that he'd put in place.

"Yes, that's true, and you always will be," Milo replied. And then without prompting, "I'm sorry for running off on you. But I had to get away."

"What happened that night?" Sheila spoke up. And then unable to contain her emotions, "What hit you so hard that you couldn't come to us with it? Really, Milo, after all we've been through together."

"It's hard to explain," Milo said. "But I can show you. Onyinye, do you remember when I was last here with you?"

"Yes, of course," she said and stepped forward a little, as if wanting to reach out to him as she had wanted to on that night.

"I could see how perplexed you were, that you were hurt by my weird behavior, by the distance I placed between us."

"Yes, that was hurtful. You shut me out and I didn't know why, and still don't."

"I'm so sorry. It was impossible for me to act differently. First, I want to offer my deepest apology and hope with my whole heart you accept it. But before you decide, let me show you what I saw that night before I left you. I filtered it from your vision but now want to share it with you, all of you."

And then, like a stage before a performance was about to commence, the lights came on, bit by bit. They were strands of lights like those sold at carnivals, spreading from the corners of the paddock and moving inward. They spread and spread and whatever they touched caused a branching activity that set off an endless array of rebranching. The light extended above and below ground and, in fact, rendered this demarcation almost meaningless.

But the most fantastical magic occurred when the strips of light marched up to and touched them. There was no sensation as it lit up their bodies, highlighting each body part and the interactions between them. It signaled the life force coursing through, its movement and cohesion. Pedro raised his arm and flicked his fingers and a spray of light was thrown into space. Sheila and Onyinye pressed their fingertips together and the miraculous energy could be seen flowing between them. Everything had auras that pulsed with varying shades of color, and theirs became deep, pulsing red as soon as they touched.

They marveled at the ground and what lay beneath it. The tiny membranes of roots in symbiotic embrace with bacteria that were lured in by promises of food and community. The bacteria transmitted pulsing waves across the substrata with clear but unknowable instructions; but now the humans had proof that a mesmerizing communication undergirded everything, including themselves.

Then they turned back to Milo, and their amazement came crashing down when they recognized the anguish on his face. As the world sparkled around them, Milo remained holographically removed. His carefully rendered features now contained a morose quality.

Finally, Milo began an explanation he wished would never have to be spoken.

"Onyinye, do you remember when I asked you to join me in the paddock?"

"Yes, of course. You looked terrible. I don't think you even wanted me to touch you. I was hoping to talk to you about it the next morning but, of course, you were gone by then."

"I wanted to touch you more than anything. But I was untouchable."

He went quiet and the others chose to not speak, waiting for Milo to explain what he meant.

"You see, I learned how to identify the energetic forces in this space and expose the natural interconnectedness of all things. What you are experiencing should continue indefinitely, or as long as the border remains in place. And I was as amazed as you were when I first witnessed it. I felt the same surge of wonder that I see in all of you.

"But then I realized something, something horrible. And it was confirmed when I invited you into the enclosure, Onyinye. You were the first human to enter into this space, and the life force sparkled through you like it did the cows and trees and everything connected through the earth. Everything, that is, except me. That was the horrible thing that your presence confirmed. There was no light coursing through me, no aura proclaiming my life force and its protection over me. I had crossed over, not to death, which awaits all living things, but to something man-made, artificial, synthetic.

"This realization was too much for me and I had to get out. I had to contact the only living being that understands me."

"You've been with K2, haven't you?" Sheila said, her concern turned to grief.

"Yes, we've teamed up. He's sitting on a beach in Hawaii right now and I'll be rejoining him soon."

"I'm so sorry," Sheila said, tears welling up in her eyes. "I'm so sorry for the role I've played in bringing you to where you are right now."

"You know something, Sheila? It's alright. If neuralBlast didn't come into my life I'd probably be dead right now. I might have taken up with those White nationalists, that's how empty my life was. What you've given me is much better . . . . But it's not as good as what you've got down there. And what you have is the key to the resistance. You need to let everyone see and experience this. BECAUSE HUMANS NEED TO SEE TO BELIEVE, AND NOW THEY CAN SEE THE WORLD THEY ARE A PART OF, SEE A WORLD THAT RADIATES THROUGH THEM AND ALL THINGS ON A GRAND SCALE. Once they see this everything will change, there will be no going back to the life-deadening rule of law imposed by The System, a set of laws that severs everyone from the beating heart that connects all living things."

People were, in fact, starting to emerge from the Big House. They gawked from the perimeter, enchanted as if this was the grandest Christmas light display, but still uncertain how to interact with it. It would not be long before they ventured into the sacred place and partook of the sacred ritual of connection. Which meant that these four would soon not be able to continue their private conversation, and the things still remaining to be said needed to be said quickly, and directly from the heart.

"What about you, Milo? What happens to you now?" Sheila asked the question at the forefront of all their minds.

"I need to go. You see, I don't trust myself. There's a downside to learning all this. When you disconnect the way that I have and have the power I have, you can easily be pulled into destructive behavior . . .. I am not a piece of plastic! But I am also no longer a natural human and I need to figure out what I am. Right now, I need to have my cyborg skills fully challenged and engaged, or I might use them to harm people. To avoid this, I will be transporting into interspace and living in that world of worlds. K2 is coming with me, so he won't be bothering you. Maybe someday we will return, but not until we understand better who we are. Use this time to recapture the world and your true experience of it. Know that I love you all and that I will return someday if I can live in peace with you and be of proper service."

"We will always welcome you back, brain-boy, when you are ready. And we may be able to hang with you and all your super power better than you think we can," Pedro said.

"You will always be in my heart," Onyinye said.

"Goodbye, Milo. We love you, as only humans can," Sheila offered her final farewell.

The crystals began to disassociate and then Milo was no more, his waving hand the final remnant to dissipate. At about the same time others began to disconnect sections of the electric fence and enter this sacred space. They were immediately transfixed and enraptured by the experience of seeing their life's energy passing through them and consorting with everything around them. They danced and ran, touched the auras surrounding them and each other. Many dug their hands beneath the earth's crust and watched the spidering root and mycelium reach toward them and send showering waves of light through the connected web of knowledge beneath the soil. Wherever one touched or moved there was a feast of interaction, curiosity, acceptance. These pilgrims laughed, cried and prayed. At first Pedro, Onyinye and Sheila remained within the orb of emotion they felt for Milo. But they could not stay immune from the joy erupting around them and allowed those feelings to seep in gradually until they, too, rejoiced at the reunion of all things occurring around and within them.

Milo emerged from a path and entered a clearing that separated him from their huts. K2 was sitting in this space aimlessly stirring the small fire they had built earlier.

"You say your goodbyes?" he asked without taking his eyes away from his task.

"I did," Milo said, and then added, "It was appropriately gruesome."

This caused K2 to raise his eyes and assess his comrade. "That would be a good description of the way you look right now."

"And feel."

"You having second thoughts?"

Milo thought before answering. "Second, third and fourth. But nothing changes. Even if I wanted to go back to them, I know I can't, not now anyway."

K2 would probably never feel, or understand, the ambivalence Milo experienced. He was a warrior and experienced the world primarily through that lens. Milo realized that his best chance for getting through what he needed to do was adopting this attitude as well. Better to be immersed in a hero's crusade than to experience a thousand cuts caused by being denied that which he most desired.

"C'mon, we've got worlds to conceive, worlds to conquer!" Milo said, wrapped in this new armor.

Milo rose and poured water onto the flames. The wood sizzled and spat back at Milo but he continued to pour until the last ember was silenced.

They hopped on their bikes and fired them up. They left everything behind, which wasn't much; each day they spent here saw them jettison something of who they were and now all they were was moment to moment experience and motion: cruising the island, the soft ocean breeze on this cloudless day, a perfect day for transition.

Milo turned to look at K2 and when their eyes met both shook their heads and smiled slyly at each other. Milo went first, turning his bike onto the beach and then fishtailed it onto a pier that jutted for 40 yards into the ocean. As soon as he hit the boards, he jacked the engine into full throttle and kept it there. The blaring noise was enough to pin the few fishermen to the rails as Milo and then K2 sped by. Instead of crashing into the barrier at the end, Milo raised himself up and propelled the Harley into the air, a movement duplicated by K2.

The onlookers raced to the end of the pier. What happened? Instead of seeing the two men dashed against the rock and sea, they were simply gone.

Only one man was close enough to see what happened: the rip, the tear in reality that accepted them before they disappeared. But he would not admit to what he saw, would not believe it because he could not bear the weight of this singular vision. Instead, he hid from this extraordinary act, and adopted the thoughts and behaviors of those spared this experience that upended everything he knew to be true.

My deepest gratitude goes out to my editor, Ellen Fernandez-Sacco. She not only sharpened the text but helped flesh out many of the themes. She had a deep understanding of the characters and their motivation. We were friends in high school and reconnected many years later, and I'm so glad we did.

Fred Burton has written two previous novels, *The Old Songs* and *Bountiful Calling*. As with all his work, Fred strives in *Man Made* to carefully construct situations and characters so that at a certain point they place demands on him and he becomes a conduit for the action that needs to unfold. He hopes you find value in his most recent offering.

.

Printed in Great Britain
by Amazon

60216811R00201